The Incredible Flight of the Osprey

Osprey

OSPREY TRILOGY

THE INCREDIBLE FLIGHT OF

THE OSPREY

AN INTERSTELLAR MYSTERY

BOOK ONE

DJ Albrecht

Water Valley Press

Water Valley Press

Published by Water Valley Press
2086 Vineyard Drive
Windsor, CO 80550

Bible quotations are taken from the <u>World English Bible</u> - a Public Domain Book.

ISBN13: 978-0-9600265-1-7

Cover design by Brandi Galuzzi https://brandigaluzzi.myportfolio.com

Printed in the United States of America

ACKNOWLEDGMENTS

Friends and family are priceless gifts and deeply appreciated. Special thanks go to Kim Taylor and Laura McIntyre for their proofreading skills. I appreciate David Domenico, Bobby Albrecht, Brandi Galuzzi, Everett and Sharon Stockton, and Bill McIntyre for valiantly serving as Beta readers. If this story has any merit, it is due to their insightful comments and encouragement. Finally, thanks to Brandi Galuzzi for her excellent cover design.

Contents

Prologue

Plesetsk Cosmodrome – December 14, 1968

olonel Sergei Golovkin struggled to control his racing heart. He sat atop the Soyuz 7K-L1S3 spacecraft, now designated Zond 7. It was hard to believe, but here he was, destined to be the first man to journey from Earth around the Moon and back. Sergei would come within 1,100 km of its surface before returning. Even better, this mission would keep the Soviet Union ahead of the United States in the space race.

Concentrate on your breathing. Breathe slow, deep breaths. Relax, he thought, not wanting to alarm the flight surgeon monitoring his vitals.

Ignoring the hissing, knocking, and vibration of valves opening and closing around him, he thought about how this came to be. He, Sergei Golovkin, joined the class of cosmonauts in training as their political officer. As such, he was embedded with the other cosmonauts. He took all the necessary flight training for the Soviet Manned Circumlunar Program. However, he was not scheduled to fly into space. He was not even included on the official list of cosmonauts. His only official duty was to ensure that each cosmonaut adhered (at least publicly) to the behavior expected by the <u>Peoples' Party</u>.

Everyone knows that the Zond 5 and Zond 6 spacecraft flights around the Moon were successful with animals on board. It's only natural that Zond 7 would carry a man this time, he thought. He smiled as he recalled everyone's surprise when it was announced that he would fly Zond 7 around the Moon. Sergei understood that the others never considered him to be one of their own. Some even mocked his zealous devotion to the revolution and the Party.

They're just a group of arrogant flyboys – not that much different from their snobbish American astronaut counterparts. Well, they can just go to hell! I'm going to the Moon! Sergei relished the sweet feeling of vindication washing over him. He always believed that his devotion to the Party would someday be rewarded. But this was beyond his dreams. His gloved hand bumped his spacesuit pocket that contained his own 'Pilot-Cosmonaut of the USSR' medallion, given to all cosmonauts that fly a mission for the Soviet Union.

He thought, *My boss, Alexei, must be more powerful than either Boris or Igor to get me selected for this trip over the entire Cosmonaut Corps.* He shook his head. *It must have been some argument over who would have the honor of being the first man to travel around the Moon. I wish I could have heard it.*

At that very moment, a somber trio of Alexei Chestof (Chief of Political Officers), Boris Dementyev (Director of Cosmonauts), and Rurik Zharkov (Chief Spacecraft Designer) were grimly watching the final launch preparations in the Launch Control Center. They did not share Sergei's view of reality.

They knew that the Zond 5 flight was a success. But not so with the Zond 6 flight. The reality was that upon re-entry, its parachutes failed to open, causing the re-entry vehicle to crash in a way that would be fatal to any living creature on board. Worse yet, the crash did not kill anything. The animals that were on board (turtles, fruit flies, and such) were already dead. They met their demise because an O-ring had failed during the flight itself, causing the cabin to depressurize (These details were conveniently overlooked by the official press release.) They also knew that Zond L1S-2, which launched earlier, on the 3rd of July, suffered a first-stage failure. Another fact that failed to be reported.

The actual debate between Sergei's boss and the others responsible for Sergei's fate was not over who would receive the "honor" of being the first man to fly around the Moon. Instead, they argued over the wisdom of even *sending* a Cosmonaut on Zond 7. Rurik argued that both problems with Zond 6 had been identified and resolved. Boris argued that the final secret accident report on Zond 6 was not completed, and other safety issues might be discovered. However, they were so close to winning this phase of the space race with the Americans, and letting it slip away with a timid decision, was too much for Rurik or Alexei to bear. Alexei sided with Rurik and argued that the Soviet window (to be the first around the Moon) was closing fast as the Americans moved up their own attempt to reach the Moon.

Seeing the three men standing off to the side, Igor Bastov (Chief of Mission Control) recalled the debate as if it had just happened.

It had started innocently enough when Igor asked, "Comrades, is this to be a human flight or not? Remember, as Mission Control Chief, I cannot authorize this flight as human worthy unless all three of you agree."

Rurik had said, "I certify that this spaceship is human-worthy. We have corrected both the O-ring failure and the parachute failure."

Boris countered, "I disagree. We must wait until the accident investigation is completed before declaring the Soyuz spacecraft human-worthy. I'll not risk any of my Cosmonauts on this spaceship until the investigation is complete and its final report submitted."

"By then, the Americans will be eating ham, eggs, and green cheese on the Moon," Alexei argued. "Our intelligence indicates the American Apollo program will attempt to fly around the Moon this December."

"And the source of our intelligence is?" Igor asked.

"An Associated Press Release," Alexei shrugged.

"Oh, now that's a reliable source," Boris snorted.

Alexei ignored Boris's sarcasm. "Just think of how being the first to send a man around the moon will enhance our reputation around the world."

Boris retorted, "I don't see how being the first country to send a man to the moon and bring back a corpse enhances our reputation. Only a fool would send a man in that vehicle before the accident report is completed."

"Since there's no agreement between you three, we'll not launch a cosmonaut on this mission," Igor said.

"Wait a minute," Alexei interjected. "Boris, you said you wouldn't risk one of your cosmonauts. Would you agree to a launch if it did NOT put any of your cosmonauts at risk?"

"Sure, as long as my cosmonauts aren't at risk, I'd support this launch," Boris said, "In fact, if you're fool enough, you can send anyone you want up in that craft as long as it isn't one of my men!"

No sooner were the words out of his mouth than Boris realized his mistake.

"Excellent, Boris!" Alexei exclaimed, "Let's send my cosmonaut. Comrades, you heard for yourselves that Boris will support sending my cosmonaut around the moon."

"You don't have a cosmonaut," Boris said, knowing full well that Alexei did.

Alexei's lips curled into a smirk. "Have you forgotten Sergei Golovkin? He completed all the required training with your men, only he reports to me, not you. I propose we send him to be the first man to fly around the Moon."

Igor recalled seeing the triumphant smirk cross Alexei's face as Boris gave a long sigh. "If you want to risk Sergei's life on this fool's errand, so be it. I, too, will agree that the vehicle is human-ready."

Igor had thought, *Interesting play, Boris. You know that your cosmonauts will be furious because you let Sergei go ahead of them. You must be pretty sure this mission will fail. Let's hope you're wrong.*

Igor mentally returned to the present moment as he resumed monitoring the launch preparations. As he did, Sergei, unaware of the misgivings and tensions between those responsible for his fate, continued his part of the pre-launch procedures.

"Sergei, this is Olga of Launch control. Come in. Over."

"Olga, this is Sergei. I copy. Over."

"Sergei, this is Olga. We're testing our communications with the down-range tracking stations. Your flight will also be tracked by both the Bezhitsa and Ristna tracking vessels. Over."

"Olga, this is Sergei. I copy. Over."

Royal Observatory, Edinburgh, Scotland

Unknown to the Soviet team at Plesetsk, their secretive pre-launch activity was being monitored by another set of ears in the West. Those ears belonged to one Lindsey McDonald, a stocky, red-headed Scott. He was a researcher who worked at the Royal Observatory in Edinburgh, Scotland. He was also fluent in Russian. He had tracked each of the Soviet space efforts since before Yuri Gagarin first flew into space.

After overhearing the Soviet transmissions between Launch Control and the downrange tracking stations, McDonald telephoned his friend, Philip Becker, in Halifax, Nova Scotia. Philip was a tall, sandy-haired Canadian working at the Burke-Gaffney Observatory. After checking, Philip confirmed the movement of the Bezhita, a Soviet tracking vessel, off the Sable Islands. This was a sure sign that an actual flight was about to take place.

"That settles it, Philip," Lindsey said. "We are on for tonight. It is so overcast here that I won't be able to see anything. But I'm dialed in on their frequency to monitor the pre-launch and post-launch transmissions and give you a running account by HAM. I need you to be our eyes in Halifax. Donald Paxton told me he was doing some work at the Teida

Observatory on the Canary Islands. I'll ring him up and ask him to be our eyes down there."

Later, when Philip and Donald settled in at their respective locations, the three friends began their own count-down procedure via HAM radio.

"VE1PB, this is GMLMD. Can you hear me well enough, Philip?"

"GMLMD, this is VE1PB. I hear you loud and clear, Lindsey."

"How's the weather in Halifax?"

"The sky is clear here," Philip answered.

Donald Paxton signed in by saying, "GMLMD, this is MWPAX. May I join you two?"

"Good to hear your voice, old chap," Lindsey replied, "I'm picking up conversations between Launch Control and the launch vehicle. Sounds like a manned flight. I think Ivan* may be trying to beat the Yanks to the Moon."

"Think they'll try and land?" Donald asked.

"I don't think they're trying to take the biscuit by landing on this flight. It sounds like Ivan only has one man on board. It's probably just a fly-by mission. Still, they'll be the first to send a man around the Moon," Lindsey answered.

Donald said, "I've been monitoring some blokes in the States and just heard an odd thing. They've spotted a Russian tracking vessel just off the coast of Cuba. They think it's the Ristna."

"That explains why it wasn't spotted with the Bezhitsa up here," Philip said. "Why in the blooming world would Ivan move the Ristna to CUBA?"

"Not sure. It could be the Russians are trying something different. We'll have to stay sharp if we are going to see anything," Lindsey said. "By the way, Donald, how's the weather in the Canary's?"

"Warm and clear in any direction," Donald replied. "I bet the Yanks'll be pissed if Ivan beats them to the Moon!"

"Got that right," Lindsey agreed.

"Ivan's cosmonaut must survive the launch first. They've had a considerable bit of trouble with their newest booster of late," Philip observed.

"Okay, chaps," Lindsey said, "the final countdown just started. Five, four, three, two, one, liftoff. They have liftoff. So far, so good. This fellow, Sergei, is reporting that all gauges are in the green. Flight control is reporting all systems are Go—."

Donald interrupted, "Sergei? Who's Sergei?"

"Meaning?" Lindsey asked.

"There is no Sergei on the official cosmonaut list," Donald said. "I know. I've got a list in front of me of all the cosmonauts Ivan has, and there's no Sergei on it!"

Lindsey said, "That's strange. *I wonder what it means*, he thought.

He continued, "Oh, Sergei is experiencing some buffeting. The rocket is starting to pitch a little. The shaking is more violent. Okay, everything seems to be settling down. They are approaching time for stage separation...." After a very long pause, Lindsey continued. "Here we go. Five, four, three, two, one. Stage separation is successful. The second stage is firing as it should ... it looks like Sergei is on his way to the Moon.... Oh, scratch that! They're parking the spacecraft in a low earth orbit for now."

"What went wrong?" Philip asked.

"It doesn't sound like anything went wrong. The controllers are carrying on their normal chatter," Lindsey said with a relieved sigh.

---

* Cold war term for Russian

Low Earth Orbit

What a ride! Sergei thought. Despite all his training, he was not prepared for the excitement of the launch. *How do the Americans say it? It was an 'E-ticket' ride?* He wondered. His next thoughts were on just how beautiful the earth was from his vantage point. He was glad that Mission Control had worked a parking orbit into this mission. It gave him more time to enjoy the view.

His thoughts were interrupted by Launch Control. "Sergei, this is Olga. Come in. Over."

"Olga, this is Sergei. I copy you. Over."

"Sergei, this is Olga. Our Launch Control Chief and your boss send their regards and congratulations on a job well done so far. Over."

The mood in the Control Center had lifted. Even Boris, ever the pessimist, felt his spirits rise, despite seeing a smug smile pasted across Alexei's face.

"Olga, this is Sergei. Please acknowledge my appreciation of their comments. Over."

"Sergei, this is Olga. I copy you. You will remain in parked orbit until you reach the following coordinates 25.0000° N, 71.0000° W. We will launch you to the Moon from those coordinates. Over."

"Olga, this is Sergei. I copy you. I will launch to the Moon from over coordinates 25.0000° N, 71.0000° W. Over."

"Sergei, this is Olga. That is correct. The estimated time of your departure will be midnight, local time. Over."

In Scotland, Lindsey could hardly believe their good luck as he relayed the Soviet transmissions to his friends. "Great! Given the coordinates and the timing, you chaps get to view the whole event. What a lucky break!"

Donald said, "Are you sure it's luck? It sounds like Ivan wants to start to the Moon within sight of Cape Canaveral. Kind of like poking a stick in the eyes of those NASA chaps."

"25.0000° N, 71.0000° W. You know what that is?" Philip asked.

"That's somewhere around Cuba," Donald said. "So?"

"So? To be more precise, those are the coordinates for the center of the Bermuda Triangle." Philip answered.

"What? Don't tell me you've suddenly gone superstitious," Lindsey said.

"I'm not superstitious!" Philip balked, "I'm just saying bad things have a way of happening around the Bermuda triangle."

The other two just laughed.

"Even if there is anything to the Bermuda Triangle legends, Sergei isn't *around* the Bermuda triangle – he's miles *above* it," Lindsey said.

Just before the appointed midnight hour, the three friends were in position to observe the historic event. Both Donald and Philip had their telescopes trained on the Zond 7 spacecraft.

Lindsey asked, "How's she look, Donald?"

"She's a thing of beauty. I see her distinctive elongated bell shape body and her solar panels extended like rectangular wings."

"I second that," Philip agreed. "I think I can make out her small communications dish mounted on the side of her nose."

"Look sharp! I think Ivan is starting to count down," Lindsey commanded.

Plesetsk Cosmodrome

"Sergei, this is Olga. Are you ready to proceed? Over."

"Olga, this is Sergei. All looks well here. I'm ready. Over."

"Ristna, this is Olga of Launch Control. Do you have a visual on Zond 7? Over."

"Olga, this is the Ristna. We have a clear visual on Zond 7. Over."

"Ristna, this is Olga. Very good. Over."

"Sergei, this is Olga. All your tracking stations are online and receiving your telemetries. The Ristna also has visual contact with your ship. Launch Control is giving me the order to let you proceed. Over."

"Olga, this is Sergei. I copy you. Over."

"Sergei, this is Olga. Commence a 15-minute burn on my mark. Five, four, three, two, one, MARK. Over."

"Olga, this is Sergei. The burn has commenced. I feel the acceleration of the craft. It is smooth and increasing. Over."

"Sergei, this is Olga. We're now ten minutes into the burn. All system indicators here are good. What are you seeing, and how are you feeling? Over."

"Olga, this is Sergei. My ride is smooth. I am looking back at earth, and it is beautiful. The stars are spectacular. Over.

"Sergei, this is Olga. We have four more minutes before ending the burn. What are your readings? Over."

"Olga, this is Sergei. All my gauges are in green. I am beginning a roll to align with the Moon. The Moon is—GOOD GOD, NO!"

"Sergei, this is Olga. The Moon is what? Over."

Silence.

"Sergei, this is Olga. I didn't copy your last transmission. Over."

Silence.

"Sergei, this is Olga. Can you hear me? Over."

Silence.

"Sergei, this is Olga. What's your status? Over."

Silence.

"Tracking vessel Ristna, this is Olga. Do you still have a visual on the Zond 7 craft? What do you see? Over."

"Olga, this is tracking vessel Ristna. We've lost visual. I repeat, we have lost all visual contact with Zond 7! Over."

Royal Observatory, Edinburgh, Scotland

Lindsey was shaken by the increased alarm in the Launch Control and tracking station transmissions. His concentration was broken by Donald asking, "Philip, what are you seeing?"

"Nothing. And you?" Philip answered.

Donald agreed, "Nothing either. This is freaky. One minute I am watching a rocket burn … the next, I see absolutely nothing. The rocket just disappeared!"

"You mean it dropped over the horizon," Lindsey interjected.

"Hell, NO!" Donald exclaimed. "There is no horizon about it. One second it was high in the sky. The next second it was gone."

"It can't just be gone," Lindsey said with disbelief. "Maybe the rocket burn ended?"

Philip said, "Look, the telescope I am viewing is powerful enough to see the ship after the burn stops, and I DO NOT SEE THE SHIP!"

"Same here. Don't ask – the night's crystal clear," Donald agreed.

"WOW," Lindsey said. "Ivan's tracking stations are going nuts."

"What's Ivan saying?" Philip asked.

Lindsey replied, "The Ristna just reported again that it's lost all visual contact. The other tracking stations are all reporting that the telemetry readings stopped. The flight safety officer reports that no distress signal is being received. Neither the Launch Control Center nor any of the tracking stations are receiving radio transmissions from Zond 7 on any frequency. Do you think the ship exploded and disintegrated?"

"If it had, we'd have seen a burst of some kind, and we'd now be looking at a debris field, but there is no debris," Philip said. "Had it been struck by a meteorite or other space debris, we would have seen the impact and a debris field."

"What about an explosive decompression that pushed the Zond suddenly off course?" Lindsey wondered aloud.

"An explosive decompression would kill the cosmonaut, but it would not stop the ship from sending telemetry signals," Donald answered. "Besides, I've been scanning the entire area, and I see nada, zip, nothing. This ship is gone. No trace."

"Donald's right – there's no doubt about it," Philip added. "That spaceship is gone!"

"Where did it go? What happened? What does this mean?" Donald spurted out as his mind raced through all the possibilities.

"I've no idea where it is or what happened," Philip said. "But I do know what it means. It means Ivan's just lost his chance to beat the Yanks to the Moon."

Plesetsk Cosmodrome

Hours had elapsed since the final partial transmission from Sergei had been heard.

The mood at the Launch Control Center had moved from desperate – when contact with Sergei was first lost – to somber as the grim reality set in that the Zond 7 craft was lost. The dour quartet of Alexei, Boris, Igor, and Rurik began discussing what to do next.

"Is there anything left that we can do?" Alexei asked. "Can we launch a rescue mission?"

"No," answered Igor. "No other vehicle can be made ready to launch for a rescue attempt. Even if there was one, we have no idea where Sergei is. We can only ensure that word of this mishap never goes beyond this room."

Igor failed to notice that tears were silently streaming down Olga's face. He said, "Olga, please inform all the tracking stations that we have concluded our test launch and tracking exercise, simulating an actual manned mission. Pass along my appreciation for their work. Tell them that with their help we found and will correct some serious flaws in our communications systems. Thank you."

Quietly, to the other three men near him, Igor said, "For the record, Zond 7 has yet to be launched. Today was simply a communications test as well as a rocket engine firing test which we'll designate as Zond LIS 3."

"What of poor Sergei?" asked Alexei.

"Ah yes," Igor answered with a long sigh. "Next week, we'll announce the sad news that Colonel Sergei Golovkin, a true hero of the People, had an unfortunate training accident over Siberia. That will be that."

The Mission

Three men sat huddled at a table eyeing Today's News Channel's (TNC) breaking news ticker. They were dressed casually enough, but their haircuts and demeanor gave them away as military or ex-military. The news ticker read:

"BREAKING NEWS JACQUES BEAUREGARD STRIKES AGAIN! The renegade space pirate's latest victim is the Russian Federation space freighter Aist. Pravda confirmed that the infamous pirate captured the vessel two weeks ago when it lost all communication with Space Station Freedom. Beauregard is now believed to be holding it for ransom somewhere inside the Asteroid Belt between Mars and Jupiter."

BAM! Vice Admiral Dennis Robinson's hand struck the table with such force, it caused his two companions to jump. "You crazy son of a bitch!" the flushing Vice Admiral exclaimed. "I'll get you yet, damn it!"

"You'll need to excuse my friend, Lewis," Retired Admiral Justin Carter explained to NASA Mission Controller Lewis Wright, who had nearly spilled his drink. "With Dennis, it's personal. You see, during the Asteroid Conflicts, Jacques Beauregard was his best starfighter squad leader. But Beauregard and his squad went rogue at the end of hostilities. Since then, Beauregard's been occupying himself by capturing merchant vessels for ransom and disrupting trade between here and Mars."

"A regular thorn in the Admiral's side, I suppose," Lewis replied.

"A royal pain in the ass is more like it!" Robinson corrected.

Lewis chuckled as he took a fresh look at the two men. They had summoned him from Johnson Space Center in Houston all the way to this tavern in the heart of Georgetown. Robinson was a stout, unsmiling character with intense green eyes. His title was Special Security Advisor to the President. He was known for his quick, often foul, temper and mouth. His friend at the table, Justin Carter, was a rather portly Skunk Works Program Manager. He was currently responsible for building and deploying two new classes of spaceship. One was the new Alpha Class transport. The other was a Black Project space frigate with the latest in weapons technology. Lewis had heard a rumor that the two projects had more in common than just their shared program manager.

"This transport is just the latest in a string of captures made by Beauregard since our unsuccessful Delta Force raid on his training facility six months ago," Carter said.

"That stupid Ivan had it coming," Robinson interrupted, speaking again of the unfortunate Russian transport. "He refused to wait for the next convoy to form up. Said it would only slow him down. Look at where that got you, you stupid bast—"

"Convoy?" Lewis asked, interrupting the angry Admiral.

"Yeah, son," Carter replied. "It's like when we sent American ships to England during World War II. The Navy had all merchant ships form up into convoys of dozens of ships. As a group, they traveled to England accompanied by U.S. and British warships to avoid being sunk by German U-boats."

"And how's that working?" Lewis asked.

"About the same as it did back then," was Carter's response. "It's not perfect, and it takes a lot of military resources, but it's better than the alternative. It slows down the trade between our Mars outposts and Earth.

Of course, none of this would be necessary if we could just capture and neutralize Beauregard."

"And that brings us to you, Mr. Wright," Robinson added.

"What does this have to do with me?" Lewis asked.

"Everything, young man. Everything," Robinson smiled.

Lewis, who had never seen the Admiral smile before, was decidedly uneasy about where this conversation was heading.

"Our last two attempts to neutralize Beauregard ended in failure because he was forewarned about where and when we were going to strike," Robinson said. "Too many people and departments, not to mention governments, were involved in our planning and execution. This time we want a smaller strike team. I want you to organize it. It can't have more than five members. Six tops."

Lewis gave a low whistle. "You can't even launch a military spacecraft with that few people."

"Exactly!" Carter exclaimed. "That's why we'll use an actual transport mission to Mars as our cover. Only you, your team, and we will know what the real mission is."

"You're serious?" Lewis asked.

"Absolutely. Our plan's code name is TF-76." Without missing a beat, Robinson asked, "What do you think, Captain?"

What can I say? Lewis thought. "I'm all ears, Admiral," he answered.

"This time, we'll nail that Jacques clown for sure!" Robinson said. Leaning forward and licking his lips, Robinson continued, "Here's the plan: Lewis, we want you to be the mission controller. Select the best commander at your disposal. He—"

"Or 'she,'" Lewis corrected.

"Or 'she.'" the Admiral frowned, "will be taking our most advanced battle technology on a resupply mission to Mars with a skeleton crew. It will be disguised as a merchant marine spacecraft. The new Alpha Class transport, to be specific. It'll travel alone, instead of in a convoy. We'll say that it's outfitted with a new faster engine, and we're relying on its speed to avoid intervention by pirates. Its published manifest will list items that any pirate will find hard to resist."

"Kinda like the Aist," Lewis smiled.

"Yes, like the Aist. But this is all a ruse," Carter said. "Your commander must have a minimal but battle-hardened crew, trained in the use of the latest ship-to-ship combat technology."

"I wasn't aware that the Alpha Class transport has ship-to-ship, or any, combat technology, for that matter," Lewis said.

"The standard Alpha transport doesn't," Carter said. "But this one's not standard. Think of it as a transport platform that carries much of the latest ship-to-ship warfare technology we developed at the Skunk Works."

"Jacques will be drawn in, thinking he is attacking a single merchant marine vessel. Having a skeleton crew will reinforce this idea," Robinson said. "Before he knows it, your crew will have the best of him. He'll be trapped and out-gunned. Jacques must either surrender or be destroyed. It's the perfect plan," he concluded with a self-satisfied smile.

"Just like a new video game," Lewis also smiled. His sarcasm was lost on the admirals. "It sounds good on paper," Lewis continued. "But, have you thought of what happens if he succeeds in boarding our ship? Having a skeleton crew and all."

"Not a problem. Won't happen," Carter responded. "The only direct external entrance to the crew cabin is the portside portal. The entry chamber is impervious to energy weapons and is blast-proof. If he's fool enough to try and blast his way in, the exterior door will give way, sucking him into space before the chamber's interior door fails."

"What if he forces his way through the cargo hold via either its rear door or its top hatch?" Lewis asked.

"Even better!" Carter answered. "We've designed internal weaponry to protect the cargo hold. It'll be a virtual kill zone, should he try to pass through it."

"Sounds like you're more interested in a dead pirate than in a captured one," Lewis said.

"We didn't say that," Carter winked. "But sometimes certain outcomes just can't be helped."

"It's the perfect plan," Robinson repeated. "We've thought of every contingency. Nothing can go wrong. What do you think, Captain?"

Two admirals concocting the "perfect plan" to kill a pirate, Lewis thought. *I should worry.* But all he said was, "Count me in, sir."

Carter smiled. "Excellent. Now that we have you onboard, there's one other minor detail you need to know." He leaned forward. Motioning for Lewis to do the same, he lowered his voice. Just above a whisper, he said, "We believe there may be a mole inside NASA that's feeding information to Beauregard. So be careful. If he gets wind of our plan, all bets are off."

"Any idea who?" Lewis asked.

"Not a clue," Carter shrugged.

His words sent a chill down Lewis's back.

Houston, Texas

As he flew back to Houston, Lewis was haunted by the thought of how casually the fate of a man could be decided over a meal and a few drinks. The idea of a mole in NASA feeding information to Beauregard added to his angst. He landed at Houston's Hobby Airport, where his friend, Captain Matthew Dirksen, met him outside the security gate.

"So, how's DC, Lewis?" Dirksen asked. Captain Dirksen, known by his friends as Matt, was tall and muscular. Other than his thinning blond hair, he could pass as a pro football linebacker. Lewis and Matt had met at the Academy (Lewis being a senior when Matt joined). They also served together during both the Lunar and Asteroid conflicts. But their friendship was solidified during the time they spent together as instructors in Top Gun school. With his aversion to meetings and paperwork, Matt stayed in the field, advancing to the rank of Starship Captain. Now Matt was one of

NASA's senior captains. Lewis's career, however, led him down the path to management. He was now one of the most respected NASA mission controllers. The fact that Matt and his wife named their son after Lewis was a testament to the closeness of their relationship.

"Not sure, Matt," was Lewis's reply.

"Not sure?" Matt questioned as he eased the car into traffic, turned on the autopilot, and leaned back. "You were pretty excited about the DC invite when I gave you a ride to the airport a couple of days ago. I told you that no good ever comes from being called back to DC."

"I know," Lewis admitted. "I got caught up with the idea that the admirals were letting me in on a special secret."

"Now you're saying the secret's not so special after all?"

"Oh, it's special all right," Lewis began, but then he paused to admire the SkyDome as it rose above the city and hovered over Clear Lake. The SkyDome was a dinner and dance club that occupied a half-domed air vehicle that placed its patrons in the sky for a two-hour trip. What made it stand out was the fact that the dance floor was clear. Dancers got the feeling they were dancing on the clouds — or at the least floating in the sky. Lewis never tired of watching the graceful vehicle in flight.

"Beautiful, isn't it?" Matt interjected when he noticed where Lewis was looking. Never one to waste much time admiring beauty, he continued, "Now tell me about that special secret."

Lewis smiled and picked up his train of thought. "It could be a priority ticket getting you back to Mars and see your wife and Lewis Jr. They call it the perfect plan – one where nothing can go wrong."

"I hear a 'but' coming."

"But, thinking about it on the flight back, I realized that what makes their secret plan so special is that if something does go wrong, it's my career on the line – not theirs."

"Like I said, no good ever comes from getting called back to DC."

Lewis nodded but said nothing. After a few moments of thoughtful silence, Matt's curiosity got the best of him. "What's the plan, and how do I get a priority ticket to Mars? You know all solo flights to Mars have been canceled because of that Beauregard character. The next convoy won't assemble up for at least four months, and I'm anxious to see my wife."

"That could be arranged. But first, we need to catch us a pirate. Interested?"

Matt didn't need to think about it. "Hey buddy, if it's my ticket to Mars, count me in."

Lewis smiled and thought, *Careful what you wish for, my friend.*

The Meeting

T he hot, humid air of August draped over Houston like a wet blanket. But that didn't compare with the heaviness of yet one more meeting in the stuffy NASA briefing room. A bead of sweat wandered down the back of the muscular neck belonging to Captain Matt Dirksen. As a rule, he did not like meetings. This one was no exception. He sat rigid, eyeing his superior officers as they discussed different agenda items about his mission. Across the table sat Dr. James Silvertongue, Special Counsel to the President. He had called this meeting to be briefed on the mission's progress (TF-76). Matt would be flying. He was a tall, slender, silver-haired man. He preferred to be called "Doctor," as he held a Ph.D. in Psychology and had published numerous scholarly works on the psychology of space travel. He was an advisor to the President (an old college buddy) on all things related to space flight. To a stranger, he was refined, politically correct, and had an intelligent air about him. To those who worked around him, he was smug, genteel, and annoyingly arrogant. He fancied himself an expert in the field of Space Exploration. On the other hand, Matt considered him an over-rated bureaucrat, whose lack of practical experience left him out of touch with the realities of space travel.

To Silvertongue's right sat another James. Admiral James Christopher Morris II, NASA's Interplanetary Program Chief and Commanding Officer of the US Space Force. A man of average stature, this James also carried himself with an aristocratic air. He preferred to be called JC. His detractors said that JC was an appropriate nickname because he acted like he thought of himself as the Son of God. Once Matt had been overheard saying, about him, "Hmph, Morris's no Son of God. He's the son of something, but it's not of God."

Admirals Carter and Robinson rounded out those sitting at the table. The balding and perennially grouchy Admiral Gerald Hornsby, Commander of the Astronaut Corps, sat along a wall behind the table with other senior staff members. In the corner of the room, also a little away from the table, lounged Matt's boss and friend, Lewis Wright. He was the Mission Controller for this mission.

Lewis was feeling unsettled as he took in who was sitting around the room. It seemed no matter how hard he tried to ignore it, the thought of *what if Beauregard's mole is in this room right now?* Kept entering his mind. He glanced across the room behind Matt. There sat, along the wall, Commander Barnabas Maalouf, selected to be the Osprey's pilot. The two became friends during the Asteroid Conflict Lewis caught his eye and gave him a slight nod. A broad grin spread across Barnabas's face. Except for Matt, who had selected Barnabas, no one else in the room knew who Barnabas was.

Check out the TNC feed; Barnabas texted Lewis.

Lewis pulled it up.

Today's News Channel (TNC) was running a brief segment on mission ST-86, which was the cover story for mission TF-76. TNC was reporting that the purpose of the mission was to test a new type of space engine. Matt's small team would be flying a new class of space freighter. It featured a new engine and would attempt the fastest run ever made from Space Station Freedom to Outpost Charlie on Mars. Once there, the team would deliver supplies and experimentation equipment. As the meeting progressed, TNC was reporting details about their pending attempt to reach Mars and discussing the probability of Jacques Beauregard intercepting the craft before it reached its destination. Vegas odds were set at 2 to 1 against a safe arrival on Mars by Matt's crew. A bored Lewis knew all this because he was, at that very moment, surreptitiously eying the news report on his smartphone. He thought, *Wow, such creative reporting. They're discussing details about this mission that even I don't know about, and I am the Mission Controller.* He texted Barnabas. *Got the feed. Where do they get this stuff, anyway?*

"Gentlemen," Silvertongue began, "as you know, the purpose of this meeting is to discuss the progress of mission TF-76. It is to be undertaken by the United States Spaceship (USS) Osprey. This is a new space freighter, under Captain Dirksen's command. Underneath a superstructure that looks like a long-haul freighter lies all the combat and thrust technology developed for our new unnamed class of military frigate. The USS Osprey is designed to out-run or out-gun any pirates that roam the space routes between Earth and Mars. We'll use the Osprey and its cutting-edge technology to capture the notorious Jacques Beauregard and transport him to a prison at Outpost Delta on Mars. If capture is not possible, the Osprey will simply destroy the vile pirate and continue to Mars with a cargo of geological and botanical experiments, tools, and various supplies."

"Before we continue," Silvertongue droned on, "I'd like to extend my gratitude to Captain Dirksen for volunteering to command the USS Osprey on this mission, despite the danger. I commend his love of country and devotion to duty."

Lewis thought, *the only things driving Matt are his love of flying, the challenge of capturing a pirate, and a strong desire to see his wife and their son.*

"Ahem … I'd like to say, secrecy is of the utmost concern," Morris said.

Secrecy? If secrecy is the utmost concern, half the people in this room would be out, Barnabas texted.

With a meeting this big, the mole must be in this very room, Lewis replied.

Including me? Barnabas texted.

Especially you, Lewis shot back.

Lewis's attention returned to Morris, who was saying, "Even so, we need to fly a diverse and inclusive team. That's why we have chosen to review Captain Dirksen's crew selection. Though I would not wish to impinge on your authority as ship's captain, Mr. Dirksen," JC continued (as he impinged on Matt's authority). "I believe crew selection is so critical that we should at least *review* who you wish to be part of this mission. But first, let's review the broad aspects of what needs to be accomplished...."

As the interminable meeting wore on, Lewis let his mind wander. He reflected on the staging of this meeting. As with many larger organizations, the actual decisions were made away from these formal meetings. Frequently, formal meetings served to "socialize" the previously reached decisions, to remind everyone who was in charge or both.

Lewis looked up. From their body language and eagerness to be heard, it seemed that Silvertongue and Morris were using this meeting to demonstrate their position and status. This thought amused Lewis because the real power in this room was held by the two admirals. They had already agreed on a detailed course of action, weeks before this meeting. — a fact that Lewis had learned in a previous dinner with the two admirals. Its purpose was to "bring Lewis up to speed" on their latest adjustments to their plan. "Bring up to speed," in this case, was a euphemism for telling the veteran mission controller what he was expected to do. Lewis responded by recommending Matt to command the mission. The admirals said they wanted to "get the ball rolling," and Lewis knew Matt enjoyed rolling balls.

"CAPTAIN WRIGHT," Morris's voice seemed to boom as it instantly snapped Lewis's attention back to the meeting at hand.

He felt the blood rising up his neck as he said, "Huh?" and noticed all eyes were on him.

"Mr. Wright," Morris intoned, "we have yet to hear from you on this subject. Please share your thoughts on this very important matter. What do you have to say?"

What do I say? Lewis thought as his heart skipped a couple of beats. *I don't even know what they're discussing! What to say, what to say?*

"Well sir," Lewis began, then paused, looking slowly around the room. His mind raced for an answer that wouldn't give him away. It seemed that everyone had already spoken. "I believe that every aspect has already been touched upon. I'm afraid that anything I say will only repeat what's already been mentioned. So, I have nothing further to add, sir."

Matt coughed to hide his laughter at his friend's discomfort.

"Captain Dirksen, was there more you wanted to add?" Morris asked.

"No, sir," Matt said. "A sip of water just went down the wrong pipe."

"Very well," Morris replied. "Let's move on to the next agenda item: reviewing Captain Dirksen's crew proposals. Admiral Robinson, please lead this aspect of the discussion."

Smooth recovery. Very smooth, Barnabas texted Lewis.

Robinson chewed on his unlit cigar as he browsed the holographic dossiers of the proposed crew. An agitated Matt tugged at his collar and continued to sweat as he waited and shot a glance at his friend in the corner. Lewis caught his glance and returned a slight smile and thought, *Sorry, buddy, I know you shouldn't have to vet your crew selection before a bunch of NASA bureaucrats, but I couldn't stop it.* Lewis noted that Matt's right leg was bouncing. Lewis knew that only happened when the captain was nervous, frustrated, or angry.

Today, Lewis thought, *he's all three.*

"Ahem," Morris began, "Captain Dirksen. I've examined your proposed crew … ah; I still need to be convinced they are up to the task at hand. Admiral Robinson asked me to play devil's advocate as you argue your case."

"As you know, there is strength in diversity," Silvertongue interjected with a thin smile.

"Uh, yes, James," Morris continued. "Let's begin with your selection of Payload Specialists Hilda McDermott and Marc Smith. I appreciate their notable accomplishments in their … uh … fields of endeavor. But, given the physical danger this mission will encounter, is it wise to carry two civilians?"

In response, Matt called up a hologram on the table. It showed Hilda, an athletic woman in her late 30's with short red hair, a Roman nose, and a strong jaw. She was taking down an opponent by tossing them over her hip during a hand-to-hand combat exercise. The intensity of her eyes revealed that she had little sympathy for her opponent.

"Mr. Morris," Matthew's leg continuing to bounce, "Hilda McDermott is not only a well-respected Botanist but also an ex-Marine Gunnery Sergeant. As such, she taught small arms marksmanship and advanced hand-to-hand combat techniques. Not to mention that she earned the silver star for her exploits during the Asteroid conflict."

"Really?" Carter exclaimed as he looked more closely at the hologram. "You're saying she's that good?"

"She holds a black belt in Taekwondo," Matt responded.

"And Marc Smith?" asked Morris.

At Matt's command, the hologram began showing Marc, a tall, muscular man with a boxer's nose, bent at the knees and waist, locking arms with a larger opponent. They grappled for a few seconds. Suddenly, Marc moved to the side of his opponent, drove forward, grabbing his opponent's knees, lifting him, then drove him to the ground. A big grin covered Marc's sunburnt face as he helped his opponent to his feet.

Didn't know a big guy could move that fast, Lewis texted Barnabas.

"Before becoming a Geologist, Marc Smith was a Master Sergeant in the Special Forces. His specialty was explosives. He also holds a black belt in karate. Like McDermott, he served with distinction during the Asteroid conflict," Matt said.

"In short, he's very good at blowing up rocks," Lewis interjected. His failed attempt to lighten the mood was met with silence. He wondered, *did anyone in the room even read the reports Matt provided ahead of time?*

"Publicly, these two are just a couple of scientists on their way to Mars with several experiments on board. Their military service and credentials are not part of their published bio's. They'll give any unsuspecting pirate trying to board us more than a little grief," Matt said.

"Two ordinary scientists. This is good. Good start, Captain," Silvertongue affirmed.

"You selected Lieutenant Commander Barnabas Chidi Maalouf as your mission pilot?" Robinson asked. The hologram showed a tall cheerful-looking, 40-something Western African with a spectacular smile.

They're talking about you, my friend, Lewis, texted Barnabas.

Yes, they are, Barnabas texted back.

"Yes, sir. His specialty is flying long haul-freighters. He flew troop transports during the Lunar War and was also awarded the 'flying cross' during the Asteroid conflicts. He holds the highest score in the pre-qualifying tests on the Osprey's simulator," Matt answered.

"I heard a rumor that Commander Maalouf is a member of the Coptic Church. Isn't it risky having a cult member on board?" Silvertongue inquired. "Don't get me wrong. I'm all for diversity. I'm just wondering."

You're a cultist, now are you? Lewis texted Barnabas.

So, it seems Barnabas texted back.

"Mr. Silvertongue," Matt spoke up while trying not to roll his eyes. "The Coptic Church is no cult. It's an orthodox Christian Church dating back to the first century. Coptic simply means African."

"Lewis smiled at his friend's deliberate use of "Mr." instead of Doctor when addressing Silvertongue.

"I suppose it wouldn't hurt to include one of those religious types," Silvertongue mused.

Very generous of Silvertongue, Lewis texted.

It's my winsome smile, Barnabas replied.

"Reviewing your co-pilot and weapons officer," Morris said, "tell us why, besides her looks, you would select Lieutenant JG Marci Gonzalez?"

The hologram now showed a stunning brunette with shoulder-length hair, sparkling brown eyes, and a radiant smile. Marci could have stepped out of a fashion magazine. She was animated in answering the questions about why she chose to be an astronaut.

"It appears she could be quite the social butterfly," Morris observed. "I've heard she's been recently observed in the company of a variety of young officers at the SkyDome."

"Yes, I believe with your nephew HJ," Robinson quipped, causing Morris to frown.

"Lieutenant Gonzalez is indeed extroverted. However, she's hardly a social butterfly. When it comes to flying, her handle is 'Ice Queen.' She finished top of her class at the Academy and went on to complete Top Gun training. No one, absolutely no one, can match her weapon systems skills. This fact was confirmed by her score in the Osprey weapon systems control simulation tests."

"But she has no actual combat experience," Robinson stated.

Matt frowned and shifted forward in his seat. "She does, sir. She flew with distinction toward the end of the Asteroid Conflict." He paused, looking intently at Robinson before saying, "In fact, she also flew fighter cover for the last raid on Beauregard's hideout. She took out two pirate fighters and covered the damaged troop transport, Charlie as it returned from the raid."

Admiral Robinson's face turned dark at the reference to his last failed effort to capture the pirate. But he kept his composure and said, "She sounds like a winner, Captain."

Each one around the table nodded their consent.

"That's settled," Carter said. "Now, let's look at your Tech Officer."

"I have a suggestion, Admiral," Morris interrupted. "He graduated third in his class at the academy. His specialty was weapons and tactical countermeasures. He participated in the last raid on Beauregard's hideout. He also has extensive experience in the handling of munitions. He has been trained in the operations of the Positron Reactor. I think this makes Lieutenant JG Homer Jaeger a vital addition to your team."

Matt couldn't hide his surprise and displeasure with Morris recommending his nephew for this assignment. Matt didn't even have a chance, yet, to make a case for his choice.

Watch your step Matt, Lewis thought. *Aggravating Morris could be a career-ender.*

Matt took a deep breath. "Lieutenant Jaeger is a strong candidate, sir," he admitted. "And, under most circumstances, he's a logical choice. However, Chief Petty Officer Joshua Torres is an expert in supporting the new class of frigates represented by the Osprey. He's so well qualified that he led the team that developed the Osprey simulator."

"Did Chief Torres wash out of the Academy's Spaceship Pilot program?" Morris asked.

"Not exactly, sir," Matt replied. "He was at the head of his class when an accidental explosion damaged his eyesight. So, he failed his subsequent physical due to his impaired vision. Technically it's a wash-out, but it wasn't due to lack of skill or effort. In fact, after being released from the Academy program, Chief Torres applied for and was accepted as a noncommissioned officer responsible for all Academy's flight simulators. A position he's held for three years."

"Sounds like a good pick to me," Carter said.

There was a murmur of approval in the room to which Morris responded, with a frown, "Chief Torres is your Tech Specialist."

"Thank you, sir," Matt replied.

"You're welcome. Just remember he's your choice," a disappointed Morris said. "Hopefully, thinking of your career, he works out."

Robinson spoke up. "Say, JC, I think it might be wise to send a weapons officer to Outpost Delta to inspect their defenses. Why not send Lieutenant Jaeger as a passenger on this mission? He can conduct the inspection. He could even lend a hand to the crew on the way."

Morris smiled, "That's a great idea. What do you think, Captain?"

"Works for me," Matt replied, with more enthusiasm than he felt.

Lewis shared his friend's disappointment. *Did we just let a mole onto our ship?* He wondered. The time had come to let Matt and Barnabas in on his own misgivings.

Preparations

The instructor's monotone delivery, combined with the warm, stuffy room, lulled Chief Warrant Officer Josh Torres into a semi-comatose state. His head bobbed as he tried to stay awake. By order of the TF-76 Mission Controller, Lewis Wright, the entire crew of the Osprey was required to attend a technology review of their ship. A torture that Josh was not spared even though he was as the ship's Tech Officer, so familiar with the Osprey that he wrote its simulation training program. Today's topic was the ship's power plant and life support.

Matt, also struggling to keep awake, noted that his entire crew and several other crews were present. He further noticed, with displeasure, that Lieutenant JG Homer Jaeger (HJ) was not in attendance. The lieutenant had ducked out because of an apparent "urgent request" by the NASA Program Chief. While technically not a crew member, HJ could be an asset on this mission, but for his aversion to participating in the training exercises.

"The Alpha class transport vessel is outfitted with the latest version of the Z56 Positron Reactor," the instructor droned on. "This is more efficient and safer than the nuclear reactor it replaces."

"How are positron reactors safer than nuclear reactors if they use anti-matter as fuel?" Hilda McDermott interrupted.

"They are for several reasons," replied the instructor. "First, they are less complicated, so fewer things can go wrong. Second, nuclear reactors, and their spent fuel, stay radioactive for years after being used up. Also, the kill zone for an exploding Positron Reactor is only a few kilometers, versus the many miles associated with that of a nuclear reactor."

"Either way," Marc interjected, "anyone on the spaceship is definitely in the kill zone."

"This is true," the instructor replied.

"Peachy. That's just peachy," another student remarked.

The class laughed.

Seeing the puzzled expression on several other students' faces, the instructor continued, "The engine itself is safe. The danger comes from our ability to store the anti-matter fuel. The positron fuel reacts with any kind of matter to create energy. So, it must be stored in a magnetic field. As long as that magnetic field is intact, all is well. But if that field loses enough strength, the anti-matter escapes, causing an out-of-control reaction."

"What does that mean?" Hilda asked.

"It means that the engine explodes, taking out the surrounding half dozen kilometers," Matt replied.

The instructor said, "This shouldn't happen. The Z56 Positron Reactor diverts a portion of its power to keep the magnetic fuel container stable. The engine must be in either thrust mode or standby mode. Either way, it provides the energy to keep the magnetic container stable."

"What if the engine shuts down before all the anti-matter is used?" asked another student.

The instructor said, "The magnetic field weakens and allows the anti-matter to escape, causing an explosion. That's why the Alpha Class transport is equipped with an emergency engine-compartment-ejection system. The system separates the entire engine compartment from the rest of the transport. It pushes it to a safe distance away from the crew. It's activated from the pilot's console."

"What if that doesn't work?" Hilda asked.

"Why, Gunny?" Josh said. "I never knew you to be such a pessimist."

"Just asking," Hilda replied.

The instructor came to her defense. "That's a good question. In a worst-case scenario, the emergency ejection can be triggered from the engine compartment itself as a failsafe option. That's it for today. Class dismissed."

As they filed out, Josh turned to Hilda. "He forgot to mention that the poor shmuck who triggers the ejection from the engine compartment dies when the engine blows."

Hilda shuddered at the thought.

"Which is why I'm a weapons officer and not a tech officer," Marci interjected as she passed them both. "The tech officer is the shmuck who gets to hit the Eject Button. Sucks to be a tech officer, right, Chief?"

"That was harsh," Hilda said to Josh.

"Naw, it's just an 'ex' thing," Josh replied.

"Really? She's an 'ex'?"

Josh watched Marci walk away. "Sad, but true."

Aboard the Osprey-Sim

The Osprey shuddered from the impact of pirate-extraordinaire Jacques Beauregard's energy weapons. The Osprey's pilot, Barnabas, rolled the ship down and to the right to avoid the second round of energy bursts – part of Beauregard's surprise greeting.

"Drones away!" Marci shouted amid the din of emergency alarms and impact warning bells. The drones swarmed toward Beauregard's array of spaceships, causing all but his lead ship to break off their attack on the Osprey. With the drones harassing the other enemy ships, the lead ship closed rapidly on the Osprey.

"Port shields at 75%, Captain," Josh reported.

"Divert power from the starboard shields to the port side, Chief," Matt replied. "Commander, try and keep that ship to our port side."

"Aye, sir," was the reply from both Josh and Barnabas.

Beauregard's lead ship kept closing in, firing its weapons at full force. Even though the Osprey's port shields were still holding, the pirate's ship was now close enough to set off more collision alarms.

Matt frowned. "He's trying to close on us faster than I expected. He thinks we can't beat him at close range."

"Captain, I'm repositioning thrusters to move us laterally away from that ship. Trying to keep it to our port side," Barnabas said.

"No good, Commander," Josh interrupted. "The ship is still closing. It's as if we are drawing it in with a tractor beam."

"You're right. I think the bogie using a tractor beam on us," Barnabas replied.

"That shouldn't work on us," Marc said. "We're the bigger ship."

"Doesn't matter that we are the larger vessel. The beam acts like a lasso that pulls the bogie towards us. Now that it's locked in, we can't pull away," Barnabas said.

"Smith, McDermott, prepare to repel boarders," Matt commanded.

"Aye, Captain," Marc and Hilda took up their positions, creating a cross-fire to welcome any hostile boarders.

"Focus, everyone," Matt said. "Beauregard is aiming to board us. Commander, how good are you at swatting flies?"

"Flies? What? Oh, I catch your meaning, Captain," Barnabas said after a moment's hesitation. "I'll give it my best shot."

The danger of shooting had become too great. A direct hit on either ship would cripple both vessels. Everyone's weapons fell silent as the pirate ship maneuvered to dock at the Osprey's port-side docking station.

Barnabas said, "Lieutenant Gonzalez, set your energy weapons to 12 o'clock high and prepare to fire on my mark."

"Aye, sir," was her puzzled response.

"Chief, read me the distance to the pirate ship," Barnabas said. "I need to know when he's eight feet from our dock."

"Aye, sir. They're at 50 feet."

Barnabas turned off the ship's anti-collision program and went to manual override. Then he gently tilted the Osprey's stubby port-side wing up 30 degrees as if inviting the Pirate to dock. The pirate ship cut its engines and tractor beam power as it prepared to do just that.

"Status of the tractor beam, Chief?" Barnabas asked.

"Sensors indicate that it's off."

"I see maneuvering thrusts," Marci observed. "Looks like they are lining up to dock."

"Very good," said Barnabas. "Distance, please, Chief."

"They'll be at five feet on my mark: four, three, two, one, MARK."

At that moment, Barnabas used his wing thrusters to execute a quick 210-degree roll. The Osprey shuddered as its stubby wing caught the much smaller pirate ship and slung it around like a rock. More alarms sounded from the impact. The pirate ship spun out of control, straight overhead, rushing away.

"Lieutenant, commence firing on my mark," Barnabas commanded.

"Aye, sir," Marci responded.

Josh said, "We'll be outside our mutual kill zone in five seconds, sir!"

"Thanks, Chief. We're at five, four, three, two, one, MARK!"

"Firing now!" Marci exclaimed.

"Keep firing until you take that rat down," Barnabas ordered.

An orange fireball erupted from the pirate's hull. "He's hit!" Josh shouted.

Marci smiled. "Just like skeet shooting, only I forgot to say 'pull.'"

"Well played, you three," Matt said. "All hands, damage report."

"Portside wing is badly damaged, but our compartment seal is holding," Josh replied.

"I've lost all my port thrusters," Barnabas answered.

"Very good. We seem to be clear of threats," Matt concluded.

"Not quite, sir," Josh corrected. "We've drifted too close to the planet's surface and are beginning an unplanned re-entry."

"Prepare to engage the main engine. It's time to bid this place farewell." Matt watched the remains of the pirate vessel begin their descent. "Five, four, three, two, one, fire!"

There was a disturbing silence. "The main engine's not responding," Barnabas reported.

Matt frowned. "Try again. On my mark: four, three, two, one, fire!"

Silence.

"Okay, kids, strap yourselves in and prepare for an unplanned re-entry procedure," Matt said. "Five, four, three, two, one, fire retros."

The reassuring sound of retro rockets and a familiar tremble of the ship assured the crew that all was not lost yet.

This ought to be interesting. Trying to land this ship with only the fore, aft, and starboard thrusters, Barnabas thought.

The captain echoed his thoughts by saying, "Bet you wished you had those port side thrusters about now, huh, Commander?"

The whole re-entry was a white-knuckled affair for Barnabas. Sweat beaded on his forehead as he struggled to keep the craft stable with the correct angle of attack. At times, he had control. At other times, the Osprey tried to tumble out of control. All the while, the planet's surface was rising to meet them way too quickly.

The craft shimmied and shuddered and began to tumble again. Finally, it slowed up, righted itself, and began to descend much like a leaf floating back and forth to earth. The craft came to rest with a thud. The entire ship shuddered one last time, and the ceiling panel just behind the commander's seat fell to the floor.

Matt unstrapped himself from his seat in the flight simulator and nodded. "We survived yet another simulated attack. Good work. I'll tell

Mission Controller Wright we're ready to launch whenever he wants. By the way, Chief Torres, nice touch with the ceiling panel."

Josh smiled. "Just wanted to add a touch of realism, sir."

"All right, kiddos, that's a wrap," Matt said. "Get something to eat and get some rest. We have an early wake-up call to get from Houston to the space station. That is all of you except for Chief Torres. You and I need to talk."

"Whoa, looks like someone is staying after school," Marci gave Josh a wink as she and the others exited the simulator.

After they left, Josh said, "Captain, I never got a chance to thank you for choosing me as your tech officer. I know Morris wanted you to choose his nephew instead. I just wanted you to know that I appreciate the —"

"Forget it, kid," Matt interrupted, "I didn't pick you out of the goodness of my heart. I need somebody I can trust, with certain skills. That happens to be you. The fact is that–Morris and his nephew Jaeger are sticklers for following standard protocols and nothing more. Following the standard flight protocol won't work on this assignment. Listen — I am sure of two things. First, Jacques Beauregard is operating much closer to Space Station Freedom than our Intelligence department reports. Second, I believe he has a mole at either NASA or with one of its contractors. Beauregard knows all about our launch protocols and primary space routes to Mars. That means he chooses where and when to strike. I want to change that." Matt handed Josh several sheets of paper full of handwritten notes. "I've pseudo-coded alternate launch protocols."

"Handwritten, even," Josh interrupted as he took the papers. "You really do believe there is a mole afoot."

Matt ignored Josh's comment and continued, "I also have a new flight plan. It is not the officially submitted plan. Instead, we'll use a starting burn point that's never used and proceed through an area that he doesn't expect. We'll then accelerate at twice the normal rate. This'll leave Beauregard and his crews out of position and falling behind us. They'll have to scramble to catch up. If we're alert, we can track Beauregard and his crew as they close on us. We'll dictate where and when to engage him."

"Sounds good, Captain." Josh studied the new plan carefully, "But this new flight plan takes us through a no-fly zone."

"Precisely. No one will expect that," Matt said, with a twinkle in his eye.

"Yeah, but this is marked a no-fly zone due to the amount of space debris in the area."

"With Commander Maalouf's flying skills, it should be a piece of cake. We must make Beauregard scramble. It's our best chance to gain the upper hand."

"But how can we be sure they won't just let us pass rather than try and catch us?"

"I can't be sure. I'm just hoping that our false manifest list is lucrative enough to attract Beauregard's attention."

"False manifests, breach-of-launch protocol, alternate flight plans – just how much of this have you shared with the Mission Controller?"

"We've agreed on the false manifest list, but otherwise, we've only talked generalities. If this plan goes sideways, it will all be on us."

Josh grinned, "Sounds like a potential career-killer. Count me in."

"How long will it take you to reprogram the flight computers?"

"This'll take a while, sir. I'll need to access Osprey's flight computers remotely. To do that, I'll need to hack Space Station Freedom's flight-control computers and uplink from there. That'll take pretty much all night to be sure I am not detected. I guess I won't be sleeping until after we leave for Space Station Freedom."

Matt turned to leave, "Sounds like a plan. Do you need anything?"

"Some pizza and Red Bull would be nice." Josh set to work.

"Done and done."

As he worked, Josh thought about his assignment. The captain was pretty much a "by the book" guy himself. False manifests, hacking computers, phony flight plans weren't his style. If it weren't for his trust in the captain, Josh would have had serious doubts about what Matt was asking him to do.

Mission Control

Mission Control, Houston, Texas - December 14, 2068, 0800 Hours

Thunderstorms were rolling across Houston as launch day dawned. However, those in Mission Control were more interested in mission TF-76 than in the local weather. When James Christopher Morris II, Vice Admiral Justin Carter, Vice Admiral Dennis Robinson, and their personal aides arrived, the control center crackled with anticipation. The flight controllers were at their respective stations, monitoring information from Launch Control on space station Freedom. Mission Controller Lewis Wright, standing toward the back of the room, surveyed all the flight control stations from his position. He nodded toward the entourage as they filed into the observation hall overlooking the control center. Admiral Carter separated himself from the others and stood just behind Lewis on the operations center floor.

Lewis nodded toward the Communications Officer, "Are we patched in with Space Station Freedom and to the Osprey, Lieutenant?"

"Yes, sir," the Communications Officer replied. "They've just finished prepping the Osprey for launch."

"Very good, Lieutenant," Lewis said. "Switch their transmissions to the main speakers."

"Yes, sir."

Lewis nodded to Admiral Carter, who nodded and took a seat on a nearby stool.

Over the main speaker, the room could hear the transmissions between the two control centers and the Osprey.

"Mission Control, Freedom Control, come in."

"Freedom Control, Mission Control, we copy and have Captain Wright, Mission Controller, standing by. Over.

"Mission Control, Freedom Control, we copy. Welcome to the party, sir. How's the weather in Houston? Over."

"Freedom Control, Mission Controller. I copy. It's stormy down here, but I suppose you can already see that from where you sit. How's the weather up there? Over."

"Mission Controller, Freedom Control, we copy. All is quiet here. The radiation from our last solar storm passed us several days ago. Over."

"Freedom Control, Mission Controller. I copy. You're clear to proceed with the launch at your pleasure. We're standing by. Over."

"Mission Controller, Freedom Control, we copy. We'll commence with the launch directly. Over."

"ST-86 Osprey, Freedom Control, come in."

"Freedom Control, ST-86 Osprey, I copy you. Over."

"Osprey, Freedom Control, you're cleared for undocking. Over."

"Freedom Control, Osprey, we're undocking on my mark: five, four, three, two, one, MARK. Undocking is underway. Over."

"Osprey, Freedom Control, undocking looks good from our view. Do you copy? Over."

"Freedom Control, Osprey, we copy. Over."

"Osprey, Freedom Control, you're cleared to depart. Over."

"Freedom Control, Osprey, roger that. Over."

"Osprey, Freedom Control, you may begin your initial burn when you clear the buffer zone. Over."

"Freedom Control, Osprey, we copy. Over."

After twenty minutes, Freedom Control's mike came back to life.

"Osprey, Freedom Control, you've cleared the buffer zone. You're clear to adjust your heading to match your flight plan and begin with a 40% burn for departure. We're turning you over to Mission Control. Godspeed. Over."

"Freedom Control, Osprey, we copy. Beginning departure protocol on my mark: five, four, three, two, one, MARK. <static> Over."

"Osprey, Mission Control, we're tracking your flight. Let's run through the post-departure checklist. Over."

"Mission Control, Osprey, <static> we are <static> issues <static> dropping into parking orbit for the time<static>...."

"Osprey, Mission Control, we didn't copy your last transmission. Please repeat. Over."

"Mission Control, Osprey, we are dropping into <static> orbit. Over."

"Osprey, Mission Control, do you need to re-dock? Over."

"Mission Control, Osprey, negative, we don't need to re-dock. Our <static> flight computers aren't in sync. We're dropping into a low earth parking orbit and will attempt to re-sync the computers. If we're not successful, we'll request permission to re-dock. Over."

What are you doing, Matt? Lewis thought. To the mission controllers, he said, "Gentlemen, get eyes on the Osprey ASAP. Use any tracking assets you need, but keep that ship in your sight."

"Osprey, Captain Wright, Matt, what the heck is happening? Don't take any chances with your flight computers. We have eyes on you but be ready to scrub your flight if those computers don't sync. Do you copy? Over."

"Captain Wright, Osprey, Roger that. I'll keep you informed. <static>"

"Why don't you scrub the mission, Captain Wright?" Carter asked.

"No reason to just yet, sir," Lewis replied. "We'll let them straighten things out from parked orbit rather than interrupting other scheduled arrivals and departures. Only ... if all three computers can't be synced in time to meet our launch window, do we scrub. Mission Control, see if you can't hurry things along."

"Yes, sir," came the reply.

"Mission Control, Osprey, be advised that your launch window is rapidly closing. Missing that window makes it impossible to reach the correct Hohmann transfer orbit. Over."

"Osprey, Mission Control, copy that. Over."

Time seemed to drag on as other flights came and went from Space Station Freedom. Carter sat in a chair behind Lewis. Finally, Osprey's channel crackled to life.

"Mission Control, Osprey, all three computers are synced at 0800 hours, and we are ready to begin our departure protocol. Over."

"Osprey, Mission Control, you're cleared to depart. What are your coordinates? Over."

"Mission Control, Osprey, we are above coordinates 25.0000° N, 71.0000° W. Over."

"What? No!" Admiral Carter exclaimed as he flew off his stool. "They can't burn from those coordinates. It's against protocol to depart from there. Tell them to stop!"

Lewis shot an inquisitive look at the admiral and nodded to the Flight Controller.

"Osprey, Mission Control, do not depart from your current coordinates. Over."

"Mission Control, Osprey, we didn't copy your last transmission. <static> We are beginning our departure protocol. We'll begin our burn on my mark: five, four, three, <static> MARK. Commencing burn. Over."

"Osprey, Mission Control, your burn puts you in a no-fly zone. Abort your burn. Copy?"

"Mission Control <static> we are not...<static> Please retransmit."

"Osprey, Mission Control, abort your burn and adjust your heading. Do you copy?"

"Mission Control, Osprey, we didn't copy your last transmission. We're increasing our burn to 80%. <static> Please <static> your last transmission. Over."

Lewis asked, "Flight Control, do you have a visual on the Osprey?"

"Affirmative, sir. Our observation posts see the Osprey clearly. All looks well, except their acceleration is much faster than normal, and they're entering the no-fly zone."

"Freedom Control, Mission Control, do you have eyes on the Osprey? Over."

"Mission Control, Freedom Control, we copy. She's in our sights, and her telemetry readouts are normal. Everything looks good except for their radio transmissions. Over."

Lewis looked at the admiral, who had turned deathly pale. "Flight Control, keep a visual on the ship and try to raise them again."

"Osprey, Mission Control, do you read me? Over."

"Mission Control, <static> Osprey, we are having difficulty hearing you. <static> Over."

"Osprey, Mission Control, you're entering the no-fly zone. Correct your course and come about ASAP. Over."

"Mission Control, Osprey, we didn't copy your last transmission. We're" <static>. The static was replaced by extended silence. The mission controllers exchanged worried glances.

"Mission Control, Osprey, do you copy? Over."

Silence.

<static> "are braking and sliding past a primitive space vehicle. It has a distinctive elongated bell-shaped body <static> solar panels <static> extended like rectangular wings. The <static> has Russian letters that would be USSR if written in English. Do you copy? Over."

"Osprey, Mission Control, we copy. You're maneuvering past a primitive space vehicle believed to be of Russian origin. Did you sustain any damage? Over."

"Mission Control, we still have a visual on Osprey and think we see the vehicle it just missed," a tech observer reported.

"Mission Control, Osprey, we're just a little shaken up. We have no damage to—"

"Osprey, Mission Control, we lost your last transmission. Please repeat. Over."

Silence.

"Osprey, Mission Control, do you copy?"

Silence.

"Osprey, Mission Control, report your position and status. Over."

Silence.

"Osprey, Mission Control, do you copy?"

Silence.

"Sir, we've lost communication with the Osprey," the Communications Officer reported.

"Sir, this is Flight Control. We've lost all telemetry from the Osprey."

"Any automated distress signals?" Lewis asked.

"No, sir," came the response.

"Sir, the tracking stations are reporting they've lost all visual contact with the Osprey," the Communications Officer reported.

A chill ran down Lewis's back. "Check with Freedom Control."

"Freedom Control, Mission Control, do you have a visual of the Osprey? Over."

"Mission Control, Freedom Control, negative, we've lost all visual contact. Over."

"Freedom Control, Mission Control, any sign of explosion or collision? Over."

"Mission Control, Freedom Control, we copy. That's a negative. One minute she was there; the next, she was gone. Over."

Turning to his control center, Lewis asked, "Did anyone see debris? Or an explosive flash or any indication of what happened with her?"

"No, sir. All our tracking stations report that she was there one second and gone the next. She just disappeared."

"Damn!" Lewis exclaimed. He glanced at the Admiral, who had slumped back into the stool, his face still ashen. Lewis turned and faced him. "Admiral, you need to tell me what you know about coordinates 25.0000° N, 71.0000° W, and about what just happened out there!"

Lost Control

Space Station Freedom - December 14, 2068, 0800 Hours

The earth-rise was stunning. The planet stood out as a brilliant blue gem against the black velvet curtain of space. However, its beauty was lost on the crew of the Osprey. They were busy working down their pre-launch checklist. Captain Matt Dirksen looked over his team with satisfaction. Everyone was in their spacesuits, buckled in, and engaged with the tasks at hand. He paused just long enough after the last pre-launch task was checked off the list to relish the moment. He never got over the excitement of starting a new mission. Besides, he was on his way to see his wife and son. First, he just needed to finish the small task of capturing or eliminating a very cunning pirate.

"Okay, kiddos," he said to the crew, "it's showtime. Commander Maalouf, would you do the honors?"

"Glad to, sir," Barnabas replied. "Freedom Control, Commander Maalouf, ST-86 Osprey is ready for departure and standing by for your orders. Over."

"Osprey, Freedom Control, we copy. When Mission Control comes online, we'll commence your departure procedures. Over."

"Freedom Control, Osprey, we copy and will stand by. Over."

Matt glanced back and smiled at Josh. "Waiting is the hardest part. Hopefully, it won't be too long, Chief."

"ST-86 Osprey, Freedom Control, come in."

"Freedom Control, ST-86 Osprey, I copy. Over."

"Osprey, Freedom Control, you're cleared for undocking. Over."

"Freedom Control, Osprey, we're undocking on my mark: five, four, three, two, one, MARK. Undocking is underway. Over."

"Osprey, Freedom Control, undocking looks good from our view. Do you copy? Over."

"Freedom Control, Osprey, we copy. Over."

"Osprey, Freedom Control, you are cleared to depart. Over."

"Freedom Control, Osprey, roger that. Over."

"Osprey, Freedom Control, you may now begin your initial burn when you clear the buffer zone. Over."

"Freedom Control, Osprey, we copy and are preparing to commence our burn. Over."

"Osprey, Freedom Control, you have cleared the buffer zone. You are cleared to adjust your heading to match your flight plan and begin with a 40% burn for departure. We will be turning you over to Mission Control. Godspeed. Over."

Matt gave a slight nod to Josh, who switched to their alternate flight plan.

"Freedom Control, Osprey, we copy. Beginning departure protocol on my mark: five, four, three, two, one, MARK. <static> Over."

Nice touch, Chief, Matt thought. *Radio issues will make it easier to explain why Mission Control instructions weren't followed. You can't follow a directive if you hear static.*

"Osprey, Mission Control, we're now tracking your flight. Let's run through the post-departure checklist. Over."

Just then, an alarm went off. "Captain, there's a computer sync exception," Barnabas said.

"Chief, what are you seeing?" Matt asked.

"Our flight control computers aren't in sync, sir," Josh reported. "Protocol says we can't depart until all three computers are in sync."

"How long will it take to re-sync the computers, Chief?" Matt asked.

"Forty minutes to an hour, sir," was the response.

"Commander, put us into a parking orbit over Earth until the problem is resolved."

"Sir, wouldn't you want to re-dock instead?" Barnabas asked.

"No, I'm not giving Mission Control the chance to delay this mission for further tests," Matt said. "Drop into parking orbit while I notify Mission Control of our intentions."

"Aye, sir," Barnabas said.

"Mission Control, Osprey, <static> we are <static> computer sync issues <static> dropping into parking orbit. Over."

"Osprey, Mission Control, we didn't copy your last transmission. Please repeat. Over."

"Mission Control, Osprey, we're dropping into <static> orbit."

"Osprey, Mission Control, do you need to re-dock? Over."

"Mission Control, Osprey, negative. We don't need to re-dock. Our <static> flight computers are not in sync. We're dropping into a low earth parking orbit and will attempt to re-sync the computers. If we're not successful, we'll request permission to re-dock. Over."

"Osprey, Captain Wright, Matt – what the heck is happening? Don't take any chances with your flight computers. We have eyes on you but be ready to scrub your flight if those computers don't sync. Do you copy? Over.

"Captain Wright, Osprey, roger that. I'll keep you informed. Over <static>...."

True to his word, Josh had the flight control computers re-synced within the hour. "We're set to go on your command, sir," he reported.

"Mission Control, Osprey, all three computers are synced at 0800 hours, and we're ready to commence departure protocol. Over."

"Osprey, Mission Control, you are cleared to depart. What are your coordinates? Over."

"Mission Control, Osprey, coordinates are 25.0000° N, 71.0000° W."

"Osprey, Mission Control, do not <static> current coordinates. Over."

"Did you catch that last transmission, Chief?" Matt inquired.

"Not clearly, sir," Josh replied.

"Mission Control, Osprey, we didn't copy your last transmission. Please retransmit. Otherwise, we're beginning our departure protocol. We'll begin our burn on my mark: five, four, three, two, one, MARK. Commencing burn. Over," Matt transmitted.

"Osprey, Mission Control, your burn puts you <static>. Abort. <static> Copy?"

"Mission Control, Osprey, we're not receiving a clear transmission. Retransmit. Over."

"Osprey, Mission Control, <static> burn and adjust <static> Copy?"

"Mission Control, Osprey, we did not copy your last transmission. We are increasing our burn to 80% of maximum. Please repeat your last transmission. Over."

"Osprey, Mission <static> you read me? <static>...."

"Can anyone make out what Mission Control's saying?" Matt asked.

"Mission Control, Osprey, we're having difficulty hearing you. Over," he transmitted.

"Osprey, Mission Control, you are entering the no-fly zone. <static> ASAP. Over."

"Mission Control, Osprey, we did not copy your last transmission. We are—"

Matt's transmission was suddenly interrupted by a cacophony of alarms sounding off. The Osprey's sudden deceleration threw all the astronauts hard against their seat harnesses. The ship jerked up and to the left, trying to avoid crashing into an unknown object, causing the astronauts to be slammed back into their seats. All Matt could transmit was a "Whoa!" The pained screeching of metal on metal filled the cabin as the Osprey clipped the interloping object. She began coming to a stop just beyond the source of her distress. All onboard could see what appeared to be an elongated bell-shaped body with two solar panels fully extended like the wings of a plane. The ancient spacecraft looked to be intact and relatively unscathed. Even the Russian lettering was visible on its side.

"Can anyone read Russian?" Matt asked.

"I can, sir," Marci volunteered. "It says USSR, whatever that means."

"It means that this is an ancient space vehicle. Circa 1960's, I think," Barnabas said.

"And you know this how, sir?" Marci asked.

"I'm a bit of a space history buff, Lieutenant," Barnabas confessed.

Matt said, "I'll report this. Someone, silence those damn alarms."

"Mission Control, Osprey, we just activated the crash avoidance maneuver protocol. We're braking and sliding past a primitive space vehicle. It has a distinctive elongated bell-shaped body and solar panels extended like rectangular wings. The side has Russian lettering that would be USSR if written in English. Do you copy? Over."

"Osprey, Mission Control, we copy. You're maneuvering past a primitive space vehicle believed to be of Russian origin. Did you sustain any damage? Over."

Matt clicked the mike off. "Damage reports, everyone."

"No damage to flight-control computers. No structural warnings," Josh reported.

"All green on my console," Marci reported.

"Flight controls, engines, and thrusters are all good," Barnabas said.

Matt nodded. "Good! I'll let Mission Control know we're good. Then we'll get underway. Begin with a 20% burn on my mark, Commander."

"Mission Control, Osprey, we're just a little shaken up. We have no damage to—"

Matt's transmission was interrupted by the Osprey's acceleration, seemingly on its own.

"Commander," Matt barked. "I said on 'my mark!'"

"I'm not doing anything, sir."

"Then bring it to a full stop!"

"It is!"

The Osprey continued to accelerate on its own. First, twisting to the right and then to the left. Then beginning to roll while still picking up speed. Each astronaut was forced ever deeper into their seat as the vehicle gained momentum at an alarming rate. The craft itself groaned under the pressure. Barely staying conscious, Matt saw a kaleidoscope of colors passing by the vehicle's portals. Josh was fighting the urge to throw up. Barnabas was fighting the stick to regain control of the ship. Finally, with Barnabas and Matt both working the controls, they stopped the rolling and righted the craft as it accelerated. Other than keeping the vessel from rolling, the commander and Captain had no control. The ship continued, on its own, for another half hour.

Then as suddenly as the wild ride started, the computers died, and the ship quickly decelerated, slamming its occupants against their harnesses. The rear of the craft lifted as if kicked forward by an invisible force. For a moment, it seemed the Osprey's tail would flip ahead of its nose. The ship shimmied and shuddered and began to tumble like a poorly kicked football. Finally, it slowed up, righted itself with a violent lurch, and began to descend much like a leaf floating back and forth to earth. The craft came to rest with a thud. The entire ship shuddered one last time, and the ceiling panel just behind the commander's seat fell to the floor.

Lost

Location, Unknown

Josh was still struggling to control his churning stomach. He looked at the ceiling panel on the floor. *At least I got that part of the simulation right,* he thought.

Matt was gathering his senses from the unexpected roller coaster ride. *What can possibly go wrong? Where was this on your list of possibilities, Admiral?* He thought bitterly. *So much for your perfect plan.*

"Is everyone okay?" Matt asked.

His question was greeted by a chorus of groans and moans.

A look out the windows showed the craft to be resting on a plateau or mesa of some sort. The sky was soft pink, like that of an early morning. The clouds had a reddish tinge. There appeared to be giant outcroppings of gems – cliffs of alabaster, topaz, and jade to the ship's right. Their surfaces were very smooth, with sharp angular edges. Between the spaceship and the cliffs rose a forest of strange trees. They looked like giant, colorful peacock feathers. They grew amidst a topiary of red "trees" that looked like they had been sculpted by a very creative gardener.

What stood out the most was the silence. All was quiet – in fact, too quiet. Josh thought, *There should be a slight hum of the engine sitting at idle, but the entire ship seems to be completely shut down.* He looked over at Matt. As their eyes met, Josh saw Matt's eyes widen. "The anti-matter container!" they shouted together. Josh bolted from his seat and headed toward the engine compartment.

"Commander, what's the status of the engine and the anti-matter container?" Matt asked.

"Sir, I've no readings. The master console's dead."

"Commander, arm the emergency-engine jettison unit."

Barnabas shook his head. "Sir, I'm unable to arm the jettison unit."

"Understood, Commander," Matt replied as he saw Josh exiting the ship's bridge. "Chief, turn on your O2 pack in case the engine room atmosphere is compromised!" he shouted at Josh. "Check the container status and arm the engine jettison by hand."

"Aye, sir," Josh slid to a stop, turning on his auxiliary O2 pack. "Oops." He tripped and bumped into the portside emergency evacuation portal lever. The outer door popped open with a dull thud.

"What was that, Chief?" Matt asked.

"Crap, I just accidentally triggered the starboard escape hatch door," Josh admitted.

"Whatever. Right now, just get a reading on the engine and the anti-matter container!" Matt ordered. "We're out of time if that container unit fails. Check in over the central com link."

"Aye, sir," Josh pulled himself through the compartment doorway.

"Everyone else, stay strapped in, in case we need to separate from the engine compartment," Matt ordered.

"What's going on, Commander?" HJ asked.

Barnabas frowned. "If you'd ever attended our training, Lieutenant, you'd know that a failed anti-matter chamber causes things, like this ship, to go BOOM."

"Sweet!" HJ said.

Josh entered the engine compartment. He felt his knees go weak as he saw that the magnetic field gauge was falling toward the critical stage. Any further drop and the anti-matter would begin to escape, starting an uncontrolled reaction. Breathing hard, Josh hit the communications button.

"Captain, you need to begin the jettison procedure now!" he said. "I'm exiting the compartment right now. Over."

Silence.

"Captain? Do you read me? Over."

Silence.

A glance at the gauge confirmed that the magnetic force was still weakening. His last resort was to press the manual eject override button. Josh knew that the ejection would trap him within the "kill zone" when the anti-matter was released. But it was the only way to save the others. He took a deep breath.

At least I won't feel anything, he thought.

Josh flipped the safety cover open and reached in to hit the ejection switch. A tap on his shoulder startled him. He stopped his motion and turned to look. He saw no one behind him. He turned back to the task at hand. Again, he felt a distinct tap on his shoulder. This time he jumped as a chill went down his spine. A persistent hum came to his ears. He wondered, *Could the engine be back on in standby mode?* Gathering his wits, he checked the gauges one last time. To his surprise, the gauges showed that the magnetic field was gaining strength. One of them was already back in the green. The others were moving steadily up toward green.

A dazed Josh returned the ejection switch cover to its closed position and double-checked the gauges. They had all returned to green. He began to shake as he wandered back to the bridge.

"What did you find, Chief? Why didn't you report over the com?" Matt's voice boomed.

"The com link's down, sir. But the anti-matter containment field is holding steady."

"How can the whole ship shut down, but not the anti-matter containment unit?"

"Perhaps it's just the main computers that shut down, sir," Barnabas answered. Turning to Josh, he asked, "You okay, Chief? You look like you just saw a ghost."

"Didn't see one, but might have felt one," Josh replied.

The rest of the crew were beginning to rouse gingerly from their seats. Hilda noticed that Barnabas took a moment to bow his head and make a sign of the cross before getting up.

"What just happened, Captain?" Marc asked.

"Not sure," Matt answered. "Stations, everyone. I want a damage control report from each of you ASAP."

The damage reports were negative, with three exceptions. This meant that the life support systems controlling air and water generation were not working. The situation was serious, and if the planet could not support human life, it would soon become critical.

"McDermott, do you have a gas-sampling kit with your gear?" Matt asked.

"Yes, sir, stashed in the Cargo hold," she replied.

"Grab it and take a sample of the atmosphere outside the ship, if you will," Matt ordered.

"Aye, sir, I'll get right on it."

While Hilda set to work, Barnabas and Josh took a short break and joined the others. The conversation quickly turned to their unexpected journey.

"You don't suppose this is the work of Jacques Beauregard, do you?" Marci asked.

"If it is, then he's a highly underrated pirate," Matt said. "I'm sure it's not him."

"I think we may have just experienced a wormhole," Barnabas ventured.

"Felt like an out-of-control roller coaster," Marc said.

"Interesting choice of analogies, Sarge," Matt said

"I hate roller coasters. So, it makes sense to me, sir."

"I thought wormholes were only theoretical, the stuff of science fiction," HJ challenged.

"Yeah," Marc added, "I read that wormholes form and then collapse after a very short time. They're either so small or so unstable that no one could safely pass through them."

"With the right conditions, one might traverse a wormhole and survive, except for tossing their cookies," Barnabas corrected.

"What do you mean, Commander?" Marci asked.

"I believe it was in the mid-'80s. Yes, that's when Kip Thorne and one of his graduate students showed that it's possible to pass through a wormhole consistent with general relativity. Of course, only if it has enough 'exotic matter' with negative energy to keep it open."

"And you would know this detail, Commander, because...?" HJ asked with a smirk.

"I read it somewhere – probably on Wikipedia," Barnabas said.

"Don't let him fool you, Mr. Jaeger," Matt interjected. "The commander here has a Ph.D. in Astrophysics. He's forgotten more on the subject of wormhole theory than I'll ever know."

"Really?" Marc said. "Commander, do you think we actually went through a wormhole?"

"It seems like that's what we experienced. But there's a catch," Barnabas answered.

"And that would be...?" Marc pressed.

"Most knowledgeable researchers agree that it takes more 'exotic matter' to stabilize a wormhole than can be formed naturally," Barnabas replied. "It would take highly advanced technology to create enough exotic matter to do the job."

"Are you saying someone from an advanced civilization or some form of intelligence opened the wormhole for us?" Marc asked.

"So, it seems," Barnabas agreed.

"Where are you going with this?" HJ asked.

"Nowhere," Barnabas answered. "I'm just saying that theoretically, a wormhole can't be traversed naturally. So, some form of intelligence and advanced technology is needed to make this happen."

"Connect the dots, Mr. Jaeger," Matt interjected. "We could be the unwitting guests of an advanced civilization."

"Or of some supernatural beings," Hilda added as she rejoined the group. "The question is, are they benevolent or malevolent?"

Marci ran a hand through her hair. "Now that's a sobering thought."

Aboard the Osprey

SHIP'S LOG December 14, 2068

Entry by Captain Dirksen:

After being drawn through what might be described as a wormhole, the Osprey came to rest upon what appears to be a tall plateau on a small planet. While she has no structural damage, the crew cannot connect with the central computer, which seems to be offline, or worse yet, dead (as are the two backup computers). Fortunately, the ship's engine is idling in standby mode, so its magnetic fuel container remains intact.

It seems that we arrived at midday. The light is beginning to dim as I make this entry. Osprey's life-support system is not functioning (a result of the primary computer failure), denying us access to fresh air. The food-and-water-dispensing system is also locked. My most significant concern is whether or not we can breathe the air on this planet as our available supply on the vessel is extremely limited.

In attempting to reboot the Ship's computers, we only received meaningless error messages.

Utilizing a test kit from her supplies, our biologist, Hilda McDermott, took a sample of the atmosphere. The results are disappointing. The sample ratios should be about 78% nitrogen, 21% oxygen, less than 1% carbon dioxide. The least amount of oxygen needed to support human life is about 17%; anything less than 16% and we pass out. According to her test, the atmosphere is 78% nitrogen, 7% oxygen, and 15% carbon dioxide. While no poisonous gasses were detected, we would not survive long outside on so little oxygen.

Situational Assessment:

The ship seems to be structurally sound. The Life-support system is offline. All access to food and water is locked down, and there is no way to regenerate the oxygen supply. The central computer and backups are unresponsive. Unless we can figure a way to scrub the carbon dioxide and extract enough oxygen from the atmosphere, our situation will become critical.

END OF ENTRY

As the day wore on, Josh and Barnabas continued to try restarting the computers. Their lack of progress frustrated Josh and irritated Matt. Even the ordinarily unflappable Commander expressed angst over their situation and lack of progress.

The rest of the crew took notes and pictures of their new surroundings from the Osprey's portals. It was hard for them to resist staring at such an exotic sight. The outcroppings around them were sparkling in the light, but no sun was visible. The feather trees occasionally swayed in the breeze. Behind them, some wispy clouds, white with a pink tinge, floated by.

"Strange," Hilda observed. "The plant life is predominately red and orange. I would expect more greens."

"And there doesn't seem to be any animal life, like birds and such," Marci added.

"Did you see that?" Marc asked.

"What?" Barnabas asked.

"A shimmering column," Marc said. "Maybe it's that chameleon technology."

"Chameleon technology?" Barnabas asked.

"It's a new cloak that blends with the background and covers the heat signature of a soldier," Marc explained. "There, I see it again over there."

"I can't see anything," Matt observed.

"I don't think it's shimmering," Hilda said. "It looks more like shafts of light."

"You may be right, Gunny," HJ said. "It's hard to tell in the daylight."

"But, there's something or someone out there," Marc insisted.

There was a growing sense that they were being watched. The appearance of circles of light shining on the floor or wall across from a portal confirmed this. The lights were about the size of a dinner plate and moved in a slow random motion before disappearing. Sometimes the light would be yellow. Other times it would be red or blue. Matt's body language, terse commands, and gruff demeanor revealed his frustration with the situation.

"At least the engine and fuel system are holding in standby mode," Barnabas said, trying to ease Matt's mood.

"No matter," Matt growled. "Chief, don't give up on those computers."

"Sir, I'm on it." Josh crawled under his workstation and opened an access panel.

"The rest of you, get off your asses and check this ship out top to bottom. Make sure it's still structurally sound," Matt barked.

The hapless crew once again set to work, looking for evidence of structural compromise.

"What's the point?" HJ complained in a low voice. "We've already done a damage assessment. Besides, if the structure had been compromised, we'd be dead by now."

"You don't know that for sure, Lieutenant," Marci said. "Actually...." She paused, looking at the master console.

"Actually, what?" HJ asked. Then he looked at Marci's expression. "What the hel—" He was interrupted by Marci, who asked, "Chief Torres, what are you up to?"

Josh looked up from under his workstation. "What do you mean?"

"Look at the main console, Chief, and tell me what you did," Marci pressed.

The console was displaying:

"Вы дети света или дети ночи?"

"What're you talking about?" Josh answered, with a puzzled look on his face. "I still can't get the computers to boot. That console doesn't even work. It has no power."

"What do you see, Lieutenant?" HJ asked.

"It's Russian. It's a question about children," Marci replied. "I think it says, "Are you children of the light or children of the night?"

Just as the others got within sight of the console, the message flickered and disappeared.

"You saw that, didn't you?" Marci asked.

"Saw what?" Hilda asked.

"The message on the console," Marci replied.

"No message. Just a couple of flickers on the monitor," HJ said.

"It was clear as day," Marci insisted. "It was Russian for 'are you children of the light or children of the night?' I—"

"Now we know what you *think* you saw, Lieutenant," Matt said.

"There was no *think* about it," Marci insisted. "Didn't anyone else see the message?"

Everyone shook their heads no. "It's all right, Lieutenant," HJ said. "We're all under a lot of stress. Right—"

"Don't patronize me!" Marci exclaimed. "I know what I saw."

Matt steered Barnabas aside and asked quietly, "What do you make of this?"

"Either the lieutenant is seeing things or...."

"Or what?"

"Or, it means we no longer control our own ship," Barnabas said.

Darkness was beginning to descend over the crippled spacecraft. Outside, the night was dim but not dark. It felt almost like a summer's night in Alaska. Inside, it was difficult to see. Fortunately, the flashlights seemed to be working. Matt had the crew make one more physical check for damage. Once he was satisfied that the ship was airtight and in no immediate danger, he set the night watch. He took the first watch and assigned Josh to take the second watch.

The Second Watch

No one could shake the feeling that someone or something was watching them. One by one, each castaway drifted into a fitful sleep. Toward the middle of the second watch, the wind came up and rocked the craft. The rumble of thunder could be heard moving closer. A squall overtook the Osprey with a downpour of, hopefully, drinkable water.

The storm roused Hilda, who found Josh on the observation deck.

"Are you children of the light or children of the night?" Josh asked no one in particular. "I wonder what it means."

"Do you believe the lieutenant saw that writing?" Hilda asked.

"I do," Josh said. "Maybe someone's trying to communicate with us."

Hilda shuddered. "Creepy thought, Chief."

Marc joined Hilda and Josh. "I don't know about that, but I could sure use a smoke right about now."

"Too bad the captain confiscated all your cigarettes," Hilda said. "We're about to run out of air, and you're thinking about your smokes."

"I'd just like one last one before I check out," Marc said.

Matt joined the group. "That's easy. Feel free to step outside anytime and have your final smoke, Sarge. What's happening?"

"Not much, sir. I'm watching the aurora borealis, just like I used to as a child back home," Hilda said.

"No, you're watching something *like* the aurora borealis," Josh said.

"No, I mean that I see exactly what I used to see back on earth, only closer," Hilda said.

"Yeah, but not the same colors," Josh challenged.

"Even the colors are the same – mainly strong yellow-to-green light with red at the very top," Hilda insisted.

"You mean white-to-pink colors," Josh said.

"No, I mean yellow and green sheets of light, just like on earth. See for yourself, Chief." Hilda was starting to get irritated.

Josh looked out the window, "You're right. But this doesn't make sense unless … Captain! We need to recheck the atmosphere outside!"

"He's right," Hilda chimed in. "I know what you're thinking, Chief!"

"What? I don't follow," Marc said.

"The Aurora! It's green and yellow and red like on earth!" Hilda said.

"So?" Matt asked.

"So? So!" Hilda responded. "Those are the colors given off by oxygen and nitrogen when they get agitated. Carbon dioxide gives blue-white to pink color light. If this air has as much carbon dioxide as our earlier test showed, the aurora should be white-to-pink with a little green."

"But it's not," Josh said. "It's got the same colors as we would see if we were on earth."

"Don't just sit around like a flock of gawking geese. McDermott, break out that test kit of yours and take another sample," Matt ordered.

"Aye, sir!" Hilda leaped out of her chair.

Hilda used the evacuation port to take another sample. Surprisingly, this time it indicated there was enough oxygen in the atmosphere to support the astronauts. "Here're the readings: 78% nitrogen, 20% oxygen, and 2% carbon dioxide," she reported.

Marc rubbed his temples. "How can this be? First, the atmosphere has too much carbon dioxide and not enough oxygen. Now the ratios are almost reversed. Was the first test wrong?"

Hilda said, "Here's a thought — on earth, plants use the light energy from the sun to create their food. You know it as 'photosynthesis.' Well, in doing that, the plants consume carbon dioxide and give off oxygen. But, at night, the process reverses, and the plants take in a little oxygen and give off carbon dioxide. What if the same process is at work here, only in reverse? Here the energy source is provided after dark, causing the plants native to this place to give off oxygen at night and to release carbon dioxide during the day."

"I suppose," Matt said. "But, how do the plants do this in the dark?"

Hilda said, "That's simple. The energy source that causes these plants to create their food could be a wavelength of light that we can't see with our eyes. It could be ultraviolet or infrared light or even radio waves."

"Bottom line, Captain," Marc commented, "I think I'll take you up on your offer and step outside for that smoke now."

The Admiral's Story

Johnson Space Center, Houston, Texas

Lewis turned and faced Vice Admiral Carter straight on. "Admiral, you need to tell me what you know about coordinates 25.0000° N, 71.0000° W, and what just happened out there."

"Aside from it being the coordinates of the Bermuda Triangle?" the admiral asked.

"The Bermuda Triangle? Now THERE'S a conspiracy theory," Lewis said. "Go on."

Carter took a deep breath. "It was on this very day in 1968. We were in the middle of a race to the Moon with the USSR."

"The USSR?"

"The United Socialist Soviet Republic – Russia. The Russians tried to launch a man around the Moon ahead of us. It was known as Zond 7. It was lost with a cosmonaut on board."

"I don't remember reading about it."

"You wouldn't. Officially, it never happened. The official report stated that the Zond 7 launch was a communications exercise, in preparation for a future attempt to reach the Moon."

"That makes no sense," Lewis said. "All of the Zond vehicles are accounted for. Even the one that was left in storage."

"That's just it. At the end of the Cold War, no Zond vehicle was found in storage. One was listed on the official inventory, but it was never found."

"What really happened?"

"According to the spooks at Langley, listening in, the Russians were trying to send a man to the Moon. This was verified by some British amateur astronomers."

"For real?"

Yes. On the evening of December 14th, the actual launch occurred. Ivan put the Zond spacecraft into a low parked orbit. Then, when it was over the exact coordinates from where the Osprey started today, he set off toward the Moon. Only a few minutes into its flight, the Zond 7 disappeared without a trace, just as the Osprey did moments ago."

"You're kidding!" Lewis exclaimed.

"No, I'm not kidding. And this was no fluke. We also lost unmanned crafts, starting from those same coordinates. Once was by accident and twice by experimentation. That's why that quadrant is a no-fly zone."

"I've never seen this documented anywhere."

"You won't. This is a matter of national security. It's top secret. It is officially designated a no-fly zone because of the amount of space debris located in that quadrant."

"How convenient," Lewis observed.

"I'm afraid they're gone, Captain. They're all gone."

"I'm not buying that!" exclaimed Lewis. "Not for one minute! Attention, Flight Safety. This is Captain Wright. Get a fix on the last known location of the Osprey."

"Captain, this is Flight Safety. Will do, sir."

"Flight Rescue, this is Captain Wright. Prepare to depart. Coordinate with Flight Safety and take an armed boarding squad along, just in case."

"Captain, this is Flight Rescue. That'll delay our departure by at least twenty minutes."

"Flight Rescue, this is Captain Wright. No matter, just do it!"

"Yes, sir. This is Flight Rescue. Out."

"Do you think this is a wise course of action, Captain?" Carter asked.

"I haven't lost a crew on my watch yet, sir. I don't intend to start now," Lewis replied.

"Flight Rescue, this is Captain Wright. When you are ready to depart, be sure to approach the target with extreme caution."

"Captain Wright, this is Flight Rescue. Extreme caution. We copy."

"Mission Control, this is Captain Wright. Be sure to patch me into your communications with Flight Rescue when they launch."

"Yes, sir, Captain. This is Mission Control. Out."

Minutes dragged by as the captain and Admiral waited for the rescue mission launch. Finally, the speaker came to life.

"Uh … Captain Wright, this is Mission Control. Flight Rescue is experiencing mechanical difficulties. It looks like their launch will be delayed, sir."

"Mission Control, this is Captain Wright. What's your new estimated time of departure?"

"Captain Wright, this is Mission Control. We've got the right parts on-site, but it could take a while to … uh … install them, sir."

"Mission Control, this is Captain Wright. Just tell me when you think you can launch the rescue team."

"Captain Wright, this is Mission Control. We … uh … are being advised … uh … sir, that it could be five hours before the repairs are completed."

"Mission Control, this is Captain Wright. Did I hear correctly – five hours?"

"Captain Wright, this is Mission Control. That's affirmative. You heard correctly, sir."

Damn! Lewis thought. *How much worse can this get?*

With the Lost Osprey

The rest of the first night passed with the Osprey's crew stretching their legs just outside the ship. At the sound of a second approaching rain squall, they hustled to set out various containers and canvas (found in the cargo hold) to collect rainwater. As the dawn approached, Matt called everyone into the ship and closed it up. Tension subsided with the knowledge that at least there was air and water in this strange place. Matt encouraged the crew to rest for a few hours.

The second day was well underway when Matt pulled the crew together to take stock of their situation.

"Listen up, everyone. We caught a break, being able to open the ship last night. Being able to breathe the outside air, at least sometimes, takes some – only some – urgency from getting our computers back online." Matt looked at Josh.

"Sir, what about water and food?" HJ asked.

"I wouldn't worry too much, Lieutenant," Matt answered. "If we are careful, the water that comes with the evening showers may be all the water we need for now. As for the food, there's a quantity of foodstuffs destined for Mars in our ship's cargo bay. So, we won't starve."

"Uh ... Captain," Josh interrupted. "Food may be an issue."

"What?"

"The food containers destined for Mars are locked down tighter than our life support system," Josh said. "Only the containers holding our personal gear are accessible."

"What? You've gotta be kidding, Chief."

"No, sir," Josh said. "Apparently, they think we, as a crew, have sticky fingers."

"Great. Who stowed food along with their gear?" Matt asked.

Everyone looked down. "I brought some beer," Marc offered.

Matt shook his head and took a deep breath. "Food may be an issue, but it'll have to take a second seat to our security. What we need to concentrate on now is our security. We're being watched. We've no idea if it is by hostile eyes or what their capabilities are."

Barnabas said, "If I may, Captain, I think—"

"Not now, Commander," Matt interrupted. "I'm assigning you all to three teams of two, with special tasks for today. If all is quiet by nightfall, we'll assess our situation and investigate the area around our ship. First team – Gunny McDermott and Sergeant Smith – test and review all our personal weapons. See what's working and what isn't. Second team – Lieutenant Gonzalez and Chief Torres – see if you can get any of our ship's weapon systems to work independently of the main computers. Team three – Commander and Lieutenant Jaeger – I want you to scour the cargo hold for edible foods and drinks. Questions?"

"Sir, do you think someone is planning to attack?" HJ asked. "Given that the only form of life we've seen so far is of the plant variety."

"Can't say, Lieutenant," Matt replied. "But someone is shining light beams around. They just haven't shown themselves yet. Commander, you were about to speak when I interrupted you. What're your thoughts?"

"Captain, it seems we did survive traveling through an actual wormhole, and it most likely was held open by some technology from an advanced society."

"Really, Commander?" HJ spoke up. "Travelling through wormholes still can't be proven mathematically."

"Maybe what can't be proven mathematically can still be experienced. Do you have a better explanation, Lieutenant?" Barnabas asked.

HJ was silent.

"If we were helped through a wormhole by other intelligent beings, why aren't they trying harder to communicate with us?" Marc asked.

"Odds are, they're watching us closely. Perhaps to see how intelligent we are. They may be the ones who disabled our ship," Barnabas said.

"Or, the trip through the wormhole could've done that," Marci said.

"True," Barnabas agreed. "Either way, they must know our ship is disabled, and we're not going anywhere. They probably also know we depend on our ship to survive. Maybe they want to see how resourceful we are."

"Or, this is like a game to them, whoever they are," Hilda said.

Marc said, "Or, following the commander's premise, that an advanced civilization held the wormhole open for us, we may be the objects of some experimentation. You know the first rule of observation is, 'Don't let the observers interfere with what is being observed.'"

"You're saying that they're observing us like we are test rats." HJ frowned. "That's just stupid. We are a helluv-a lot smarter than rats."

"Sure, we are, but are we smart enough to hold a wormhole open?" Hilda said. "Ever think that we aren't the most advanced creatures in" – she looked around — "in whatever universe this is. Don't forget the adage 'never underestimate your adversary.'"

"So, now this supposed advanced civilization is an adversary?" HJ questioned with a hint of sarcasm.

"I'm just saying we don't know what kind of intelligence we're dealing with and whether they're hostile or not," Hilda replied.

"Regardless, we need to be alert," Matt concluded.

"But, Captain, isn't the rescue ship already on its way to pick us up?" HJ asked.

"Do you see a rescue ship, Lieutenant? They'd have been launched within hours of our disappearance. We've been here for the better part of a day and all night. Still, there's no sign of a rescue ship. We can't count on a quick rescue, so we need to be self-sufficient. Now, let's get to work." Matt turned and left the crew cabin.

Later as the day was winding down and the teams completed their tasks, Hilda, Barnabas, and Marc went to the galley to relax.

"I'm just wondering, Commander — if you have a Ph.D. in Astronomy, shouldn't we be calling you 'Doctor' instead of 'Commander'?" Marc joked. "I bet you never imagined you'd be flying through a wormhole into another world."

"Not hardly, Sarge," Barnabas said. "But, life's a journey. Might as well enjoy the trip."

"Even if we don't know where it ends?" Hilda asked.

"Why worry, Gunny? It's all in God's hands," Barnabas said.

"That's a very … uh … Christian thing to say," Marc observed.

"Guilty as charged," Barnabas shrugged.

"Seriously, Commander," Hilda pressed. "How can you, with an advanced degree and all, still believe in God? Don't you see a conflict of interest between science and religion?"

"Not so much," Barnabas answered. "The scientific process helps unlock how this universe, whichever one we're in now, works. The operative word being 'how.' It helps us observe specific processes at work. From that organized observation, we can come to understand the natural cause-and-effect relationships at work around us."

"Tell me something I don't know," Hilda quipped.

Barnabas said, "To believe in science is to believe that the Universe is organized and to some degree predictable. If it isn't, the scientific process is of little value. Science explains the 'how,' but not the 'why' behind the 'how.' Is there a purpose to what's happening? Do we have a purpose? Scientists may try to answer those questions, but science doesn't. To answer those questions, we must—" Marci's shout interrupted him.

"Come quick! Here's another message!" she exclaimed, staring at the central console, which read:

"Высокая дорога ведет к Свету низкую дорогу к огню."

Just as the others reached the Bridge, the screen appeared to flicker and fade to black.

"What? I don't see anything," Marc said.

"It was right there, I swear," Marci pointed at the monitor.

What did it say?" Barnabas asked.

"It was Russian and said, 'A high road leads to the Light a low road to the fire.' I'm certain of it," Marci insisted.

"Are you sure?" Hilda asked

"Don't question me. That's what it said," Marci stated, anger flashing in her eyes.

Josh looked questioningly at Barnabas, who shrugged.

.

The Plateau

Location, Unknown

The first whole evening and day passed without incident. Matt sat down to pull out his tablet and make an entry in his ship's log. *Talk about old-school,* he thought. *I should be able to speak to the ship's computer.*

SHIP'S LOG December 15, 2068

<u>Entry by Captain Dirksen:</u>

There is still no sign of intelligent life (other than messages Lieutenant Gonzalez thinks she saw on our central console). I want to be sure the air is breathable again tonight. If so, I plan to send out three teams to explore our immediate surroundings. I'm sending buckets with each team in hopes of retrieving drinkable water. To be safe, I will limit their time out of the ship to four hours, about half of the eight hours of relative darkness. The first team will be Lieutenant Gonzalez and Gunnery Sergeant McDermott. They will explore the trail that leads from mid-ship, across the meadow, into the forest. Gunny's skills as a botanist will be helpful in a search for edible plant life. Commander Maalouf and Lieutenant Jaeger will be the second team. I am sending them on the rim trail leading from the fore-ship along the edge of this plateau toward a significant outcropping. Hopefully, they will find water or a better view of our surroundings. Master Sergeant Smith and I will explore the rim trail that leads from the ship's aft. It looks to have the most interesting geological elements. I am assigning Chief Petty Officer Torres to remain and set up the distress beacon (I hope he can at least get that activated) and to stand watch over the ship. Each team has a flare and whistle to use in case they need help.

Situational Assessment:

Our concern over losing the life support system has been alleviated by:

- Knowing this planet's air is breathable at night.
- Our ability to collect rainwater.

I am still concerned about:

- Where is our expected rescue ship? We are setting up our distress beacon tonight. It seems to function correctly under its own power.
- There is a lack of a consistent supply of drinkable water.
- The fact that we have virtually no food.
- None of our ship's armaments function here.
- None of our personal weapons work except for a couple of Glocks and our survival knives. I've ordered everyone to carry their survival knives when off the ship. Gunny and the Sarge are to always carry their Glocks.
- Owe are still unable to get our computers up and functioning.
- Lieutenant Gonzalez's belief that she saw another message that said, "The high road leads to the light, the low road to the fire." I'm not sure if someone is trying to communicate with us or if the lieutenant is affected by a growing sense that we are not alone.

END OF ENTRY

As the pale pink of daylight gave way to the bluish-purple of the evening, Hilda ran one more test to confirm that the oxygen level was safe for exploring. When the results indicated that it was, each of the three teams moved out, leaving a somewhat dejected Josh to stand watch.

Matt and Marc followed the rim trail, running from the aft of the crippled Osprey. Marc stopped periodically as they walked to examine clusters of semi-precious stones. Occasionally, he would scoop up a sample and look at it more closely, then toss it into a pouch he had slung across his shoulder. Watching him at work, Matt asked, "Why does a highly decorated Master Sergeant retire early to take up geology?"

Marc gave Matt a look. Matt said, "Just curious, Sarge. Didn't intend to pry."

The Sergeant shrugged. "It's not much of a story, sir. I enjoyed my time in the service. But it was time to grow up and follow my passion. It just happens I have a passion for rocks."

"Blowing them up or classifying them?"

"Both," Marc said with a wry smile. "I was a bit of a problem child that way – at least to hear my Mom talk."

"What exactly does a problem child look like?"

"When I was young, my Dad would take prospecting trips and leave me behind. My Mom would be doing things with my sisters, leaving me to my own devices. One time—it was the day after the fourth of July—my friend Eddy and I collected all the leftover fireworks we could find. We crammed the unspent powder into one giant tube on our back porch. Then we took some string soaked in gas and stuck it in one end of the tube. We planned to light the fuse and toss our tube into the hen yard next door to scare the hens. We lit the fuse on the porch and discovered a great truth – gas-soaked string makes for a very fast fuse. The fire jumped immediately from our match, along the string, to the tube of black power. We were lucky to get off the porch before the whole concoction blew up."

"Wow! Anybody lose a finger?"

"No, but I was deaf for at least five minutes. My ears rang for a week. Eddy and I came away unscathed until Mom found us. Grandpa's wicker rocker wasn't so lucky. Our tube blew a hole in the back of it. After dishing out our punishment, my Dad suggested that if I wanted to spend time with explosives, it would be better to build rockets than bombs."

"Wise man. Of course, you did what he said and bought a rocket kit."

"No way, Captain. Rocket kits are for amateurs. We made our rockets from scratch. We even cooked up our own rocket fuel using saltpeter and sugar."

"It's a wonder you didn't burn your house down."

"No, but we did take out the neighbor's hen house. To perfect the nozzle, we strapped rockets with different nozzles to an old sawhorse in the backyard. One of our nozzles worked so well that the rocket broke its strap and headed straight toward the back of our house. At the last second, it veered left, flew straight into our neighbor's henhouse, and blew up."

Matt smiled. "Bet the hens were upset."

"Some of them were pretty fried. The ones that survived weren't nearly as pissed as our neighbor. She called the cops. By the time the dust settled, my Mom told Dad that the only way he could ever go prospecting again would be if he took me with him."

"Tough luck for an aspiring rocketeer."

"You'd think so. But I loved it. I'll never forget my first prospecting trip to the Rockies with my Dad. We found some beautiful aquamarine specimens. We were so excited, you'd think we'd struck the mother-lode. On our next trip to the Wah Wah Mountains, we found some red beryl. As a kid, I just knew that I'd continue prospecting and die a rich man."

"Or die a young man," Matt said. "I mean if your prospecting luck wasn't any better than your luck as a rocketeer."

Marc smiled, "My Dad introduced me to all kinds of rocks on those trips. That's when I picked up my love for prospecting and geology in general. When I enlisted, I hoped I would be sent to other moons or planets, where I could study their geology."

"That's quite the story. Have you seen anything like this back on earth?" Matt motioned to their surroundings.

"Not even close. These formations resemble the crystal formations at home, only on a massive scale." Marc pointed to an outcropping of eight hexagonal crystals that ranged from 20 to 36 feet in length. "Look at that aquamarine outcropping over there."

"Aquamarine?"

"It's a greenish-blue variety of beryl. It forms hexagonal crystals. What makes it unusual here is its sheer size. Creating aquamarine requires heat and pressure for a very long time. I'm not sure how to explain the forces that created such a large, exposed gem."

Matt held his arm out to stop Marc before he stepped off the edge of a large crevice. "Thanks, Captain," Marc said. I was so caught up in my surroundings, I forgot to watch where I was walking. What happened to our trail?"

"It just ended. This crevice is too large to jump, the outcropping you were looking at is blocking us from moving to our left, and there's nowhere to go on our right unless…."

"Unless what?"

"Look over there." Matt pointed his powerful flashlight over the edge of the crevice. About 40 meters below them was a wide trail leading along the cleft into a colorful series of semi-precious gem columns. Flickering lights could be seen about 100 meters ahead as the path rounded a curve. "What do you think that is, Sarge?"

"Hard to tell. It could be the lights from a community. It could be campfire lights. It could be a sign of civilization or an encampment."

"Think we could get down to that trail?"

"I might have enough rope in my climbing gear back at the ship, sir. Maybe we can pick up that trail someplace nearer our ship."

"Good idea," Matt agreed as he started backtracking along the edge, keeping his light on the trail below.

As they walked, Marc said, "Sir, may I ask a question?"

"What is it?"

"I heard that as a fighter pilot, your handle was 'Rawhide.' How'd you get it?"

Matt smiled. "Simple. I paid my way through college breaking wild horses and working the rodeo circuit. My specialty was roping calves. Captain Lewis gave me that handle when I was late reporting back from leave one time. I cracked a couple of ribs getting tossed by a bronco I was trying to break. Why do you ask?"

"No offense, sir, but some of the guys back at the Cape were talking. They said you ride your crew so hard that you give them raw hides."

Matt smiled despite himself. "What do you think, Sarge? Am I living up to my reputation?"

"Not entirely, sir."

"It sounds like I need to pick up my game."

They were halfway back to the ship when a thundershower overtook them. Being exposed, the companions got drenched. Even though the temperature was temperate, the rain chilled them to the bone. They continued following the path that seemed to end about 15 meters below them, close to the aft of the Osprey.

"Captain, I could grab my gear, and we could rappel to the trail here," Marc suggested.

"We've got less than two hours left before we have to call it a night. Let's get dried off. You can organize your gear, and we'll start fresh tomorrow night. Those lights aren't going anywhere. I'd rather approach this a little more cautiously. We'll use a three-man team instead of just the two of us. I think we'll use Lieutenant Jaeger."

"Chief's still in the dog house?"

"For the moment, yes. Torres should've had the computers up by now. Why do you ask?"

"He looked pretty disappointed that you had him stand watch while the rest of us got to be out and about," Marc observed.

"What are you thinking, Sarge?"

"Thinking you might want to toss him a bone, sir."

"What do you suggest?"

"There's about an hour-and-a-half left before we reassemble. Why not let the chief climb the hill just inside the forest to the right of the trail Jaeger and Commander Maalouf followed?" Marc pointed just beyond the Osprey. "It looks to be a ten-minute walk from the ship, and he will be in sight of the ship during his climb. Not sure he'd find much, but it lets him get out and about for a short while."

"I suppose you're right, Sarge."

The Forest Hill

When they boarded the ship, Matt said, "Chief, get ready to move out. I have an assignment for you!"

Josh had a spring in his step as he crossed the field toward the outcropping he was to climb. It wasn't very far, but just getting away from his technical problems, even for an hour, was a relief. After a short walk, he entered the forest of peacock trees. From the moment he entered the forest, he felt as if he were being watched. The sound of gentle swishing brought him to a quick stop. It was the breeze rustling the feather trees. Josh started to walk again, being more vigilant. Then he thought he noticed something moving. Feeling the hair begin to raise on the back of his neck, Josh stopped again and looked more carefully. This time he caught a glimpse of movement out of the corner of his eye. He looked more directly at the feather trees and saw what looked like a shimmering shadow passing through the trees.

"Hey," he yelled. "Stop!" He started to walk toward the object. He slipped on the rain slickened ground and fell. As he hit the ground, he could have sworn that he heard a chuckle. Josh got up gingerly and thought he saw a weak shaft of light quivering among the feather trees.

He was trying to decide if it was real or just his imagination when he saw it start to move away. Or so he thought. He couldn't be sure.

"Wait," he implored. "Don't go just yet. I need to know who you are."

"Oh, do you now?" was the reply.

Was it a voice, a whisper, or a thought? It was an intriguing sound with a unique cadence. Did it sound like a resonating organ pipe or the echoing of a small waterfall? He wasn't sure. He needed to hear it again.

"Who are you? What are you?" he asked. His questions were met with silence. No matter how hard he looked, he could no longer see anything. Still feeling a little unnerved when he reached the outcropping, he cautiously started walking up the narrow path. It was wet and slippery. He was higher now, and the path curved along the edge of the outcropping. A large crevice opened on one side of the trail. The further Josh walked, the broader and deeper the crevice grew. Josh looked over the edge and gave a low whistle. *I'd sure hate to take a header down there*, he thought as he looked up. There it appeared again, a dim shaft or beam of light to the side of the path. Josh stopped, unsure of what to do or if he even saw anything real. He blinked a few times. It was still there – a beam of light with no apparent source.

Josh heard, "Don't go any further." Was it a whisper of the wind? Was it imagined?

Josh moved forward past the beam of light. It seemed to waver as he passed by. He could have sworn he heard another chuckle. The path was narrow and the wet surface slick. Suddenly, Josh slipped and fell awkwardly against the cliff wall. Trying to control his motion, he overcompensated. Josh lurched off the path, falling over the edge. Josh's first thought (other than he was about to die) was that his fall was a little slower than he expected. Given the depth of the chasm, Josh wondered if his entire life would run through his mind before hitting bottom. Just then, he felt something like a lasso wind around his right ankle. Josh looked up at his feet and saw they were wrapped in what looked like a luminescent rope. It was attached to the shaft of light he had just passed. Another set of glowing ropes were snaking toward him. The cords wrapped around his back, gently halting his fall. Now they were lifting him and setting him down on where the narrow path began. He thought he heard another chuckle. This was followed by a voice.

The voice said, "You'd best leave flying to creatures with wings." It wasn't just any voice. It was a soft, echoing sound, much like a rippling brook.

Josh sat up and gathered himself, "Who are you? What just happened?" Josh asked, his heart still racing.

"I believe I just rescued you," the voice answered with a laugh.

Josh nodded his head and asked, "Who are you?"

"My name is Vigilo. I am a Custodes."

Josh thought, *Custodes? Isn't that Latin for watchman?* He couldn't help but smile as he recalled his Latin. "Quis custodiet ipsos custodes? *Who watches the watchers?*"

"The Circitor, *Overseer*, of course," Vigilo responded without any sense of irony. "Our Circitor is named Taxiarchis. You are the one your Circitor calls Chief Torres, are you not?"

"I am," Josh agreed. "My formal name is Chief Petty Officer Joshua Torres. I'm the chief technical support NCO for the spaceship Osprey."

"Welcome to Portae, Chief Petty Officer Joshua Torres."

"My friends just call me Josh."

"Is not your Circitor also your friend?" Vigilo asked, "He never calls you Josh."

Josh nodded. "I don't know, Vigilo. I never really thought about it that way before. What do you do, Vigilo?'

"I watch, hence my name."

"Watch what? Are you watching us? Why are you watching us?"

"Of course, I'm watching you," Vigilo said matter-of-factly. "It's my job. I find you and your companions quite entertaining and very odd. I think I'd enjoy watching you even if it weren't my job."

"Why's it your job to watch us?"

"Taxiarchis is deciding if it is safe to let you pass."

"Let us pass?" Josh asked. "In what solar system is the planet portae located? We don't want to pass. We just want to return home."

"Try not to think of this as a planet. Rather think of it as a custos turris, *watchtower,* or an outpost or watchman's station. We guard the other systems from the war zone."

"War zone?"

"You refer to it as the Solar System."

"I don't understand. The Solar System isn't a war zone."

"Then why's your ship armed? Why'd you test your weapons when you arrived?"

"It's complicated," Josh admitted.

"We're tasked with watching and testing to see if you're safe to let by or if you'll spread the rebellion to other places," Vigilo said.

"Kind of like keeping us in quarantine?"

"Like quarantine," Vigilo agreed. "It is a challenging job."

"How's that?" Josh asked.

"You're all hard to see. Some of you are harder than others. You're all very shadowy and wispy with an occasional spark of color. That makes it hard to see your expressions. Your voices are also tinny and lacking in expression."

Josh was puzzled. "Is this for real? What about me?"

"Mostly, this is true. Now that we have been talking, you are easier to see. But the cheerful one who sits in the front left seat — he's easy to see. He's shadowy but sparkles often. But the one who sits in the rear right seat, the one who thinks he is all-knowing, isn't so easy to see. He hardly ever sparkles."

Josh wasn't sure he liked the direction of this conversation. Trying to press his point home, he said, "We're from Earth and want to return."

You mean "Tierra, the rebel planet," Vigilo said.

"It is? Josh asked.

"Yes! It's full of misery, discontent, and violence. That's not the way it was designed."

"If I'm a potential rebel from a rebel planet, why did you save me?"

"I was told it isn't your time to die … just yet."

"Not my turn to die? Do you know when it's my turn to die?

"I don't know. Wouldn't be allowed to say if I did."

Along the Rim Path

Barnabas and HJ walked along the rim path leading from the front of the ship. It followed the plateau's rim for several hundred yards or so until it reached the base of an alabaster outcropping. They stopped to pick up a couple of fallen branches to use as walking sticks.

"What was that?" Barnabas asked with a start.

"What was what, Commander?"

"It was a rumbling sound."

"That's just my stomach. Seriously, I could sure use a nice hot meal."

Barnabas shook his head. They resumed their trek. The trail began to descend gently at first, then more steeply. Soon they walked with a vertical wall of alabaster on their right and the edge of a cliff on their left. The trail was smooth, with occasional tufts of vegetation on either side. What "vegetation" there was amounted to colorful lichens. Even in the dim light, the lichens displayed orange, yellow, and red interest points against a background of pale alabaster. The men would have taken note of this if they weren't concerned about navigating the narrow path. HJ slipped and lurched close to the edge. Barnabas caught his arm and helped steady him before he fell into the abyss.

"Thanks. This could be treacherous when it gets wet."

"Got that right, Lieutenant."

"Sir, Marci tells me you're quite the pilot. You seem to enjoy it."

"I'm living my dream. I've wanted to fly in space since I was a teen."

"Marci says that your battle maneuvers in the simulator are smooth. How'd you end up as a transport pilot instead of a fighter pilot?"

"When I was young, my brother and I used to take our dog, Skip, and sneak into the local landfill to hunt rats with our .22s. Later, when I was on leave, just before starting flight school, we met up. We decided to go rat hunting with Skip like we did as kids. We were wandering over a pile of debris when suddenly, a huge gray streak darted under us. We started blasting away as fast as we could until we realized the streak we were shooting at was our dog. Fortunately for Skip, we were such bad shots we never hit him. That's when I decided, being a fighter pilot or weapons officer shouldn't be in my future. I love flying among the stars. Just don't ask me to shoot at anything."

HJ chuckled, "I'll keep that in mind."

"What about you? Why do you want to be a fighter pilot?"

"My story isn't as good as yours. I just love the whole package."

"The whole package?" Barnabas asked.

"Yeah. Don't get me wrong. I love flying and fighting in combat. But, I also love the perks of being a fighter jock: the babes, pay, and parties. It's like being a rock star. The way I figure it, you only go around this life once. You might as well grab as many of the perks as you can along the way."

"That's it? There's nothing more to life than what you can get out of it for yourself?"

"Naw, Commander. No disrespect intended. I know you're religious and all that. But I don't buy all that mystical, altruistic crap. If we can't observe it, then it doesn't exist. What does exist … is the opportunity to enjoy ourselves without getting hung up on societal expectations, morays, and all that bull."

"How do you mean?"

"Don't get me wrong, Commander. I'm as good as the next guy, better than most. It's just that I don't want to be held back, by some moralizing cleric, from grabbing life by the horns and giving it a good shake. I enjoy good food, fast women, and lots of toys. You know the old saying, 'He who dies with the most toys, wins.'"

Barnabas said, "Hmm. I know that he who dies with the most toys still dies."

"I suppose so. I don't plan on dying any time soon, and I plan to add to my collection of toys and babes along the way."

Barnabas smiled, "I catch your drift, son."

As they progressed, the distinctive smell of rotten eggs rose to greet them. "Sulfur," Barnabas said under his breath. The trail took a turn, and the smell of hot tar was added to the already putrid mix.

HJ grimaced. "Commander, you really ought to take a shower."

"After you, Lieutenant," Barnabas retorted with a slight smile.

They looked down the trail and saw white smoke drifting toward them. It looked like it was coming out of the side of the alabaster wall. The duo approached the source of the smoke and found it was coming from the mouth of a small cave. The air exiting the cave was steamy and hot. The cave itself was small, with walls angled toward a point about ten feet above the ground. It was wide enough for three men to enter shoulder to shoulder. Not that they would want to. A black gooey substance oozed down the center of the floor, out onto the trail, and spilled over the cliff's edge. It was a mix of black ooze and grayish-white and yellow lumps.

"I wonder what's oozing out of that disgusting cave?" HJ dipped his walking stick into the mix and raised it to his nose. "It's definitely tar."

"What do you say we check inside?"

"Not sure I'm up for that. It's pretty foul in there. I'm not even sure we could breathe."

"Your choice, Lieutenant. We don't have to go in very far."

A flash of lightning and clap of thunder made them both jump. The sound of an approaching rain squall settled the debate as they both jumped inside. The rain came in sheets, steaming as it hit the tar on the trail. They hunched to either side away from the center while gagging on the fumes of hot tar and sulfur. The torrid stench blew on them from deep inside the cave, making them even more miserable. Fortunately, they successfully avoided the tar and sulfur oozing down the middle of the narrow passage.

"Perfect timing, eh, Commander? Even the weather's on your side."

"It's better to be in here than out on that narrow trail in this downpour," Barnabas said.

"Yeah, unless you want to breathe," HJ coughed. "Nothing is more sickening than the smell of rotten eggs and burning rubber."

"You're right. It's hard enough to breathe by the mouth of this cave. It wouldn't be wise to go in much deeper."

"I'm okay staying here until the rain passes. What are those chalky yellow and white lumps in the middle of all that goo?"

"Don't know." Barnabas looked closer. "I think it's brimstone."

"Brimstone?"

"Lumps of sulfur. Some call it brimstone as in 'fire and brimstone.'"

"So, in a manner of speaking, we're at the mouth of hell."

"Looks as if," Barnabas agreed.

HJ bent down and looked further into the cave. It took a turn. "I'm pretty sure I see an orange-like glow coming around the corner."

"The fires of hell, perhaps?" Barnabas asked, mostly to himself.

"What?" HJ asked.

"This could be a useful find," Barnabas said, changing the subject.

They moved a little further toward the back of the cave. Something glittered against the light from HJ's flashlight. He scooped it up.

"What is it?" Barnabas asked.

"It's a medallion of some sort."

"Where'd this come from?"

"No clue," Barnabas said. " a Russian medallion circa the 1960s, maybe."

"How do you know this stuff, Commander?"

"I'm just a space travel history buff. Say let's collect some of this tar in our bucket?

"To what purpose?" HJ asked.

"Fuel for a cooking fire. So you'll get that hot meal, after all."

"We kinda need food to cook, don't we?"

"One thing at a time, Lieutenant. One thing at a time."

"While we're at it, Commander, why don't we use some of this tar to turn our walking sticks into torches?"

"Excellent idea. But how do we light the tar?"

"Easy, sir," HJ grinned. "Marc asked me to keep his second cigarette lighter safe in case the captain confiscated his first one."

With a flick of the lighter, HJ set off both his and Barnabas's torches. It was with no small sense of accomplishment that the two companions started back toward the Osprey.

"We've done good, Lieutenant," Barnabas said, with a big smile spreading across his face.

"We sure did, Commander," HJ agreed.

Through the Forest

Hilda and Marci followed the path that began mid-ship and led straight into the forest of feather trees.

"What kind of trees are these?" Marci asked.

"Not sure. They could be related to a fern or a different species."

As they continued to walk through the forest, the path rose a little then began to angle gently down into a glade. A wide variety of flora began to open before them. A carpet of grasses was broken occasionally by clumps of small ferns. The ground was softer, with more spring than that in the forest. Small trees were scattered about, along with what appeared to be berry bushes. This place was different from the rest of their plateau. It was dominated by plant life with an occasional outcropping of beryl. The far end of the glade appeared to be occupied by a very tall outcropping of granite.

Hilda motioned for Marci to stop. "This area holds real possibilities."

"For what?"

"For food, of course!" Hilda used her flashlight to point out the possibilities. "That clump of weed looks like wild parsnips or carrots." She refocused her light. "Over there could be some field garlic. I think those bushes may have edible berries, and that looks like a pistachio tree. Let's get busy."

The women began harvesting wild parsnips, purple carrots, and field garlic. Then they moved to some bushes. Hilda verified that the berries were partridge berries. They also found a small wild plum tree, growing plums that were a little larger than cherries.

"I haven't seen a wild cherry plum tree in years," Hilda commented.

"Does this strike you as odd?" Marci asked.

"What?"

"Here we are foraging for edible food, but there's no sign of animal life at all. No birds, no small mammals, no animals of any kind."

"Come to think of it," Hilda agreed, "I don't hear any insect sounds or the sound of frogs croaking. In a place like this, back on earth, we'd be hearing frogs croaking and insect noises."

"If there're no animals around, can we be sure this stuff is even edible?" Marci asked.

"No guarantees, Lieutenant."

"That's not the assurance I'm looking for, Gunny."

They were harvesting pistachios when a rain shower overtook them. A flash of lightning and a boom of thunder got their immediate attention. They ran toward the granite outcropping for cover. The downpour began just as they arrived. They found a shallow cave in which they sheltered from the storm. They sat on the sandy floor with their backs to the wall. The storm raged a few feet away. It was raining so hard they could not carry on a conversation over the noise. After twenty minutes or so, the storm passed as quickly as it came.

They had just stepped outside the cave when Marci stopped Hilda. "Do you hear that? I'm not sure, but it sounds like falling water."

They made their way to the source by scrambling over some boulders. Their effort was rewarded by finding a rock pond of water fed by a small, twenty-foot waterfall. Suddenly, a new sound captured their attention. It sounded like the chugging of an old steam engine. They climbed around the first pond. Below it was several other ponds with steam drifting out of them. The distinct odor of rotten eggs filled the air.

"Cool," Hilda commented, "Here's a series of water springs."

"Yeah, but can we drink this water?"

"Not sure. I'll take some samples and run tests back at the ship. Do you hear that?"

"Hear what?"

"The sound of the waterfall is quieter now. It must be fed only from rain runoff."

With their water samples collected, the duo began their trip back to the ship. Hilda stopped one more time. "Wow! Here's a cranberry bush. We gotta get some before we leave."

"What about that plant over there, Gunny? It looks edible."

"Not so fast." Hilda bent over and studied it closer. "This won't do. I think it is a Cycad. They may look edible, but they are poisonous — just like that wild almond tree next to it."

"Are you sure the almond tree is poisonous?"

Hilda looked around and found an almond that had dropped its husk and was almost ripe. She split the shell, bit down on the nut, and then spit it out, making a face. "Oh yeah, it has that bitter taste. Bitter almonds contain glycoside amygdalin which turns into prussic acid, a.k.a. hydrogen cyanide, when eaten. It doesn't take much of that chemical to kill you."

"How is it you know all this stuff? I know botanists study plants, but your field knowledge is pretty amazing."

"It's a bit of a story," Hilda said.

"No problem. It'll take a while to get back to the ship. We've got nothing but time."

"My father was a Master Gunnery Sergeant for the corps. He was always away, moving up the ranks. When he was deployed — which seemed to be all the time — Mom and I stayed with her parents on their small farm. My Grandpa was a horticulturalist."

"A what?"

"A horticulturalist — someone who works with farmers and gardeners to help improve their crop yields and resistance to insects, diseases, and such. He worked as an extension agent for Colorado State University. My Grandpa shared his experiments with me and even let me help. That was fun. But even better, his favorite hobby was foraging. We'd go on these long hikes into the foothills. There he'd teach me which wild plants were edible and which weren't. Sometimes we'd take along some spices. He'd build a cooking fire and create meals out of what we'd foraged. Mostly they were simple stews. Sometimes they were quite tasty. Other times not so much."

"Sounds like he was more of a father than your father."

"Bingo! When I was young, I felt like I was a disappointment to my father because I was not the boy he wanted."

"No brother then?"

"Three sisters, but no brother. As I got older, I obsessed over making my father proud of me. I joined the corps. I worked my butt off. I didn't just pass my physical training minimums; I maxed out on the scoring. I became a Gunnery Sergeant and thought that would get his attention. But he barely acknowledged my accomplishments. I think I volunteered for multiple deployments during the Asteroid conflict, in part because I wanted to impress the old man."

"How'd that work out?

"Didn't go as expected. He never tried to contact me, even though we were in the same theater of war."

"Sorry to hear that. But, I'm sure it impressed him when you won the Silver Star, though."

"You'd think. But the chump didn't even attend the ceremony."

"Ouch!"

"In some ways, my deployments changed my life," Hilda commented.

"How so?"

"Two things happened. First, the young lieutenant I was serving under was shot by a sniper while we were on patrol. He died in my arms. I still can't get over the unfairness of it. I've seen many soldiers die, but this was different. The lieutenant only had a month left in his deployment. He was good-natured, kind, and full of life. He was leaving the corps, heading home to run the family business with his dad. His fiancé was beautiful. They were to be married in Paris and honeymoon in Polynesia. He had the perfect life ahead of him, and he did nothing to deserve dying like that. It got me thinking. Then, when I returned from that deployment, I learned my Grandpa had passed. So I re-evaluated where I was and where I wanted to be. I was tired of trying to impress my dad and answering to a bunch of grumpy old officers. When it was time to re-up, I didn't. Instead, I decided to do something that helped me feel closer to my grandpa. I used the G.I. Bill to get a degree in botany. And here we are. The best part is it pissed my old man off when I resigned the corps."

"Quite the journey,'" Marci observed. "I'm sure glad you're here. We need your talents."

"Thanks," Hilda replied. "I am too. This is a botanist's paradise, and it would drive my father crazy to know that I abandoned the corps. only to sign on with NASA to fight a pirate."

"Why did you sign on, anyway?" Marci asked, motioning around them. "This wasn't part of the plan."

"No, it wasn't, but you won't catch me complaining. I'm a Botanist, after all. To be honest, even though I left the corps. I miss the fighting and hope I can still get in on a good one."

"Even if it means answering to a grumpy old captain?" Marci asked with a smile.

"Yeah, there's that. The captain isn't so bad. I get that he's stressed that the mission objective is completely blown, and there's no rescue in sight. Then there's the commander. He's not such a bad guy either. But he's too cheerful and relaxed for my taste. Makes me wonder what he knows that we don't."

"Maybe you should ask him sometime," Marci offered.

"Maybe I will."

A rustling in the bushes caught their attention.

"Just the wind?" Marci asked.

Hilda drew her Glock. "Or maybe a creature in search of food."

"Now's not the time to investigate, Gunny," Marci said. "Times up, and we need to get back to the ship."

"Yeah, I suppose you're right, Lieutenant."

Who's in Charge?

Location, Unknown

Once again, Matt removed himself from the rest of the crew. He needed to update the ship's log. He wasn't ready to share all of his entries just yet. After gathering his thoughts, he wrote:

SHIP'S LOG December 16, 2068

Entry by Captain Dirksen:

It is almost evening, and all is quiet. This is our second full day stranded on the plateau. Last night's forays were productive: Commander Maalouf and Lieutenant Jaeger discovered tar and sulfur to fuel torches and a cooking fire; Gunnery Sergeant McDermott and Lieutenant Gonzalez found some possibilities for food and drinkable water; Master Sergeant Smith and I found a promising trail that starts about 35 feet below our current position and appears to lead down to civilization. We are planning to rappel to it tonight, using the sergeant's gear. I will be sending Lieutenant Gonzalez and Gunnery Sergeant McDermott back to gather more water and food.

Note on drinkable water: Our tests indicate the water samples retrieved by Gunnery Sergeant McDermott and Lieutenant Gonzalez are safe to drink. However, the sulfur content makes the water taste and smell like rotten eggs. Another, purer source is preferable.

Chief Torres's state of mind concerns me. He reported a 'conversation' with a beam of light. I'm sure he believes what he saw and heard. But I think his continued failure to solve the Osprey's technical problems weighs too heavily on him. Commander Maalouf isn't in complete agreement with my assessment. But he does agree we need to monitor the chief's condition carefully.

Situational Assessment:

There is no change to the ship's status. Animal life may exist, but this has not been confirmed. No sign of intelligent life other than cryptic messages superimposed on our computer's primary monitor from time to time. Between the air at night, food, water, and fire that we've discovered, our odds of sustained survival are greatly improved. Several concerns:

- Still waiting on a rescue ship.
- Monitoring Chief Torres's mental state.
- Still puzzling over the messages Gonzalez thinks she sees.
- Wondering who's in charge of this place.

END OF ENTRY

The afternoon turned to evening. The crew gathered just outside the ship to have their first cooked meal since landing in this strange place. It fell to Hilda and Barnabas to cook the vegetable stew.

"Hey, just because I'm a botanist doesn't mean I should be the cook," Hilda complained.

Barnabas said, "No worries, Gunny. I love cooking. We can team up."

"That's good," Marci said. "I don't cook, and I'm not volunteering to do the dishes."

Matt said, "Chief Torres draws clean-up duty tonight." Upon hearing chuckles and sighs of relief, he added, "But that duty will be rotated among everyone."

Marc joined the rest of the crew. "Hey Captain, did you see there's a new message on the console on the Bridge?"

"Not funny, Sarge," Marci said. "I don't need you mocking me."

"I'm not mocking you, Lieutenant."

Everyone made their way to the Bridge and gathered around the monitor. To their surprise, the message was still there. It read:

"si descendunt, habes fugere."

"Funny," Marci said, "I don't recognize it. It's not Russian."

"It's Latin," Josh said.

"Do you know what it means, Chief?" Matt asked.

"It means I'm not seeing things after all," Marci said.

"That too, Lieutenant. What does it mean, Chief?" Barnabas asked.

Josh said, "I think descendunt means descend or go down. Fugere means flight or flee. I think habes makes it imperative."

Matt said, "In English this time, Chief."

Josh said, "I think it means, 'If you go down, you have to fly.' Maybe 'If you go down, you have to flee.' I'm a little rusty, so I'm not sure."

"You know this because you're a great expert in Latin?" HJ asked.

"I'm no expert, but my Dad insisted I study Latin as an undergrad."

"Why Latin? It's a dead language," HJ said.

"That's what I said, Lieutenant. But my dad insisted. It was a condition for him to pay my tuition. Go figure."

"Hmm … why are the messages in Latin now, instead of Russian?" Barnabas wondered.

"Maybe whoever's watching us is probing how complete our language skills are," Marc offered. "Just a thought."

"Vigilo sometimes speaks to me in Latin," Josh said.

HJ rolled his eyes. "Here we go again, Josh and his imaginary friend, the light beam."

Josh's eye's flashed, but he kept still.

"Enough already," the captain said. "We need to eat and get on with my plans for the evening. We haven't much time."

The crew returned to their meal. The lit torches scattered about, and the cooking fire gave the feeling of an evening Bar-B-Q among friends.

However, one taste of the stew removed any similarity. The meal itself was filling but bland. When HJ commented on its taste, Barnabas smiled. "I said I loved to cook. I didn't say I was any good at it."

"Buck up. At least we're not starving," Matt said.

After the meal, Matt laid out his plans for the evening. "Listen up, everyone. Tonight, we'll divide into three teams. Gunny and Lieutenant Gonzalez, I want both of you to go back and gather more food and water."

"Again, Captain? Really?" Hilda started to complain.

Matt cut her off, "Tomorrow, we'll rotate that assignment. Commander and Chief, you'll clean up the camp and set out receptacles to catch potential rainwater. Look for more buckets in the cargo hold."

"Will do," Barnabas answered. "I'd much rather drink fresh rainwater than that rotten egg water from the pond. No offense, Gunny."

"None taken, Commander," Hilda replied.

"When you're done, stand by. We may need help descending to the trail," Matt said.

"We'll be sure and keep the torch on for you, sir," Barnabas said.

"Lieutenant Jaeger, Sergeant Smith, and I will try and reach the trail below us and see where it leads. Again, let's plan on being back in four hours. Questions? Good, let's get to it!"

Through the Forest

Hilda and Marci set off across the meadow toward the forest. As they went, Hilda grumbled, "Some things never change, Lieutenant!"

"Meaning?"

"Meaning the captain sends us, the women of the group, off to gather food and water while he and the boys get to go play on the rocks."

"Hadn't occurred to me, but I see your point, Gunny," Marci agreed.

"This is a unique group to fly and fight with. I mean it in a good way."

"No fighting so far, Gunny. I hope it stays that way."

"One never knows, with all those strange messages showing up. I know somebody's toying with us. I feel it in my gut. At some point, they'll make their move. What do you make of the chief's 'conversations' with an alien being? Do you think he's losing his marbles?"

"I don't know what to make of it. I believe Torres thinks what he saw is real. But...."

"But what?"

"He's acting differently on this trip. I should know — we go back a ways."

"How's he different?"

"I can't put my finger on it, but he's not himself," Marci said.

"Could it be HJ, Lieutenant? They don't seem to be the best of friends."

"There's history there."

"Are you part of it?"

"Never thought of it that way, until now. I suppose I am. Not sure I want to go there."

"No worries. If you don't want to talk about it, I understand."

"That's okay. It's all pretty much public knowledge. At least the captain knows about it."

"He doesn't share everything he knows," Hilda said.

After a pause, Marci said, "The three of us were in the same class at the Academy. We were a very competitive group. The top position went back and forth between Josh and me in the first couple of years. We ended up together in various simulator exercises. Pretty soon, word got around that we were an item."

"Were you?"

"We hung out some, even went on a few dates, but nothing serious. We were just good friends."

"Is that how Josh viewed it?"

"I think so. Why do you ask?"

"I've seen the way he looks at you when he thinks no one is watching. You may not choose to notice, but those looks say he thinks of you as more than just a friend."

"The truth is I'm not that close to Josh now. I respect his skills and have no problem working with him, but we're not friends. At least not like we used to be."

"What happened?"

"Things changed when Josh washed out of the Academy."

"Just how do you go from top of your class to washout?"

"A training accident messed up Josh's sight to the point that he failed his flight physical."

"What happened?"

"Our team was on a live-fire demolition exercise. We had infiltrated behind enemy lines and set the charges to bring down our target. Josh was going to cover our retreat. The first charges were supposed to go off away from Josh, so he could escape after we were in the clear. At least that was the plan," Marci said.

"Let me guess," Hilda interjected. "Things seldom go as planned."

"Exactly. Josh was in the correct position, HJ and I had set the charges, and Josh began firing to cover us. We just got clear, and HJ detonated the explosives as planned, but some of them went off in the wrong order."

"Meaning they blew up in Josh's face."

"Yes. Had they been full charges, he'd have been killed right then. Fortunately, these were flash and smoke charges, so Josh survived intact. But his face received second and third-degree burns. He was temporarily blinded and needed plastic surgery to repair the damage. He used to be quite handsome, and the surgery helped some, but you can still tell serious damage was done to his face. With careful treatment, he regained his sight. It just wasn't good enough, soon enough for him to stay in flight school."

"Wow, Lieutenant! And HJ pulled the trigger. That explains a lot."

"Yeah," Marci agreed. "The charge delays weren't clearly marked, so they were easily wired wrong. But HJ pulled the trigger, so Josh blamed him for the accident. It got pretty ugly between those two."

"I can see that. Do you think HJ was negligent?"

"No way! But Josh raised such a fuss, a full inquiry was called."

"Wouldn't one have been called anyway?"

"I suppose," Marci admitted. "Anyway, the inquiry found that the markings on the explosive delay settings were confusing. HJ was found innocent of negligence. The manufacture was fined and ordered to label their gear more clearly."

"How'd Josh take the findings?"

"Not well. He couldn't let it go. I got tired of defending HJ to him. So we parted company. I only deal with him on a professional basis now."

"Too bad, but I get it. What about HJ? He seems to be more than a friend to you. I've seen the way you look at him from time to time."

"Is it that obvious?"

"Yeah, Lieutenant, it is."

"He's a hunk, isn't he? Outside work, we see a lot of each other. I do love him and believe he feels the same about me."

"Has he said how he feels about you?"

"Not in so many words, Gunny. Of course, when we're on duty together, it's strictly business. He's just another officer as far as I'm concerned. There's no room for personal feelings when we're on a mission."

"Good luck with that," Hilda said quietly.

"What?"

"Easier said than done," Hilda answered.

A sharp crack rang out before Marci could reply. The women dropped what they were doing and started running back to the ship.

Marci panted, "Who fired that shot?"

"Couldn't have been one of us. Sounded like a rifle shot. All we have are sidearms." Hilda picked up the pace and drew her Glock. "I just hope we get there in time to help!"

Along the Ridge

Marc was ready to go as soon as the evening meal was finished. He had spent the day retrieving and organizing his climbing gear. He felt like a kid about to go on his first camp-out. Josh watched wistfully as Marc gathered his gear and set out with the captain and HJ.

Barnabas caught Josh's look. "Don't worry, son — if we hustle, we'll be done with kitchen patrol soon enough. We'll still have time to join them."

"I think the captain is still pissed at me for not getting the computers back online."

"It's not personal. He's just in a bad mood because he really wanted to get his hands on a pirate, then be off to Mars to see his wife and son. Now, who knows when he'll be able to do either. He takes his frustration out on you because you're the only one that could get the computers going again. But it is what it is. He knows you've done your best, and no one else on this team could do any better—"

"It's not just that. I don't think he believes Vigilo is real."

Barnabas shifted uncomfortably. "Perhaps he's still processing it all."

"You believe me, sir. Don't you?"

"I believe you believe what you saw and heard."

Josh pressed, "But do you believe it actually happened?"

"Honestly, I'm trying to wrap my mind around it. You're talking about a completely different life form than what we know, with an intelligence that we can only imagine."

"So, you think it was my imagination."

"I didn't say that, Chief. I'm in no position to say that."

"I understand. I'm not even sure it really happened myself."

"So…," Barnabas searched for something else they could talk about, "I hear you attended the academy with Lieutenants Gonzalez and Jaeger."

"I did."

"I also heard that you were at the top of your class."

"I was."

"You must've been passionate about flying."

"I'm passionate about traveling in space," Josh said. "In fact, I have dreams about flying in space. Have had for years."

"So how is it you're a chief and not a commissioned officer?" Realizing he had just succeeded in replacing one awkward topic for another, Barnabas quickly followed up with, "I'm sorry, Chief. That's none of my business."

In silence, they finished cleaning and storing everything. When they secured the ship, being careful to keep the portal door propped open, Josh said, "That's okay. It's a bit of a tale, but it explains why it's important to me to do right by the captain."

"Go ahead," Barnabas said as they started out to catch up with the climbing team.

"We — HJ, Marci, me, and several other cadets — were part of a live-fire exercise. We were to slip behind enemy lines at night, destroy a structure, and withdraw. At least, that was the plan that we, as a team, drew up. It was the perfect plan."

"Perfect plan. I've heard that before," Barnabas interjected.

"The plan was good, but its execution was, let's say, lacking. Some of the flash devices went off too soon and too close to my position. As you can see from my facial scars, I was badly burned. I was also temporarily blinded. When my sight did come back, it wasn't good enough to stay in the flight program."

"Could you've stayed and become a navigator or weapons officer?"

"I could've, but I was messed up, depressed, and bitter. I pretty much gave up and left the Academy. It got, well, complicated."

"In what way?"

"The structure our squad was to blow up ran from north to south. Marci and HJ set the charges. I was at the south end of the structure to cover their retreat. The charges were supposed to start at the north end to cover me as I retreated. But, HJ's charges started from the south and blew up in my face."

"Wow! Sounds like he screwed up, and you paid the price!"

"That's how I saw it," Josh agreed.

"You must've been pissed."

They stopped to admire the evening light show in the sky.

"I was. To make it worse, HJ gave me a nickname — Scarface. After I got out of the hospital and saw him, he expressed no remorse or responsibility. 'Tough break, getting yourself blown up like that is all he said like it was my fault. We exchanged some pretty-heated words, and there was an investigation. But HJ didn't even get a reprimand. The formal cause of the accident was that the markings on the explosives and sequencing charts were too 'confusing' and hard to follow in low-light conditions. The manufacturer was fined and required to make their markings clearer." Josh had a hint of bitterness in his voice.

"Go figure. Still sticks in your craw?"

"It did. It still does if I dwell on it too long. But I'm trying to move on, thanks to Captain Dirksen."

"What did he do?"

"At the time, he was one of the instructors at the Academy. He showed an interest in me when no one else did, even after I dropped out. He helped me get my mind off what I couldn't do and figure out what was important. I thought I only wanted to fly spacecraft. He helped me realize that what I really wanted was to travel in space. The captain helped me see that I enjoyed tech support almost as much as flying. He told me that it could be my ticket to travel in space. He encouraged me to get an advanced degree in hydrology. It was my major as an undergrad. Later, he helped me re-enlist as a non-commissioned officer and work up the ranks as a Tech Support Specialist. He got me so busy, I had no time to wallow in self-pity."

"Good plan. What then?"

"The day I qualified as a Tech Specialist, the captain told me, 'Son, you need to move on from the accident. I know you're angry with HJ, but there's no room in the Space Corps for bitterness against any of its officers. Let go of your anger. It'll free you up to concentrate on achieving your goals.' He promised to make room for me if I did. He warned, 'Keep dwelling on how HJ wronged you, and you'll likely kill your chances of getting into space.'"

"If the captain is anything, he's direct. How'd you take it?"

"I was a little put off at first. But I figured that with what he had done for me, I could at least give it a shot."

"How's that working for you, now?"

"I'd be lying if I said I was totally beyond it. But I'm in a better place now than I was."

"Are you saying you've forgiven him?" Barnabas asked.

"Honestly, Commander?"

"Honestly."

"It's a work in progress. Someday I hope to be able to answer yes."

Just then, they got to where the others were. Matt was looking over the ledge. HJ was a little further away along the ledge, near an outcropping.

"How's it going, Captain?" Barnabas asked as they approached.

"Not as well as we'd hoped. The Sarge rappelled to the path below, right by the Osprey. But the wall angles inward, making ascending back up challenging at best. He thinks our best move is to set a climbing path up over there." Matt pointed to where HJ was standing.

"Anything we can do to help, sir?" Barnabas asked.

"Yeah, Chief, go see if Lieutenant Jaeger needs a hand belaying the sergeant."

"Yes, sir," Josh replied as he moved quickly to stand by HJ. "What's up, Lieutenant?"

"Not much, Torres," HJ answered, looking around at the ground. I'm about to lower a rope to the Sarge. He's about to ascend, but I need to place an anchor bolt to tie onto before I belay him. I set one already, but it's too close to the edge, and it made an odd sound as I was placing it. Ah, here's a good spot."

"Do you know what you're doing, sir?" Josh asked, "Shouldn't you start with two anchors?"

"Back off, Torres!" HJ hissed. "I know what I'm doing. Look around," he motioned with his arm at the barren terrain. "No trees, no boulders. My only choice is to set a bolt to anchor us, and we're losing time. Besides, I only need it to help me keep my balance as I belay the Sarge. It's not like it'll be under a bunch of pressure. Jeez! You're acting like an old lady."

"Sorry, Lieutenant," Josh replied. "I'm no expert at this. I was only asking."

"Understood. When I get the Trubolt set and the anchor in place, help me harness up."

After the anchor was set and HJ was harnessed up, Josh asked HJ if there was anything else he could do.

"I've got things well in hand and don't need your help," HJ said. "Rope!" he shouted to Marc below as he tossed the rope over the edge.

"Got it ... clipping ... up rope," Marc said.

"Mind if I check out some of this gear, Lieutenant?" Josh asked.

"Knock yourself out," HJ answered. "On belay," he shouted to Marc.

"Climbing," Marc yelled.

"Climb on," HJ shouted.

Josh looked around. A few feet from HJ's most recent anchor, Josh spotted a small outcropping of what looked to be topaz. *I wonder if this'll make a good anchor,* he thought. Josh began copying HJ's anchor rigging using the outcropping as a natural anchor.

They could hear Marc shout, "Take! I'm setting a piton," followed by the pinging sound of his Piton hammer driving a piton in place.

"Watch it!" HJ said to Josh, who inadvertently brushed his back.

Before Josh could reply, Marc shouted, "Climbing!"

Just within earshot, Matt was peering over the edge with his flashlight.

"Bet you wished you were part of the action, Captain," Barnabas said.

"What do you mean, Commander?" Matt said with a thin smile. "Why, I'm holding the flashlight, of course."

"Exciting stuff. I see you've also been practicing your calf-roping," Barnabas pointed at a coil of rope by Matt's feet.

Matt gave him a sheepish grin. "Busted. It's boring doing nothing but watching the sergeant and lieutenant work. I had to do something to pass the time."

"I guess you can take the captain out of Wyoming, but you can't take Wyoming out of the captain."

"There's more truth to that than you know. Were you aware that I got suspended one time for breaking in a wild horse?"

"No, sir, I didn't know that."

"It's true. It was two days before I was scheduled to command a mission. The Mustang I was breaking tossed me, I busted three ribs. I missed the launch as a result. NASA was less than pleased. They banned me from riding horses again while I'm still flying. So, here I sit, roping imaginary horses while watching those young bucks climb on the rocks."

Barnabas motioned toward HJ and Josh. "Think it wise to team those two up?"

"Climb on!" HJ shouted at Marc.

Matt said, "They don't have to like each other, but they must learn to work together. They could be a good fit. Torres is detail-oriented and competent, but Jaeger is a more creative big-picture kind of thinker."

"Interesting take, Captain. I can see why you selected Torres over Jaeger. But I'd still be concerned, given their history."

"Trust me, Commander, I'm more troubled over Jaeger's recent history with Lieutenant Gonzalez than I am over his history with Torres."

"That being?"

"That being, they're quite the item, clubbing at the Sky-Dome."

"The Sky-Dome?"

"I forgot you're not familiar with Houston. The Sky-Dome is a club that looks like a half dome on the waterfront. Every other hour it lifts off and moves out over Trinity Bay, hovering about 100 feet above the water."

"That's impressive."

"The most impressive part is that the dance floor is a clear polycarbonate material. It gives the illusion of walking on air. It is one of the hottest nightspots in town. It is frequented by Jaeger and any number of girls, until recently. Lately, he's been seen exclusively with Gonzalez. A romance between crew members makes me uncomfortable."

"I hear you."

"I'm also concerned about the cryptic messages we keep receiving. It makes me wonder who's in charge, our watchers or me."

"Call it a gut feeling, but I think you're right to be concerned, sir."

They heard Marc shout, "Take. I'm setting another piton," followed by the pinging of his piton hammer tapping another piton into place.

"Excuse my impertinence, sir, but, given your suspicions, do you think it wise to leave the ship unguarded?"

"I thought about that. I figure that whoever's watching must know we are virtually defenseless. If they intended to harm us, my guess is, they would've done it by now —"

"CRACK!" Both men instinctively ducked at what sounded like a nearby rifle shot.

HJ felt the effects almost immediately. First, there was a rumbling, then an invisible force jerked him forward. Fortunately, the anchor attached to his harness kept him from pitching off the cliff. Unfortunately, the force pulling on HJ loosened the anchor. He could feel it starting to slip. He also saw he was now at the very edge of the cliff. A portion of the plateau had broken away and tangled in the climbing rope.

"Rock! Rock!" he shouted to Marc.

Marc felt the broken part of the plateau give way, drop him, then hang up. At first, he thought he was falling.

"Falling! Falling!" He shouted while thinking, *why isn't he belaying me?* Seeing the broken column following him down and hearing HJ yell "Rock! Rock!" helped him understand that he was tangled with a chunk of the plateau. Now he was only held up by a single man. Marc knew that his fate would already be decided if the gravity here was as strong as it is on Earth. *I wonder how long HJ can hold on?* he thought as he began examining if he could untangle himself from the mess and escape.

The sound of the outcropping splitting off caused Josh to look behind him just in time to see HJ jerk forward. In one motion, without thinking, Josh reached out with one hand and grabbed HJ's harness. With the other hand, he caught hold of a loop in the rigging he had just attached to his topaz anchor. He winced under the force that was trying to pull HJ over the edge. It was stretching his arms apart.

"Hang on, HJ. I've got you!" he shouted as he started shaking from the strain.

"Don't let go, Torres!" HJ shouted back, feeling like the force was going to drive the rope through his back.

"What the hell are you doing, Chief?" Matt yelled. "You're pushing Jaeger over the cliff!"

Matt noticed that the cliff was closer to HJ and Josh than it should be.

"I don't think the chief's pushing. I think he's holding the lieutenant," Barnabas said.

"Your right; something's wrong with the cliff. Part of it is missing or...." Matt finally saw what was happening. "It's broken free! Where's the sergeant? Sarge, can you hear me? Are you okay?" Matt shouted.

"I'm fine, just hangin' out down here, sir." The very calmness of Marc's voice, the one most in danger, settled Matt's nerves.

"Sarge, can you get free?" Matt yelled.

"I'm pretty tied up at the moment, Captain. Any way you could get another rope to me? I could use it to swing away from this mess."

"Captain, could you rope him in?" Barnabas suggested.

"Should've thought of that myself." Matt grabbed the rope by his feet and looked over the edge gauging the distance. "Sarge ... put an arm up, and I'll try and lasso it."

"Hell, I'll put both arms up."

The first attempt came up short. The second was on target, sliding over both arms. Marc grabbed the rope and secured it under his armpits. Then he set about trying to free himself. His harness and gear were so entangled with the rock, Marc had to embrace it harder to gain enough slack to undo the buckles. The broken piece of the outcropping was swaying back and forth, making Marc's maneuvers even more challenging.

"I'm nearly free. I think I'm about twenty feet above the trail. Right now, this pillar that has me is balancing on the edge of the trail. If I bail, the change in the rock's center of gravity will pitch it over the trail and yank HJ down with it," Marc shouted.

"I'll worry about that, Sarge," Matt said. "You just get to that trail. I'll belay you as you climb up. Commander, grab your knife and get over to where HJ is. On my word, cut that rope."

Barnabas grabbed his knife and ran to where HJ was. "Hold on, guys — we've got a plan."

"Better be a fast plan. I can't hold it much longer," HJ panted.

"What he said!" Josh nodded toward HJ.

"Whenever you're ready, Sarge," Matt shouted.

"I'm away," Marc shouted as he launched himself from the pillar. He aimed for the trail. Marc noticed that his fall wasn't as fast as he expected. A sharp pain ran up from his left ankle when he landed. He fell backward and yelled, "Up rope!"

"On belay!" Matt yelled with more confidence than he felt.

Somehow Marc found himself safely on the narrow ledge. He shouted, "Climbing."

"Climb on," Matt shouted back.

It was a challenge to climb with an injured ankle, but Marc made steady progress. The pillar pitched back and started swaying more from Marc's jump. This only added to HJ's and Josh's agony.

When Matt thought Marc was out of danger from the dangling pillar, he yelled, "Commander, cut the rope."

"Yes, sir." Barnabas attacked the rope. He was careful to steady the taut rope with his hand on the plateau side of his knife. Barnabas thought *it wouldn't do to be holding onto the side of the rope that's going over the cliff.* He was surprised at how challenging the rope was. Barnabas was cutting but seemingly without effect. He bore down harder.

HJ was wincing in pain, saying, "Hurry, Commander!"

Josh felt his arms coming out of their sockets and prayed, "God, I know I haven't been to Mass in years and can't remember the last time I even thought about you, but if you're there, I could sure use a hand about now."

Just then, the rope snapped, sending the pillar crashing over the trail's edge and catapulting HJ and Josh in the opposite direction. They landed flat on their backs. The force of the rope end that Barnabas held pulled it clean through his clenched fist, giving his hand a nasty rope burn.

At about the exact moment, Marc's head popped above the plateau's edge. "Hey, Captain," he said, with a huge grin, "now I know what one of those calves you rope feels like."

Matt said nothing. He just sat down and let out a long sigh of relief. Then he grabbed Marc's shoulder to help him clamber back onto the plateau.

The noise of the pillar bouncing as it fell into the abyss continued for a while. Finally, it gave way to silence and an occasional light cracking sound.

Hilda and Marci arrived. Hilda rushed up first with her weapon drawn. She surveyed the scene and saw the captain sitting on the cliff's edge next to Marc, lying on his back with his knees bent up. The commander was further away, kneeling by the edge of the cliff, nursing his left hand. Away from the edge of the cliff, both HJ and Josh were sprawled on their backs. She said, "How can just one shot cause all this havoc?" Then, realizing that no one was shot, she holstered her weapon and started toward the two young men lying on their backs. Marci brushed by her and hurried straight for HJ.

"Are you alright?" she asked as she knelt beside him.

Hilda walked by HJ and asked the same question of Josh — who was beginning to sit up.

HJ smiled. "Just a little shaken up, Marci." He noticed that both women were closer to him than Josh, although Hilda had her back to him, and raised his voice. "Hey Torres, what'd I tell you? I'm just a babe magnet," he gloated.

Hilda rolled her eyes and took a calculated step backward, landing directly on HJ's outstretched hand.

"Ouch!" he exclaimed in pain. "Watch it, Gunny."

"My bad. I guess I just got caught up by your magnetism, Lieutenant," she gave her foot a slight twist as she stepped off his hand.

"Everybody in one piece?" Matt asked as he and Marc walked up.

His question was met with a chorus of grunts and moans.

"Good! Let's gather up what's left of the Sergeant's gear and get back to the ship."

Josh sat up and started to shake as what just happened settled in.

"Easy, Chief." Marc steadied Josh, who rose to his feet, then promptly sat back down. Marci helped HJ up while Barnabas joined the group.

"What happened?" Hilda asked.

Marc shrugged. "I was trying to set a rope to help everyone climb from the trail below, back onto the plateau. I think that setting some pitons in the cracks may have split part of the outcropping. It fell away. The captain and HJ saved my bacon."

"The important thing is that everyone's alright and out of danger," Marci said.

"Not so sure about that last part," Barnabas said.

"What do you mean, Commander?" Matt asked.

"Listen closely, sir. Do you hear an occasional noise like ice cracking? There it goes again — did you hear it?"

"Yeah, so?" Matt asked.

"The commander's on to something." Marc bent over the spot where HJ had set his second anchor. It had disappeared into the crevice that had just opened. "Stress fracture, maybe."

"Here's another." Barnabas pointed with his flashlight toward a spot near where HJ was when the cliff gave way. Several cracks were radiating from that spot. Barnabas followed one that was larger than the others. His companions watched as his light beam illuminated the direction of that crack heading straight for the Osprey.

"What do you think, Sarge?" Matt asked. "You're the geologist."

"Hate to say it, Captain, but our little adventure tonight may have destabilized this portion of the plateau."

"Meaning what?" HJ asked.

"Meaning that these cracks could travel further, causing more of the plateau to open up and fall away," Marc answered.

"Worst case, Sarge?" Matt asked.

"Worst case? Judging by the direction and size of a couple of these cracks, half the ground the Osprey is sitting on could break off."

The sound of a sharp crack and slight tremor emphasized his point.

Desperate Times

Onboard the Osprey

Josh struggled to keep his feet. The first tremor nearly threw him to the floor. He shook his head to clear it. Alarms were sounding. He heard the captain calling his name.

He was saying, "Josh get over here. We need your weight to keep the ship from sliding off the plateau!"

Josh struggled to get to the port side where most everyone else was. The angle of the deck was too steep for him to walk. He dropped to his hands and knees and crawled toward the others. Something was wrong; someone else was missing from the group. He heard HJ calling for help from the starboard side of the ship.

"Don't leave me!" HJ yelled, "I'm being sucked in! I can't get out!"

Josh saw that HJ was halfway out of the starboard portal, holding on for dear life. Josh tried to anchor himself and reach down to grab HJ's arm.

"No time, Chief," Matt yelled. "I need you. You can't help him now."

Just then, HJ grabbed Josh's arm and yanked him down. Josh felt himself tumble out of the ship into the darkness with HJ's hand shaking his shoulder, crying, "Chief, Chief, CHIEF!"

Josh came to with a start. "Wake up, Chief." It was the Sarge. "Jeez, man! You scared the bejeebies outta me!"

"Sorry, Sarge — bad dream." Josh rubbed the sleep from his eyes.

"Must've been a beaut," Marc said. "No matter, I was about to wake you. We need to hurry, or we'll be late for the noon meeting."

"Noon meeting?"

"Yeah, no sleeping in this morning, Chief. The captain's too worried about those cracks heading toward the ship to wait for our usual time. He wants ideas on how we can stop them."

Just as they entered the ship's bridge, they noticed that a new message was waiting on the console for them.

Για κάθε φορά που υπάρχει μια σεζόν μια εποχή για να μείνει μια σεζόν για να φύγει

"What does this message say?" Matt asked.

Barnabas smiled, "It's Greek to me, Captain."

"Very funny, Commander," Matt said.

HJ said, "The commander's right, Captain."

"How'd you know?" Marc asked.

"Easy. My mother is Greek, so I learned the lingo as a kid," HJ answered. "The message says, 'For every time there is a season for a time to stay a season to go.'"

"Could be appropriate for our discussion," Marc commented.

A somber mood hung over the team as the discussion turned to the approaching cracks.

"Sarge, how certain are you that the flaw in the rock will extend this far?" Matt asked.

"I can't be certain, sir." Marc looked at the somber faces gathered around the flight deck. "The rock we're dealing with here appears to have more semi-precious gem qualities than I'm used to seeing—"

Matt interrupted, "Meaning?"

"Meaning that it's harder and more brittle than normal rock, with definite facets. Last night we may have split a facet—"

"Split a facet?" Matt interrupted again.

"Think 'fault line,'" Marc answered, with more calm than he felt. "If this is true, the integrity of the ground the Osprey sits on is compromised. I don't think it'll take much for it to break away."

"Options?" Matt asked.

Hilda said, "We need to move everything we can off this ship ASAP."

"Is it safe to set up camp in the meadow?" Marci asked.

Marc said, "Most likely. The meadow looks to be supported by a different rock structure. I'll need to verify it, but most gemlike areas don't support plant life, other than some lichen."

Hilda said, "Might be better if we move closer to our source of food and water."

"Of course, those options don't account for the fact that we still need this ship to keep breathing during the day. Is there any option where we don't abandon ship?" Matt asked.

HJ said, "Doesn't look like it, Captain. Is there some way we can stop the fracture?"

"Is that possible, Sarge?" Matt asked.

"In my opinion, sir, it's not possible."

"Maybe there's a refuge around here, where the oxygen level stays up during the day," Marci suggested.

Barnabas agreed, "The lieutenant may have a point, sir. Perhaps the messages yesterday and today serve as a warning. Today's message reinforces yesterday's."

"Meaning, Commander?" Matt asked.

Barnabas rubbed his chin. "If memory serves me correctly, it read 'If you go down, you must 'fly' or 'flee.' We climbed down, so I'm guessing it's advising us to flee. It could be that there is a refuge just waiting to be discovered."

"I've got it!" Josh exclaimed.

"I'm listening," Matt said.

Josh asked, "What if it's a play on words, sir?"

"A play on words?"

"Yes, we flee by flying. We'll fly the Osprey to the edge of the forest on the meadow."

HJ frowned. "That would be poetic, Chief. Forgetting just one minor detail — THE OSPREY CAN'T FLY, MORRON!"

"Easy Lieutenant," Matt cut in. "What are you thinking, Chief?"

"In my effort to bring the computers online, I never tested the maneuvering thrusters," Josh said. "We might be able to bypass the computer and use them to move the ship."

"How?" Matt asked.

"The ship has four banks of thrusters — fore, aft, port, and starboard. Each bank has a junction box where the thrust signal from the computer can be disconnected. In its place, we have a remote controller that we use to test-fire each of the thrusters in the bank. We can test each thruster during normal maintenance without interfering with the IT guys working on the computers. I have a test controller onboard that we can use."

HJ sighed. "That's crazy, Torres. Everyone knows thrusters are used for maneuvering in space. They're not powerful enough to lift a spaceship this heavy."

Barnabas said, "Sounding like a broken record here. But, if you'd bothered to attend our training sessions, Lieutenant, you'd know these thrusters are powerful enough to do what our Chief is suggesting."

"And don't forget, gravity isn't as strong here as on Earth," Marc said.

Looks like I'll need to revisit my comment about our Chief thinking outside the box, Matt thought. To Josh, he said, "Let's get moving, Chief. Tell us what you need. We'll gather it up while you test your theory. If your theory holds, then you can show us what to do."

HJ said, "I hate to rain on your parade, Captain, but—"

Matt cut him off, "Then don't."

HJ was undeterred. "Seriously, doesn't the thrust tester communicate to one thruster at a time, Chief? How's that going to lift the ship?"

"You're right, Lieutenant," Josh admitted. "But I'm going to set the control switch to broadcast to the entire bank at once."

"I'm not trying to be a wet blanket, but the thrusters only lift the Osprey. Without the computer, how do you plan to move it to the meadow?" HJ asked.

"That's easy, Lieutenant. I'll rig up a mechanical lever to angle some of the starboard thrusters outward. That'll be enough to nudge the ship to the meadow. CRAP!"

"What is it, son?" Barnabas asked.

"I was planning to connect the test controller to all four banks of thrusters. But the safest way to make this work requires two controllers. We only have one."

"What's a controller made of?" Marc asked.

"In simplest terms, Sarge, it's a rheostat connected to a power source and a switch to distribute the signal. I have a spare switch. I've got everything I need to jury-rig one, but I don't have the rheostat."

"I've got a rheostat," Hilda said. "It's part of a simple incubator I use for some experiments I planned to run on Mars."

"That'll work," Josh said.

"Only if we get done before the fault gives way. Let's get moving!" Matt urged.

Aboard the Osprey

SHIP'S LOG December 17, 2068

Entry by Captain Dirksen:

These are desperate times. We risk losing the Osprey to severe fracturing of the plateau's structure. So we need to move the Osprey closer to the forest, away from the plateau's edge. Thanks to Chief Torres's clever use of the ship's positioning thrusters, we may have a chance to make this work.

Lieutenant Gonzalez and Commander Maalouf will control the ship's thrusters to move the Osprey out of danger.

Situational Assessment:

No sign of life in the Osprey's computers. No sign of animal life. No sign of intelligent life, other than the cryptic messages mentioned before. Several concerns:

- There is still no sign of a rescue ship.
- The crew's stress level is high.
- We must succeed in moving the ship, or she'll be lost.

END OF ENTRY

The evening was well underway when the test controller and the jury-rigged controller were connected correctly. When all was set, the captain and crew took up their positions. Marci was to control the fore and aft bank of thrusters and both the starboard and port-side lifting thrusters. Barnabas would control the modified port and starboard thrusters that would move the hovering ship sideways toward the forest. Matt and Hilda would be the spotters that would direct Marci and Barnabas during this maneuver. Marc, HJ, and Josh were positioned outside with flashlights to mark where the captain hoped to place the Osprey.

"Thanks, guys," Josh said to Marc and HJ as they waited. "I couldn't have done this if you hadn't positioned the port and starboard thrusters for me."

"Glad to help, Chief," Marc replied.

"Just hope it works, Torres," HJ grunted.

"Everyone in position?" Matt asked. After receiving the unanimous agreement, he said, "On my mark, Lieutenant, put this ship into a low, even hover. Five, four, three, two, one, MARK."

The ship shuddered, then rocked back and forth some. Finally, it felt like an unseen hand was lifting the Osprey ever slightly clear of the ground. Its motion was like that of a fishing boat drifting on the ocean.

"Steady, Lieutenant," Matt said. "Now, Commander, begin moving toward the forest at your pleasure."

"Beginning the maneuver now," Barnabas replied.

A second invisible hand pushed the ship sideways but too fast. The side of the starship angled down. The ship's hull complained as it scraped the ground. Barnabas eased up.

"More lift please, Lieutenant, on my mark," Barnabas said.

"Aye, sir."

"Five, four, three, two, one, MARK!" This time both Marci and Barnabas increased thrust together. Marci sneezed, causing her hand to jerk. That motion accelerated the lift too quickly, causing Barnabas to over-correct. The Osprey began to swing wildly and headed directly at Josh, who was the closest "target." He dove out of the way. Barnabas and Marci quickly killed their power, dropping the Osprey hard on the ground. HJ and Marc laughed at Josh, lying on his face.

"Not funny," Josh said.

"I thought it was funny. You, Sarge?" HJ said.

Marc smiled. "Yeah, I thought it was funny. Great reaction time, Chief. Only the bird set down a dozen yards away from you."

Josh sat up and brushed himself off. "It sure looked like it was heading straight for me."

Matt shook his head. "Let's try this again without sneezing."

"Aye, sir," a crestfallen Lieutenant replied.

"On my mark, Lieutenant … put this ship into a low, even hover. Five, four, three, two, one, MARK!" The unseen hand began lifting the Osprey clear of the ground.

"Steady as she goes, Lieutenant," Matt said. "Okay, Commander, start moving us toward the forest over there."

The second invisible hand pushed the ship sideways. It moved too fast, and the side of the vessel angled down. Again, the ship's hull complained as it scraped the ground. The commander eased up.

"More lift please, Lieutenant," Barnabas said.

"Aye, sir."

Both Marci and Barnabas increased thrust together. The ship moved closer to the forest before it started to keel over.

"We're going over, sir!" Marci exclaimed.

"Cut your thrust, Lieutenant!" Barnabas commanded as he eased off his thrusters, and the ship settled down. "We made progress, Lieutenant, but we're not there yet. I figure if we do this a few more times, we'll get where we need to be," he said as he thought *if we don't flip this bird over in the process.*

"I agree about flipping the bird, Commander," Marci commented.

"Did I just say that?"

"You did," Marci replied

Barnabas shook his head. "Note to self — start thinking more quietly. Lieutenant, are you ready to go at it again?"

"I am, sir."

Barnabas and Marci repeated their maneuver half a dozen times before Matt gave the order to shut the thrusters down. The flight crew let out a collective sigh, realizing they had made it to the edge of the forest. The Osprey seemed to be out of danger for the moment.

Matt said, "Okay, everyone, take what's left of the night and relax." Under his breath, he said, "Sarge, did we move her far enough?"

Marc shrugged, "Don't tell the crew, but I'm not sure."

The Edge of the Forest

A pre-dawn thunderstorm rolled in and hung around most of the day, depriving the crew of their needed rest. Finally, it passed on to reveal the daytime pink sky giving way to a typical bluish evening sky.

The crew gathered for their assignments. The smell of their evening meal drifted through the open door. "Ugh!" HJ exclaimed. "Not carrot and parsnip stew again. This is getting old."

"I heard that," Barnabas (the crew's default cook) said from outside. "If you don't like it, you can always wash it down with some fresh rotten-egg-tasting water."

Marc said, "Ah, what I wouldn't give for a drink of fresh Rocky Mountain spring water."

"There's such a thing?" Josh asked.

Marc replied, "You bet. I remember hiking near the tree line with my cousin. We came across a spring with fresh cold water bubbling straight out of the ground. Talk about thirst-quenching. I've never tasted water that good since."

"Sounds good to me," Josh commented.

"Skip the spring." HJ licked his lips. "I'll take a dark ale made from some of that Rocky Mountain water. I wish I could have a cold pint right now. What about you, Commander?"

Barnabas smiled. "I'm more of a white wine kind of guy."

"To make wine, you need grapes," Marci said. "My favorite is a concord grape. Nothing like it or the jelly it makes. I wish I could have a handful of those grapes right now."

HJ said, "You can't make white wine out of Concord grapes."

"No, but I've got a friend who makes wine out of frozen grape juice," Josh said. "He claimed he finish the whole process in only one month."

"That sounds like some high-class stuff," HJ said.

"Must be why he called it the thirty-day wonder," Josh deadpanned. After a long silence, he shook his head. "Jeez, you're a hard audience."

"I think the lieutenant was merely speaking of her favorite fruit," Hilda said. "Mine is persimmons. I wish I could have a couple right now."

"Speaking of fruit, I wish I could get my hands on some figs or pomegranates," Matt said as he sat down.

Josh said, "Fruit's good. But I wish I could sink my teeth into a freshly-roasted ear of sweet corn."

"Toss some sweet potatoes in with that corn you're roasting, Chief. If I had a wish, I'd wish for some of the roasted sweet potatoes instead of these parsnips," Barnabas said.

"And he's the cook," Matt said.

Marci looked at the ship's console. "Look, there's our daily message."

It read: "Να προσέχεις τι εὐχεσαι."

"More Greek?" Josh asked.

HJ replied, "Yeah it is."

"What's it say?" Matt asked.

HJ replied, "Be careful what you wish for."

SHIP'S LOG December 18, 2068

Entry by Captain Dirksen:

Thanks to Lieutenant Gonzalez and Commander Malouf's ability to improvise with their crude controls, we succeeded in moving the Osprey closer to the forest and away from danger, for the moment. That exercise took virtually all evening. Tonight, I am only ordering short forays to be out for half the night. The teams and assignments will be as follows:

Lieutenant Gonzalez and Master Sergeant Smith will return to the area first explored by Gunnery Sergeant McDermott and Lieutenant Gonzalez. Their task is to retrieve the food and water that was harvested last night but left behind.

Lieutenant Jaeger and Gunnery Sergeant McDermott will be sent down the one trail not yet explored. Perhaps they will locate a wider selection of food and more pleasant water.

Commander Maalouf and I will return to the cave that produces tar to restock our supply of fuel.

Chief Torres will remain with the ship. He needs to reconfigure the positioning thrusters to be flight-ready.

Situational Assessment:

There is still no sign of animal life. I'm sure we are being watched by some sort of intelligent life. It only communicates with us through cryptic messages. Curiously, the last two "communications" seemed to be a coordinated warning and helpful clues. Hopefully, tonight's exploring will give the crew a chance to relax after yesterday's stressful events. Still concerned over:

- Lack of a rescue ship that must have been launched by now.
- The tactical location of the ship is less than ideal.
- Who or what is generating our daily "messages." Today's message, "Be careful what you wish for," is especially disconcerting because of its timing.

END OF ENTRY

Along the Rim Path

Matt and his second-in-command walked together in silence. "Sir, if you don't mind my asking, what's your thinking in selecting the teams tonight?"

"Why, Commander? Got a problem with my choices?"

"No, sir, just curious."

"McDermott already taught Gonzalez what to look for and what to avoid when gathering food. So that task can be handled by Gonzalez and

Sarge. McDermott is now free to explore the new trail with Lieutenant Jaeger."

"I guess that you're not teaming up Gonzalez and Jaeger any time soon, are you?"

"No. I'm not."

"You think he's a bad influence on her?"

"Yeah, she's got real potential. But Jaeger's a distraction, and there's just something about him. Not sure what, but I just don't trust him."

"Perhaps it's his sense of entitlement or his less-than-stellar work ethic."

"Could be. Maybe I just don't like the kid. That's not good."

"Don't feel too bad, sir. I've got a sense that the feeling is mutual. Just how does one get the name, Homer Jaeger? No wonder he goes by HJ."

"His mother is Greek, and his father's German. Ladykiller looks from his mother and a lousy disposition from his father. It's quite the combo."

"Doesn't bode well for Lieutenant Gonzalez, not that it's any of our business."

"It's not, Commander, as long as their personal feelings don't affect their performance."

Changing the subject, Barnabas asked, "What about the chief?

"I've held his feet to the fire long enough. I'm sure yesterday's efforts drained him mentally. I think he needs some downtime tonight."

"Makes sense, sir."

"I'm glad you agree. I value your opinion, which is why we are teamed up tonight. I want to discuss our situation without being overheard."

"What's troubling you, sir?"

"I believe that whoever opened the wormhole is keeping us here."

"Agreed."

"A rescue ship should've been here by now. Whoever let us in may not be letting our rescue ship through. I expect they'll eventually communicate with us more directly rather than through some strange messages."

"Except for Josh's watcher," Barnabas said.

"Except for Josh's watcher. What's your take on all this? If his watcher's real, there must be more. How is it only the chief can see a watcher?"

"Ever heard of the 'Invisible Gorilla Test'?"

"No."

"Early in the 21st century, a couple of researchers created a short video in which six people, three in white shirts and three in black shirts, pass basketballs around. The viewer is asked to watch and count how many times the people in white shirts passed a basketball. As the video progresses, a black gorilla strolls into the middle of the action, faces the camera, and thumps its chest. Then it leaves, being visible for at least nine seconds. You'd think that the gorilla would be seen by everyone watching the video."

"One would think."

"At least half the people who watched this video were so focused on counting the number of passes, they missed seeing the gorilla at all. To them, the gorilla was invisible."

"Your point, Commander?"

"My point is that when we look at our surroundings a certain way, looking for a specific object, we can totally miss seeing something else that's obvious. Gunny, the Sarge, and we are trained to look for specific threats like we've seen in the past. The chief has no such constraints. He was just out for a walk, so he may have been able to see what we missed."

"What about our two Lieutenant love birds?" Matt countered.

"You know what they say: 'Love is blind.' I'm not trying to prove anything other than what the chief is seeing could be real."

"Interesting. I'm also concerned about the cohesiveness of our team."

"Under the circumstances, I think it's okay, sir."

"I sense that the chief is in his own world, that Jaeger's attitude is getting worse, and he's distracting Gonzalez."

"Gunny and Sarge?"

"They're finding this place a little too interesting. What are your thoughts, Commander?"

"Hmm … You know I have your back, sir. Gunny and the Sarge are troupers. They'll hang in there. But, they're also scientists in a strange new land, begging to be explored. I imagine that from their point of view, our mission is toast."

"Which it is."

"Yes, sir. Of course, they could be distracted by their research. Lieutenant Jaeger is a different story. He's the type who likes hitting the easy button. I should say the easy-out button. He'll jump ship at his first opportunity. That'll put Lieutenant Gonzalez in a bind. Her heart'll be with him while her head'll be with the team."

"And Chief Torres?"

"He's a team player, so no worries there. You think there's another source of O2 around here, sir?" Barnabas asked.

"I'm afraid that if there is, it'll be a challenge to keep everyone near the ship."

"That's a problem?"

"I have a gut feeling. If we have a chance to escape, or whoever is holding us decides to let us go, our window of opportunity will be short. I want everyone ready as a team, near the ship, so no one's left behind."

"Good point, sir." *Sadly, we don't always get what we want,* Barnabas thought.

Near the Osprey

For once, Josh was not disappointed at having to stay with the ship. He finished resetting the maneuvering thrusters and stepped outside. He carefully set the block to keep the portal door from shutting. As he did so, he thought, *the engineers really need to modify the design of this hatch. If it were to slam shut, there'd be no way in.* He didn't even mind having KP duty by himself. After the stress of the day, it felt good to do some mindless work to help unwind. With his chores done, he sat back next to the ship and watched the nightly light show. As before, the silent curtains of light danced across the sky. They swayed to and fro, in movements choreographed to some unheard music. Fully relaxed, Josh was drifting off to sleep when he noticed a singular beam of light separate itself from the greenish curtain in the sky and drift down until it stood directly in front of him.

"Good evening, Josh."

"Vigilo, is it you?" Josh asked.

"It is," was the reassuring reply.

"I was beginning to think I imagined you," a relieved Josh said.

"Imagined? What does that mean?"

"It means to think of something that isn't real."

"Why would you think I'm not real?"

"It's just that … no one believes me, and I've never seen anything like you before."

Vigilo chuckled. "It can't be helped that the others are slow in their perception. They've all seen our messages. They should've believed you by now."

"Why are the messages in different languages and always a riddle?

"The riddles are a nice touch, don't you think?"

Josh wondered how such a non-human voice could sound so flippant. "Why the riddles? Why don't you just say what you mean?"

"It's, how would you put it, not rocket science. Riddles play two roles. They help us understand your puzzle-solving skills and how well you follow our advice. So far, you are better at the former than the latter. These messages are also designed to stay in your memory. You never know when they may be useful later. Here's a question. If the messages weren't coded, would you have taken them seriously?"

"Sadly, probably not," Josh answered.

"Unfortunately, my friend, events are about to take a serious turn, and we need your help. We'll continue with the riddles, but you must also give your companions a critical warning."

"Why me?"

"I don't know. I just know Taxiarchis chose you," Vigilo answered.

"None of this makes sense to me."

"The ways of Taxiarchis often don't make sense, at first."

"What do you want me to say?" Josh asked.

"Two of your friends are discovering a beautiful garden as we speak. In that garden, they'll feel at home and safe. But danger is lurking nearby. Tell them NOT to wander into the cave that they will find."

Josh asked. "Why can't we enter the cave? What's the danger that is lurking nearby?"

"I can't say, my friend. I can say that you have a responsibility to convince your friends that they face grave danger if they enter that cave."

"Why me? Why not a Watcher?"

"They're more likely to believe one of their own than one of us."

"But why would they believe me? They already think I'm crazy and that you are only a figment of my imagination. They'll never listen to me."

"My friend, you must give this warning. That is your responsibility. If you don't, sanguis eorum sit super manus."

"Their blood is on my hands?" Josh responded

"Yes. But, if you do warn your friends, and they choose to ignore you, then their blood is NOT on your hands."

"You're starting to scare me."

"There's no reason to be frightened if you warn your friends about the cave. Can you do this? Will you do this?"

Josh swallowed hard. "This I can do, but I'm sure they won't listen."

Through the Forest

It took a little while for Marci and Marc to arrive at their destination. Marc was still nursing a tender ankle and using a walking stick as a cane.

"Not fair of the captain to make you walk with me, Sarge," Marci sputtered.

"No worries, Lieutenant. He knows I'm still pretty wound up. The last thing I want to do is just sit around and do nothing."

"I suppose so. You had a very close call."

"Closer than you think. I haven't mentioned this to anyone, but I should be dead, along with the captain."

"What do you mean?"

"When I hit the ledge from my jump, I bounced backward before I could get a handhold or my balance. I knew that there was way too much slack in the rope. Had I fallen much further, it would have snapped taut and yanked the captain off the plateau above me."

"What happened?"

"I felt myself falling, saw the slack, and thought this is it, when I felt a second rope around my waist pull me back, to where I could grab a handhold and steady myself. I swear I felt the rope but never saw anything when I looked down."

"Okay, you're starting to creep me out, Sarge."

"Didn't mean to do that, Lieutenant."

"No worries. I have my own strange story, and we're looking at it."

"Looking at what?"

"This is the cranberry bush Gunny and I were standing by when we heard the plateau break away." Marci pointed at the bush in question. "Do you see food scattered about?"

"No, Lieutenant."

"What do you see?"

"I see orderly piles of vegetables and fruits, with a couple of water containers carefully arranged. Everything seems to be in order. What's so strange about that?"

"When we heard the noise of the cliff breaking, we dropped everything and ran. Stuff scattered everywhere. Someone has been here and carefully organized everything." Marci started to look around. Marc joined her as they looked, in an expanding circle, for footprints other than those of Marci and Hilda. "Was someone following us the other night?" Marci wondered.

"More importantly, are they watching us right now? Huh? What is that sound? Do you hear it, Lieutenant?"

"It's nothing, Sarge, just the rustling of the feather trees by the wind, I think."

"Are you sure it's not an animal?" Marc drew his Glock. "Do you see a shimmering?"

"A what?"

"A shimmering, like the heat waves you see looking down a country road in the summer. The latest type of camouflage worn by soldiers causes just such a shimmering."

"I don't think so," Marci squinted her eyes. "It might just be your imagination."

"Maybe you're right, Lieutenant. Just the same, I suggest that we quickly gather everything here and head back to the ship," he proposed while looking harder at the trees and undergrowth.

Marci shuddered, "Good idea Sarge."

Last Unexplored Path

HJ and Hilda were walking down the last unexplored path. It led them among the peacock feather trees.

HJ said, "You're looking mighty fine tonight, Gunny."

Hilda seemed to ignore him but picked up her pace.

"Hmm, maybe we could hook up after we get off this rock," HJ said as he followed.

"I believe, Lieutenant, you already have a girlfriend," Hilda said, without looking back. "And I believe she's along on this trip."

"Maybe. But maybe she's just my plus one. Maybe I'm still looking for someone like you to be my girl."

Suddenly, HJ felt an unseen force yank back on his ankle. He lost his balance and crashed through the underbrush to the ground.

"Hey Gunny, I was just kidding around. No need to take me down!"

Hilda chuckled, "That wasn't me, Lieutenant. Just chalk it up to your own clumsiness."

"No, you grabbed my ankle from behind," HJ sat up.

"And just how did I manage that, seeing as I've been in front of you this whole time?"

HJ held up his hand. "I don't know, just help me up,"

"You're no cripple," Hilda said, looking his way.

HJ started to speak but stopped when he saw that Hilda was looking past him.

"What're you looking at?" he asked as he followed her eyes.

He saw that his fall had carried him to the fringe of a lush meadow. It ran up to a spectacular emerald-colored wall of outcroppings. Hilda stepped around HJ, who scrambled to his feet and followed. A trail meandered through the meadow, ascending gradually to the outcroppings. They followed the pathway to a narrow gap in the emerald wall. Each of them ducked through the portal and stood on the other side, surveying what lay ahead. HJ let out a low whistle.

"I think I smell, jasmine. No, maybe I smell—"

"Did you hear that?" HJ interrupted.

"Hear what?"

"Shhhh … just listen. There it is again!"

"What?" Hilda asked. "Wait, do I hear birds singing?"

"Sure, sounds like it," HJ agreed. "I think we have a game-changer!"

"Huh?" How's it a game-changer?"

"What do birds need to survive?"

"Water, food, air, that's why we would only hear them at night. That's when there's oxygen for them to breathe."

"That's my point. Where do they go during the day? They still need to breathe."

"Wow, you're right. If we find where they go during the day, we find a source of oxygen!"

And I'll be free of that damnable ship and its captain Ahab! HJ thought.

The Garden

Aboard the Osprey

The bounty lying in front of the crew was mesmerizing. Ripe figs, dates, concord grapes, persimmons, and pomegranates made for a medley of rich colors. Red potatoes, sweet potatoes, red cabbage, and wild corn rounded out the fare.

"Wow, my stomach's already growling just looking at all this stuff!" Marc exclaimed.

"I don't think even the commander's cooking will ruin our next dinner," Hilda added.

"Ouch! A little harsh, you think, Gunny?" Marci asked.

"Just speaking the truth, Lieutenant," Hilda replied.

Barnabas laughed, "Well said, Gunny."

Marci said, "Looks like everyone got their wish."

"Except for those who wanted a tolerable drink," Marc said.

HJ passed around two fluid containers, "Maybe, maybe not. Try this."

Marc took a sip from the first container. "Did you go to Colorado or something? This tastes like pure Rocky Mountain spring water."

Barnabas took a sample from the second container. "Interesting, I taste an excellent Riesling but with a hint of seltzer. It's different, but not bad at all. Where'd you get this?"

"From the garden, of course," HJ said.

"So, everyone got their wish after all," Marci concluded.

"Pretty much," Hilda agreed. "It's strange that the fruits we found are in various stages of ripeness. I've never seen fruit trees that had blossoms, buds, young fruit, and ripe fruit all at the same time, but these do."

"Impressive," Barnabas said.

"The place is spectacular!" Hilda exclaimed. "It looks like a crater of colorful glass that has been transformed into an enormous garden. I think the walls are made of gemstones. You'll love it, Sarge!"

Matt asked, "Is the garden natural? Or was it planted and is being cared for?"

"That's a good question," Hilda said. "It's not manicured like a formal garden. But it has a design that's purposefully casual, almost careless. You'll have to see it to understand what I'm trying to say."

"Walk us through it, Gunny. What will we see?" Matt asked. The rest of the crew leaned forward to better hear Hilda's answer.

"There's a beautiful meadow leading toward a wall of rugged outcroppings that look like they were carved out of emeralds or green glass. A gap in the wall opens to a sunken garden surrounded by these outcroppings. The garden is about the size of a football stadium with fruit trees growing in a clover field. A stream runs through the middle of the grove. Toward the far end is a waterfall. Small pools of liquid are at the base of the outcropping. They're amber in color, like gold, bubbling up. That's where we found the beverage that the commander likes—"

HJ interrupted, "She's leaving out the best part."

"That is?" Matt asked.

"Birds! We heard songbirds."

"So?" Marc asked.

"Think about it, man," HJ said. "Birds can only breathe oxygen. Where do they go during the day to find their O2? If we follow them, we will find a constant source of oxygen!"

Matt said, "Not so fast. Did you see any birds, or just hear what you thought were birds?"

HJ stiffened. "I know we heard birds, Captain."

"You didn't answer my question, Lieutenant. Did you see any birds?"

"Not actually," HJ admitted.

"Then, we'll just have to check that out, won't we?"

Josh listened to the conversation as it unfolded. He could feel his pulse quicken and a knot form inside his stomach. *What Vigilo said is coming true, and I'm not ready to deal with it!*

"That'll do for now," Matt said. "Thanks for the report, Lieutenant and Gunny. Grab a snack." He motioned to the produce in front of them, "then get some rest. We have a busy night ahead of us exploring the garden."

The team reluctantly broke up. Later as everyone retired for the day, they failed to notice the display panel.

It read: Todo lo que brilla no es oro

[All that Glitters is not Gold]

No one slept well due, in part, to the exciting news from HJ and Hilda and in part to a powerful storm that lingered most of the day.

SHIP'S LOG December 19, 2068

Entry by Captain Dirksen:

Lieutenant Gonzalez and Sergeant Smith retrieved the produce left behind earlier. Their report that they found the food carefully organized reinforces my belief that we are not alone and are being watched.

Commander Maalouf and I retrieved a good supply of tar for torches and cooking.

Lieutenant Jaeger and Gunnery Sergeant McDermott discovered a hidden garden. They also reported hearing birds which could lead to a consistent source of oxygen. The whole team wants to explore this garden. After conferring with Commander Maalouf, but against my better judgment, I will not require anyone to stay behind to guard the ship. Tonight, we will all investigate the garden as a team.

Situational Assessment:

Lieutenant Jaeger believes there might be a cave that provides a constant source of oxygen behind the waterfall. Tonight, we will try to confirm his assessment by leaving several torches burning in the cave. Several concerns:

- There is still no sign of a rescue ship.
- Will the crew be ready when/if we get a chance to leave?
- Chief Torres seems agitated and withdrawn. He appears to be in his own world.

END OF ENTRY

After a simple meal, the crew set out for the garden. HJ and Marci led the way. They were followed by Hilda and Marc. Watching them, Barnabas turned to Matt, "If I didn't know any better, they look like two couples off on a moonlight hike."

Matt was thinking about the events that happened just before the start of this adventure. First, he noticed HJ breaking out his spacesuit. "What the hell do you think you're doing, Lieutenant?" Matt demanded.

"Just breaking out my space suit, Captain," HJ said. "I'm going to use it to explore the garden after the sun comes up in the morning."

"No way, Lieutenant," Matt stated. "What're you thinking?"

"It's simple, Captain. I'm going to spend the daylight hours in the garden and follow the birds to their source of O2."

"Stow it, Lieutenant."

"But, sir, how else are we going to find the source of the O2?"

"We'll use our tar torches to test for O2. We'll leave them in the cave. If the cave has oxygen, the torches will still be lit when we return tomorrow. Now stow your spacesuit."

Instead of stowing the suit in its usual place, HJ hung the suit, helmet attached, on the side of the entry portal, while muttering obscenities under his breath. Matt chose to let HJ's behavior go for the time being. Later he told Barnabas, "That kid's looking for an excuse to just do his thing."

When the crew arrived at the garden, they stood just inside the entry and stared in amazement. What they saw was more spectacular than Hilda's description.

Barnabas broke the silence. "Looks like we're in the Garden of Eden."

"The what?" HJ asked.

"Garden of Eden," Marc echoed.

"What's that?" HJ asked.

"Garden of Eden. It's where Adam and Eve first … oh forget it." Seeing HJ's blank stare, Barnabas quit explaining and shook his head.

"Think of it as Nirvana," Hilda said.

"Nir what?" HJ asked.

"Nirvana, a place of idyllic happiness."

"Huh?"

Hilda looked at Barnabas, who shrugged his shoulders. "What we mean is the garden is pretty. That you did well, Lieutenant."

"Oh, I did, didn't I?" HJ replied.

Hilda clenched her jaw and rolled her eyes but said nothing.

Josh was thinking, *I need to warn everyone! I could use a drink to settle my nerves.* "I'm thirsty," he said. "Let's have some of that light amber drink you told us about, Gunny."

"Follow me," Hilda replied as she walked down the main path that runs along the outcroppings toward the waterfall. She stopped just before arriving at the waterfall. To her right were a series of small pools filled with amber liquid. The color was very light in the top-most basin and darker in the lower pools.

"Help yourself, Chief. Just be careful of the darker pools. I think they are more potent."

"Potent is good," Josh took a deep drink of the darkest pool. "Whoa, that packs a punch!"

"Don't say I didn't warn you." Hilda left to investigate some of the fruit trees scattered about the garden.

The others gathered around and sampled some liquid from the lighter pools. After a while, as they compared notes on the different drinks, Josh said, "Permission to speak, Captain?"

"What is it, Chief?" Matt answered.

Josh saw everyone looking at him and froze. His mind had gone blank. "I, I can't remember, sir," he stuttered.

Everyone laughed. "You need to lay off that stuff, Chief," Barnabas warned with a smile.

Marc gravitated toward the walls recording the variety of precious and semi-precious stones he found. HJ led the others toward a waterfall located at the far end of the Garden. The path wound around a large pool of water.

"There, Captain," HJ pointed. "I think I saw a shadow fly toward the back of the waterfall."

"The back of a waterfall often holds a cave entrance," Barnabas said.

The path narrowed as it ran between the garden wall and the pool of water. HJ hurried ahead, slipping a couple of times on the trail, now wet from the waterfall's mist. He disappeared behind the water. After a few moments, he reappeared. "I found a cave!" he shouted.

The shout triggered a thought in Josh's mind. He had already consumed a lot of 'amber ale,' as he liked to think of it.

He thought, *Must warn the others! They're in danger! What do I say? Why is this place spinning? That's it! The cave is full of danger; no one should go in!* He swayed as he attempted to get to his feet and staggered down the path to the waterfalls, shouting as he went.

"St, st stop, stop!" he cried.

The sound of Josh's voice caused those by the waterfall to stop and turn to face him.

He thought *They've stopped. That's good. There're many more of them than I remember.*

"I've bean er bebe, I've been instrupted to to warm you that cove is too too … there's danger in there! You no can go im," Josh stuttered. "Please do not ent … ent … go im," he pleaded.

"Who told you this? Your imaginary friend?" HJ jeered.

"He's not imagiery. He's my fiend, you friend," Josh said.

Why's everyone just standing around. Why is the ground moving so much and no one notices? Am I the only one to see there's an earthquake? Why is Marci looking at me that way? It's HJ's fault. I'll teach him. If I can only get at him with a good swing.

Someone said, "the chief is drunk." *They're lying! I'm not drunk, but someone keeps hitting me,* Josh thought.

Josh made a lunging swing that caught HJ by surprise. He backed away but tripped over a boulder and fell hard. HJ was up, in an instant, landing punches of his own on Josh, who defended himself surprisingly well, given how drunk he was.

"That's it!" Matt separated the two combatants. Barnabas grabbed Josh from behind in a half nelson and spun him away from the others.

HJ backed off. "He started it, Captain."

"I saw the whole thing, Lieutenant. We'll straighten it out in the morning. In the meantime, if you find birds in, or going in the cave, set some torches."

Matt turned to Barnabas, "Let's get the chief back to the ship."

Matt and Barnabas partly supported and partly carried the semi-conscience petty officer out of the garden. Both men were silent until they were close to the ship.

Josh groaned and started to throw up. Both officers stepped aside to avoid the mess. Matt supported Josh by his belt as he knelt and continued to heave. They continued their trek. Once they got to the ship, the chief began to heave again.

"We'll leave him out here for now. There's no reason to smell up the ship," Matt said.

"I'll watch him for you, sir."

"No. I'll keep an eye on him. Cook me up some parsnip stew. I'm starving."

Barnabas smiled, "Be glad to, Captain Iron Stomach."

The Storm

Aboard the Osprey

Matt again removed himself from the rest of the crew. This was more by force of habit than by the need for privacy. There was little to report, and the team already knew the details he planned to write.

SHIP'S LOG December 20, 2068

<u>Entry by Captain Dirksen:</u>

This is the sixth day of our confinement to the plateau. Today's message on the console was in Greek: **Προτού η ημέρα αυτή είναι η ζωή ή ο θάνατος επιλέξουν τη ζωή.** Lieutenant Jaeger helped translate this entry. In English, it means: "Before you, this day is life or death. Choose life." No one has a clue what the message means. If I didn't know the chief any better, I'd think he was playing some kind of trick on the crew. At times, I even doubt he has tried everything he could to get the Osprey's systems back up and online. Hope we find the cave torches burning.

<u>Situational Assessment:</u>

- No real change from yesterday or the day before.
- Still no firm contact from whom or whatever is watching us.
- Would sure like a visit from any rescue vehicle.

END OF ENTRY

Josh spent the better part of the afternoon making work in the cargo bay. He entered the engine compartment several times to check on things, even though the control gauges remained in the green. His head was still pounding, and his stomach was in no mood for food. The memory of last night, what little there was, was depressing. *I made a total fool of myself,* he thought. *What's worse, I botched the job of warning everyone about the danger in the cave so badly, no one will ever believe me now.*

Joh jumped at the sound of the compartment door opening. Commander Maalouf entered and found Josh on his knees. He looked worse than Barnabas had expected. "Looking for something, Chief? Barnabas asked. "Or are you losing your cookies?"

"Not funny, Commander. I'm just stowing some tools we used to set up housekeeping when we arrived."

The door opened and shut with a thud as Hilda entered.

"Please, a little quiet." Josh grabbed his head.

Hilda said, "Hey Chief, didn't know you're the religious type."

"Huh?" Josh rose to one knee.

"Just thought you were praying. What's up?"

"Not much," Josh said. "I'm just straightening up in here."

"How're you feeling, Chief?" Barnabas asked.

"How do you think, Commander?" Catching the commander's look, he quickly added, "Sorry, sir. I forgot how bad a hangover feels."

"Tying one on tends to do that," Hilda said a bit too cheerfully for Josh's liking.

"What do you need, Gunny?" Josh asked.

"Oh, nothing, Chief. I'm just looking to stow away my stash of peyote pods for some future experiments."

"I didn't know that peyote had pods," Josh observed.

"They don't. But these seem to be very close relatives to peyote. Something like this is rumored to exist in South America. This is the first time I've found any. When the pods burst, they release hallucinogenic pollen into the air."

"I don't remember you harvesting anything last night, Gunny," Barnabas said.

"I made the discovery after you and the captain escorted party boy, here, home."

Josh complained, "You're giving me grief for overindulging, but it looks like you're stashing enough peyote to get the whole crew high."

"No, Chief," Hilda shook her head. "Like I said, I'm saving it for an experiment. Besides, this is spiritual stuff."

"How's that?" Barnabas asked.

"You wouldn't understand, Commander, but Native American Indians ingest peyote as part of their religious ceremonies. It enhances their spiritual experience.

"Thought that you aren't the religious type," Josh said.

"I'm not. But that doesn't mean I'm not spiritual. Not that you or the commander would know anything about native religious practices or spirituality. No offense, Commander."

"None taken, Gunny."

"Perhaps I know more than you think, Gunny," Josh said.

"Like what?"

"That rumor about peyote pods in South America is true."

"How'd you know? Hilda asked.

"I've got a friend who works on drinking-water projects in South America. He told me that he's seen a few native rituals, first hand, and mentioned the bursting pods," Josh explained.

"Have you seen them yourself?" Hilda challenged.

"Yes. My friend showed me several empty pods when we were reviewing his design for a new filtration system. I thought he was just pulling my leg. From what you say, I guess he wasn't."

Barnabas said, "Chief, you're multitalented. I forgot that you're an expert in hydrology."

"I'm impressed. Now, if we can just keep you sober enough to make something of yourself," Hilda teased.

Josh held his head. "Ugh! Don't remind me."

"Look, Chief," Barnabas said, "we're a little worried. You were way over the top yesterday. You probably owe Lieutenant Jaeger an apology."

"I know, Commander, but you don't get it. I was told in no uncertain terms to keep all of us out of the cave. That there's death in that cave."

"By whom? Your imaginary friend?" Hilda said.

Josh could feel his irritation growing. "If Vigilo is imaginary, how'd he know there was even a garden before you announced it?"

"The chief has a point, Gunny. Look, Chief, you can't hide here forever. At least join us for our daily briefing."

"The commander's right," Hilda said.

"Okay, but I'm not up for exploring the garden or cave, sir."

"I don't think that'll be an issue after last night's performance. I'm sure the captain will be more than happy to assign you to guard the ship," Barnabas said.

Josh breathed a sigh of relief.

After the rest of the crew left to visit the garden, Josh cleaned up and stowed everything. The sky seemed darker for some reason. Perhaps it just matched his mood. After Josh's chores were done, he stopped and watched the sky. The aurora displays always fascinated him. He thought about heading up the hill to find his friend, but after his little episode last night, he was ashamed to admit he screwed things up. The night was unusually still. Hoping his friend wouldn't drop by, Josh decided to start a fire to pass the time. As he did, a thought kept crossing his mind, *Check behind the Osprey.* At first, Josh didn't think anything of it. Then he felt a shudder and heard a rumble. It sounded like a distant freight train behind the Osprey. He got up, walked behind the ship, and looked over the expanse beyond the edge of the plateau. What he saw sent a chill down his back. Bearing down on him was a massive storm. Constant lightning illuminated it, and It filled the sky. By now, Josh was used to the occasional squall, but this was far more intimidating. The thought, *Warn the others! Must warn the others,* ran through his mind as he took off at a run toward the garden.

In the Garden

The intrepid crew was again struck by the sheer beauty of the Garden. As they walked toward the cave, Hilda saw something of interest and fell behind the others. She knelt to examine some cactus-like plants growing next to the path. Marc returned to where she was kneeling.

"What's up, Gunny?"

"These plants," Hilda lifted some buttons. "I think they're related to the peyote plant, but a different variety than what I collected last night."

"Peyote?"

"Yeah. North and South American natives use it to enhance their metaphysical worship experience."

"Metaphysical worship experience?"

"Get high," Hilda said.

"That I understand. How do you get high on this stuff anyway?"

"It is usually ingested by chewing. Why? You want to get high?"

"Naw, just wondering. Why are you so interested?"

"These specimens have the appearance of peyote but also have some kind of pod." Hilda gently squeezed a small pod. It popped open, releasing a small cloud of grey-green dust. "Well, what do you know? This could deliver the goods by inhaling."

"Thinking of some self-testing now, are we, Gunny?"

"Thinking of testing it on you."

"Funny, Gunny."

"I need to grab more samples to add to my collection from last night. I've got a set of experiments in mind," Hilda said. "This should liven up the next ISEB conference I attend."

Marc asked, "The wha—"

Hilda said, "International Society of Environmental Botanists."

"Want some help gathering this stuff?"

"Sure, Sarge. Just be careful not to squeeze the pods. They seem to be very sensitive, and there's no telling how potent the pollen is. I need as many as we can carry. I'm sure that when we leave this place, I won't get a chance to return for more."

"You mean, if we get to leave," Marc corrected. "Whoever controls this place hasn't revealed himself or his intentions. And, he sure has our ship out of commission."

"Hey, it could be a she, not just a he. It could even be Josh's friend."

"Imaginary friend, you mean."

"We don't know that for sure."

"Whatever. I think we're like field rats captured for observation. Once he, she, whoever it is, finds out what they want to know, they'll let us go."

Hilda smiled. "Unless they want to find out what we taste like. Gotta hope they don't want to cook us."

"Not funny."

"I think it's funny."

"Stop smiling, Gunny. That just isn't funny.

The rest of the crew walked further down the familiar path toward the waterfall.

"Permission to inspect the cave, Captain," HJ requested.

"We'll get to it a little later, Lieutenant," Matt replied. "First, I want you to climb to the top of the waterfall and look around."

"Too what purpose, sir?"

"To see beyond where we are now." Matt had an edge to his voice. "Your eyes are better than mine, and from that high position, you can check for any signs of civilization."

"Sir, not to question your authority," HJ argued. "But, I don't think it is worth—"

"Then don't! Don't question my authority. Just do it. The sooner you do, the sooner we examine the cave."

"I'm on my way, sir!" HJ started climbing the rocks that were to the right of the waterfall.

Matt and Barnabas exchanged glances. "Commander, I want you and Lieutenant Gonzalez to go in the cave and determine if the torches are still burning. Then scout to see which directions we should explore."

"Directions, sir?" Barnabas asked.

"Yes. we'll break into two pairs and explore two directions at the same time."

"Very good, sir," Barnabas followed Marci behind the waterfall.

"Captain," HJ yelled. "I'm at the top now but not seeing anything."

Matt yelled, "Look slightly to your right, Lieutenant. If my sense of direction is correct, that's the area that Sarge and I were looking at a couple of nights ago. See anything over there?"

"No. Wait, I do. I see lights about five to ten kilometers away. Cool."

"What do you mean by cool, Lieutenant?"

"I see lights, like a city. I also see occasional streaks of light angling down to the city and then back up from the city."

"Streaks of light? What do you mean?"

"Think of watching the lights of planes landing and taking off again at night, only these are beams of light taking off and landing." HJ scrambled back down.

"Interesting. How long do you think it would take to get there, Lieutenant? Could we get there and back in one night?"

"We could get there and back here in one night, sir. But I don't think we can make it to there and back to the ship in one night."

"Very good. Let's join the others in the cave."

Matt and HJ found Barnabas and Marci talking toward the back of the cave entrance.

"Good news, sir," Barnabas reported. "All the torches are still burning. It seems that the cave contains O2, even during the day."

"Yes!" HJ gave a fist pump.

"This is good news, Commander. Anything else?" Matt asked.

"It's decision time. The cave has three paths leading away from this point. We only have two parties. Which paths do you want us to follow?"

In the Garden

When Josh crested the rise at the garden's entrance, he began yelling, "Back to the ship! Everyone back to the ship!"

He ran up to Marc and Hilda. "Hurry, Sarge, hurry, Gunny!"

"What's going on, Chief?" they asked in unison.

"Hu, huge storm rolling in," he bent over, gasping to catch his breath.

"We get squalls almost every night, Chief," Marc said.

"Bigger, much bigger," Josh blurted out, still gasping.

The urgency in his voice spurred them to action. Hilda grabbed up her specimens while Marc turned toward the cave. "I'll warn the others in the cave."

"No, Sarge! I must warn them!" Josh ran toward the cave.

A blinding flash of lightning met Marc and Hilda as they arrived at the Osprey. Its impact almost knocked them to the ground. A sudden gust of wind threatened to upend the spacecraft.

"We need to tie her down, Gunny!" Marc shouted. She gave him the thumbs up as they dove into the ship to retrieve some rope.

Josh's reception at the cave wasn't as cordial.

"What the hell, Chief! I told you to stay with the Osprey!" Matt exclaimed. "Why'd you disobey my orders?"

By this time, Josh's chest was heaving to get air. "Storm coming, sir," he huffed, "must get to ship, huge storm." He fell to his knees, gasping.

"We've had storms before. We can just wait it out in here," HJ said. "Hold it. Are you drunk again, Chief?"

"No, sir," Josh was still gulping air. "You've gotta believe me. This storm's different. Wind, strong wind. We need to secure the ship!"

Something in his whole demeanor gave Barnabas pause. "The chief has a point. If the storm upends the ship, we'd be in a world of hurt."

Matt paused for a second more, then he ran toward the cave entrance. "Let's move. Everyone back to the ship now!"

"This is a crock!" HJ spoke up. "It's a freak'n crock! Captain, you're so hung up on your ship you can't see this cave is safer in a storm. It's risky just getting from here to there. We need to stay in the cave."

Usually, this outburst would evoke the captain's wrath. But no one heard HJ. Everyone had already left, following Matt as he ran toward the ship. "You're all fools, every one of you," HJ yelled as he sat on a rock and took a drink of elixir.

The gale-force wind made it hard to run down the path. Lightning started striking at unnerving intervals. The group arrived at the Osprey to find Hilda and Marc struggling to hold onto a tie-down. The wind gusts were too strong for them to finish tying off the ship, which kept swinging back and forth like a teeter-totter. Finally, with everyone pitching in, the spaceship was tied off securely to nearby trees and rocks. As the crew began piling into the Osprey, the first torrential downpour began. Matt was about to shut the door when he looked around and counted the team. "Who's missing?" he asked. Then answering his own question, he said, "Where the hell's Lieutenant Jaeger?"

"Wasn't he right behind us?" Marci asked.

"Apparently not," Barnabas answered. "He must have taken up residence in the cave."

"He better not have!"

"Hey, Captain, don't be too frustrated with HJ. We can just leave him behind when we get the chance to leave," Josh quipped.

"I HEARD THAT, JOSHUA!" Marci shouted.

"I was just joking," Josh replied.

"Were not! I can tell by your voice. You're still pissed at HJ!"

"Why's the chief pissed at the lieutenant?" Marc asked.

"Joshua was hurt in an explosion, and he still blames HJ."

Josh said, "Hey, I'm not the one who set the charges in the wrong order. That's on HJ."

"The inquiry cleared HJ, and you know it. You're just bitter because your injuries washed you out of the flight program."

"I'm not bitter Marci, I'm moving on."

"Hardly! You still hate him!"

"Granted, we're not best friends, but I don't hate him. Honest," Josh said. But Marci didn't hear. She had already left for the crew cabin.

"Talk about a woman's wrath," Marc started but was interrupted by shouting over the storm. Looking out the doorway, he saw HJ stumbling toward the ship. Now HJ was kneeling on the ground, his chest heaving as he tried to get air into his lungs. Marc and Josh jumped into the storm and helped HJ onto the Osprey. Once HJ was onboard, they wrestled the door closed.

"You're hurt!" Marc exclaimed, seeing blood dripping from HJ's hand and arm onto the portal's anti-chamber floor.

"It's nothing. I just scraped my knuckles on a rock when the wind knocked me down.

Josh tossed some gauze and disinfectant to Marc, who went to work on HJ's hand and arm. "Looks like too much blood to be just nothing.

You've got a puncture wound on your arm. How many times were you knocked down?"

"Lost count. Thanks for helping me up, guys."

"No problem. We're just glad you're okay," Josh said.

Really? I wonder, Marc thought as he wrapped HJ's hand.

The storm ebbed and flowed all night. At one point, the lightning was replaced by colorful beams of light that wandered randomly between the Osprey and the plateau's edge. They were accompanied by rumbling that was more like notes from an organ than actual thunder.

Shortly before daybreak, the storm subsided, leaving behind an eerie silence. The trail to the garden was all but obliterated by fallen trees and storm debris. Matt observed the mess. "No time to clear that mess now. We'll attack it tomorrow night."

"Do you suppose someone's trying to tell us something, Captain?" Barnabas asked.

Matt looked around. "That's what I'm beginning to think."

A Final Test

Location, Unknown

The crew was enjoying a meal from the bounty they brought back from the garden. *Even Maalouf's cooking can't spoil it*, Matt thought as he slipped away to write an entry in his log.

SHIP'S LOG December 21, 2068

Entry by Captain Dirksen:

Last night we discovered a cave that appears to be the source of O2. We confirmed the presence of birds of the Raven variety. The torches, with enough oil/tar to fuel them through the day, were found to be still burning upon our return. Thus, we believe that the cave retains O2 as hoped. Tonight, we will examine the Garden and cave more thoroughly. I am giving each crew member specific tasks in collecting and categorizing specimens. The only exception is Chief Torres. I am leaving him to guard the ship. His continued conversations with his imaginary friend have me concerned. They seem harmless enough and help relax the chief. Still, I will request a full psych assessment when we return to base.

Today's 'communication' with us was:

καλούν σε μένα την ημέρα της κόπο ? Θα σας παραδώσει, και θα με τιμήσει - Α Ω

According to Lieutenant Jaeger, it is Greek and means:

"Call on me in the day of trouble; I will deliver you, and you will honor me." It is signed, "Alpha Omega."

There is no consensus on its meaning other than it seems more of a warning than a directive. Maybe it's an offer to help. If it is, how do we acknowledge we even need help?

Situational Assessment:

Our tests indicate the Cave has a consistent supply of O2. I've yet to decide if it warrants relocating our operations to the Garden or not. Other concerns include:

- Chief Torres's mental state.
- Lieutenant JG Jaeger's insolence.
- Can we leave this place as a team should the opportunity arise?

END OF ENTRY

"Listen up," Matt said, "today we're going to be more organized as we examine the Garden and Cave. I want a catalog of the botanical life in the Garden. Lieutenant Gonzalez, team up with Gunny and begin collecting and indexing samples."

"Yes, sir," Marci and Hilda replied in unison.

"Sarge, I want you to begin collecting and categorizing the mineral and gem deposits. I'll help you as I can. I'll also collect fluid samples for later testing."

"Will do, sir."

"Commander and Lieutenant Jaeger, explore the cave. Map it as far as it is reasonable. Log the variety of life and gems you find. See if you can't find where the birds we saw are nesting."

Barnabas said, "Yes, sir."

HJ said, "Okay, sir. But it seems a pretty large task for one evening."

"It is," Matt said, "so, we'll return each evening until we're finished."

"It'd make more sense to stay in the cave over the day instead of walking back and forth each evening," HJ complained.

Matt shot HJ a glance. "We all need the exercise. Especially you."

"Sir, what about the chief?" Barnabas asked

"Chief Torres is to stay with the Ship."

"If only you could hold your booze, Chief, you'd be going with us," HJ whispered.

"I wouldn't be going in that cave if I were you," Josh said.

HJ laughed. Barnabas, who overheard the exchange, shook his head. The team gathered what they needed to accomplish their tasks and set out walking to the Garden.

When Josh finished his chores for the night, he stepped out of the Osprey. He lounged outside, admiring the aurora. Josh dozed off, then came to with a start. He'd slept hard for much of the night. Josh wandered toward the hill where he first met Vigilo. Why he wasn't sure, but he felt he just needed to talk with his friend. *If only I can find him,* Josh thought.

His friend was waiting for him on the now familiar hill. When Josh got close to Vigilo, he sighed, "I screwed things up big time."

"What does 'screwed it up' mean?" Vigilo asked.

"It means I got drunk, shot off my mouth, and generally became a jerk. Now nobody believes me."

"Did you warn them about the cave?"

Josh thought that there was anxiety in Vigilo's voice, but he wasn't sure. "I did, but I didn't convince anyone to stay out of the cave. I failed."

Vigilo consoled, "My friend, you did your part. It matters not how well you did. What matters is that you tried. Now, all is in motion. Your little band has one more test to take."

"Why all these tests?"

"We're discussing your final disposition," the Watchman said.

"So, you still aren't sure if your boss'll let us enter your domain?"

"You misunderstand our dilemma. The question isn't about letting you visit our domain. There's no way you'll be allowed to do that. No, the question we are now pondering is whether to allow you to return to yours."

"But I thought we're friends. You saved my life. How can you not go ahead and let us go?"

"I am your friend. But this is not about friendship. This is about protecting those whom we are charged to keep safe."

Josh began to feel the heat of being slighted at this turn of the conversation. He wanted to say, "Who are you to imply we're a danger to your charges? Who made you our judge, anyway?"

As if his mind was being read, Josh heard Vigilo's soothing liquid voice say, "Don't take offense, my friend. It's not for us to judge whether you are good are bad. That weight must be carried by our Creator. Our job is only to assess the risk you present to those we protect. You tell me. Are not the seeds of rebellion, resentment, and pride evident within your landing party?"

Josh paused and reflected. "Yes, you're right, even as I think about myself. I'm guilty as—"

A blood-curdling scream interrupted him. He immediately recognized it as Marci's voice. He took off at a run. His conversation and all else fell from his mind. It focused only on one thing. He thought *Marci's in trouble. I need to get to her now!*

Had he been listening as he ran, he would have heard Vigilo's parting comment, "Ah, my friend, your final test has begun. God's speed."

Exploring the Cave

In the Garden

Upon arriving at the garden, the crew found several disturbing changes. A massive tree lay across the very spot where Marc and Hilda were harvesting peyote the night before.

"Wonder if we would've been hit by that tree if Josh hadn't warned us," Marc mused as the group walked around it.

The cave vestibule had also changed. The same places where the crew stood when Josh arrived with his warning were covered in debris from a fallen stalactite.

"The chief did well in warning us," Matt observed.

"Maybe someone doesn't want us here after all," Barnabas said.

The evening passed quickly. In the garden, everyone was occupied with research tasks. The most interesting assignment fell to HJ and Barnabas.

Only the vestibule of the cave had been examined the night before. Tonight, the two explorers, armed with powerful torches, were exploring deeper into one of the cave's three main tunnels. HJ was bouncing with joy as he finally got to explore more of the cave. Barnabas didn't feel the same. He couldn't shake the unease brought on by Josh's warning. The cave was full of sights, sounds, and smells unrivaled in Barnabas's previous experiences. "It certainly smells much better than the cave we found a few nights ago," he commented.

"Got that right, Commander. What's that sound? Do you hear it?"

"I hear it. It sounds like a chorus of flutes. Wait, do I hear water?"

"Yeah, that's it," HJ agreed."

Barnabas pointed to a large corridor that ran a little to their left. "I think It's coming from there."

They walked along the corridor a short distance. HJ stopped and pointed his torch at one of the anti-chambers. "What do you make of all these side chambers?"

"Your guess is as good as mine. They're not deep, but something very big's growing in each chamber."

"It looks like a couple of oversized daylilies that are bent to the ground. Their petals are as big as mattresses." HJ sat on one and stroked it with his hand.

Barnabas sniffed the air. "What's that smell?"

"Orange blossoms, maybe?"

"I think you're right. Let's move on before we run out of time," Barnabas turned to go. Suddenly, he felt something solid brushing past the back of his head. He lunged to the ground as a couple of more shadows flew past. "What the—"

"It's just birds," HJ captured one in the light from his torch.

"Scared the heck out of me," Barnabas brushed himself off. "I think that's a sign that the dawn is coming. We need to join up with the others."

"Seriously, Commander? We just got started. We could spend another hour here easily with no harm."

"Sorry, Lieutenant, but you know that's not the protocol. The captain was quite clear that we are to reassemble when the birds start coming into the cave." Barnabas knew HJ was right but felt increasingly nervous about staying in the cave despite its beauty.

"This sucks, Commander. Just when things are getting interesting—"

"Zip it, Lieutenant. We follow the captain's orders, period. Now let's go." Barnabas turned and walked back toward the cave entrance. HJ followed, grumbling under his breath.

The group of explorers joined up by the garden springs. By the time Barnabas and HJ arrived, the others had already begun to refresh themselves with a drink.

Marc raised his cup. "A toast to a successful start."

Matt smiled but said, "We need to get back to the ship and rest up. It'll take several more days of work to complete our tasks."

"Why not just stay in the cave, Captain?" HJ queried.

"Your question is noted, Lieutenant. But we'll continue to spend our days together, at the ship."

"That makes no sense, Captain," HJ protested. "If we just stay here, we'll be able to start earlier and work longer, rather than traipsing back and forth to the ship."

"Enough, Lieutenant!" Matt said. "We'll use the ship as the base for our operations until our mission is over."

"Our mission ended several days ago when we got stranded," HJ argued. He could see Matt's body language but ignored the warning. "Besides, I'm only along for the ride. Part of your mission was to deliver me safely to Mars, but you failed that. So, don't give me any 'until this mission is over' crap—"

Barnabas interrupted, "Shut up, Lieutenant! The captain is your senior officer, and I'm placing you on report for insubordination!"

"Whatever."

"Whatever, SIR," Barnabas said.

"Whatever, sir."

The rest of the group was stunned into silence by the exchange. Marc attempted to break the tension. "Captain, may we take a few minutes to relax before returning to the ship? Gunny had a couple of things she wanted to show me, sir."

Matt shook himself back to Marc's question. "Sure, Sarge. Don't wait too long, or there'll be hell to pay." Matt turned to leave. "Commander."

"Sir," Barnabas responded as he fell into step alongside Matt.

Once they were out of earshot, Barnabas said, "That's it, sir? You're not going to let that snot-nosed kid get away with that kind of insolence? How do you know he'll even return to the Osprey this morning?"

"I don't, Commander. He is right; technically, he's not part of the crew. As much as I want to bust him in the chops for his insubordination, we can't forget he has a doting uncle in high places."

"Unless he initiates the action," Barnabas suggested.

"He's too smart for that. No, he'll just keep goading and grousing."

"Do you think you can motivate him to return to the ship each day?"

"I do. I'll schedule our debriefings on the ship for mid-afternoon."

"How does that get him back to the ship?"

"Did you guys find anything worth sharing?"

"Yes."

"Does Lieutenant Jaeger love to hear himself share?"

"Yes."

"Does he enjoy watching Lieutenant Gonzalez talk?"

"Yes."

"Problem solved, Commander."

"What about tonight? You didn't schedule anything for tomorrow."

"Tonight is a test if you will. If anyone can't be trusted to follow me, they'll show it by not returning to the Osprey tonight."

"Do you really want to know, sir?"

Garden Cave

There was an awkward pause after the captain and commander left. Once they were out of sight, HJ gave a salute in their direction, "So long, Captain Ahab."

"Oh, HJ, don't be that way," Marci chided.

"Be what way? He's just a flyboy officer with too big an ego and too small a brain."

"Listen to what the lieutenant is saying. At least consider her career," Marc said.

"Stay out of this, Sarge. This is just between the captain and me, and he is not my boss."

"You'd like to think so, Lieutenant. But, given your relationship with Lieutenant Gonzalez, intended or not, your actions reflect on her, and he is her boss."

"Back off, Sarge," HJ warned.

"I'm just saying, Lieutenant," Marc said, "it's your call.

Marci tried to break the tension, "Come on HJ, show us the cave."

"Sure, Sweetheart," HJ replied. "Sarge, Gunny, coming with us?

"I guess. Why not?" Marc replied.

Hilda shook her head. "Sarge, you forgot. I've got something I want you to see."

"That can wait. You gotta see the cave. It is fantastic!" HJ said.

Marc thought for a minute. But, when he caught a certain look from Hilda, he said, "You two go ahead, we'll catch up in a few."

"Have it your way, Sarge. Come on, Marci, I've also got something I want to show you."

Marc and Hilda wandered in the garden and stopped at a tree with green and bright orange fruit. The skin was smooth.

"You drug me away just to see a tree with orange balls?" Marc asked.

"I drug you away because you don't need to piss off the lieutenant."

"Our discussion wasn't that bad, was it?"

"Trust me, it was heading south sure enough. It wasn't going to end well. So just buck up and join me for a little while."

"I suppose you're right," Marc conceded.

"This looks interesting, and I'm a little tipsy,"

"I've got a bit of a buzz going also," Marc said.

"How do you know?"

"Easy — you're starting to look attractive, Gunny."

"Funny guy. Try this. It may help." Hilda handed him a greenish orange ball.

"Nice try, you taste it first."

"Whatever." Hilda picked a reddish-orange ball and took a large bite. "Yum, just like I remembered. They're Persimmons; sweet like a mango, but they have an aftertaste like honey."

Marc followed suit and took a mouthful for himself. He gagged and tried to spit it out. "What are you trying to do, kill me? This tastes like bitter cotton!"

"Of course," Hilda continued as if nothing ever happened, "if you eat a Persimmon that isn't quite ripe, you get a mouth full of bitter cotton. That's why you always want to eat a fully ripe fruit — not a greenish one, like what you have."

"Very funny." Marc took a bite from Hilda's fruit after she handed it to him. "Wow, this really does taste good."

"It's one of my favorites. But you must wait until it's ripe. Otherwise, it's pithy and tasteless."

"You knew that the one you gave me was too green," Marc accused.

"Guilty, but you'll never make that mistake again. Experience is a great teacher."

"What's the lesson?"

"Don't debate a snotty-nosed lieutenant. It's as satisfying as eating a green persimmon."

"And what does a ripe persimmon represent?"

"Hanging with me," Hilda giggled.

"They walked a little further together, enjoying the beauty of the garden and each other's company. Drawn by the sound of water, they found themselves in front of the garden's waterfall.

"Shall we spend the night, I mean day here?" Marc asked.

Hilda took a deep breath. "Tempting, but the captain was pretty insistent that we should return to the ship. We need to hurry if we're to make it before daybreak."

"HJ has a point," Marc said. "Technically, the mission as originally conceived is over, and we're marooned. So, technically, we aren't under Captain Dirksen's command anymore."

"It's not much of a technicality. The fact is, whether we achieve our goals or not, we still answer to the captain. That holds until we return to base, or he releases us from his command."

"Yeah, you're right. Besides, I've been military long enough that the one thing, maybe the only thing, I am good at is following orders. Let's just drop in to say goodbye to the lieutenants and head back to the ship."

"They're returning with us, aren't they?" Hilda asked.

"They should, but I have a feeling they won't."

Marc and Hilda ducked behind the waterfall and entered the cave. As they walked deeper into the cave, they were impressed by the powerful fragrances and soothing sounds. They found HJ and Marci and told them of their intention to return to the ship. HJ invited Marc and Hilda to spend the day with him and Marci in the cave. But surprisingly (or perhaps not), he did not try and persuade them when they declined his invitation. As they were leaving, Hilda paused to take a long look at the giant flowers scattered in the alcoves connected to the main path.

Marc stopped by her side. "Beautiful, aren't they."

"Hmm," Hilda said as they wandered back into the garden. "Those flowers look very familiar. I just can't place them."

"Maybe it'll come to you when you sober up."

"Maybe we should pick up our pace. I thing … er … think it's starting to lights out, I mean getting light out."

"We are out," Marc said as they locked arms and swayed slowly toward the ship.

When Hilda and Marc stopped by to announce their departure, Marci and HJ were examining some colorful gemstones they had found. HJ was making grand gestures of presenting a gem to Marci, who giggled and accepted it. They, too, were feeling a buzz from the golden liquid they had been drinking. HJ was glad Marc and Hilda left for the ship, so he could be alone with Marci. As soon as he was, he took Marci's hand.

"Hey, Babe, come here. I have something special to show you."

"What?"

"It's a surprise."

They walked unsteadily down the main corridor. As the duo walked HJ again heard the chorus of flutes.

"What do you hear?" he asked.

"It sounds like you hired someone to serenade us with a flute. It sounds beautiful."

"The best is just ahead," HJ led Marci to one of the anti-chambers.

"What do you think of all these side chambers branching out from the main path?" HJ stopped and pointed his torch at one of the anti-chambers.

Marci gasped when she saw the giant flowers in the anti-chamber. There was a cluster of three flowers. One was white with streaks of orange. It smelled like orange blossoms and had orange berries on the end of its pistil. Another was white with streaks of red. It smelled like raspberries and had red berries on the end of its pistil. The final one was white with purple streaks. It smelled like grape jelly and had purple berries.

HJ jumped onto the middle flower with its red berries. "The petals feel like a great mattress, Marci. Join me."

Marci sat beside him as he picked a red berry and gave it to her. It tasted like raspberry-flavored honey. "It tastes wonderful," she said. She thought she felt the flower vibrate gently each time HJ picked a berry. "These are so relaxing. I feel almost like I'm floating."

"Only the best for my Babe," HJ leaned over and began to kiss her. She didn't resist at first. But after a short while, she broke it off. She knew what he wanted but decided she wasn't going to be that easy.

"Not so fast, lover-boy," Marci slid off his flower pedal and climbed up on the one that had purple berries. She sat on her knees and sampled a purple berry. Again, the flower seemed to shudder slightly when she picked a berry. *That's odd*, she thought.

"This one tastes like grape soda," she observed with a yawn.

"Don't be that way," HJ pleaded and tried to pout. He rolled over on his stomach with his feet pointing toward the throat of the flower. He propped himself up on his elbows and began to undress Marci with his eyes while munching on some red berries.

Marci didn't notice. She was sampling another berry, thinking how sleepy she was, when she heard a strange noise from HJ's flower. She turned and began to scream.

Near the Osprey

"I figured as much!" Matt said, "Those clowns are all spending the day at that damnable cave! And where's the chief? Off with his imaginary friend again?"

"Easy, Captain," a subdued commander said. "There's still time for everyone to return. You know the chief has never been late yet."

Just then, Hilda and Marc appeared, singing a boisterous and off-tune version of "What do you do with a drunken sailor?"

"You guys are plastered," Matt scolded.

"Yes, that we are, sir," an unperturbed Marc replied.

"Aye, and lovin' it, sir," Hilda agreed.

Barnabas chuckled. "You'll be paying the price in a few hours."

"Right again, sir, but right now, I'm feel'n no pain. How about you, Gunny? Are you feel'n any pain?"

Hilda's brows were furrowed. Being deep in thought, she did not hear Marc's question.

"Where are the others?" Matt demanded.

"Oh, they stayed behind, sir," Marc answered.

"Why didn't you bring them with you, Sarge?"

"Well … uh …," Marc stammered as he looked down. "They outrank me, sir."

"Damn! That's disobeying a direct order!" Matt exclaimed. "I've got a good mind to take Jaeger behind the woodshed, and I don't mean metaphorically."

"What about Lieutenant Gonzalez, sir?" Marc asked.

"I'll be sure to deal with her too. But Jaeger is behind all this."

"Steady, Captain. Don't forget his connections."

"Damn his connections. I'll bring him up on charges. When I am through with him, he'll be busted from the corps!"

"I agree this is insubordination, sir, but at least we know they're safe in the cave and not out doing something crazy," Barnabas turned and began to enter the Osprey.

"No, wait!" Hilda said. "It's coming to me now."

"What?" Marc asked.

"The flowers in the cave," Hilda answered. "They're unusual, I kind of recall, but I just can't put my finger on it. That's it! They're Monkey Cups. They're giant Monkey Cups."

"Great Gunny," Matt said, "the pretty flowers in the cave are giant Monkey Cups. So?"

Hilda wasn't listening. She was still thinking. "They're unusual because a Monkey cup is one of the few flowers that's carnivorous." Her eyes widened as she spoke. "Captain, we need to get them out of there, NOW!" She grabbed Barnabas from the Osprey portal as she turned to run toward the cave. She pulled him so fast he kicked the door block, which kept the portal door from closing. Matt and Marc scrambled to catch up.

"I don't get it," Matt said. "So, the flowers eat insects."

"Normal ones do. But these are enormous. They won't settle for a few flies. HURRY EVERYONE!" Hilda shouted.

A blood-curdling scream placed an exclamation point on her words.

The Mouth of the Beast

Garden Cave

Josh was the first to arrive. Breathing hard, he followed the screams to the anti-chamber where Marci and HJ were captives. To his horror, he saw HJ struggling with plant tendrils. His legs were half-hidden by the flower petals that were starting to engulf him. One tendril was wrapped around his waist, another around his chest. A third tendril was wrapping around his left arm, and a fourth was creeping toward his neck.

HJ yelled, "Help me! Help me! I'm being sucked in! I can't get out!"

Josh drew his rescue knife and started helping HJ when he noticed Marci. She was halfway out of her flower. But she was trapped by a couple of tendrils around her legs. Another one had wrapped itself around one of her arms. Still, another was almost at her neck. She was struggling to reach HJ. "Save him, Josh!" she shouted.

Josh could tell that Marci was also losing her battle. The tendril had reached her neck and cut off her air. He went straight toward her and cut at the tendril that was around her neck.

HJ tried to speak again, but all that came out was a gurgling noise. His eyes were starting to bulge with the pressure. Josh finally got the tendril cut through and tossed it aside.

Marci pleaded, "Don't let him die! You can still save him. I'm okay."

"No, you're not!" Josh started to slash at the other tendrils with his knife. No matter how furiously he slashed, the tendrils kept slowly pulling Marci back into her flower.

"Please, I'm begging you, Josh. Please help HJ."

Just then, the others finally arrived. The captain looked over the situation, thinking, *This can't be happening!* He began shouting commands. "Gunny, help the chief!"

"Aye, sir," Hilda drew her knife and jumped into the fray. After slashing a couple of tendrils, she heard Josh shout, "A little help, Gunny!"

She drew her Glock and tossed it to Josh, who fired a round at the tendril holding Marci by the arm. The sound was deafening. It severed the tendril and then began ricocheting around the anti-chamber.

"Sarge, Commander, follow me!" Matt ordered as he drew his knife and leaped onto the flower that was trying to consume HJ.

They both followed him into the battle.

Josh fired another round at the throat of the flower. Again, the sound was deafening, but the flower was unaffected. That round ricocheted and glanced off Marc's already sore ankle.

"Ouch!" Marc yelped.

"Stow, the Glock before your ricochets, kill one of us!" Matt ordered.

"Sorry, sir," Josh replied as he reached over and holstered Hilda's gun for her.

"Careful of the slender tendrils. They've got stingers that have a numbing agent," Hilda gasped as she sliced a tendril that was creeping around Josh's waste.

It seemed like an endless struggle. As soon as one tendril was cut, another appeared and took its place.

"The thinnest tendrils are the easiest to cut, Captain!" Josh shouted.

"Careful!" Hilda added. "They're the ones with stingers!"

"Got that right, Gunny!" Marc agreed. "I just got whacked by one, and my whole side's going numb."

Matt yelled, "Get after it, men! We're losing the lieutenant!"

HJ's eyes were glazing over. His face was beginning to turn blue. Barnabas tried to hack through the tendrils around HJ's chest, while Marc tried to cut one that had slipped around his neck. Matt tried to peel back the petals. But that wasn't working. Unlike the tendrils, the petals would not cut. They were firmly and slowly closing over HJ's legs. This action was pulling him further down into the throat of the flower. Matt tried to crawl in and use his shoulder as leverage to reverse the petal's motion. All he got for his trouble was a tendril wrapping itself around his arm.

"A little help?" he called.

Marc grabbed the tendril and began cutting on it as Barnabas grabbed Matt's legs and pulled him free. Then they set back to work.

In desperation, Marc placed his Glock against a tendril, wrapping itself around Barnabas's waist, and fired. The round severed the tendril. But it also ricocheted, grazing Matt's head.

"Sorry, sir," Marc holstered his gun and went back to hacking at the plant with his knife.

Meanwhile, Hilda and Josh were frantically trying to free Marci. Tendrils kept appearing and attaching themselves to anyone within a few feet of Marci's flower.

"Lieutenant, try and pull yourself away," Hilda ordered." Chief, you go after the tendrils around the lieutenant while I cut the ones that are trying to grab you."

"Good idea, Gunny. I think that the lieutenant passed out."

Josh got one last tendril cut, freeing Marci. She slid, limply, out of the flower onto the floor. Quickly, he and Hilda jumped down and drug her away from danger.

"The lieutenant's free!" an exhausted Josh yelled.

Matt said, "Good work, Chief! Now you get her out of here while you can. Gunny, get over here and lend a hand."

"Aye, Captain," Hilda replied. To Josh, she said, "Good thing you got here when you did. Otherwise, we would've lost her."

"I can help you too, Captain!" Josh shouted.

"Negative, Chief. No telling what else is lurking around here. Get the lieutenant out of the cave NOW!"

"Yes, sir!" Josh lifted Marci gently and stumbled toward the cave entrance. He noted the captain's wisdom as he almost tripped over a tendril, trying to wind around his ankle.

Hilda entered the battle to save HJ by cutting tendrils from her companions as they struggled to free HJ. Arms were growing tired. But each combatant pushed through the pain to save their companion. At one point, Marc stood on a bottom Petal and tried to push the top pedal back. A tendril trying to wrap around his leg tripped him up. He fell to the ground and winced in pain as he rolled his sore ankle. The flower was relentless. It had pulled HJ in up to his armpits. All three of the men grabbed a petal and together tried to pull it back. But it was too strong for them and barely budged. Finally, Hilda felt HJ's jugular with her finger. She found no pulse. All eyes were on her. She shook her head. Matt began swinging at random tendrils. Then, looking at the exhausted team, he said, "Let's go. We're too late. We can't do any good here."

As they retreated from the cave, they felt other tendrils reaching for their feet. Just outside the cave, they found Josh cradling Marci's head as she lay on the ground.

"How is she?" Matt asked.

"I think she'll be okay, sir. "Her pulse is strong. Her breathing is shallow but steady. Where's the lieutenant?"

Matt shook his head, "Let's move out. We don't have much time left."

As they cleared the entrance to the garden, Matt noticed that the storm clouds rolling in were tinged with an ominous predawn pink. He dropped to the back of his crew to help push them forward. *Will we make it back to the ship in time?* He thought. He surveyed the bedraggled group.

Barnabas and Hilda were supporting Marc, who couldn't put weight on his twisted ankle. Josh, staggering from exhaustion, was carrying an unconscious Marci, fireman style.

"Hurry!" Matt urged. People were taking several steps then pausing for several breaths. "Deeper breaths ... take deeper breaths," he said, resisting the urge to pant himself. His lungs were beginning to burn.

Josh stumbled and went to one knee. The thought that his fall may have caused Marci's head to hit the ground sent a surge of adrenalin through his tired body. He scrambled to his feet with a renewed determination to get her safely to a place of refuge.

Finally, the group broke through the forest and, with relief, approached the Osprey. Hilda and Barnabas, still supporting Marc, were the first to reach the portal door.

Hilda exclaimed, "What the hel—"

Barnabas interrupted, "It's locked!"

"Can't be!" Matt staggered forward.

"Sure enough, Captain," Marc confirmed.

Think, Matt thought. *There must be a way in!* No ideas came to mind.

The daybreak was upon them. Josh was already breathing heavily. His lungs were on fire, and his head felt light. He gently laid Marci on the ground and sat down beside her. Placing her head in his lap, he leaned over and kissed her on her forehead. Then he laid back and thought, *Well, Vigilo, I guess we failed your last test.* As he was losing consciousness, he thought he heard, "maybe not, my friend."

Matt stood helplessly and observed Josh's actions. He looked over toward the others. His body was still, but his mind was racing. *This is just a problem. I can solve this. I need to slow down and solve this problem,* he thought. He noticed that Hilda and Barnabas let go of Marc, who was hopping on one foot. Hilda was looking on the ground for something to use as a lever to pry the door open. *That'll never work,* Matt thought.

171

Barnabas patted both of his companions on the back and staggered over to Matt. "It was a good run, Captain. You're a good man. It was an honor to serve under you." He kneeled and took on a prayerful pose with a faint smile on his face.

Marc joined Hilda in looking for a lever of some kind. Suddenly he stopped, tapped Hilda on the shoulder, and pulled out his survival knife. Seeing his motion, Hilda pulled hers out as well. Together they began to pry at the portal door. Realizing the futility of their efforts, Hilda slammed her knife to the ground and began to swear again. An angry tear found its way onto her cheek. Marc dropped to the ground and started to laugh.

"Just what the hell's so funny?" Hilda asked.

"You. I never realized, before now, how cute you are when you get mad."

"What? We're dying here, and you're laughing because I'm cute?"

"It's not you, Gunny. It's the irony of our situation."

"How so?"

"All this time, we've worried about defending against an attack. Whoever wanted to take us out didn't need to attack. They just locked a door. Pretty clever, don't you think?"

Hilda sat down next to Marc, laid her head on his shoulder, and locked his arm in hers. "Clever, Sarge," she agreed. "Clever indeed. Aren't you longing for one last smoke?"

"Naw. Trying to quit, it being bad for my health and all. They say it'll take years off of your life, right?"

"Now that's funny," Hilda said, with a weak smile as she drifted off.

Matt fell to his knees. "Where's the rescue ship?" He asked out loud. "If you exist, God, I'm not deserving, but couldn't you give the crew a little help here?"

Silence.

"Could use a little help. It would be appreciated."

Silence.

"God, do you exist? If you do, we need you. I need you!" was his last thought before he heard a roar, like a strong wind, then blackness rushed in.

The morning light fell on several beams of light, hovering over the prone astronauts. A different colored beam settled over each figure.

Rescue or Recovery?

Johnson Space Center, Houston - December 14, 2068, 1500 Hours

Lewis paced back and forth. "Seven hours!" Lewis spit the words out in frustration. "What else can go wrong? We've been through the rescue drill hundreds of times. It's never taken this long to launch a rescue vehicle."

"Patience, Captain, patience," Carter said. "This particular rescue must be approached with the utmost caution, given the grim history of flying in this quadrant."

"I know, Admiral, I know."

An exchange over the main speaker drew their attention.

"Mission Control, Phoenix One, come in."

"Phoenix One, Mission Control, we copy. Over."

"Mission Control, Phoenix One, we're approaching the last known position of the Osprey but don't see any sign of it. Over."

"Phoenix One, Mission Control, we copy, what about the other vessel. The one they reported seeing? Over."

"Mission Control, Phoenix One, we see it at about three o'clock. It's about two hundred meters away. It's as they described. Over."

"Phoenix One, Mission Control, we copy, approach slowly with extreme caution. Over."

"Mission Control, Phoenix One, we copy, our shields are up. Weapons are ready. Over."

"Phoenix One, Mission Control, we copy, any sign of the Osprey or its debris? Over."

"Mission Control, Phoenix One, Still no sign of the Osprey. Is this a rescue or a recovery?" Over."

"Phoenix One, Mission Control, to be honest, we're not sure. Over."

"Mission Control, Phoenix One, still no contac— THEY'RE COMING RIGHT AT US!" <Static> <sound of alarms> "crash avoidance activate—" <static>

"Phoenix One, Mission Control, what's your status?"

<static>

"Phoenix One, Mission Control, do you copy?"

Lewis said, "Crap! Not again!"

Carter frowned. "I warned you, Captain."

"Mission Control, Phoenix One, we just avoided the Osprey. She shot out of nowhere like a bat out of hell!"

"Phoenix One, Mission Control, we copy, what's her condition and yours. Over."

"Mission Control, Phoenix One, we're both at full stop. We are above her and about one hundred meters beyond. We're fine. She seems to be intact with no visible damage, but we still can't raise her on our radio. I'm not sure, but it looked like someone just ejected from the Osprey into space."

"Phoenix One, Mission Control, did we copy correctly? Did you say ejected? Over."

"Mission Control, Phoenix One, roger that. I can't be sure, but it looks like an untethered astronaut was moving away fast. Whatever it was, it's out of sight now."

"Phoenix One, Mission Control, are you sure about what you saw?"

"Mission Control, Phoenix One, still not sure; a lot was happening all at once. But, I think that's what we saw. Over."

"Phoenix One, Mission Control, we copy, can you hear anything using your listening devices? Over."

"Mission Control, Phoenix One, we copy, right now all's quiet, please advise. Over."

The communications officer looked at Lewis, who nodded. The communications officer turned back to his console. "Phoenix One, Mission Control, you are go to hard dock and board the Osprey. Be careful. Over."

Mission Control, Phoenix One, copy that, dock, and board. Over."

Several minutes passed without any word from Phoenix One.

"We didn't lose the Osprey, Admiral," Lewis said, with relief written over his face.

"That's good. But we still don't know if we're dealing with a rescue or a recovery."

"With apologies for stating the obvious. It's too early to tell, sir."

"Mission Control, Phoenix One, docking is completed. Jeez. We're picking up all kinds of sounds now! It sounds like a riot in that ship. We're preparing for a hostile boarding. Over."

"Phoenix One, Mission Control, copy that. You're free to board at will. Over."

"Mission Control, Phoenix One, we're forcing the cargo door right now! Over."

Returning or Awakening?

Onboard the Osprey

Matt's dreamless slumber was interrupted by a rocking motion and insistent alarm. His head ached. As he rubbed it, he looked down and found himself in his spacesuit and buckled in place. He looked around and saw that, excepting HJ, the crew was in their spacesuits and at their stations. Everyone was moving slowly as if they were coming out of a stupor. The Osprey was humming and returning to life.

"Captain, look!" Josh pointed at the central computer monitor."

In English, a two-line message on the monitor read:

```
"You are welcome to leave NOW"
"DO NOT RETURN UNDER ANY CIRCUMSTANCE!"
```

"There you have it, kids," Matt said. "That's our cue to bug out! Commander Maalouf, begin our check-off procedure and prepare to launch."

Barnabas smiled. "Yes, sir! We don't need to be told twice."

"Wait!" Marci exclaimed. "HJ isn't here. We can't leave without HJ!"

"I'm sorry, Lieutenant," Barnabas said. "Lieutenant Jaeger didn't make it."

"What do you mean?" Marci asked.

Marc said, "We couldn't rescue him, Lieutenant. He was dead when we left him."

"No, that's not true!" Marci said. "That can't be true!"

"It is. I'm not even sure how we made it," Hilda confirmed. "The last thing I remember is being locked out of the ship."

Barnabas said, "Yet, here we are. Even in our space suits, and I have no idea how."

"No, NO! This is just a bad dream. I have to go get him!" Marci unbuckled her restraints and started for the port side evacuation chamber.

"Hold up, Lieutenant," Matt said. "We gotta get out of here while we can!" Seeing that Marci was intent on leaving, he said, "Chief, you're the closest, hold her back before she opens that portal and gets us all killed. Commander, get this ship moving!"

"Aye, sir," Josh unbuckled and tried to catch Marci. By the time he reached her, she was peering out the interior door to the portal chamber.

"There he is! He's sitting in the corner. We have to let him in!" Marci reached for the open lever. But Josh blocked her reach.

He said. "That's not him Marci, it's just his suit. He's gone."

"No, I don't believe you! You have to save h—"

An invisible force interrupted her as it pushed her and Josh hard against the rear bulkhead. The others felt that same force pressing them hard into their seats.

"We're underway, Captain. Apologies for no formal countdown."

"A little warning would've been nice, Commander," Matt observed. "Please steady the ship if you will."

"Sorry, sir, but after I lifted her from the ground, I lost control," Barnabas said.

"Meaning?"

"Meaning, she's flying on her own."

"Damn," Matt swore, "I hope we're heading in the right direction."

A wave of nausea swept over Matt as the ship rocked and rolled through a spectacular kaleidoscope of color. He heard a cacophony of alarms as the Osprey complained at the way it was being treated. The ship was not flying well. It pitched and rocked almost out of control.

"Don't you have any control of the ship, Commander?" Matt asked.

"Not yet, sir."

"Get it under control quick. This feels like a bad carnival ride!"

Suddenly, the ship lurched up and to the starboard as a fresh set of alarms sounded.

"What the he—" Matt started to say.

Barnabas said, "The crash avoidance system's kicked in. We've just missed an inbound ship and are maneuvering around a stationary object. I bet it's that old USSR craft! It looks like we are back where we started!"

Matt felt his body strain against his safety harness as Barnabas fought to bring the Osprey to a stop.

"Kill those alarms, Commander. Chief, find out what's crashing around in the cargo hold and secure it!" Matt ordered.

"On it, sir," Josh pulled himself away from Marci and rushed toward the cargo hold. Without warning, the Osprey lurched forward and twisted to a complete stop. Josh fell against the emergency eject lever. The portside portal exit door sprung open, sucking every loose item in the portal's antichamber into space, including HJ's spacesuit. Fortunately, the interior door to the transfer portal was secure, saving the crew from disaster.

"What was that?" Matt demanded.

I accidentally activated the portal door. I'm re-securing it, we but lost HJ's—"

Marci screamed, "You killed him!"

"It was just his suit," Josh said.

"NO! He's in there. You left him there to die!" Marci launched herself from the rear bulkhead and tackled Josh. "You pushed him out like a piece of garbage."

She was on him like a cat, beating, clawing, biting, and kicking. Josh rolled to face her, trying to fend off her blows.

Marc unbuckled and pushed out of his seat. He moved to get Marci off Josh as he did; he pressed hard on his bad ankle. It gave way, and he crumpled in pain.

"Gunny, break it up," Matt ordered.

"Aye, sir," Hilda pushed herself over Marc and reached for Marci.

More alarms sounded.

"What the hell?" Matt asked.

"I think we're avoiding that Soviet Craft again," Barnabas said.

"That doesn't make sense. It's a stationary vehicle, and we're at a full stop," Matt said.

Everyone was quiet for the moment. There was the sound of metal scraping against metal. This was followed by a series of loud thuds.

"Do I hear sounds of metal dragging across our ship from outside?" Matt asked.

The fight to the rear of the command deck resumed with the combatants bouncing around trying to gain leverage. Josh and Hilda struggled to restrain Marci without hurting her. Their shouts and grunts intensified. A different set of alarms began ringing.

"Captain, we're being boarded!" Barnabas exclaimed.

The cargo hold door crashed open.

"EVERYBODY FREEZE!" a fully suited Marine ordered.

Josh found himself looking up the barrel of a very large gun.

Matt's voice boomed, "Who the hell are you?"

"Gunnery Sergeant Bradley from the USS Phoenix, sir. We're rescuing the crew of the USS Osprey! Raise your hands slowly and move away from your station. You too, Commander."

Barnabas frowned. "I'd say you're a day late and a dollar short."

"Silence!" Sergeant Bradley watched as his men helped everyone untangle themselves. "Who's in charge here?"

Debriefings

Debriefing Facility, Johnson Space Center

"This makes no sense, Captain." Robinson stared intently into the debriefing room.

"You're telling me, Admiral," Lewis said.

The two men were observing, through a one-way mirror, the debriefing of a seemingly confused Captain Matthew Dirksen. Lewis stood with his arms crossed and rubbing his chin thoughtfully. "Sir, I'm still trying to wrap my head around what's going on."

Admiral Carter joined them. "Everyone has the same basic story. Some of the details differ. Each person has a unique perspective. But the overall story is consistent. They all talk like this is a standard mission debrief."

"Yeah, it all sounds pretty normal. Sucked into a wormhole, trapped in a strange, other-worldly place full of giant gems, strange primitive plants; stranded for seven days with a disabled ship, only able to breathe outside at night, which by the way was dim, not dark; watched by strange unseen beings; taunted by mysterious messages; attacked by man-eating plants; passed out due to lack of oxygen; awakened while returning through the wormhole. Yeah, Admiral, nothing to it. Just another uneventful seven-hour mission," Lewis said.

"Did the whole crew go crazy?" Robinson asked.

"The better question is, what are they smoking, and why aren't they sharing?" Lewis said.

"Not funny, Captain. This is graver than you think," Carter said.

Robinson said, "Wright may not be far from the truth. It sounds like they all hallucinated. They're adamant that they were gone a full seven days."

"I admit that hallucinating makes more sense than their stories," Carter said. "But we need to take their story as wild as it sounds, seriously. Think of what would happen if the public ever found out that a gateway to an advanced civilization exists this close to Earth."

"Don't tell me you even think that these crazy stories are credible, Justin," Robinson said. "The crew is delusional."

Lewis said, "That's hard to believe, sir. They're a reliable crew."

"Son," Robinson said, "the physical evidence just doesn't support their story. They were gone for only seven hours. How do you get seven days out of seven hours? I spoke to the officer who led the boarding party. He says the Osprey's cargo hold is a mess. Things were not well secured. It'll take a while to sort it all out. Hopefully, when that is done, some clues show up."

"What about the ship's manifest?" Carter asked.

"No help there. It doesn't line up with the actual contents in the cargo hold. You wouldn't know anything about that, would you, Captain?" Robinson asked.

"We had two manifests, sir; one for general publication and one that was our actual record. They've got the wrong one," Lewis answered. "What's this about a crime scene investigation anyway?"

Robinson said. "We have a missing and presumed dead astronaut to account for. And, honestly, do you find the crew's explanation satisfactory?"

"No, sir. I just can't believe anyone's guilty of a crime," Lewis said.

"I agree with the captain," Carter said. "Before we go off impeaching the integrity of the crew, we need to take a hard look at the possibility they're telling the truth. If they did encounter another intelligence, then we're dealing with Pandora's box."

"What do you mean, sir? Lewis asked.

Carter said, "Think about it. Did they provoke these beings to retaliate? Did they stir the curiosity of these beings enough to pay us a visit? If what our crew says is correct, we could be facing a powerful force over which we have no control."

"I'm not sure I agree with you, Justin," Robinson said, "but we can all agree that we have two issues to deal with. First, we need to get at the truth of what happened, and second —"

"We need to control what the public hears," James Silvertongue interrupted as he walked in. "How'll the public react if the crew's story gets out?"

"Good point, James," Carter agreed. "There's only one conclusion you can draw from their story. An advanced civilization renders our best technology impotent and whose portal is within our moon's orbit. It would undoubtedly set off a public panic."

"Well put, Admiral," Silvertongue said. "For the sake of the public, we need a believable story. One that accounts for the loss of an astronaut but doesn't reveal their version of events."

"Will it preserve the careers of the surviving crew?" Lewis asked.

"It'll save the careers of most of the surviving crew," Robinson said.

"Most of the surviving crew?" Lewis asked.

Silvertongue said, "My dear Captain, all we have right now is a missing astronaut and a confused crew telling an unbelievable story. No one looks good, not even you!"

"Especially not you as Mission Controller," Robinson added.

Silvertongue said, "We need a good story with drama and a hero — that being our dearly departed astronaut and an appropriate villain. Someone has to take the fall for this."

"Our society's sense of justice demands it," Robinson said.

Silvertongue said, "You're too good a man, with a still promising career, to take the fall, my dear Captain. No, you won't do. We need someone more closely related to our fallen hero. Someone on the crew. A saboteur, perhaps. Someone with an ax to grind."

Lewis felt both grateful that his superiors wanted to preserve his career and yet guilty for feeling such gratitude.

"Someone with the wherewithal to render the entire crew helpless while they do their dastardly deed," Robinson said.

"Yes, my dear Captain," Silvertongue said, not noticing Lewis grimaces at his continued use of the phrase 'dear Captain.' "The rest of the crew as victims. Excellent! That has a minimal impact on their careers."

"Except for the scapegoat. Their career is toast or worse," Lewis said.

"Small price, Captain," Silvertongue said with a smug smile. "After all, we must be faithful to preserve the public trust in our program and with this administration."

Lewis shook his head and thought, *If I hear you say 'my dear Captain' one more time, I might just punch that smirk right off your face!*

Robinson said, "Now that we've settled that, gentlemen, where's the nearest pub? I've got a powerful thirst, and it's not for water!"

On their way out, Lewis looked back at his friend in the interrogation room. *What really happened up there, Matt?* he thought.

Debriefing Room C, Johnson Space Center

Matt reviewed the transcript of his debriefing on an iPad. He picked up a stylus and started to sign the statement.

"It's pretty much what I recall," he affirmed to the intelligence officer across the table.

"Are you sure, Captain?" The officer asked.

Matt caught the unbelief in the officer's voice and sat back, looking hard into his eyes.

"What exactly do you mean?" Matt asked.

"For starters, you failed to explain the mess in your ship's cargo hold or the fight that was going on between three of your crew when we boarded. Frankly, Captain, do you expect me to believe that all this, this yarn you've been spinning, happened in just seven hours?"

"Seven? What do you mean, seven hours? We were gone for a full seven days! Just ask any of the crew."

"They agree with you all right. It's just that by our time, you were out of contact for just seven hours. Which would be long enough for all of you to get your stories worked out."

Matt's face began to flush. "What? Now you're saying we made this stuff up? The wormhole must've placed us into some kind of time warp."

"Nice try, Captain. Unfortunately, the ship's chronometer matches Mission Control's time exactly. Seven hours, not seven days."

"Look, I can't explain that," Matt said, his voice rising. "But I know this statement is accurate. I resent you implying that I'm trying to cover up something or being anything less than honest." He was starting to lose control. "Where are you going with this anyway, colonel?"

"Relax, Captain. Look at it from my perspective, a missing astronaut, amazing stories about wormholes, lost planets, and man-eating plants. What do you expect me to believe?"

"I certainly don't expect you to believe I'm a liar!" Matt threw his stylus across the room. It clattered to the floor. The officer was unfazed.

"Go ahead," a seething Matt continued, "you weren't there, I was, I'd like to know just what you do believe you son of a—"

The Colonel cut him off, "I'll tell you what I believe. I believe the truth is found in a story that accounts for the evidence. So far, the evidence doesn't back your story."

Matt said, "I have five eyewitnesses that'll back me up on this."

"That's just it. Following the physical evidence often gets us closer to the truth than what witnesses say. They can be so unreliable."

Matt wasn't sure what angered him the most, the colonel's words or his unemotional arrogance? Matt decided it was both. In any case, he knew that he needed to calm down.

"You're the man with all the smarts in this room. You tell me, where's the evidence taking you?" he asked.

"Logically, your story doesn't make sense. Now, before you go off again, let me finish. Your premise is all wrong. Wormholes are theoretical. They've never been experienced—"

"Before now," Matt interjected.

"They've never been experienced," the colonel continued. "According to the theory, had you actually experienced one, you'd all be dead. I'd say the evidence indicates there was intentional foul play at work. It's just," he paused, seeming to collect his thoughts.

Finally gaining a little self-control, Matt asked, "It's just what?"

"It's just that we can't figure out if you're part of all this or not."

"Part of what?"

"Part of a plot to cover up the murder of Lieutenant Jaeger."

"What! You think Lieutenant Jaeger was murdered?" Matt's recently gained control started to slip away.

"That's where the evidence seems to be taking us, Captain. Of course, there's more evidence to collect, but we do have a person of interest."

"Who?"

"It's a little too early to say. You'll know soon enough when we make an arrest."

"In that case, you might as well just arrest me and get it over with," Matt demanded.

"Why'd you say that, Captain?" A suddenly interested Colonel asked.

"I am the ship's Captain. Ultimately, I'm responsible for all that happens with my crew."

"Your sentiments are admirable," the colonel said, with more condescension than necessary, "but you're not our person of interest."

"Then are we through here? Am I free to go?"

"Yes, Captain, we're through here. You're free to leave."

Matt stood up. "Good, 'cause I need to find a pub and get a drink."

"I've reviewed your records, and you don't drink anymore."

"My record just became outdated."

Crime Scene Investigation

Hanger A, Moon Base 12

Captain Paul Allen, Chief Investigative Officer, approached the spacecraft. *The Osprey looks a bit like a caged bird,* he thought. Hanger A is a fully pressurized and secured hanger. The Osprey was towed here by a space salvage barge to keep it away from prying eyes. As little as there is, the Moon's gravity also made the crime scene investigation easier on the investigators.

Master Chief Susan Ward greeted the captain, "Welcome on board, sir. We've been expecting you for a while."

"I've been detained by an agitated Admiral. This place looks like my teenage daughter's bedroom." Allen surveyed the mess in the Osprey's cargo hold. The contents of several storage units lay about. Several types of unidentified liquid puddled among broken containers on the floor. The air smelled of wine mingled with tar and fresh peyote.

The chief said, "Hate to disagree, but it looks and smells like my son's workout room."

"That too," Allen agreed. "Where's Chief Henson?"

"I sent him and the rest of the team to examine the bridge, sir."

"Afraid they'd contaminate the crime scene, here?"

"Something like that. By the way, why are we treating this as a crime scene anyway?"

"A spaceship disappears for seven hours, then reappears, missing one astronaut and the crew fighting amongst itself. Must be a crime there somewhere. Bring me up to speed. What've you found in this mess?"

"It isn't as widespread a mess as it looks."

The captain raised an eyebrow.

Ward said, "What I mean is that the supplies, addressed to Mars, are intact. Their storage units were locked down tight until I opened them to take inventory. Only a few storage units, belonging to the two scientists, have sprung open."

"How? Caused by the impact of a sudden stop, perhaps? Opened by the crew?"

"Most likely, they were opened but never properly secured."

"Anything missing?"

"Hard to say, sir. Nothing seems to match the official manifest. Crews never keep a list of their personal items."

"Find anything unusual?"

"I did. I found what I think is some form of peyote residue."

"What do you mean, some form of peyote?"

"Its pods from a type of peyote found in South America. This stuff is a very potent airborne powder that's released if the pods pop. It looks like that is just what happened. Rumor has it that this stuff can leave its users highly susceptible to suggestion."

"Suggestion?"

"Yeah, like being hypnotized."

"Hmm. That'd explain the Admiral's theory. Have you read the crew's debriefing notes?"

"Started to, sir. I skimmed over them. They read like a sci-fi story."

"Yeah, but their stories are fairly consistent. Keep looking and see if you can find any corroborating evidence scattered about."

"Such as?"

"Climbing gear, rope, fruit, used O2 test kits, that kind of stuff."

"I guess this circa 1960's Russian medallion qualifies."

"Yeah, it could. Depends on who handled it. Check for prints."

"Will do," the chief said. "Sir?"

"Yes?"

"What's the Admiral's theory?"

"The crew was disabled; the lieutenant was killed on board, and his body dumped into space. At least that's the short version," Allen said.

"Who would do that?"

"From the rescue team debrief and a grieving Admiral's mind, it would be Chief Torres."

"Wow! Has the Admiral shared this with anyone else?"

"As far as I know, only me. Let's keep it that way."

"Consider my lips sealed, sir."

"Thanks. I'll check the Bridge." Captain Allen bounded in the light gravity down the passageway to visit the rest of his team. Arriving at the Bridge, he found Chief Henson reclining on Commander Malouf's seat with his feet propped on the ship's console.

Chief Henson bounced to a standing salute. "I could get used to this, sir. I understand that the captain of these birds basically watches as his crew does all the work."

Captain Allen returned the salute and chuckled. "That's not even the captain's chair, Chief. Let's get to it. We know there was a load of peyote that possibly contaminated the onboard air supply. This would affect everyone on the crew—"

Henson interrupted, "Unless they were using their local air tank, sir."

"True. Have someone check the O2 levels in each oxygen pack."

"Already done. All tanks are full, except for Torres's tank."

"How long has his supply been used?"

"Ten to fifteen minutes. Each tank should hold sixty to sixty-five minutes' worth of O2. Torres's level sits at about fifty minutes left."

Allen said, "The peyote pods burst, spreading hallucinogenic powder through the HVAC system, disabling the crew. Except for Chief Torres, who was breathing his own O2. After fifteen minutes, the crew's disabled, leaving him free to do whatever."

"What, sir?"

"Nothing, just following a theory. Have you viewed the initial debriefing holograms?"

"Yeah, I did, sir."

"What do you think?"

"If you're wondering whether they're covering something up, I think they could've settled on a simpler story."

"Mass hallucination?"

"That's just as farfetched as their stories, sir."

"I suppose, Chief, let's see where the evidence leads. What does the onboard flight recorder show?"

"Matches everything we got on our ground-based systems, including a seven-hour gap."

"It just stopped recording for seven hours?"

"Sure did, sir."

"How about the captain's log?"

"Here, it's on this tablet. We checked. Only his fingerprints are on it."

"Now that's old school. Why use a tablet when you can just speak your status report directly into the ship's computer?"

"Perhaps he wanted to keep his comments off the record, or he was convinced the ship's computer wasn't working."

"Did you read it?"

"Saved that for you, sir, although we did crack the password."

"Thanks, let's see what Dirksen wrote. Hmm. Reads like he posted seven daily updates."

"Can't be, sir."

"Look and see, Chief. All his entries are dated on different days."

"We checked the timestamps on the meta-data here." The chief pointed to the tablet screen. "Each entry is timestamped for the same day one hour apart."

"That's weird. Dirksen acted like these entries were on different days. Why?"

"Maybe he thought his entries were on different days, sir."

"What else do we have?"

"We found the water and food dispensers locked down. Probably due to the crash avoidance protocol. They haven't been reset."

"Anything on the console?"

"Yeah, one of the compartments has been opened. The tamper seal's broken, sir."

"Which one?"

"The one that accesses the thruster overrides." Henson opened the compartment door."

"Why would you tamper with the maneuvering thrusters?"

"Don't know. This panel is usually only opened to test individual thrusters. Maybe they felt they need to test, and oh!"

"Oh?"

"Sir, here's a control lever marked, "stealth," with on, off, dark, and cloak options."

"What the heck? This ship doesn't have a cloaking device. I never read that in the technical specs," Allen said.

"Uh … must be an undocumented feature, sir."

"This panel provides access to both the thruster testing AND to activate an undocumented cloaking device?"

"Yep, that's the way it looks, sir."

Captain Allen mused, "That could explain the Osprey's sudden disappearance and reappearance. It certainly makes more sense than testing individual thrusters. Okay, give me a rundown on what else you've found so far."

"Here's what we've got, Captain. For starters, no water or food was dispensed."

Just then, a Petty Officer walked in from the Crew Quarters.

The Petty Officer said, "The shipboard telemetry shows no miles traveled between the time the Osprey disappeared and when it reappeared. Here's our list, sir." She handed her tablet to Captain Allen. The list read:

- No water or food was dispensed.
- Shipboard telemetry shows the ship at a full stop during the unaccounted-for time.
- Evidence that the Central computers may have been hacked on the eve of the mission.
- Shipboard computer logs look normal but have a seven-hour gap.
- Ship's computer functions checkout as normal.
- The maneuvering thrusters function normally.
- The engine was found in the idling mode. No state change triggers were logged.
- Telemetry shows no unusual activity other than the crash prevention maneuvers.
- Only Lieutenant Jaeger's spacesuit is missing.

"As is Lieutenant Jaeger," Captain Allen said. "All in all, this doesn't seem to support the crew's statements, except for the missing space suit."

"Sir, we just started examining the bridge-to-cargo hold passageway and portside entrance portal. So far, it looks like Chief Torres caught the brunt of Lieutenant Gonzalez's wrath. Most of the bits of cloth belong to his uniform. See here, these scuff marks on the seats and walls look like they came from Gonzalez's shoes as she tried to gain leverage on Torres."

"A hard thing to do in weightless space," the Petty Officer said.

Chief Henson said, "Yeah, but, judging from the bruising on Torres's throat, noted on his medical exam, I'd say she was about to get the better of him. He's lucky that Gunnery Sergeant McDermott grabbed her ankle and twisted, breaking her leverage."

"I bet that some of this blood spatter belongs to Torres. Grab some samples." The captain opened the door between the passageway and the portside exit portal.

Another investigator bent over to take a sample, lost his balance, and hit the emergency escape lever. BANG! Everyone jumped at the sound of the portal's external hatch opening.

"Jeez, man!" Captain Allen exclaimed. "Be careful. If this ship were in orbit, we'd all be floating in space about now."

"Sorry, sir," the investigator said.

"Do you think that's how he did it?" Chief Henson asked.

"Did what?" The captain asked.

"Killed the lieutenant and disposed of his body?"

"Where's the murder weapon?"

"Good question, sir."

"What's on the floor here in the anti-chamber?" the captain asked

"Looks like some drops of tar, some scuffs of dirt, and, whoa, there's some more dried blood," the Petty Officer answered.

"Get samples of everything and test to see who that blood belongs to," the captain said.

"Bingo!" the fallen investigator said from within the Ship's passageway. He stood up, holding a gun.

"Where'd you find that?" the captain asked.

"It was lodged under this chair."

"Whose is it?" the Petty Officer asked.

"Probably McDermott. She was wearing an empty holster when the crew was picked up," Chief Henson replied.

"Does it have a full clip?" Captain Allen asked.

"Negative. Two rounds are missing," the investigator replied.

The chief gave a low whistle.

"What?" Captain Allen asked.

Chief Henson said, "Traces of gun powder were found on Torres's sleeve according to his post-flight exam."

Allen said, "Check for prints. I'm buying a round for the whole team if they belong to anyone other than Torres."

The chief asked, "Where're the shells?"

"Floating in space with Lieutenant Jaeger," the captain suggested.

The Petty Officer said, "Here's a scenario: the shooter drags Jaeger, who's passed out due to peyote, into the anti-chamber, shoots him, puts him in his spacesuit, shuts the interior portal door, hits the emergency escape lever, and BAM! Jaeger and the spent cartridges are floating in space, never to be seen again. What do you think, Captain?"

Captain Allen said, "If that turns out to be Jaeger's blood, I think Chief Torres better find himself a damn good lawyer."

Thoughtful Admiral

Johnson Space Center, Houston, Texas

Lewis rushed into Admiral Carter's outer office. The admiral's assistant scowled, "It's about time you showed up. You're late, and you know how he hates to be kept waiting."

"Couldn't be helped. Traffic was a bear," Lewis said, irritated at the assistant's attitude.

The assistant frowned. "Whatever. He said to send you in as soon as you arrived."

Lewis straightened his shoulders, prepared for the impending reprimand, and entered the Admiral's office.

Lewis found Admiral Carter intently studying a holographic recording of Josh's debriefing. Carter motioned him over without looking up. Lewis watched Carter's body language for a moment. "Good afternoon, Admiral."

Carter looked intently at Josh's holograph. "Fascinating."

Lewis said, "I thought you and Admiral Robinson considered Chief Torres's account — let's see if I can remember the wording. Oh yes, — 'metaphysical bunk.'"

"Don't be impertinent. Those were Admiral Robinson's words, not mine. I'm concerned that Chief Torres's account, and that of everyone else on the Osprey, is more truth than fantasy."

"But the hard evidence doesn't support their stories," Lewis said. Seeing a disapproving look from the Admiral, he quickly added, "just playing devil's advocate, sir."

"Six different versions of the same account are pretty hard evidence."

"They do have their discrepancies, sir."

"Minor discrepancies, mainly the kind that creep in, because each account is from a different point of view as to what's important and what isn't. There're no major contradictions, yet enough differences to make it hard to believe they conspired."

"Point taken," Lewis said. "But this is a singular event. We've no precedent, and the rescue ship found no evidence of a wormhole portal."

"You're skeptical because this is a unique event with no precedent?" the Admiral asked.

"Exactly. I'd like to believe, sir, but something like this has never happened before."

"The big bang theory was a singular event that set our known universe in motion. Do you believe in it?"

Lewis said, "I do, but that's different."

"How?"

"There's evidence to support it."

"But no evidence to support the chief's testimony?"

"Not the same kind of evidence. Basically, we're relying on human testimony, which can be flawed, sir."

"Maybe not all that flawed, Captain. Ever heard of John Colter?"

"No, sir."

"He was a member of the **Lewis and Clark Expedition** but left to join another group of fur trappers. Later, he set out on his own, passing through a portion of what's now Yellowstone. Colter was wounded in a battle with some Indians before making it to Fort Raymond. There, he recovered and talked about seeing geysers of hot water and bubbling mud pots. They said these sightings were the delirious imaginings of a wounded man. They mocked his story by calling the region he passed through 'Colter's Hell.' Here's an eyewitness account dismissed for years as a 'tall tale' because there was no known precedent. It was a singular event if you will."

"With all due respect, Admiral, you don't strike me as a metaphysical philosopher. Where are you going with all this?"

Carter said, "No, I'm not one of those kinds. I'm saying it's foolish to dismiss eyewitness accounts too quickly. Colter wasn't considered a credible witness, so Yellowstone's mud pots and geysers were believed to be a fantasy for years. But it turns out he was right. Unfortunately, some, in high places, don't consider your crew to be credible. So, we're going down this crazy trail of creating an alternate reality."

"And you? What do you think, Admiral?"

"I think we have six highly trained, brave men and women that agree on all the major points of the events they witnessed. They're staking their careers and reputations on these claims. We must allow that they might just be correct. The fact is, I'm inclined to believe they are."

"If that is true, why are you allowing us to go down this, as you put it, 'crazy trail' of creating an alternate reality? No offense intended, sir."

"None taken. If what the Osprey's crew says is true, we have a situation that must be held secret, at the highest level, for only those with 'a need to know.' Should the public ever hear their story, panic would break out. The political fall-out would be enormous. Now being fed to the public, the alternate reality provides the perfect cover for a very disconcerting truth. Besides, I have something else in mind for your crew, depending on how they deal with the challenge of saving Chief Torres."

"That leaves me with three questions, sir."

"Yes?"

"First, what do you know that these analysts don't? Second, if you consider this a highest-level secret with a 'need to know,' why are you talking with me? Finally, what do you have in mind for my crew?"

"You and I both know about the earlier disappearances, as I told you in the control center. That information is so highly classified that even the analysts assigned to investigate this incident don't know about them. In answer to your second question, you 'have a need' because I'm assigning you to quietly look for verification. If Captain Dirksen's account is true, what happened to him and his crew probably happened to the other vehicles that disappeared. Here's the list of missing vehicles, including the ill-fated Russian spaceship, which we already saw. I want you to find them and bring them back for analysis."

"What about the Russians? They won't take kindly to us retrieving their ship."

"They're not to know. Use a minimum and very trusted crew. No outside observers on board. Understood?"

"Copy that, sir. About my third question?"

"My intentions for your crew? First things first. Let's get on with the recovery mission. Those flying this mission may be observed by various astronomers at observatories around the world. So, this'll be listed as a recovery mission. The space junk that endangers your crew must first be cleared. Each item on that list is a 'danger to your crew.'"

"My cover story, sir?"

"Your story is that you'll be trying to locate and recover the body of our latest space hero, Lieutenant JG Homer Jaeger. I've no doubt JC and his inner circle will want us to try and retrieve the lieutenant's remains."

"Really?"

"Yes, I know JC, and I am pretty sure how he'll play this event."

"If what the Osprey's crew says is true and if we're able to find it, who knows what'll be in the lieutenant's suit. A broken and half-eaten body sounds kinda gruesome," Lewis said.

"Good point. Of course, this whole affair may get pretty gruesome before it's over."

"Meaning?"

"Meaning Lieutenant Jaeger may not be the only casualty."

Preferral of Charges

"Upon the preferring of charges, the proper authority shall take immediate steps to determine what disposition should be made thereof in the interest of justice and discipline, and the person accused shall be informed of the charges against him as soon as practicable." – Article 830.30.b Uniform Code of Military Justice

Johnson Space Center, Houston, Texas

Thunder of an approaching storm could be heard by the occupants of one of NASA's drab tan conference rooms. James Morris II and Admiral Gerald Hornsby eyed the others around the conference table. To their right was Vice Admiral Dennis Robinson. Next to him was James Silvertongue. Then came Captain Lewis Wright and Retired Admiral Justin Carter. Directly to Morris's left sat a newcomer, Captain Brian Bitters, from the Judge Advocates Office (JAG).

Morris said, "By now, you've all heard that the debriefing of the Osprey crew has taken a distressing turn. There are major discrepancies between the crew's statements and the physical evidence found on the Osprey. We basically have a flight that disappeared for seven hours and returned with an astronaut missing."

Silvertongue said, "I don't need to tell you that this is unacceptable."

Then don't tell us! Lewis thought.

Silvertongue continued, "Word of Lieutenant Jaeger's demise will be out soon enough, and we have no clear story about what happened on board that ship."

"No clear story?" Robinson snorted. "Hell, we have no IDEA what happened!"

"No, Dennis," Morris resumed control of the meeting, "but we do have clues, and a story is starting to emerge. That's why I invited Captain Bitters, from JAG, to explain where we are in the investigation." Turning to Captain Bitters, he asked, "Captain, what've you found?"

"Sir, we've collected a variety of disturbing clues," the chubby, balding Captain said. "First, we found among the mess in the cargo hold a significant amount of peyote."

"What do you mean by significant?" Robinson asked.

"Enough to get the whole crew high. We also found that Chief Torres's reserve O2 canister was used for about 10 to 15 minutes. If he was using his reserve oxygen at the time the peyote was released into the air, he wouldn't have been affected by it."

"Interesting," Morris said. "Is there more, Captain?"

"We found that Gunnery Sergeant McDermott's weapon had been recently discharged."

"What did she shoot?" Carter asked.

Bitters said, "We don't know. We do know she didn't fire her weapon. Chief Torres did."

"How do you know that?" Lewis asked in disbelief.

"We found powder residue on the chief's uniform sleeve. We found no powder residue on Gunnery Sergeant McDermott. And, the chief's fingerprints were on the weapon. We failed to find any shell casings or bullet holes anywhere within the vessel."

The room was silent. *This is going sideways fast!* Lewis thought.

Bitters said, "We believe that the ship's computer was hacked. The 'presentation view' of the ship's flight plan was unchanged. BUT … the actual flight plan itself was different."

"Meaning?" Morris asked.

"Meaning, sir, that the flight plan being viewed on the monitors at Mission Control was a view of the original plan, NOT the updated plan which the vessel was following. The only way that can happen is to manually alter the flight plan without updating the 'presentation view.' Such events are normally logged with the ID of whoever did the updating. However, in this case, there's a four-hour gap in the logs the night before the Osprey's launch."

"And this techno mumbo jumbo means?" Morris asked.

"It means that someone intentionally changed the flight plan without authorization, hid the change from the mission controllers, and erased any evidence of who they were."

Morris said, "There's only one crew member capable of such actions."

Seeing the direction this was taking, Lewis spoke up, "So far, all we've heard as evidence is a variety of physical clues. The crew's unanimous description of events paints a very different picture. That must also be considered."

"Come, come, Captain Wright," Morris said. "We all know that eyewitnesses are notoriously unreliable. Besides, the accounts are hardly unanimous. Not everyone has been thoroughly interrogated, er, debriefed yet. And don't forget, we may never know Lieutenant Jaeger's account."

That's crap! Lewis thought. He was about to respond when Admiral Carter caught his eye and shook his head no, ever so slightly. Lewis blinked and sat a little straighter.

Carter gave him a chance to compose himself by saying, "James, we share your grief over losing your nephew. How can we help?"

Morris replied, "Thank you, Justin. If you, with the help of Captain Wright, can find Lieutenant Jaeger's body, it would be of great relief to myself and my sister."

Carter said, "Captain Wright is already putting together a team for such a mission." Lewis nodded his head in agreement.

"Thank you, Gentlemen," Morris said. "As for the rest of us, and based on your inquiry to date, what do you recommend, Captain Bitters?"

"Sir, I believe there's probable cause that Chief Torres endangered his ship and murdered Lieutenant Jaeger. I recommend that as his commanding officer, Admiral Hornsby have him court-martialed."

What the hell?! This is just wrong! Lewis thought as he felt his anger rising. He leaned forward to object but stopped when he felt Admiral Carter's firm grip around his wrist.

"Gentlemen, I concur with Captain Bitters. Do I see any objections?" Morris looked around the table.

Seeing none, he concluded, "Good. Gerald, would you be so kind as to prefer charges against Chief Torres?"

"Consider it done, JC," Hornsby said.

The room fell silent as the gravity of what just happened sank in. Morris broke the silence. "I propose that we adjourn to the Fireside Room for dinner and to discuss our tactics moving forward. That is, except for our good Captain Wright, who'll be busy searching for HJ's body."

Carter said, "If you don't mind, James, I'll stay to review Captain Wright's plans."

"Suit yourself, Justin," Morris said as everyone stood to leave.

As they filed out, Lewis overheard Silvertongue's satisfied comment, "As they say, 'any good story has to have a villain.' It looks like our problem is solved."

"Wait, Admiral. You can't just leave them alone. You know what they're about to do to the chief," Lewis pleaded.

"Patience, Captain. Morris has already made up his mind. I don't need to be in that meeting to guess what his next play is."

"What is Morris's next play?"

"Preferral of Charges."

"That's why you have to go with them and stop this!" Lewis insisted.

"I understand your concern, but it doesn't work that way. 'Adjourn to the Fireside Room for dinner,' is code for, 'let's plan how we're going to hang Torres.' Unless you want to help them lay their plans, we best stay on the outside looking in."

Lewis slowly shook his head no.

"I didn't think so. I don't want to be part of that either. I want to get to the truth."

"How's that going to help the chief, sir?"

"It's not. At least not right away. Remember, I have plans for your crew. But first, they need to prove themselves by saving the chief from what Morris is planning to do. Will they have the chops to help him or not? If they do, I can use them. If not, they're of no value to me."

"What plans?"

"In due time, Captain. In due time. Meanwhile, we must get at the truth of what happened."

"How do we do that?"

"Just like we discussed, we find the body and the satellites that disappeared before. Hopefully, then we can corroborate your crew's story and get closer to the truth. Of course, it could be the chief's guilty, like Morris and his clique believes. But we'll never know they're wrong, and the crew's story is true unless we find the objects that may have been through the wormhole before. Morris and company have certainly closed their minds to that possibility."

"But your mind is open?"

Carter said, "Yes, the crew's testimony, combined with those old satellites, will establish the truth of what's out there."

"No disrespect intended, Admiral, but what is truth?"

"For me, and hopefully you, truth is knowing what, in fact, happened. For some of our friends, it's more relative."

"How do you mean?"

"For Silvertongue, truth is a good public relations story. If the story holds together, he'll decide it's true. For Morris, truth is a story that vindicates his nephew and doesn't conflict with his view that traveling through a wormhole is the stuff of science fiction. Truth for that obnoxious JAG officer—"

"You mean Captain Bitters."

"Yeah, Bitters. Truth to him is whatever it takes for him to advance his career." Carter held up his hand. "Before you ask how I know, I can see it in his eyes."

"See what?"

"Ambition. If you're not careful, it'll blind you to the truth. Bitters views the group retiring to the Fireside Room as a circle of influence that he wants to join. He'll do anything to be inside that circle of 'movers and shakers.' Those already on the inside know it, so they'll use his ambition to make him do their dirty work for them."

"Including framing an innocent man, sir?"

"Yes, even framing an innocent man."

"What about Admiral Robinson?"

"Robinson is gruff, but he's scared. To face the truth, you must be brave. He's afraid the crew is right, so he'll buy into any reasonable alternative and call it true."

"You're saying he is a coward?"

"Not at all. I've served with Robinson on the battlefield. He's no coward in battle. What I mean is that it takes a special kind of bravery to admit your view of things is wrong. Robinson is only open to a 'truth' that matches his world view."

"Sounds like you're saying no one really wants to know the truth. They just want to cover their butts or reinforce their beliefs, even if it finds an innocent man guilty."

"Sadly, yes. You just stated what I've been trying to say quite well."

"There must be something we can do, Admiral!"

"The situation has taken on a life of its own. We'll see how it unfolds and trust that your crew can find a way to short-circuit Morris."

Lewis sighed. "Basically, the chief is screwed."

Carter nodded. "Basically. Unless what your crew finds corroborates your team's testimony."

"And there's nothing else we can do?"

"Other than finding that space junk, not much unless...."

"Unless what?"

"Unless you're a praying man or know one," Carter looked hard at Lewis. "Judging from that look on your face, Captain, the chief may not have a prayer.

The Plan

Officer's Club, Johnson Space Center

T he Fireside Room was a much-coveted mahogany-paneled space. It was located adjacent to the central atrium of the Officer's Club. Accessed by double French doors, it featured a river rock fireplace, an array of overstuffed leather chairs, and an elaborately carved dinner table. It gave off a faint aroma of furniture polish and leather. When not in use, the doors remained open with the posh interior on display. A velvet cord strung across the doorway reminded casual observers they could look but not enter. In theory, any officer could reserve this room for special occasions. Practically speaking, Monday, Wednesday, and Friday evenings were always reserved. When pressed, the steward would only offer other evenings as an alternative. He would never admit that Admiral Hornsby held a permanent reservation for that room on behalf of his close confidant James Morris.

The wait staff played a game called "who's in and who's out," based on who accompanied James Morris to dine in the fireside room. Some were regulars. Others came and went. The game consisted of laying small bets on whether a newcomer would even hang on as a regular for more than a month.

The attendant removed the velvet cord to allow Morris and his entourage access. As they passed, the attendant said, "Good evening, Mr. Morris. Will you be having your usual?"

"Yes, thank you, Carlton," Morris replied.

The steward was about to close the doors when Bitters stopped him. "A tall Lieutenant should be here soon. You need to let him in."

"Very well, Captain." The steward closed the doors.

The group had just given their drink orders when the doors opened to let Lieutenant Maynard Hinsdale enter. The tall, dark-haired JAG officer did a poor job of hiding his excitement at being invited to join this exclusive group. The invitation alone stroked his ego and his ambition. *Everyone knows that being part of JC Morris's circle leads to ample opportunities,* he thought. *Finally, cultivating my friendship with Bitters is paying off. He's such a self-centered boor. But I'm in now, and that's the main thing.*

At the same time, Bitters was approaching Maynard thinking, *Don't look so smug, Hinsdale. You may think you're in, but you need to pass muster with Morris first. Don't make me the fool for suggesting you by screwing up.* With a smile, Captain Bitters offered Maynard a limp hand in welcome. "Gentlemen, may I introduce Lieutenant Maynard Hinsdale, my associate in the JAG office."

The audience offered a subdued welcome as the two JAG Officers took their seats.

Morris nodded. "Welcome to our little band of progressives, Lieutenant. You've joined us at a good time. We may have a use for your ... uh ... talents."

Maynard straightened slightly in his chair, enjoying the warm feeling of being needed.

"As I was saying," Morris continued, "we need to review how we intend to handle our little problem, James."

Silvertongue said, "Thank you, JC. We must move quickly and streamline as much of the pre-court-martial activity as possible. We must release a compelling story to the public. One that leaves no room for doubt. This is, I might add, a very compelling and salacious story, full of jealousy, revenge, and a mean-spirited villain."

"Why must we hurry?" Maynard asked.

Hornsby snorted. "Two reasons, Lieutenant. First, to keep order in the ranks with swift justice. None of that drag-it-out-for-years crap. Swift justice. Second, we don't ever want that other story to leak out."

"Other story?" Maynard asked.

"You know," Hornsby frowned. "The story we don't talk about."

"Oh, that story, sir. That story. Gotcha, sir," Maynard said, knowing full well that he had no idea what the Admiral meant.

Silvertongue said, "It's paramount that we not appear to be denying Torres his rights. We need to deal with notifying the chief of the charges against him."

"Done," Hornsby said. "Brian did that in my presence earlier today. The chief was somewhat disoriented. I suppose that comes with sleep deprivation."

"Don't tell me that you've tortured the lad," Silvertongue said.

"Who said anything about torture?" Hornsby asked. "His cell just happens to be in the noisiest part of the detention center, next to where the guards are blasting heavy metal music at all hours. Not to mention a lighting system that flashes on and off during the night. The electricians just can't seem to figure it out."

"Well done, Horatio," Morris chuckled.

"Regardless, he must waive his right to an Article 32 Hearing," Silvertongue said. "It would also help if the chief opted out of attending his preliminary hearing."

"We need to draft a plea bargain to my liking," Morris said. "Twenty-five to life in prison should do."

Bitters said, "Why not press for a conviction? I'm sure I can get one."

Morris said, "Not so fast, Brian. The safe play is to lead the chief to sign a plea bargain."

"Who would sign a plea bargain that gives them life in prison?" Maynard asked.

"Someone who thinks they're getting the death penalty," Morris said.

"I can get a conviction," Bitters insisted.

Morris said, "I don't doubt your skills, Brian. But juries, even handpicked ones, are unpredictable. It's too risky. Besides, Gerald failed to line up my favorite Judge to run the trial."

"Who?" Robinson asked.

"Grant Coon, an old golfing buddy of mine."

"Hey, I can't help it if Coon just had back surgery and can't preside," Hornsby said.

"No matter. We need a plea bargain," Morris said.

Silvertongue cleared his throat. "Gentlemen, the real question before us is how to get Torres to waive his right to an Article 32 Hearing."

"And opt-out of his preliminary hearing. Yes, James, we heard you," Hornsby said.

Maynard found himself caught up in the conversation, "I agree with Mr. Silvertongue."

All eyes turned to him as Morris said, "That, my good Lieutenant, is your contribution to our little project."

"Pardon me, sir?"

"May I enlighten him?" Bitters asked.

Morris nodded, "You may, I'm off to prepare our star witness. So, I'll bid you all a good evening." Then he walked out the door.

With an air of superiority, Brian said, "It's like this, Lieutenant — we'll work in tandem. The admiral will appoint you as Torres's Defense Counsel and me as the Prosecutor. You're the good cop; I'm the bad cop.

You gain the chief's trust. And convince him he needn't bother with the Article 32 hearing or the preliminary hearing."

Maynard swallowed hard as he realized that admission to this little band of progressives came with a cost.

Hornsby said, "So, you'll be working more closely with Brian than, ah, normal."

"Uh, yes, sir," Maynard answered.

"You realize this is highly unusual. So, it mustn't leave this room," Hornsby said.

"Yes, sir."

Hornsby asked, "You won't let us down, will you, Lieutenant? Can we count on you?"

"No, sir, I won't let you down. Er, yes, sir, you can count on me."

"This all sounds good," Robinson said. "but without a body or an eye witness, how do we make anything stick?"

"Won't need to. Our good friends here are going to get a sweet plea-deal done," Silvertongue patted Maynard on the back.

Robinson was unconvinced. "I hear you, James. But what if our good friends fail?"

Hornsby said, "Don't worry, Dennis. We've got it all worked out."

"You found the body?" Bitters asked.

"No," Hornsby said. "Just as good. JC found an eye witness."

Reality or a Dream?

Debriefing Facility, Johnson Space Center

arci looked around the debriefing room. *So, this is what it's like to be arrested and interrogated,* she thought as she took in the stark room. It had a two-way mirror along one wall, two straight-back chairs, one table, and one microphone. *I answered all these same questions during my first debriefing days ago. Why a second round, unless they want to charge me with something?*

"Lieutenant?" her interrogator interrupted her thoughts.

She analyzed the boyish figure seated across the table from her. Technically, they were the same rank. But his boyish face made her wonder just how long he had been out of the Academy. She tried to focus on what he was saying, despite his irritatingly high-pitched voice.

"Don't you see my point?" he was asking. "There's no way the events you described can be real. You must've been dreaming."

"How do you know what is real and what isn't?" she challenged. "You weren't there! You haven't even been in space, have you?"

Before her inquisitor could answer, there was a tap at the door. He excused himself and stepped out. Marci sat and stewed over his self-important attitude and condescending choice of words. Worst of all was the fact that he refused to believe her story, an experience shared by the entire crew with each of their debriefing officers. Curiously, when he returned, his tone changed.

"Okay, Lieutenant. I can't say I understand how difficult your experience was, and I'm having trouble following your details. So, help me out here. Of all that happened over the seven hours in question—"

"Days," Marci corrected.

"Days, seven days in question, what was the most troubling event?"

"That's easy. Chief Torres made no effort to save Lieutenant Jaeger!"

"No effort?"

"No!" Marci exclaimed. "He just turned his back on the lieutenant, despite his pleas for help. He might as well have killed him!"

"That's troubling," her questioner agreed. "What should we do?"

"Josh should be held accountable," Marci demanded.

"Josh?"

"Chief Joshua Torres."

Again, there was a soft knock at the door. This time Morris entered.

"Thank you, Lieutenant. That's all," he dismissed the young officer.

"But we're not finished, sir," the lieutenant objected.

"I believe you are. I'll take it from here. Make sure the observation room is cleared on your way out," Morris turned the mike off.

To Marci, he said, "Good evening, Lieutenant Gonzalez. My name is James Morris the second. I'm NASA's Program Chief. Thank you for your time and patience with our young Lieutenant there."

"Frankly, sir—" Marci began.

"It's JC," Morris interrupted, "my friends call me JC. As I was saying, I hope you didn't find the debriefing too annoying."

"No, sir ... uh ... JC," Marci answered. "It's frustrating that my questioner wouldn't listen. He kept carrying on about me being in some kind of dream state. He was very condescending."

"Good help is hard to come by nowadays," Morris quipped.

Marci didn't laugh.

Unfazed, he continued, "There seems to be a discrepancy between your seven-day experience and our mission clock, which shows that your flight took seven hours."

"The clock is just wrong."

"Maybe, maybe not. It's just a minor detail, Lieutenant. What we must concentrate on is the need to see that justice is served."

"Your point, sir?"

"You said it yourself. Chief Torres must be held accountable."

"I did," Marci admitted.

"Do you mean it?"

"I do, sir."

"Sadly, there seems to be a pattern emerging here that may let the chief off the hook."

"That is?"

"Each crew member seems to think they traveled through a wormhole, spent a week on a mysterious planet, and lost HJ to a man-eating plant. A pretty fantastic tale, you will admit?"

"I know it sounds far-fetched. But it's true. I don't see how it lets Chief Torres off."

"First, that story is not corroborated by the physical evidence we collected from the Osprey, nor from its telemetry. I see you disagree. Before you object, know I believe that you remember seven days of experiences. But what if your memories were planted by someone else? Perhaps the chief? Perhaps by a series of untimely accidents? What if our evidence and your memories are both correct?"

"Ever consider that your telemetries are wrong?" Marci asked.

"Anything is possible, but the best theory that ties this all together is that the crew suffered from a collective experience, maybe a joint hallucination. Essentially, you all recall the same set of experiences, each from your own unique perspective."

"No way!"

"Remember, anything is possible. You, however, have an insight that no one else shared. Please, Lieutenant," Morris continued holding up his hand to keep Marci from interrupting, "did you see the chief hit the eject button that sent HJ into space?"

"I did."

"You're the one, perhaps the only, person who can place the chief in position to have caused HJ's death. You're the one person who can help hold him accountable. Just suppose, for a minute, that the chief sabotaged your trip, introduced a hallucinogenic agent through the air, and used suggestive ideas to generate new memories of a trip that never happened. He failed, however, to block your actual memory from his act of killing HJ. You're the only one that recovered from his peyote-induced stupor, in time to see him eject HJ's body into space."

"I suppose, but he may have just ejected HJ's spacesuit into space."

"Really? Do you know that for sure?"

"No," Marci admitted. "Not for sure."

"Help me out here, my good Lieutenant. We're trying to reconstruct what happened. You must think outside the box."

"The box?"

"Yes. All of you are sure your memories are of real events. What if they weren't? What if they were planted? The planted memories may well lead the inquiry. There will be an inquiry to conclude that this was no more than an unfortunate accident. If that happens, justice won't be served. You do want justice to be served, don't you?"

A confused Marci replied, "I do but, I'm not following you. Won't justice be served when the truth comes out during the inquiry? That's when Josh'll be held accountable."

"Are you sure, my naïve dear? The captain and commander don't like HJ. Can they be trusted to let the truth come out? Aren't they more interested in protecting their handpicked crew from scandal?"

"I haven't thought about that."

"Of course not. You've placed too much trust in those two. If they get their way, the chief won't be called into account. Your story as it stands, along with their scrapes and bruises, will just confirm that HJ's death was probably an accident, not a purposeful nefarious act by the chief. You do want justice served, don't you?"

"I do, but your theory is fantastic."

"As is yours and your crew's story."

"Yeah, but—"

"Think about it," JC's voice softened. "You know Torres is very creative and intelligent."

"Yeah, but—"

"And HJ took your affection from him."

"Yeah, but—"

"Look at the emotions you're dealing with now at the loss of HJ. Don't you think that the chief had emotions that were just as powerful when he realized he was losing you to HJ?"

"I never thought of that."

"Hurt, jealousy, anger, pain. These all could drive someone, like the chief, to murder the source of his pain most creatively?"

"I suppose...."

"What he didn't plan on was how much his actions hurt you. What he didn't plan on is that you, with what you saw, are positioned to be HJ's advocate for justice."

"But the story isn't what I—"

"Isn't what you think you saw? My dear Lieutenant, you can't be sure of what you actually saw, can you?"

"I thought I was. But now, I'm not so sure."

"So, the details don't quite match your memories. They'll bring justice to the chief on behalf of HJ, whom he took from you far too soon."

Marci looked down as waves of grief and anger swept over her.

"You and HJ were supposed to grow old together." Morris's voice was gentle. "The chief took that away from you. Shouldn't he be held accountable?"

Marci looked up, "Yes, he should."

"Will you do your part to hold him accountable? Will you be HJ's advocate?"

"Yes, sir. Yes, I will."

Break-in

Shorefront Drive, Channelview, Texas

A dark, non-descript sedan rolled quietly down a street of bayside bungalows. The moonless sky was dark except for the glow of city lights from across the bay. The car passed by Master Sergeant Marc Smith's bungalow and stopped near a bush at the public access to the beach. A figure dressed in black slipped from the passenger side and blended in beside the bush. The car pulled away and drove slowly around the block. It parked two doors away from Marc's residence, facing north. Its driver did not acknowledge the driver of a black SUV parked directly opposite the bungalow. "Charlie 1, this is Charlie 2. I'm in position." The driver spoke into his lapel mike.

"Roger that," he heard in his earpiece.

The darkly clad figure hurried quietly to the beach. He took up a position behind Marc's back porch using a beached kayak as cover. He whispered into his shoulder mike, "Charlie 3 here. I'm in position."

"Roger. The target is still inside, so just relax until I give the word," was the reply.

After a few minutes, Marc walked out his front door, hopped into his classic Jeep Liberty, backed out of the driveway, and drove north. The dark sedan pulled away from the curb and followed the Liberty. "Charlie 1, Charlie 2 here. I'm tailing the target."

"Roger that." The occupant of the SUV replied while rolling his eyes at the unnecessary update. "Charlie 3, you're good to go."

"Roger." Looking around quickly for anyone who might be watching, the dark figure pulled out a handgun, attached a silencer, and shot out Marc's back porch light. He waited a few seconds to see if any neighbors heard the glass shatter and came out to investigate. All was quiet, so he separated from the kayak, and still crouching, made his way to Marc's back porch. He cautiously ascended the steps, picked the lock, and disappeared through the door. Once inside, he laid an array of listening devices and cameras on the kitchen table.

"I'm ready to start, Charlie 1." The intruder set to work.

"You're clear," was the reply from the SUV.

Heading down Seventh Boulevard, Marc was unaware of the dark sedan that was following him. He tapped Hilda's number on his console.

Hilda's voice came over the radio. "Hey, Marc, what's up?"

"Not much. I'm just running a little late and wanted to let you know."

"No worries. I'm running a little behind myself. Do you think we'll have time for dinner before the show?" Hilda asked.

"Good question. I think we can still make it." Marc reached, out of habit, for his phone to check the time. "Oh crap!" He exclaimed.

"Oh crap, what?"

"I left my cell phone at home," Marc felt for his wallet. "And my wallet also."

"I take it you expect me to pay for you as well."

"No way. I'm swinging back to my house right now."

"You don't have to. I'll float you a loan, with interest, of course."

"Very funny. I don't have a choice. Our tickets require two-step authentication. So I need my phone, but it won't take long. I just left the house."

With that, Marc executed a classic "don't try this at home" maneuver. He cut from the outside lane across the three inside lanes of traffic. He could hear tires screeching as he made a U-turn by jumping the median and crossing two lanes of traffic heading in the opposite direction. The driver tailing Marc barely avoided rear-ending the cars in front of him as they braked to keep from hitting Marc. "Charlie 1, be advised that the target flipped a U-turn, and I've lost him for the moment."

"Roger Charlie 2, I'll advise Charlie 3 and keep my eyes open."

"Charlie 3, did you copy that last transmission?"

"I did. I'm ready to test my first couple of plants," the intruder said.

A Houston Police Officer, parked on the side of the road, witnessed the havoc Marc created and flipped on his lights. Fortunately for Marc, traffic didn't clear immediately, so the officer couldn't give chase right away. This allowed Marc to speed up and quickly turn off the boulevard before the light turned red. He passed a strip mall and made a quick turn into its parking lot. Marc then headed down an alley behind the mall and turned onto another alley, leading back to his neighborhood. He killed his lights and turned down another path that led to another alley, which led to a residential street. He stopped his car and waited. He heard no pursuit siren. Marc carefully drove down his street toward his bungalow. Still, without lights, he turned onto the public access path leading to the beach. He thought to himself, *just to be safe, I'll park in back. They won't spot me if they cruise my street.*

"Charlie 3 to Charlie 1 any sign of our target?"

"No, you're still clear. Just hurry it up," the SUV occupant admonished.

Marc parked behind his bungalow with his lights out, hopped out of the Jeep, and bound up the back steps. *That's odd. I know I left the porch light on,* Marc thought. Then he saw the back door ajar. A chill ran up and down his spine. He slowly entered the kitchen. He noticed some electronic gear on his kitchen table as he crept past it. Being careful to avoid the boards that he knew creaked, he rounded the corner to the hallway.

However, being warned by the sound of Marc first mounting the porch stairs, the intruder flattened himself against the hallway wall with a Taser at the ready. When Marc's shadowy figure appeared, he fired.

Marc sensed, more than saw, an initial motion and hit the floor just as the intruder fired. The Taser probes ripped his shirt as they passed over him. Marc leg-whipped the intruder, who fell to the floor with a thud. It's one thing to shoot an ex-Ranger by surprise. It's quite another to face him on the floor with only an expended Taser in hand. Several quick moves and Marc had broken the intruder's nose and almost had him in a sleeper hold. Unfortunately, within the confined space of the hall, Marc couldn't get his position right and felt the intruder slip out of his grip and run for the back door.

"Not so fast," Marc dived and grabbed an ankle. Pulling back and up, he brought his assailant crashing down on the kitchen table. Marc let go of the ankle, squared up, and moved in. As he rolled off the table, the intruder got in a lucky kick to Marc's groin. As Marc doubled over, the assailant grabbed a chair and smashed it against Marc. Marc was able to partially block the blow with his left arm. Despite the pain, Marc drove his shoulder into the intruder's diaphragm. Marc heard the air rush out of his opponent and thought he also heard a couple of ribs crack. Just to be sure, Marc started raining body punches on his opponent. Groaning with pain, the intruder managed to get his hand on his gun. Having forgotten to place the safety on, he accidentally fired a wild shot which he heard ricochet several times before he heard Marc yelp in pain. But Marc's blows didn't let up. The intruder swung his gun, catching Marc behind the ear. A dazed Marc let up, and the intruder once again tried to escape.

Marc wasn't done fighting. He spun his assailant around and slammed the hapless man's head onto the table twice. Then Marc placed his opponent in a sleeper hold. A warning thought worked into his conscience as he thought he heard a crashing noise behind him. Suddenly, Marc felt like he had been struck by lightning as 5,000 volts from a Taser hit him square in the back. Marc rolled off the first assailant, who grunted, "Thanks, Charlie 1. You could've warned me he was home."

"No time to grouse now. Grab your stuff, and let's get out."

Marc's Bungalow

"Wasn't that Jeep out back the same vehicle that was called in for reckless driving earlier?" the responding officer asked Marc, pointing at the Liberty parked on the beach.

"Sir, I'm not sure I know what you're talking about," Marc answered, trying to sound innocent. The police officer looked at him skeptically and was about to speak when he was interrupted by a very agitated NASA Senior Captain. "Good God, man!" Matt's voice boomed. "The Sergeant Major here has been assaulted, shot, and tasered, and all you can think of is a possible traffic report? If you're done here, our security team needs to do a sweep of this house."

"I've seen this dozens of times, Captain," the police officer explained. "This is a simple case where Sergeant Smith interrupted a burglary in progress. The perp ran before he had a chance to take anything. There's no need for all this fuss. Besides, this isn't your jurisdiction."

"It's not what he took. It's what he left behind that has me worried." Matt held up a small listening device. "Like this bug, we found on the kitchen floor. We're looking at an attempt to spy on a NASA employee."

"Suit yourself, Captain," the police officer replied. He handed a card to Marc. "Here's my card with your case number. I'll invite you down to the station to review my report later when you're feeling better. If you have any questions, just give me a call."

"Thank you, officer," Marc replied.

As the police officer left, Marc turned to Matt. "Why would anyone want to bug my house, sir?"

"Not sure, Sarge, but you did right to call me when you did."

"Excuse me, Captain," the leader of the NASA Security team interrupted. "We found two bugs and a camera. Other than that, the house appears to be clean. It'll take us a while to re-secure the front and back doors. Whoever broke in did a number on them. It also looks like the back porch light was shot out. Our scene investigators are on their way. Perhaps it'd be best for the Sergeant to spend the night at the infirmary."

"Sounds good to me," Matt replied. "Be sure the Sergeant gets a bug sweeper before he comes back."

"Do you think anyone would be dumb enough to try this again?" Marc asked.

"I don't know, Sarge. I just know things have gotten strange since we've returned. Hey, where you going?" Matt asked when he saw Marc grab his key fob. "Someone here'll give you a lift to the infirmary."

"I'm going to Gunny's. I need to apologize for standing her up."

Matt raised his eyebrow. "Hold up, Sarge. You're in no shape to drive. I'll drop you off on my way back to the base. Kids, these days," he added under his breath.

Downtown, Houston, Texas

"I've heard of some crazy explanations for being stood up, but this tops the list," Hilda said. The concerned look on her face gave lie to the anger in her voice.

"I'm still a little woozy," Marc took a glass of water from Hilda.

Hilda looked at Marc's leg. "You've been shot!"

"It's just a flesh wound."

"Oh, don't give me that movie-jargon bull. Lie down. I'm going to look at it," Hilda finished by pushing Marc down on the couch.

After fussing and fuming over Marc's leg, Hilda shook her head. "It hardly penetrated your thigh. Must've been a ricochet. You're one lucky dude. Who'd want you dead anyway?"

"This wasn't a professional hit by any stretch. If it were, I wouldn't be breathing right now. No, it was just some guy I interrupted trying to bug my place."

Hilda softened her voice, "You could've called, and I would've come over to your place. It would have been easier."

"Thanks, but the NASA security guys were sweeping my bungalow for bugs, and both doors are busted. It'll take them the better part of the night to finish investigating and securing the place. Hey, I'm sorry for how this whole evening turned out."

"No worries, I'll just order us some Chinese take-out."

"Thanks, Gunny!"

"It's Hilda."

"Thanks, Hilda."

"What's going on? Why is the NSA trying to keep tabs on us?"

"Why do you think it's the NSA?" Marc asked.

"Who else would it be?"

"Not sure, but there's no way this was NSA."

"Why not?"

"Tonight was the work of amateurs. The NSA grunts are strictly professionals. And pretty good ones at that. These guys were way too sloppy and not very good fighters. I had the first one taken down when the second one zapped me. Yeah, these clowns weren't that good. Has to be amateurs or old P.I. wannabe's," Marc said. As an afterthought, he asked, "Have you noticed anything unusual here?"

"Nothing strange. But life hasn't been usual since we've gotten back."

"Meaning?"

"For starters, neighbors that used to say 'Hi,' now just look the other way when I walk by. That story, by the World Enquirer, hasn't helped."

"Which one was that?"

"The headline was 'Bermuda Triangle Strikes Again: Aliens Based in the Bermuda Triangle Capture U.S. Spaceship,'" Hilda said.

"How'd they connect our parking orbit to the Bermuda Triangle?"

"Overactive imaginations, I guess."

"What sucks is, this kind of garbage can't help our careers as serious researchers," Marc said. Then he chuckled. "Think of the headlines if they heard the real story."

Hilda rolled her eyes. "I can see it now: 'Spaceship travels through a wormhole and returns with alien rocks and plants' or 'Spaceship marooned on a mysterious planet for a week.'"

"Looking back, it seems like a dream," Marc said as the food and drink started to relax him. Again, he stretched out on the couch and rested his head on Hilda's lap. "It seems like a dream, but the smells, tastes, and pain all say it wasn't."

Hilda stroked his hair. "Why'd you really come over, Marc?"

"I just wanted to see a friendly face and share a moment, I guess."

"Is that all?" Hilda asked with a wistful smile.

Mild snoring was Marc's only response. Hilda's smile broadened. She gently slid Marc's head on a pillow. She removed his shoes and covered him with a blanket. Her lips brushed his forehead as she pulled the blanket under his chin. She turned out the light and retired to her room. In the vacant apartment, across the street, listening equipment faithfully recorded the sounds of Hilda preparing for bed, just as it had the conversation she and Marc shared earlier that evening.

Fallout

Coffee Shop, Baytown, Texas

"ASTRONAUT ASSAULTED BY BURGLAR," read the headline of the newspaper that had just been slammed to the table. The man responsible for abusing the newspaper shook his head, trying to control his anger.

"What were you thinking?" the agitated inquirer asked of two rather sheepish men sitting at the table.

Though of average height, the stout red-haired inquirer seemed to tower over his two acquaintances. Thomas McIntyre was a reporter for the World Enquirer. His Scottish heritage was thought to be the source of his skepticism and stubborn pursuit of answers. He liked to think of himself as a relentless pursuer of the truth. That persistence drove Tom to sometimes use less than ethical techniques. His former employer, the New York Tribune, grew tired of defending him against defamation lawsuits. This led him to work for his current employer.

Featuring headlines such as "Psychic Predicts the World Will End in 2075" or "Ape Boy Discovered in the Amazon Rain Forest," the World Enquirer wasn't regarded as a prestigious news source. No Pulitzer prizes ever came from the World Enquirer. But Thomas, author of the "Just the Truth Zone" column, hoped he would catch that one good scoop that would return him to favor with his old boss. So far, things were not going as planned.

"We're just doing what you paid us to do," one of the men answered.

"Breaking and entering assaulting an astronaut," Thomas said, "I don't recall telling you to do any of that. I do recall saying not to call attention to yourself. What were you thinking?"

"We're just trying to get eyes and ears on Smith like you wanted."

"That worked out well. Look at you, George. What did he do? Take you to school with a baseball bat?"

"Hey, cut me a little slack. Smith's tail lost him, and he surprised me."

"I'll say he did. Put some sunglasses on and stay out of sight for a while. Next time, hire some decent help."

George shrugged. "You get what you pay for. There's no way we can get decent help on the budget you've given us."

"Who'd you get anyway?"

"Got this great deal. They're all volunteers. All we need to cover our expenses and equipment. They belong to the 'Area 51 Watch Group.'"

"The what?"

"Area 51 Watch Group. They're die-hard believers who think that the government has been communicating with aliens for years, and all the evidence is being hidden in Area 51. All we had to do was suggest that aliens might be involved in the Osprey mishap, and they were all over it. So many volunteered, we had to hold interviews and turn some away."

"All it takes is one of them to leak what we're doing, and the show's over. Not to mention your contract," Thomas said.

"Not to worry, boss. These guys are crazy committed. It's like a cult. They can be tossed in the slammer for life, and they'll never squeal. You can count on it!"

"You better count on it, or you could lose your P.I. license and trash my future. You screwed up big time."

"Maybe not as bad as you think, boss. I almost forgot to give you this," George handed Thomas a flash drive.

"What's this?"

"It's a copy of a fascinating conversation that occurred at the second target's apartment. Trust me."

"Do I even want to know how you got it? Did you break into her apartment, too?"

"Didn't have to. We rented one across the street and set up a first-class directional surveillance operation."

"What's the cost?"

"It's high, but this is good stuff."

"It had better be. I'm off to see my editor. Not looking forward to that little chat."

World Enquirer Building, Houston, Texas

Thomas was right to be concerned about meeting with his editor.

"Have you seen the latest headline ticker?" his red-faced boss demanded. "Astronaut assaulted and shot in his own home." Or this one, "Astronaut fights off intruder," or even better, "Manhunt underway for burglars who shot astronaut." You said your P.I. would be discrete. Is this your idea of discrete?"

A contrite Thomas began, "No, sir, it isn't—"

His editor interrupted, "You're risking what remains of your career and this newspaper's reputation. Why are you so hell-bent on dogging Sergeants Smith and McDermott?"

"Call it a hunch. There's something odd about this Torres court-martial. Why aren't McDermott, Smith, Maalouf, and for that matter, their captain testifying?"

"Maybe the case is so tight their testimony isn't needed."

"Maybe, maybe not. Either way, I'm positive that more happened on the Osprey than anyone's saying."

"Why aren't you also after the captain and the commander?"

"They both live on the base. It's too risky trying to get ears on them," Thomas explained.

"You may call it a hunch, but I'm beginning to think it's a little crazy. You're supposed to write headlines, not make them. Reign your guys in before this 'investigation' goes any further south than it already has."

"This wasn't what I envisioned when we started. But when you hear what I've got on this flash drive, you'll find it in your heart to forgive me."

"This better be good."

"Oh, it's good. Trust me."

"What's this little 'investigation' costing, anyway?"

"You won't like the price, but you'll agree that it's worth it once you hear what's on that flash drive."

Thomas was right on both counts.

Johnson Space Center, Houston, Texas

Later that evening at NASA, Admiral Robinson glared around the room. Assembled in front of him was the crew of the Osprey, except for Josh, who was seated by himself in prison. Lewis leaned against a table behind and to the right of Robinson, with arms crossed.

"Here's the latest from the World Enquirer website: 'Alien Rocks and Plants Return from Mysterious Planet with the Osprey.' Oh, and here's a sidebar: 'How to Survive a Trip Through a Wormhole.' Any idea how the World Enquirer got such ideas?" Robinson asked.

"You know these tabloids, Admiral," Matt replied. "They'll make up just about—"

"Not this time, Captain," Robinson cut him off. "This is too close to the story you all concocted. If someone is trying to mess with me, I'll have their head!"

Marc flushed at the exchange. He was already thinking hard. *Had someone overheard his conversation with Hilda?* He and she exchanged looks.

Robinson said, "Listen to this: 'A source close to the investigation confirmed that more happened during that fateful day onboard the Osprey. Stories of it passing through a wormhole and being marooned on the surface of a strange planet are circulating at NASA.' You know that tabloid blogs pay for stories like this all the time. If any of you think you'll make a quick buck without sacrificing your career, you'd best think again."

"It said, 'a source close to the investigation', Admiral," a heated Matt retorted. "It didn't say an astronaut. We aren't close to your damned investigation. If I were you, I'd check on your own lackeys, er, investigators, first, before coming around here and accusing my team of impropriety, sir."

Matt's indignant outburst stunned Robinson into momentary silence.

Lewis jumped in for damage control. "Uh … Admiral, I'm sure the captain here is just as frustrated by this breach of trust, aren't you, Captain?" He looked at Matt.

"Oh yeah, yes, sir," Matt said. "My whole team signed non-disclosure forms. They understand that anyone who breaks the agreement is subject to severe consequences. You can be sure, sir, that if I discover anyone from my team leaked anything, you'll be the first to hear."

Robinson said, "I appreciate your passion, Captain. I guess I can overlook that little outburst if I have your word that you'll help find and bring to justice the guilty party."

"You have my word, sir. I'll bring a SWAT team down on the perps if necessary."

"Very well, carry on." The admiral rose and left the room.

Lewis let out a sigh, "Okay, let's break it up. There's work to do."

As Lewis walked out, Marc caught up with him. "Sir, may I speak with you, in private?"

"Sure, Sarge, but shouldn't you talk with your captain first?"

"I would, sir. But you didn't promise to rat out the leaker. Captain Dirksen did."

Court-martial

General Court-Martial – Day 1, Case for the Prosecution

Josh surveyed the courtroom. The stuffy room smelled a little of old books and furniture polish. The morning sunlight played ominously off the wooden floor. The time had come for opening statements. He turned his attention to the stumpy Prosecutor, and his heart began to race.

Lieutenant Bitters wiped his forehead and turned to face the jury. "The prosecution intends to show that Chief Petty Officer Joshua Torres purposefully, and with malice, did murder Lieutenant JG Homer Jaeger. 'What?', you say. 'How can a member of the U.S. Space Corps perpetrate such a dastardly act upon a fellow astronaut?' I had trouble believing this myself, at first. But, once I viewed the evidence, I had a change of heart."

Bitters took a breath and wiped his brow. "During this court-martial, you will discover that the evidence shows, beyond a reasonable doubt, that Chief Torres had motive, opportunity, and the wherewithal to kill Lieutenant Jaeger. Furthermore, this was not a simple crime of passion. It was premeditated. The evidence will prove that Chief Torres carefully planned and executed this crime. If I may, I would like to refer to our deceased Lieutenant as HJ. That's how his friends knew this vibrant young officer."

Bitters stepped closer to the jury. "Now, the defense will attempt to spin some kind of tall tale involving wormholes, suit malfunctions, and equipment failures. But they have no physical evidence to support their fantasy. We, on the other hand, have clear physical evidence to support the fact that Chief Torres disabled the crew, hid his ship from view, murdered HJ, and disposed of his body!"

Josh sat ramrod straight, listening to his accuser. His stoic appearance belied his inner turmoil. Thoughts kept flying through his head. *What was I thinking in waiving my Article 39 hearing?*

The Prosecutor was thoroughly warmed up. He continued with passion, "Let's walk through what we intend to prove. First, let's consider the motive. It began with an age-old emotion: jealousy. The chief was madly in love with Lieutenant JG Marci Gonzalez. They were in flight school together, spending many hours alone in the flight simulator. Then HJ entered the picture, stealing Lieutenant Gonzalez's heart away from the chief."

Joshua winced. *That's not how it was exactly,* he thought. *Who am I kidding? That is the way it was. It just sounds so bad, the way he says it.*

"But there's more," Bitters continued. "There was a training accident that cost the chief the vision he needed to complete flight school. To this day, he blames the accident on HJ."

Josh's heart beat a little faster. *Not true! I've moved on, I think. I've tried.*

"Now, let us touch on opportunity: opportunity and premeditation. The chief found himself in the lucky position of being the Technical NCO for the Osprey. With this position of trust came the ability to control the whole ship, including its cloaking device. Oh wait, was it luck? It's been said, 'we make our own luck.' It sure looks like the chief did just that. After washing out of flight school, he became a Non-Commissioned Officer specializing in computers, simulators, and flight control. He pursued a relationship with Captain Matthew Dirksen. He managed to get the captain to select him for his position on the Osprey...."

Josh winced as the Prosecutor continued to detail how much control he did have over the ship. *Wow, he's making it sound like I set all this up. The captain pursued me, mentored me. This isn't the way things went at all,* he thought hard. *Where's the captain? I don't see him here. I haven't heard from him at all.*

"Moving on to wherewithal. Our investigation uncovered the fact that the chief had access to a powerful airborne hallucinogen from the peyote family. A hallucinogen that leaves its victims in a helpless state, totally open to the power of verbal suggestions."

No way! Josh thought. *Just because I've traveled to a region that has that form of peyote doesn't mean I ever even touched the stuff.* He leaned over to say as much to his Defense Counsel, who brushed him off with a hand gesture.

Why did I ever listen to this guy anyway? Josh thought. *"Don't worry, I've got a plan, just trust me," he said. I did, and now I'm screwed.*

"We also uncovered the fact that the chief discovered and used an undocumented cloaking device as the perfect cover for his scheme. We know this because we found the cloaking switch, toggled on."

Josh thought *I didn't even know it could work. I only toggled that switch on to get the Osprey thrusters to work as we needed.*

Josh's stomach churned as he heard the Prosecutor reveal his hacking into the main computer and changing the flight plan. *How'd they figure that out? Why'd the captain tell them about that? He's hanging me out to dry.*

General Court-Martial – Day 1, Case for the Defense

After the Prosecutor finished, the gaunt Defense Counsel, Lieutenant Hinsdale, rose to his feet. With a self-important air, he faced the jury.

"You've just heard an impassioned speech by the Prosecution. He spoke to motive, opportunity, and wherewithal. He wants you to believe the chief, in fact, murdered our sadly departed Lieutenant. It's an imaginative story and very … uh … plausible. But, it leaves out one important fact. There's no body. Where's the body? Without a body, how can we determine the cause of death? The lieutenant could have died through a simple spacesuit failure. Perhaps he took his own life. Is he even dead? Maybe the chief did kill him. But we'll never know because we can't examine the body."

Josh watched his smug Defense Counsel. *He made it sound so simple. "No body, no case," were his exact words. I was a fool. I should have known by his manner. He's too full of himself. He was the only person who seemed to believe my story. Bet that was all for show.*

Hinsdale said, "It's true we cannot prove that the chief did not kill Lieutenant Jaeger."

Lieutenant Hinsdale missed the odd expression crossing the Judge's face as he continued, "But neither can the prosecution prove, beyond a reasonable doubt, that the chief did kill him. Let me remind you that you can only find the chief guilty and sentence him to death if you believe it beyond a reasonable doubt. Thank you."

Josh shook his head involuntarily as the full meaning of this trial settled in.

Maynard sat down with a self-satisfied expression on his face.

The Judge gave him a questioning look and asked, "Is that it, Counsel?"

"That's it, your Honor," he replied, crossing his arms.

The Judge shook her head. "The court will recess for lunch and reconvene at 1400 hours to hear our first witness."

Everyone rose as the Judge retired to her chamber. Josh turned to his Defense Counsel and asked, "Who's side are you on anyway?"

Hinsdale smiled condescendingly. "Not to worry, Chief. My plan is beginning to come together quite nicely. Just trust me."

"It would be easier to trust you if you'd share your plan with me," Josh said.

"In due time, Chief. In due time."

As the courtroom began to clear, Josh stood and thought, *this sucks. After what I just heard today, even I'd vote myself guilty.*

General Court-Martial – Day 1, Damning Testimony

Josh sat stoically at the table for the defense. Inside he was numb. The roller coaster of emotions from the morning's opening statements left him drained. He passed on lunch. He didn't think he could hold it down.

How much worse can this get? Josh thought. As the Prosecutor called his next witness of the afternoon to the stand, Josh looked at his defense lawyer, who was texting and smiling. *Wow. Does he even care what is going on here?* The Prosecutor's voice brought Josh's attention back to the trial.

"Captain, please explain your role in this investigation to the Court."

Allen said, "I'm the CSI's chief investigative officer assigned to this case, sir."

"So far this afternoon, we've heard testimony from a variety of expert witnesses. I'm going to recap their testimony with a series of statements, Captain. Based on your review of the evidence and personal experience, please confirm if each of these statements is correct."

"Yes, sir."

"Did the telemetry readings on the Osprey match the observations of flight control?"

"Correct."

"Is it correct that though the ship disappeared for seven hours, it did not go anywhere according to the telemetry?"

"Correct."

"Is Chief Torres the only crew member who has the knowledge and ability to hack the Osprey's console control and activate the cloaking device to hide the Osprey?"

"Correct."

"Is the chief the only crew member to travel to the area in South America where he could obtain the potent form of peyote that was found onboard the Osprey?"

"That's correct."

"A form of peyote was introduced into the air system and disabled the whole crew except for the chief?"

The Judge looked at the Defense Counsel as if expecting an objection. None was offered.

"Correct."

"How do you know the chief was unaffected?"

"The chief's O2 tank is the only one that was used. It was used for about ten minutes."

"We also heard from an expert who testified that this variety of peyote leaves people open to suggestion. Does your research agree?"

"It does. The suggestion could be verbal or visual."

Josh looked over to his counsel and thought, *I've got a bad feeling. I'm getting set up to take the fall, and this guy doesn't even give a rip.*

Bitters continued. "It looks like the chief had the opportunity, but did he have the means? Captain Allen, did you find a weapon?"

"Yes, sir. Gunnery Sergeant McDermott's sidearm was found on the cabin floor, just outside the portside anti-chamber doorway."

"The same anti-chamber from which Lieutenant Jaeger's body was ejected into space?"

"That's correct, sir."

"Was it fired?"

"Yes, sir, twice."

"Any evidence that the chief could have fired the weapon?"

"Yes. Gun powder residue was on the chief's sleeve, and his fingerprints are on the gun."

"Did you find any bullet holes in the ship?"

"No, sir."

"Did you find evidence that anyone was hurt?"

"Yes, sir."

"What did you find?"

"We found blood on the portside exit portal floor. DNA testing confirmed that it's Lieutenant Jaeger's blood."

"Where are the bullets, Captain?"

"In the lieutenant's body, I suppose."

The Judge looked at the Defense Counsel waiting for an objection, based on speculation by the witness. However, the Counsel was too engrossed in his portable device to notice.

The Judge said, "Strike the last answer from the record as it is merely speculation."

"Thank you, Captain. No further questions," the Prosecutor said.

The Judge said, "Any questions from the Defense?"

The Defense Counsel looked up. "Ah, no questions, your Honor."

Josh's mind raced as the Prosecutor called an old flight school classmate to the stand. *When did I ever use Gunny's Glock?* He thought. *It all happened so fast. We were struggling with the beast; she tossed me her Glock. Yes, I remember, but did I use it? I must have, with powder traces on my sleeve. I just can't remember.* The Prosecutor's voice brought Josh back to the court. "I'm calling Lieutenant Hank Garrison to the stand."

Once Garrison was sworn in, the Prosecutor handed him several sheets of paper. "We've just heard a former witness testify that Chief Torres blamed the training accident that cost him his career as a pilot on HJ. That witness further confirmed that HJ took the chief's place as Lieutenant Gonzalez's love interest. Jealousy and pain are strong motivations for murder—"

"Get to the point, Counselor," the Judge said.

"Ah, yes, your Honor." Bitters Turned to the witness. "Please describe the documents you hold in your hands."

"These are printouts of two text messages, sir."

"To who are they addressed, and who sent them?"

"They are addressed to me. They were sent by Chief Torres."

"Do you recall receiving these texts electronically?"

"I do, sir."

"Read the first one to the Court, please."

Garrison read, "I'd love nothing more than to shoot HJ and blast his body into space!"

"Now, the second one."

Garrison read, "Right now, blowing HJ away would feel so good!"

"Do you remember receiving these texts?"

"Yes, but we were only trash—"

"Just answer yes or no, please."

"Yes."

"Your Honor, I'd like to enter these texts into evidence."

Hinsdale frowned and whispered to Josh, "You never told me about these texts."

"I don't remember them," Josh whispered back.

Hinsdale spoke up, "Objection, your Honor. This evidence was never provided to us during the discovery phase."

"Counsels approach," the Judge said.

Once they were in front of the Judge, Bitters said, "It's included in the discovery package sent to the Defense, your Honor. It's on page 127."

The Judge frowned at Hinsdale. "Well?"

"I must've missed it, your Honor."

"You may return to your tables. Objection overruled. Does the Defense wish to cross-examine the witness?"

"The Defense has no questions, your Honor."

The Judge said, "In that case, we'll adjourn and resume at 0900 tomorrow morning.

The Bailiff called, "All rise." The Judge rose and left the courtroom. Although Josh and his attorney stood, their conversation wasn't over.

"That's it?" Hinsdale said. "I'm busting my butt, and you just happened to forget that you texted a threat to kill Jaeger. What're you thinking? That could seal the case against you."

"I remember now, Lieutenant. It was nothing really."

"'I'd love nothing more than to shoot him and blast his body into space,' is nothing?"

"We were trash talking. That's all, I promise. The three of us were playing the Virtual Reality game 'Asteroids & Aliens.' HJ was beating the tar out of both of us. We were just trash-talking. Garrison was texting back worse things. Nobody mentioned that."

Hinsdale scowled.

"The timeline's all wrong," Josh said. "Those texts were sent long before the training accident. There must be something you can do. Recall Garrison as a witness. Ask how long ago those texts were sent. Ask how his return texts read. Explain how it was just innocent trash talk."

"Too late. I've already dismissed the witness."

Josh wanted to say more, but the guards stepped up to accompany him to his cell.

As they started to leave, Hinsdale said, "Looks like the noose is tightening around your neck. But don't fear, I've got an idea on how we can loosen it."

"What's your idea?"

"I'll drop by later. Trust me."

"Easy for you to say. It's not your neck that's in the noose."

Back in his cell, Josh thought, *How do I trust a guy that doesn't seem to know what he's doing? Worse yet, he doesn't seem to care about what'll happen to me. Nor does anyone on my crew. Why haven't I heard from any of them? It's not right. Well, maybe it is. After all, it's my fault HJ's dead. They probably think it's what I deserve.* As Josh lay on his cot, his thoughts grew darker and filled his mind.

Good Cop Bad Cop

Base Detention Center, Interview Room A

Josh was physically ill. He felt helpless, abandoned to face a false murder charge. He was seated in an interview room, part of the detention center. Across the metal table from him sat both Hinsdale and Bitters. Before him on the table lay an unsigned plea agreement. For the last half hour, Hinsdale was encouraging him to sign the document.

You're playing the part of "good cop." Now I know why you were so disinterested in court earlier, Josh thought. *You had no intention of mounting a defense. You were planning on making a plea deal the whole-time you son of a—*

Hinsdale's words interrupted Josh's train of thought. "Chief, are you with me? Don't you understand this is your best chance to live?"

"I'd like to speak with my captain, if I may," Josh replied. *This can't be happening. The captain will know how to make it right,* he thought.

Lieutenant Bitters spoke up, "Look, Chief, you and I both know your captain hung you out to dry. Your own attorney couldn't prevail upon either him or Commander Maalouf to testify on your behalf."

Hinsdale said, "He's right. I did my best, but none of them wanted any part of this trial."

Josh felt another wave of nausea sweep over him. Seeing his comments were hitting home, Bitters pressed harder. "Think about it. Many commissioned officers would kill to be the tech officer for your

242

captain. But he chose you. Why? I'll tell you why. Commissioned officers look after each other. Your captain wanted to do something that wasn't by the book. Like, hack into the main Space Station Freedom's computer and change a flight plan, right?"

Josh just stared blankly. Seeing no response, Bitters continued. "He chose you, a non-commissioned officer, rather than risk the career of a commissioned officer. If something went sideways, you're left holding the bag. What's worse, you're about to be convicted of murder. Your life is at stake, and no one has your back."

Josh tried to focus. He felt alone and unnerved. *Why hasn't anyone on my crew tried to contact me?* he thought. He said, "I need some time. Let me read this again and think about it."

Bitters said, "Time is something you don't have. I want a signature before I leave."

Sounds just like a bad cop ploy. The thought didn't help him feel better.

"Now wait a minute," Hinsdale intervened. "Let's give this young man a chance to sleep on it. No point in rushing things along, is there? How about giving him a couple of days?"

"No."

"Come on, Captain, give the chief a break. After all, he's signing up for life in prison."

"Okay, I'll give you two days. My star witness testifies tomorrow. You have until 1700 on Friday to sign. After that, the deal's off."

"Sounds reasonable," Hinsdale said.

"You have two days. Try and talk some sense into the chief." Bitters stood and walked out the door.

Josh slumped in his chair, feeling empty inside and very much alone.

Biker Bar

Bruce's Biker Bar, Houston, Texas

A beer mug shattered against the sooty fireplace. The sound caused a brief silence to fall over the raucous biker bar. Looking toward the bar to see who hurled the projectile, the crowd saw no fight breaking out between a dejected NASA captain and his commander. So they returned to their business, and the noise level resumed its former ear-piercing volume.

"What's up, sir?" Marc asked, trying to act like nothing happened as he and Hilda McDermott joined the two.

"Not much," Barnabas answered. "We're just buying beer mugs as we finish our drinks."

"Over-indulging a little, are we?" Marc eyed the dejected captain, who so far had not even acknowledged their presence.

Barnabas replied, "We started with a boilermaker, and it's been downhill ever since."

"I didn't know the captain drank," Hilda observed.

"Usually doesn't, but today's special," Barnabas replied.

"How so?" Hilda asked.

"My cousin videoed the chief's court-martial with a hidden camera and sent us a copy to view. It's pretty ugly."

"How'd he do that?" Marc asked. "Not just anybody can get in. Even we were shut out."

"My cousin happens to be a chaplain for NASA," Barnabas said. "As such, he's allowed certain leeway and access that the rest of us don't get."

"So, let's see it," Hilda said.

Matt lifted his head from the bar. "They're throwing the book at him. They claim he smuggled peyote on board, drugged us up, and induced a mass trance. He then fed us a story about landing on a strange planet to cover up killing Lieutenant Jaeger."

"That doesn't make any sense," Hilda said. "We were lost for a whole week. In my debriefing, they even said we disappeared."

"They claim it was only for seven hours, not seven days." Barnabas handed her a smart card. "Here, watch for yourselves."

Both Hilda and Marc's faces grew dark as they watched the proceedings.

"It gets even better." Matt tossed down an official-looking document. "Here's a copy of Lieutenant Gonzalez's deposition. In it, she states she saw the chief kill Lieutenant Jaeger, then eject him, in his spacesuit, into space!"

Hilda said, "That's not right! We need to do something."

Marc agreed. "We do! Besides smashing beer mugs, what do you plan to do, sir?"

"I may be drunk, but I still recognize insubordination, Mr. Smith."

"Here, Captain," Barnabas interjected, "let's try a new drink. Bartender, two Arnold Palmers over here, please."

"Arnold Palmer? Sure, I'll have one. Is it any good?" Matt asked.

"It's special. You'll like it," Barnabas assured. Under his breath, he leaned to a puzzled-looking Marc and winked. "It's half iced tea and half lemonade. No booze."

Marc smiled.

"We need to testify on his behalf," Hilda demanded.

"Already tried to get to the defense lawyer. He refused to even see me." Matt stated. "I also sent an eNote to the judge asking for an audience and permission to testify. But she refused. Said it violated protocol if the Defense or Prosecution didn't authorize it."

Marc's face flushed with anger. "Kangaroo Court — that's what it sounds like to me!"

"That's exactly what it is," Matt agreed. "And here's how it's going down. I'm guessing they tricked the chief into signing a waiver to an Article 32 Hearing."

"A what?" Marc asked.

"It's a formal pretrial investigation, kinda like a Grand Jury for civilians," Matt answered. "This is happening so fast; I'm sure the Article 32 Hearing was waived. No one in the chief's position would do that if they knew how important it is. Has anyone gotten in to see him?"

Everyone shook their head no. "Don't bother trying," Barnabas said. "We're all on the 'don't let them visit' list, by order of Admiral Hornsby."

Matt said, "Hornsby is out to throw the chief under the bus. I'm sure he's stacked the jury and the judge with people beholden to him."

"I heard that the judge Admiral Hornsby wanted is recovering from surgery," Barnabas said. "The judge he got is a by-the-book, no-nonsense Vice Admiral. She'll kick butt and take names. That might be worth something."

Matt said, "Maybe, but the Hornsby team'll be careful to play by the book. They won't trip up on a technicality."

Hilda said, "Isn't that still risky? Even with a stacked jury, if there's reasonable doubt?"

Barnabas said, "Good point. Hornsby will leave nothing to chance."

Matt said, "According to Admiral Carter, James Morris is behind all of this. Hornsby is just the frontman. Their team has two plays. First, they'll get the chief to agree to a plea deal that puts him behind bars for years, if not life. I bet they've already started."

"How?" Hilda asked.

"They've isolated the chief, especially from us. Then the prosecutor gives a blistering opening statement calling for a murder charge. You just saw part of it. He designs it for maximum effect on the chief, not just the jury.

"That's certainly what he did today," Barnabas agreed.

"I heard from a friend that the defense's opening argument was lame," Marc added.

"Yeah, Sarge, we just saw that part before you came. 'Lame' is generous," Barnabas said.

"Tonight, I figure that the prosecutor and defense attorneys will play good cop/bad cop with the chief. Somewhere in that conversation, a plea bargain agreement will surface, and the chief will be given, at most, a day or two to sign," Matt said.

"If he doesn't?" Hilda asks.

"Tomorrow, they'll introduce their star witness," Matt said.

"That being?" Hilda asked.

"Lieutenant Gonzalez," Barnabas replied. "She's so mad at Josh she'll be manipulated to saying anything. And who's going to argue with a grieving girlfriend?"

"I'm guessing the chief will crack after her testimony," Matt sighed.

"If he doesn't crack? What then?" Hilda asked.

"Then they'll go with their second option. They continue the case and convince the jury Torres is guilty of murder, with the help of the defense attorney," Matt answered.

Marc said, "No way! You're saying the defense attorney will throw the case?"

"Yes, way. If we can't get in and testify on his behalf, and with the power of Gonzalez's testimony, he'll fry," Matt said.

Barnabas shook his head, "It's a long shot, but I have an idea."

"So, do I." Matt started for the door. "I need to pay someone a visit."

He stopped when he heard Barnabas say, "You forget I have your keys, Captain. "Hey Gunny, why don't you be the captain's designated driver while I borrow your sergeant here for my idea?"

"Sure, Commander," Hilda caught the keys Barnabas tossed her way. "Say, Captain, why don't we stop for a cup of coffee on the way?"

Barnabas started for the door. "Come along, Sergeant. Oh, by the way, Bartender, I need that whiskey bottle over there."

"There's still over a third of the bottle left," the bartender protested. "You know it's illegal for you to take an open bottle in your car."

"I'll toss it in the trunk. How about trading a couple of Benjamin Franklin portraits for a half-full bottle of cheap whiskey?" Barnabas tossed a couple of hundred-dollar bills on the bar.

The bartender grabbed the bills and slid the bottle to Barnabas. "Works for me."

A Strange Visitor

Base Detention Center, Houston, Texas

The young guard looked skeptically at the immaculately dressed officer in front of him. "I can't allow you to visit the prisoner, Captain Maalouf."

"I don't understand, Sergeant," the tall officer replied with a big smile. "As a prison chaplain, I've never been denied access to a prisoner before."

The guard noted the captain's pristine uniform, complete with stiffly starched collar and cuffs. "Your name is on our list of those not allowed to visit Chief Torres."

"Not-allowed-to-visit list?"

"Yes, sir," the guard replied. "It's the list of those restricted, by order of Admiral Hornsby. Your name is second from the top."

"Where, Sergeant?" The chaplain asked, still smiling.

"Right here, sir," the guard pointed at the name Barnabas Chidi Maalouf. He expected pushback. But the chaplain's unexplained cheerfulness was disconcerting.

The chaplain showed his ID. "That's not me, son. My name is Johnathan Maalouf, not Barnabas Maalouf. Easy mistake, this being such a common name and all."

The voice of the Surveillance Officer sounded in the guard's ear. "Let the chaplain in."

The guard replied, "Yes, sir." To the chaplain, he motioned. "Follow me, sir." Then he turned and walked down the hall.

They stopped at another checkpoint. The corporal attending that checkpoint took Chaplain Maalouf's Bible. "You can't take anything in when you meet with the prisoner."

"What?" the surprised chaplain replied. "I need my Bible to properly discharge my duties as a chaplain."

The guard's voice was firm. "We're under strict orders to not allow anything to be taken in when visiting a prisoner. Besides, the prisoner already has a Bible in his cell."

"Yes. But is it the 'Authorized' version?" the chaplain asked.

"The what?"

"The 'Authorized King James' version," the chaplain pointed to the front cover. "This is, as you can see, the 'Authorized' version. Is the one in the chief's cell authorized?"

"I don't know, sir," the perplexed guard looked toward the surveillance camera.

A voice in the guard's earpiece instructed, "Check for anything hiding in the book. If not, let him keep it, but instruct him to return with it in his possession."

After confirming that there were no hidden papers or weapons in the Bible, the guard returned it to the chaplain. "Be sure and have this with you when you return," the guard admonished in a self-righteous tone.

"Will do, Corporal," the chaplain said as the first guard frisked him from behind.

The chaplain was led through the checkpoint door to a conference room. It was empty except for a plain table, two straight-back chairs, and a surveillance camera positioned over the door. After a brief wait, the door opened, and a smiling Josh was escorted in. His smile faded when he saw that the chaplain was not the Maalouf he expected.

"Do I know you?" Josh asked as his guard stood by the door.

"Never met before, son," the chaplain smiled, extending his hand to Josh. "I'm Captain Johnathan Maalouf, Chaplain."

"I don't remember asking—" Josh began but was interrupted by a slight wag of the chaplain's forefinger.

"I try and get around to everyone under court-martial and share some words from the Good Book," the chaplain showed his Bible. "Here, son, come sit next to me so I can show you a few passages." He took a seat with his back to the guard. Josh shrugged and pulled his chair around beside the eccentric chaplain. Johnathan opened the Bible between them. He placed the bible on the table, so they blocked it from the line of sight of both the guard and the camera over the door

"I appreciate your sentiment, chaplain, but—" Josh was again cut off by a subtle move of the chaplain's finger and an almost imperceptible shake of the head.

"Young man, you need to hear what God's Word has to say about your situation. Let's start with John 3:16 and 17. 'For God so loved the world, that he gave his one and only Son, that whoever believes in him should not perish, but have eternal life. For God didn't send his Son into the world to judge the world, but that the world should be saved through him.' You … uh … see, young man, that now's the time to listen," Johnathan said.

It seemed to Josh that the chaplain was stalling for some reason, but why? Josh decided to play along. "Uh … yes, sir, I'm listening."

"Do you believe?"

The question caught Josh off guard. "I … uh … uh … I suppose so."

"Good, because we're talking about Jesus, our captain," Johnathan said as the guard suddenly slipped out of the room. Then he smiled broadly, "Yes, our captain has a message just for you. Here it is in John 8:32. Lean closer and look here." Josh leaned forward. A carefully folded note appeared from the chaplain's starched cuff and found its way onto the Bible. The chaplain tapped the note with his finger and began to speak again.

Josh palmed the note while the chaplain read, "Then you will know the truth, and the truth will set you free."

Johnathan said, "Remember Jesus, your captain and commander, loves you and wants to set you free. Do you believe that?"

Josh gave him a puzzled look.

"Listen carefully, son. Jesus, (pause) your captain and commander, (pause) loves you and wants to set you free. Do you want to be free?"

"I do, sir."

"Praise God, the truth shall set you free, but you gotta believe!"

Just then, the guard returned and resumed his position.

"My, look at the time, Chief. I must be on my way." Johnathan rose to leave, then turned, holding a business card. "Here's my card. If you ever need to reach me—"

The guard interrupted, "Sir, you mustn't hand anything to the prisoner. I must insist. Admiral's orders."

"I understand. Good day, Chief. May you trust in God's peace and Jesus, your captain." Johnathan allowed the guard to escort him out.

The corporal let him pass the first checkpoint after making sure he still had his Bible. When the chaplain got to the second checkpoint, he noticed several chairs were scattered about the waiting area. "What happened, Sergeant?"

"It's nothing, sir. The NASA fly boy over there's plastered. He staggered up and tried to force his way in to see his aunt Jenny, who he believes is being held here against her will. We had to go to code yellow alert until we controlled him."

"Code yellow alert?"

"Yeah, it means all guards in this area must come immediately to the entrance."

"Looks like he put up a bit of a tussle."

"That he did, sir," the guard smiled.

"Say, isn't he the astronaut that was shot by some burglars?"

The guard took a closer look. "I think you're right, Padre."

"You going to throw him in the clink? Seems kinda harsh after all he's been through."

"Not sure what we're going to do, sir, but he probably earned thirty days confinement."

Loud snores were coming from the reclined figure on the bench. "Too bad I couldn't just take him somewhere to sleep it off. Save you guys a bunch of paperwork and all. Well, good day, Sergeant." The chaplain began walking toward the front door.

"What?" the guard asked into his mike. "Yes, sir, are you sure? Yes, sir. Oh Chaplain, sir, I need you to come back for a moment."

The chaplain returned to the guard. "Is there a problem?"

The guard said, "No, sir. We just got word from our Commanding Officer that he is on his way over here with some high-profile reporter. Maybe it would be best all the way around if our flyboy, over there, wasn't here when our CO arrives."

The chaplain smiled. "No worries. I'll see to it."

The chaplain walked over to where the man, in a NASA jumpsuit, lay. It took the help of one of the guards to get the drunk on his feet. He leaned heavily on the chaplain as they moved toward the door. "Whew," the chaplain said, "he sure tied one on."

"You're telling me." The guard held the door open. He watched the duo walk slowly toward the street. The man in the jumpsuit broke into an off-key version of "99 Bottles of Beer on the Wall." The guard shook his head and re-entered the building.

Johnathan struggled to keep them both on their feet. "You truly out-did yourself, Sarge. How much did you drink after all?"

"Not as much as you'd think, Chaplain," Marc Smith said. "I mostly swished it around in my mouth and poured it on my clothes."

They turned a corner. Being out of sight, the duo sat on a bench and started to laugh. "Could have fooled me," Johnathan said. "I think you did more than just swish some whiskey around in your mouth."

"I suppose I did swallow some in the process," Marc admitted. "But I remember you telling me to make it real."

"So, I did, Sarge, so I did." Johnathan got up to leave. "You okay?"

"Yeah," Marc answered. "The commander will swing by and pick me up in a few."

Johnathan said, "I must be off, Sarge. Tell my cousin 'Hi' for me."

"Will do, sir, and from all of us, thanks."

Back in his cell, Josh thought about the odd conversation he had just witnessed. *Jesus, my captain? It makes no sense. The only captain I know hasn't even been to see me. Is it possible that captain and commander could be code for Captain Dirksen and Commander Maalouf? If it is, they're a little late to the party.* Carefully he unfolded the note. It read:

"Chief, we want to help, but your lawyer refuses to call us as witnesses on your behalf. Get word to the Judge asking for a civilian lawyer. Tell her your appointed lawyer isn't working and you need a different lawyer. It is your right. We are not allowed to visit you – Admiral's orders. Whatever you do, DO NOT SIGN ANY KIND OF DEAL! The captain is working to help also, but you must get another lawyer and give us a chance to back you up – your friend, Barnabas."

Josh took a deep breath and looked at the plea deal he had almost signed and back at the note. He wondered, *Who can I trust?*

Forgiveness is it Possible?

NASA Base Housing, Houston, Texas

After coffee, Hilda dropped Matt Dirksen off outside Lieutenant Gonzalez's bungalow. He thought it best to see her unannounced, for what he thought could be a difficult conversation.

Marci opened the door to let Matt in. *Wow, she looks awful,* he thought. To Marci, he asked, "How are you?"

"How do you think, Captain? Thanks to Josh, HJ is dead, and quite frankly, life just isn't worth living anymore," Marci said.

"About that...." Matt took a seat across the coffee table from Marci. "That last night on the plateau, things got more than a little crazy. I think Chief Torres did the best he knew at the time. We fought that monster long after it had sucked the life out of poor Lieutenant Jaeger. I've thought about what I could have done differently many times, but I just don't see how we could've saved the lieutenant. We were just too late. For that, I am truly sorry."

"HJ! His name is HJ, Captain!"

"I'm sorry, HJ."

"I'm not blaming you. Josh was there at first. You weren't. It was Josh who's responsible. He turned his back on HJ until it was too late."

"I believe that Chief Torres thought he had a better chance to save you first and then move on to HJ."

"It doesn't matter. Josh needs to pay for what happened!" Marci surprised Matt by the intensity of her outburst.

This isn't going well at all, Matt thought.

Marci frowned. "I know why you're here, Captain. You came because you're unhappy with my deposition."

"Not entirely. I'm here to remind you that you're alive because of the chief. Lieutenant, er, HJ, is dead because he disobeyed my direct orders and ignored the chief's warnings."

"How dare you. How dare you, Captain, speak like that about HJ!"

Matt just looked at her. Marci responded with a defiant glare. Time seemed to creep by. Marci broke the discomforting silence first. "I'm right. You came by as soon as you heard about my deposition. You're unhappy with my story because you just want to keep Josh out of prison."

Matt rubbed his chin, "It's not just Chief Torres I'm worried about. I also want to keep you out of prison."

"I'm not the one going to prison. Josh is headed to prison, and my testimony will see to it that he stays there for a long time."

"Your perjury may or may not put Lieutenant Torres in Leavenworth, but his spirit will be free with a clear conscience. You, however, will put yourself in a much worse place. Sure, you'll walk around like a free person. But, if you don't let go of what happened, your spirit will be trapped in a dungeon of bitterness. Your desire to see Josh suffer won't be satisfied by Leavenworth or any other punishment. If you don't forgive him, you'll be the real prisoner."

"So 'forgive and forget' is your new motto, Captain?"

"No, I'm not saying forget. I'm saying grieve your loss. Be sad for HJ's demise. But forgive Chief Torres and move on."

"Easier said than done. You forget, Captain, that HJ was the love of my life. Now, because of Josh, he's dead. How do I move on from that?"

Matt did not reply.

"Yeah, that's what I thought. You sit there preaching at me about what I should and shouldn't do. But you have no clue what I'm going through. I just want justice served on Josh. Once that's done, I might be able to move on."

"Lying about what happened won't serve justice. You know Chief Torres tried to help save HJ. He was just too late. We were all too late."

"Hold it right there," Marci interrupted. "He chose to pull me out first. If he'd pulled HJ out first, we wouldn't be having this discussion!"

"You're right. You'd both be dead. It was you or HJ. There was no way Chief Torres or the rest of us were going to be able to save you both."

Marci was undeterred. "Besides, how do we know it wasn't really a dream? We don't know for sure that it all didn't happen the way the prosecutor said."

"You're right on one count. The prosecutor has it all worked out, and there is no physical evidence to support what I know happened. Still, I know what we experienced was not a dream. It'll be a cold day in hell before I change my mind!"

"I'm not so sure it wasn't a mass hallucination caused by Josh. I'll do all I can to see justice is served, and Josh pays for what happened to HJ."

Matt said, "Then, this discussion is obviously a waste of time."

"Obviously."

Matt got up to leave. "I just expected a little more loyalty toward another crew member."

"Don't lecture me on loyalty. Don't you dare lecture me on loyalty! Where was your loyalty as Josh was letting HJ die? It sounds to me, Captain ... like you're trying to guilt me into changing my testimony. Is this witness-tampering?"

Matt paused. "No. I'm only asking you to tell the truth. How you testify is totally your call. If you don't tell the truth, I just thank God I won't have to live with your conscience. Remember this, Lieutenant —

whatever you do, Jaeger isn't coming back. I regret your loss. But, I also know that, at some point, you need to accept it for what it is and move on. You think that sending Chief Torres to prison will make you feel better. It won't. Feeling better will only come with time. But time will not begin its healing until you drop your grudge."

"You gave saving Josh's ass your best shot, Captain. But I intend to see justice done."

Matt turned toward her. "You still don't get it. This is not just about Chief Torres. This is as much about you. I know the prosecutor plans to use you to crucify him. That's all he cares about. It doesn't matter to him that you'll wind up as collateral damage. I can't stop him. Only you have that power now."

"Goodbye, Captain."

"Good day, Lieutenant." Matt turned and walked out the door.

Marci watched him leave, her eyes filling with tears. In her mind, she had a nagging sense the captain might be right. But her heart wanted nothing to do with that thought.

Star Witness

General Court Martial - Day Two

Matt entered the quiet chapel. He noticed some candles near the front. He lit one and placed it by the altar, then sat down on one of the pews. He looked up as he heard approaching footsteps.

A tall officer introduced himself, "Captain Dirksen, I'm Chaplain Johnathan Maalouf."

Matt stood and shook the chaplain's hand. "Good to meet you, sir."

"Please sit, Captain," the chaplain also sat down. "How's it going with our young chief?"

"Not well. We, my crew and I, aren't being allowed to testify. Lewis, er, Captain Wright says even if we did testify, the jury would be skeptical."

"Skeptical how?"

"Traveling through a wormhole and living has never happened before. We've no physical evidence to prove that we did. Captain Wright said it was a singular event."

"And the eye-witness testimony of you and your crew is considered faulty?"

"Exactly."

"But, if I understand correctly, the prosecution plans to use the testimony of one witness, over that of four others, against the chief."

"You got it. I spoke to the prosecution's star witness. She's set on taking the chief out."

"I hear witness tampering is a punishable offense." Receiving no response, Jonathan added, "Just kidding, Captain. Didn't mean to offend."

"None taken. I tried to talk some sense into the lieutenant."

"And how'd that go?"

"Not well. It was awkward and combative. I think that I only strengthened her resolve to condemn the chief. If successful witness tampering is my crime, I suppose I'm innocent."

"Sorry to hear, Captain. She could be the final nail in Chief Torres's coffin, so to speak."

"I got the chief into this mess and can't do anything to get him out."

Jonathan nodded. "Looks that way."

"That's it?" Matt shot back. "No words of encouragement? No comments like, 'The man upstairs will make it all work out in the end?'"

"Nope."

"Thanks for nothing. What kind of chaplain are you anyway?"

Johnathan thought for a moment. "One who traffics in the truth. The truth is, you don't need to hear empty clichés. The truth is, you may have screwed up. Truth is, God will work it all out, just not the way you expect, or maybe even want. You tried to help. You spoke truth to the lieutenant in an awkward combative way. Now, it's out of your hands. All we can do is sit on the sidelines, pray, and watch things unfold. There'll be no cheap clichés from me." Johnathan smiled. "Except for the one about 'sitting on the sidelines,' or 'watching things unfold,' or 'God working things out.'" Seeing that Matt didn't smile, Johnathan took a breath and said, "But I can, and will, sit with you."

The captain was silent for a while. "Does praying even work?"

"That depends on what you mean by work," the chaplain replied.

General Court Martial - Day Two, Marci Takes the Stand

In the courtroom, Thomas Jenkins had just taken his seat and opened his notebook. When the Prosecutor stood, Thomas thought, *This trial's a sham. The defense lawyer is disengaged or just downright incompetent.*

"The prosecution calls Lieutenant JG Marci Gonzalez to the stand."

Marci stepped forward and placed her hand on the Bible.

"Do you solemnly swear to tell the truth, the whole truth, and nothing but the truth, so help you God?" the Bailiff asked.

Marci hesitated, then said, "I do."

"Be seated."

She complied.

Thomas thought; *she looks drawn and tired.* He watched her intently. *Her eyes have an almost lifeless hollow look about them.*

"State for the Court your position and role on the crew of the Osprey during its ill-fated journey," Bitters said.

"I was the weapons officer, under the command of Captain Matthew Dirksen."

"And who else was on the crew?"

"Commander Barnabas Maalouf was the pilot. Chief Petty Officer Josh Torres was the Tech Officer. Master Sergeant Marc Smith and Gunnery Sergeant Hilda McDermott were the Tech Specialists."

"Was anyone else on board?"

"Yes, Lieutenant Homer Jaeger was riding jump seat."

"Riding jump seat. What does that mean?"

"It means he was riding as a passenger to Mars."

"Explain your stated mission, Lieutenant," the Prosecutor directed.

"Objection," the Defense counsel said. "That's classified information, your Honor."

The Judge frowned. "Both counsels approach the bench."

As the counsels approached the Judge, Thomas wrote, "Note: the stated mission was challenged for being classified. How could that be? What exactly are they covering up? Possibly a secret mission?"

When they stood before her, the Judge quietly asked the Defense counsel, "What're you thinking, Lieutenant?"

"We were briefed that the actual mission was classified, your Honor. So, we shouldn't speak of it in open Court," Hinsdale said.

The Judge said, "We know the ACTUAL mission was classified. But the Prosecutor asked, 'what was your STATED mission.' That's NOT classified. By objecting, you just let everyone know that there was a reason for this mission other than the one stated. Now, get your head into the game."

As they returned to their tables, the Judge said, "Overruled. You may answer the question, Lieutenant Gonzalez."

"We were to set course for Mars with supplies for Alpha Colony."

Bitters nodded. "Moving on, what was your relationship with Lieutenant Jaeger?"

"We were friends," Marci said.

"You were friends. Were you romantically involved?"

"We were."

"Bitters leaned forward. "Describe, for the Court, the relationship between the defendant and the deceased."

"Objection," Hinsdale interrupted. "There's no body. You can't refer to someone as 'deceased' if you have no body."

"Overruled," the Judge said. "Answer the question."

Thomas noted, *The witness is shifting in her chair and staring at Torres.*

Marci said, "They got along professionally."

"They got along professionally," Bitters repeated. "What about personally? Did they get along personally?"

Marci dropped her head. "No, they didn't."

"Why do you believe they didn't get along personally?"

"The chief was hurt in an accident he thought the lieutenant caused."

"Accident? Was that the very accident that scarred Torres, impaired his vision, and got him washed out of flight school?"

Marci looked down again. "Yes."

The Prosecutor handed Marci a sheet of paper. "Please describe what I just handed you."

"It's a training-accident investigation request."

"The same accident in which the chief was hurt?"

"Yes."

"Who's the requestor for this investigation?"

"Chief Torres."

"It sounds as if the chief was very upset. What emotion would you say the chief felt most strongly?"

Marci paused and looked at Josh. "Anger. He was furious."

"Furious? Was this fury aimed at a person?"

"Yes."

"To whom was this anger aimed?"

Marci took a deep breath. "Toward HJ."

"The chief was very angry, at Lieutenant Jaeger, for causing an accident that caused him great harm. How did that affect your relationship with the chief?"

"I ended our friendship."

Bitters frowned. "You ended it. How did the chief react?"

Marci was silent. "Answer the question, Lieutenant," the judge admonished.

"He was agitated."

Thomas thought; *she's running out of steam. The Prosecutor looks like he's losing patience with her.*

"Before you and HJ became romantically involved, how close were you and the chief?"

263

"We were friends, that's all."

"Are you sure? How do you think the chief felt about you?"

Marci looked at Josh, who blushed and looked down. "Never thought about it."

"So, to be clear, how would you characterize your relationship with the defendant before meeting Lieutenant Jaeger?"

"For me, we were friends and fellow cadets. Close friends maybe, but nothing more," Marci again changed positions on her chair.

Bitters said, "For you maybe. Surely you knew that the chief had feelings for you?"

Marci gave Josh a puzzled look. "No."

Bitters handed Marci a sheet of paper. "Please describe what I just handed you."

Marci said, "It looks like several text messages, about me, written by Chief Torres."

"What do they say?"

Marci read the texts quietly but said nothing. "Answer the question," the Judge said.

Josh winced as Marci read the texts. He felt the color rise in his face as he saw Marci eyeing him. Intently.

Thomas wrote, "Do I see the witness tearing up?"

"From what you just read, how do you think Torres feels about you?"

In a soft voice, Marci said, "He ... uh ... he loves me."

"He does, big time. His love for Lieutenant Gonzalez borders on obsession. Thwarted love, jealousy, anger. These are powerful motives to do harm. It doesn't matter how Lieutenant Gonzalez felt about the chief. What matters is what the chief felt about HJ, the one who stole her heart and ruined his career. Put yourselves in his place. Feel his anger—"

BANG, the Judge's gavel sounded, cutting off the Prosecutor. "You're taking testimony, Captain. Save your assertions for your closing arguments."

"Sorry, your Honor."

"Don't let that happen again, Captain," the Judge chided.

"Let's recap. Lieutenant, wouldn't you say Chief Torres was very angry at HJ?"

"Yes, at one time."

"Angry enough to plot revenge? Angry enough to—"

"Objection!" Hinsdale said. "The Counsel is leading the witness."

"Sustained," the Judge replied.

Thomas thought, *Well, this is the first time the defense counsel is guilty of paying attention.*

"Let me rephrase the question. Were you surprised to see the chief shoot HJ and eject his body into space?"

A hush settled over the room. Marci scowled at Josh. *The time has come to make him pay,* Marci thought. *Why is this so hard?* "That's not what I saw," she said.

The Prosecutor stepped back in surprise. "Not what you saw?" he repeated. "Were you not overheard, by the rescue team, accusing the chief of killing Lieutenant Jaeger?"

"Yes."

"Did they pull you off the chief as you were beating him?"

"Yes, they did." Marci began to shake as the emotion of it all swept over her like a giant wave. She looked at Josh, who looked down, unable to meet her eyes. "Josh didn't shoot HJ."

"Then tell the Court, how did the chief kill HJ?" Bitters asked.

"He didn't kill HJ. Josh just let him die when he could have saved him from that wretched beast!" Marci exclaimed.

"What?" a confused Prosecutor asked.

Marci said, "We weren't in the Osprey. HJ died in a cave because Josh set about saving me without even trying to save HJ. I should've been the one who died, not HJ!"

Thomas noted that Marci struggled to keep her emotions in check. "If he had only tried to help HJ first—"

Suddenly, Admiral Robinson interrupted Marci by violently coughing and gasping. He held his chest and motioned that he couldn't breathe, then started to collapse.

"Objection!" Hinsdale yelled. "The witness is relaying classified information!"

"He's having a seizure!" someone shouted as the admiral slumped to the floor. Several in the courtroom rushed to help the fallen admiral.

"Order, Order!" the Judge exclaimed, banging her gavel. "Bailiff, get EMS here, NOW!"

After EMS arrived, they carried the stricken admiral out of the court, and order was restored.

Thomas's head was spinning at what he'd just witnessed. He thought, *What just happened?* He wrote on his pad, "What cave? What monster? If HJ didn't die in the Osprey, where were they? What is NASA hiding?"

The Judge said, "We've had enough excitement for one day. This court will adjourn until 0900 Tuesday morning." She rose. But, before she turned to leave, she said, "Both Counsels, I want to see you both in my chambers, NOW!"

Change of Lawyer?

In the Judge's Office

Maynard Hinsdale stood at the Judge's desk, shifting his weight from one foot to the other. Next to him stood Captain Bitters, wearing an amused look. The judge was reading something as if she'd forgotten about their presence. Finally, without looking up, she said, "have a seat, Lieutenant. You, too, Captain. I've quite the letter from your client, Lieutenant Hinsdale."

"Is that allowed, Ma'am?"

"It is when your client wants a different lawyer. A civilian lawyer, to be exact," the Judge said.

"A what?"

"A different lawyer. Defendants usually want one when they feel their lawyer is incompetent or is colluding with the Prosecutor. Of course, you wouldn't know anything about that in this case. Would you?"

Maynard bristled. "What do you mean, Ma'am? You can't entertain that request in your Court."

Bitters agreed, "Your Honor, the time for the defendant to ask for civilian representation is before the trial begins. Not now."

"Normally, yes. But I suspect the defendant has valid points. Let's go over a few."

"Now?"

"Sure, now. Consider this my way of informing you that I plan on hearing such a request next Tuesday. First, your client claims that you've ignored requests by his fellow crew members to be witnesses on his behalf. Is this true?"

"No, your Honor."

"Are you sure?"

"Yes, I am."

"Then, why do you suppose his captain, commander, and two Mission Specialists have all expressed their desire to witness on his behalf to my Bailiff?"

"They can't do that," Maynard complained.

"No, they shouldn't have, but I'll ask one more time. Did they contact you asking to take the stand on the defendant's behalf? Yes or no?"

"Your Honor, they don't fit my defense plan."

"Not even as character witnesses?" the Judge's eyes narrowed.

Her look pierced Maynard's confidence. "Uh, no."

"What's your plan?"

"Yes, your Honor. I plan to discredit the prosecution witnesses and establish reasonable doubt."

"Like you did when you cross-examined Captain Allen? Oh, wait. You didn't!"

"Uh ... I mean to discredit the star witness," he said.

"That's it?"

"It's a textbook approach."

"I'd say we've learned the law from different textbooks. I'm asking you one last time. Did the chief's captain and commander volunteer to testify?"

"Yes, Ma'am."

"But they're irrelevant to the lieutenant's approach," Bitters said.

The judge frowned at Bitters, "You would know this because...? Have you two been colluding?"

"The chief is guilty as sin!" Bitters exclaimed. "It's only logical that they can add nothing of value."

"That's not your call, Captain," the judge retorted. "Lieutenant, how do you know Torres's crew is irrelevant? Did you interview them?"

"Uh, no, Ma'am. But I read their debriefing notes."

"Is your security clearance high enough for that?"

"No. I read the redacted versions."

"Don't play games with me, you lazy son of a …." The Judge paused. "Let me get this straight. You've only seen the redacted debrief notes because your security clearance isn't high enough to read the full transcripts. But you don't feel you should trouble yourself to take the time and interview the defendant's crew? Did you also advise the defendant to waive his right to an Article 32 hearing and to skip being present at the pretrial proceedings?"

"Ah, yes, Ma'am."

"So, you pissed away his rights. That's incompetent in anybody's book unless you've been colluding with the Prosecution."

Bitters stiffened, "Your Honor, I resent that implication."

"I'm sure you do, Captain. My question to the lieutenant still stands."

Maynard's face turned red. *How did she know?*

The Judge pressed, "Who selected you for this case?"

"Admiral Hornsby, Ma'am."

"Figures. Do you expect me to believe you're trying to win this case?"

"That's not fair, your Honor," Maynard looked down. The judge sat silent. Her silence caused him to again shift in his chair. He felt exposed and vulnerable.

"I see," she finally said. "You don't plan to win, do you?"

"Ah, your Honor, I think he'd do better with a plea bargain."

"Which you happen to have in your briefcase."

"I'm not at—"

"Don't play games with me, Lieutenant. Show me the plea bargain."

"This is highly unusual, Ma'am," Bitters complained.

"Not if I'm trying to decide to replace your friend here." She nodded toward the briefcase. Maynard handed her the agreement.

"Life in prison. Why would he agree to that?"

Maynard felt the perspiration dripping from his forehead. "Uh … to avoid the, ah … death penalty."

"Which you virtually guarantee by presenting an incompetent defense. I'm moving ahead and ruling on the defendant's request, Tuesday. Bitters, I'm informing you of my intentions now. I'll inform the Jury of my decision when court reconvenes."

"You can't your—"

Her raised eyebrow stopped Maynard mid-sentence. "For the Prosecutor to get the death penalty, he needs either the body or an eyewitness. Of course, I'm guessing that you failed to share this with your client. We all know there's no body. Judging from how today's testimony was going, before that most inconvenient interruption, Bitters lost his eyewitness. A halfway competent lawyer should, at the very least, avoid the death penalty. Possibly even win."

Bitter's frowned, "I didn't lose my eyewitness, your Honor."

The judge shook her head, "I wouldn't bet on it."

Maynard looked dejected. *This is not what JC wants. What do I say to him?* His mind wandered as he saw his opportunity to stay on JC's team fading away. The judge's voice brought him back to reality.

"You have two choices. Contact and depose the chief's crew. Then, show the chief you can mount a proper defense. Or, start looking for other career options as I'll allow the chief to appoint a civilian attorney. I—"

"Your Honor, this is highly unusual," Bitters interrupted.

"Captain, if I find any evidence that you two breached your ethical obligations to give the defendant a fair trial, you'll be looking for a new job as well."

"What about security concerns?" Maynard asked.

"I can hold closed sessions if secret testimony is required."

"But, by Tuesday?"

"Convince Torres to keep you, and I'll consider granting more time to redeem yourself."

"But, our plea bargain, your Honor?" Bitters asked.

The judge frowned. "If you hadn't led him to give away his rights, he wouldn't be open to such a plea deal. This plea that you're pushing on him is no bargain." Remember, no plea bargain, no getting out of doing your duty."

Maynard said, "Ma'am, yes, Ma'am!"

"Now get to it and stop wasting my time!"

When the duo got to the parade grounds, Bitters let out a mocking laugh. "That judge is sure full of herself."

Maynard said, "I think she's not one to trifle with."

"Don't worry about her. Remember, we need to keep JC happy. We do that, and she can't touch us." Bitters looked hard at Maynard. "Whoa, don't be going soft on me now. She can't prove a thing. Just convince Torres you can defend him, and we'll be back on track. Hey, let's go get a drink. What do you say?"

"Sounds good.— Oh crap. I left my cell phone behind. Go ahead. I'll catch up." Maynard bounded back toward the courtroom.

Maynard retrieved his phone, then sat in his chair, pondering what had just happened. *The judge guessed right. I'm not doing my best to defend Torres. But the chief's guilty. JC's group and Bitters are so sure of it. Still, I don't feel right about how this is playing out.* Just then, someone else entered the room. Maynard looked up and saw a tall chaplain.

"Sorry to disturb you, Lieutenant. I left my cell phone behind."

"That's okay, Captain. So, did I."

"Pardon my asking, but are you okay? You look—"

"Beat up?"

The Chaplain shrugged, "Yeah, something like that."

"Do you have a minute, sir?"

"It's Johnathan. Johnathan Maalouf. What's on your mind?"

"Have you ever had a chance to advance your career and be part of a group that most people would kill to join?"

"I'm not sure what you mean, but this sounds like an opportunity with a catch."

"Entrance to this group requires certain … uh … compromises."

"Compromises of conscience, ethics, or laws?"

"Mostly ethics and maybe conscience."

"The group doesn't happen to be the Fireside room clique, is it?"

"How'd you know, sir."

"It's a well-known group. Even your judge knows who they are and how they operate. They're known for taking advantage of anyone who wants to join."

Maynard sighed. "So I found out. That's my dilemma — do the bidding of the group or—"

Johnathan finished his sentence, "Look after the interests of Torres."

"Yeah. What do I do?"

"Ambition is a cruel mistress. And she's knocking at your door. Ask yourself, are you willing to pay her price and keep paying it until you become entirely corrupt? Because if you give in now, it'll continue.

"Does that make me bad?"

"No. It makes you dead. It'll kill your integrity. You'll never be the lawyer you could be. The Fireside room clique is counting on your ambition to keep you in line. So, the question is, do you want your ambition to define you, control you, ultimately corrupt you, or not?"

You have no idea how hard that choice is, Maynard thought.

Two Plus Two

World Enquirer Building, Houston, Texas

The rain pelted the editor's window. He leaned forward, frowning at Thomas, who was lounging on a chair, with his feet resting on the editor's desk. Thomas had just finished outlining a new article he was writing. It cast doubt on the integrity of NASA's effort to prosecute Josh. It accused them of using him as a scapegoat to cover up some embarrassing secret. The problem was, Thomas could not identify what that secret was.

His editor asked, "What do you hope to accomplish? Or are you just trying to piss everyone at NASA off?"

"Look, chief," Thomas said, "they're hiding something. I can feel it."

"What? What are they hiding?"

"Not sure, but they're trying awfully hard to hang this misadventure on Torres."

"Doesn't all the evidence point to that? At least, according to the opening statements?"

"You know the defense has been, by any measure, lame. Color me skeptical."

"What do you know that I don't?"

"It's not what I know, Chief, as much as what they're not saying."

"Like what?"

"Like, why is only one crew member on either witness list? At least use another one or two to corroborate part of the one witness's testimony. Or, if you're the defense, call one or more to support Torres as character witnesses. Why cut them out of the proceedings altogether?"

The editor shrugged, "I don't know. Keep their careers intact if they're not needed."

"Really? What's that coughing fit this morning? It derailed the key witness's testimony right when she appeared to go off-script. And, what monster killed the lieutenant? And, how does a 'dream' become classified?"

"Good questions. They should be followed up," the editor agreed.

"I plan to, Chief. I need to shake down the Prosecutor. I've bought him a few drinks, plus season tickets to see the Rockets play basketball and the Texans to play football. The guy's a real sports fanatic. I know he's holding out on me. I'm meeting him at his favorite watering hole Monday night before court resumes on Tuesday. I'm sure he's about to spill whatever he's hiding. I can feel it. I need to push my P.I. to get more out of the two NASA sergeants. We need to get closer to their conversations. All I need are some details from either source, and you'll have a front-page story in no time!"

A well-timed crack of thunder added emphasis to his bravado.

"For the record, I never heard you talk about giving the prosecutor any gifts. As for the rest of this, tread lightly, Thomas. NASA is still pissed about your 'Stow-away from another planet' article."

"It must have hit close to home," Thomas said. "You know what they say — the truth hurts. If I were way off the mark, NASA would just laugh it off. Instead, they're all hot and bothered. So, my shot in the dark must have landed too close for comfort."

The editor warned, "Like I said, they're pissed at you and this paper."

"That's their problem."

"Your last story got under their skin. Now your latest story questions their integrity."

"You mean like Voltaire saying, 'You know who your rulers are, by knowing who you can't criticize.'"

"Precisely. I know you're aggressive. But, you need to take care. If NASA gets wind you're going down this road, you'll be in their crosshairs."

"Not like that hasn't happened before, Chief."

"Yes, but if you're anywhere close to right, they'll do whatever they can to discredit you. If you cross any legal boundary getting your info, they'll be on you like a hen on a June Bug. Trying to bug that Sergeant's bungalow was stupid. I better not hear about any more antics like that, by your P.I." Thomas's editor paused. "If NASA ever connects the dots as to who's behind what your P.I. did, they'll use it to ruin what's left of your career and this paper. That'll force me to cut the cord and leave you on your own. So—"

"Don't do anything illegal," Thomas completed his boss's sentence.

"Exactly."

"Meaning illegal."

"That's what I said. You'll be on your own."

"Illegal methods, me?" Thomas smiled and stood up. His editor frowned.

Thomas walked to the door. "Don't worry, Chief. It's only illegal if you get caught."

The editor frowned, "That's what I'm afraid of."

Plans Change

Base Detention Center, Interview Room A

Maynard burst through the interview room door. "Great news Chief! The case for the prosecution is falling apart!"

Josh replied, "I gathered that from this morning's session."

"Seriously, I've been working my butt off this afternoon."

"This has nothing to do with you and Bitters being called into the judge's office, does it?"

"What? No, well, maybe a little," the lieutenant admitted. "That's irrelevant. The point is, I have a plan that'll blow you away. I'm sure we can refute enough of the prosecutor's arguments to create reasonable doubt, if not clear you outright!"

"Go on," Josh prompted.

"I've got your captain ready to testify that he ordered you to hack the computer. Gunny agreed to testify that she asked you to fire her gun at some man-eating plant. She also admitted bringing the peyote pods onto the Osprey. I've got your commander to—"

"I want a plea bargain," Josh interrupted.

"No, what? Haven't you been listening? I'm saying we can win this case outright."

"I know. That's why I want to plea bargain."

"You're not making any sense, Chief. What do you hope to gain by pleading away your career?"

"My friends' careers, for one. If they testify, their careers are toast."

"So?" The important thing is to get you off. The judge said—"

The judge said what?"

"Nothing. It's not important."

"Let me guess. The judge said your career is over if you don't actually defend me."

"She did mention something like that. But the point is, we've got a real shot at winning!"

"At my crew's expense. No way. I'll plead guilty before seeing their careers ruined."

"Hey, Chief, no more talk of guilty pleas."

"It's that or a plea bargain. Perhaps the judge will understand if the plea we draw up is lenient enough," Josh suggested.

"Hmm ... that could work," Maynard pulled out his tablet. "Okay, what do you want me to write?"

"For starters, I want an assurance that my crew-mates are reinstated, if necessary, and first in line for future flight assignments."

Maynard rolled his eyes, "Do you want a job also? Maybe a parking space to go with it?" *My career's already toasted; it can't get any worse,* Maynard thought.

"Funny, Lieutenant. I'm just getting started."

Maynard finished the agreement dictated by Josh. *I can't wait to see Bitter's reaction to this little document.*

Officer's Club, Houston Space Center

"Some plea!" Bitters exclaimed. "This reads like a list of demands. 'Reinstate the crew; reduce the charge from murder to negligence; reduce life in prison to five years' service with some obscure non-profit in South

277

America.' Why didn't you also ask to let him cruise the world on a hospital ship? What were you thinking in drawing this up, Lieutenant?"

Maynard fought hard to keep an amused smile off his face. He was amazed at how Bitter's outburst had no effect. Maynard thought *It's surprising how I no longer care what Bitters thinks or says. I suppose it's because at this point, I know there's nothing he can do to help or hinder my career.*

"That's enough, Captain Bitters," Morris said.

Wow, Maynard thought. *Captain Bitters, that's a highly formal way for JC to address you. You must not be as close to him as you led me to believe.*

"Thank you, Lieutenant Hinsdale, for providing us with copies of the plea bargain, along with an overview of how you plan to proceed with your defense."

Maynard said, "You're welcome, sir. I'm only doing my duty as an officer of the court."

Morris continued as if he hadn't just heard Maynard speak, "I understand the awkward position the judge created for you. I also share your desire to protect the state secrets that could be exposed by continuing with this trial. If you would be so kind, Lieutenant," he nodded to the door. "We need to discuss this proposal. Nourish yourself before you leave. On me, of course."

"Thank you, sir." Maynard stood and walked out of the Fireside Hall. Once out, he turned slightly and watched the steward close the double doors. He felt relieved that he was no longer part of the group inside.

Morris looked around the room after the doors closed. "What do you think, gentlemen?"

Robinson said, "It's quite a turn of events. It requires a change in our plans, I suppose."

"It will," Silvertongue agreed. "It pretty much ruins our story if we accept this plea."

Robinson thought for a minute. "We've still got a story. It's just not as good with a clumsy klutz as it was with a true villain."

"I see your point," Silvertongue agreed. "Perhaps we could cast the Osprey's manufacturer as the villain."

"That's good. How?" Morris asked.

Silvertongue smiled, "In their haste to cut corners, they made a defective portal activation lever."

"That could work," Morris said.

Robinson agreed. "I can work with that. I must say, JC, you're taking this change quite well. I mean, given that the chief's responsible for your nephew's demise."

"Thank you, Dennis," JC said. "But I believe the chief will still be held to account."

"Whoa," Bitters interrupted. "I can't believe you're all giving up so easily. I've got this case won. It's in the bag."

"Sorry, Captain, but you have no witness; thus, you have no case," Morris said.

Bitters insisted, "I still have a witness."

Morris disagreed. "No, you lost her when she ran off-script. She'll testify that HJ was killed in a cave by some monster. I can see it coming."

"I can flip her back, sir. Even if she doesn't come around, the physical evidence is overwhelming. And I'm very good. Let me prove it."

"No doubt you are a good prosecutor, Captain. But, the standard for a conviction is 'beyond a reasonable doubt,' not 'overwhelming evidence.' You can't ensure 'beyond a reasonable doubt,' without an eye-witness or a body," Morris said.

Bitter's struggled to control his rising emotions. "Sir, I must disa—"

Hornsby interrupted, "Relax, Captain. If we continue with the trial, the rest of the crew will testify in support of the chief. They'll discuss their imagined trip through a wormhole. We can't risk that story getting out. It would ruin their careers and cause a public panic. Most importantly, it could ruin our efforts at getting future funding. No, the risk is too great."

"What's more important, Admiral, your secret or seeing justice served?" Captain Bitters asked.

Robinson said, "You don't get it, Captain. If you did, you wouldn't ask that question."

Morris smiled, "I know how we get both."

"How?" Robinson asked.

Morris held up the plea agreement, "It's right here in front of us. The Defense downgraded the charge from murder to 'negligence causing death.' We'll reduce the plea even further. Reduce it to 'negligence causing loss of government property.'"

"And that's good because?" Robinson asked.

"Because, when HJ's body is found, we can bring the murder charge without it getting tossed as double jeopardy," JC explained.

"I like it," Silvertongue said. "Serving time in South America is a nice touch. It keeps the press away from the chief until we arraign him on murder charges."

"Speaking of nosy press, there's this reporter for World News Today poking around. He may have gotten wind of the debriefing reports," Hornsby said.

Robinson said, "Don't worry about him, Gerald. If he'd gotten hold of those debriefing reports, we'd have already heard about it."

Morris agreed. "You're right. If he ever sees those reports, he could throw a monkey wrench in all our plans. There'd be hell to pay. The public would freak out, and our funding could go up in smoke."

Robinson said, "Let's hope that doesn't happen."

"All this planning has got my appetite up. I'm afraid you can't join us, tonight Captain." Morris ushered Bitters to the door. "You'll need to make the necessary arrangements to formally accept the plea bargain, right away. With the changes, we just discussed, of course."

"But there's plenty of time, sir," Bitters protested.

Morris said, "No, not a second to spare. We need to get this agreement done before they change their minds. Don't be so glum. This is just a temporary setback. When we find HJ's body, they'll have to accept our initial offer. You know, the one you failed to get Chief Torres to sign. Or maybe you'll get a second chance to plead your case."

Once Bitters was gone and the doors were closed, Hornsby asked, "Isn't finding the body worse than finding a needle in a haystack?"

Morris smiled. "Normally it would be. But I got briefed by Carter earlier today. He says their engineers have come up with a new way of searching that shows real promise. "The best part is that Captain Wright assigned the chief's crew to find the body."

"Really, why?" Robinson asked.

"Because, my friend, it's about mission security. Only the original crew or the rescue crew have been in that location. The rescue crew is on another mission, and Carter doesn't want anyone else nosing around there. He's assigning the chief's crew to retrieve HJ's body."

Silvertongue smiled. "You gotta love the irony. The crew, which Chief Torres is trying to save with his plea deal, will be the ones responsible for his ultimate demise."

Morris raised his glass, "A toast, my friends. May the crew of the Osprey enjoy a most successful recovery mission."

A Bitter Drink

Downtown Pub Houston, Texas

The Pub was dark and quiet. The after-work crowd of military officers and government contractors was about to arrive. Thomas was there, sitting a little removed from the bar. As he waited for his Monday afternoon 'drinking partner,' he went over a few questions on his tablet:

- What was the Osprey's real mission?
- What did Lieutenant Gonzalez see?
- What is NASA hiding?
- What was Gonzalez about to say when she was interrupted?

The door opened several times, and people began to trickle in. After a while, Thomas spotted his source walk in and sit at the bar. He had a manila envelope in his hand, which he set down and motioned for a drink. The bartender nodded and set a whiskey in front of him. Thomas started to get up then thought better of it. *It might be best to let the booze loosen him up a little*, Thomas thought. It didn't take long for his contact to finish the first drink and signal for a refill. The bartender complied.

Thomas walked up with a ginger ale in hand. "Celebrating, are we?"

His source eyed him, "Oh, it's you. I was hoping you'd be here. Yeah, I'm celebrating. I'm celebrating the fact that life sucks."

"Really?"

"Yeah, she's a fickle bi—."

"A girl?"

"No. Life. She lays an opportunity at your feet, then snatches it away before you can pick it up. Hey, bartender, hit me again."

The bartender said, "Your friend needs to slow down, or I'll have to cut him off."

"Tough day?" Thomas asked.

"I'll say. Spent all day running around setting up a stupid plea agreement."

"I thought you wanted a plea agreement."

"Yeah, but not this one. This isn't a plea agreement. It's capitulation. It's a surrender."

"You may want to ease off a little, so you'll be sharp for the trial in the morning."

Bitters snorted, "No prep needed. No trial tomorrow."

"Are you sure?"

"Did the sun rise this morning? The plea bargain is entered and accepted. No trial, no arguments, no conviction. All my hard work down the drain. My case is still solid. It's a winner, but noooo, everyone wants to give up."

"Why?"

"The witness screwed up."

"It sounded like she was going off-script," Thomas agreed.

"No body. They think I can't win without one. Hell, I don't need no stinking body to win this one."

The effect of the alcohol was beginning to take hold. Thomas needed to push before Bitters was too intoxicated to be of value. "What's wrong with the plea bargain?"

"It's too damn light. Don't you listen, man? He gets five years of community service. He should get life and hard labor!"

"Why so light?"

"Because they won't go for murder without a body."

"There's no way they'll find the body, is there?"

Bitters frowned. "I don't know. They dismissed me before dinner."

"That's it? They didn't give you a reason for pulling the plug?"

"They're afraid the crew will all testify to some ridiculous story, about traveling through a wormhole to an unknown planet and fighting man-eating plants."

Thomas said, "You're kidding!"

Bitters patted the fat envelope. "I kid you not. It's all in these debriefing notes."

Thomas slid the envelope into his coat pocket. "Do you think their stories are true?"

"Can't say. It's classified. Say, that didn't come from me. It could mean my career."

"Then why risk me seeing it?"

"Let's just say this … it has something to do with new plans and a monkey wrench."

Thomas motioned to the bartender and paid for both their drinks. "If this ridiculous story isn't true, how can it be classified?"

Bitters said, "Now that you put it that way, what the hell?"

Thomas stood to go. Bitters put his hand on Thomas's arm. "I need your word that you won't tell anyone about any of this."

Thomas said, "My lips are sealed," as he thought, *but my word processor isn't.*

The Raid

Downtown Houston, Texas

Ⅰt was a cloudless moonlit night outside of Hilda's sixth-floor condo. The drapes to her living area were wide open, revealing the lights of downtown Houston.

Marc pushed away from the table. "What a great dinner."

"Thanks, Sarge. Coffee?"

"Sure."

"Dessert?"

"Absolutely. Home-cooked dinner, dessert ... why are you suddenly so domesticated?"

"Why not? I wanted to talk things over with you, and I needed to make sure no one could overhear us."

"Aren't you afraid this place is bugged?"

"Nope. Did a bug sweep myself. No one can possibly be listening," Hilda said.

The guy across the street, who was listening with his Laser Microphone, smiled. *Little does she know*, he thought.

"Okay," Marc said. "What's on your mind?"

"I'm worried about the chief. What do you make of his trial?"

"You're right to be worried. I don't think the truth'll come out."

"You mean about our little stowaways?"

Directly across the street, the listener poked his partner. "Look sharp, George. I think we're about to get some good stuff."

"Hold on a second. I'm checking my fantasy football stats."

"Not now! Start that recording. The boss'll want to hear this." The listener grabbed a pair of binoculars and looked into Hilda's condo. "I'm losing a visual on the subjects."

"No worries. You forget we're picking up sound from the window vibrations, so we don't need a visual to hear them."

Marc and Hilda had moved just out of sight of the surveillance team.

"Well, what about our stowaways? Marc asked.

"It's too bad the world will never know about them."

"We never should have signed the non-disclosure agreement."

Hilda's reply was muffled by the sound of running water.

Meanwhile, a black van and several patrol cars pulled to the curb. A SWAT team scrambled out of the back of the van and ran into the lobby. Uniformed officers stepped out of their vehicles to provide crowd control.

As everyone was moving into position, a couple of black SUVs pulled up. Matt and Barnabas, along with a squad of Military Police, got out.

"Are you sure this is a good idea, sir?" Barnabas asked.

"I promised Robinson I'd bring a SWAT team down on the leakers, no matter who."

"I'm not sure this is what Captain Lewis had in mind when he told you about his conversation with Sergeant Smith. This maneuver could blowback on NASA if it goes south."

"Do you have a better idea to stop the leaks?"

"No, sir."

"Then trust me on this," Matt said as they walked into the lobby with their Military Police unit in tow.

In the Lobby, they were met by a curious police sergeant. "I thought this was a simple drug bust. What's with the military backup?" he asked.

"Drug bust? Who called in a drug bust?" Matt asked.

"You tell me," the sergeant replied. "The call came from a NASA phone, and the address was screwed up, to boot."

"I'm not sure what that's all about, Sergeant. But I need to speak to your captain."

"The sergeant pointed across the Lobby. "That would be him."

Matt and Barnabas crossed the lobby to meet the police captain.

"Good evening, Captain. I'm Captain Dirksen, and this is Commander Maalouf. We're here on a matter of national security. We got a tip on this address," Matt handed the police captain a slip of paper.

"Hold on while I check with HQ," the police captain said.

The police officer stepped away and spoke into his cell phone. After describing NASA's presence, he was heard to say, "Yes, sir. I understand. Got it, sir." He looked at the NASA officers. "You're cleared to be here. I just had to make sure. There was some confusion over this being a drug bust or some other operation."

"Understood, Captain," Matt said. "We'll stay out of your way unless you need us."

"Very well, Captain. We're good and won't need your help until we're done," the police captain said. Then he read the slip of paper Matt had given him. "Hmm, this condo unit number is the same, but the floor is different than the one we've got." He spoke into his mike. "Sergeant, here's a change to the address,"

"Got it, Captain," was the response. "We're moving into position. Are you sure this is the correct address?"

The police captain looked at Matt, who nodded. "It is."

In her apartment, Hilda handed Marc a cup of coffee. "I hope they're treating our little stowaways well. Where do you think they are now?"

"Area 51, maybe. It was quite a scuffle capturing those little buggers when we discovered them," Marc winked.

Hilda mouthed, "Stay on our script."

Across the street, the eavesdropper hissed at his partner, "Shh."

"What?" his partner asked as he rattled a bag of potato chips.

"I can hardly hear a word they're saying. Stop making all that noise!"

"Chill, man. I'm hungry."

"And I'm trying to hear what they're saying, so be quiet!"

"It doesn't matter. Our equipment's recording everything."

Suddenly, a door crashed in. "POLICE! Freeze!"

Counter Offer

World Enquirer Building, Houston, Texas

homas frowned as he entered the lobby of the World Enquirer Building. The fact that his story did NOT appear in the morning issue of the World Enquirer was the reason for his mood. *Why would my editor spike the story? It's a great piece of work,* he thought as he got on the elevator.

Thomas got off the elevator and headed to his editor's office. He spotted his editor in the middle of the suite and walked over.

"Good morning, Thomas," his editor said.

"Hmph. Why'd you spike my story?" Thomas demanded.

"What story?"

"The one I sent you just in time for my deadline."

"All we got was an empty file."

"Really? Why didn't you call?"

"I had my reasons." His editor nodded toward the conference room.

Following his editor's gesture, Thomas looked at the glass-enclosed conference room. The sight of two NASA officers and their security detail made his heart skip a beat. "So, NASA spiked my story. I'm not knuckling under to their intimidation tactics. You may have lost your backbone, but I haven't," he said. Then he marched toward the conference room.

His editor shrugged. "It's your funeral." He returned to his office.

Thomas allowed his anger and self-righteousness to take control. *These dunces are about to meet the man who'll put them in their place,* he thought. He walked through the door.

"Just who do you think you are, spiking my story?" he shouted. "You've violated my right to free speech, free press. I'll have your stars by the time I'm done with you."

Something about the admiral's smile stopped him. "I believe you just took the term 'hostile press' to a whole new level." The admiral offered his hand. "I'm Admiral Carter."

"Oh, I'm just getting started." Thomas ignored the outstretched hand. "You have no business hacking my computer and wiping out my story."

"I didn't hack your computer. As for your story, I found it in my email inbox early this morning. Here's a printout. That's why I thought it best to drop by and pay you a personal visit."

Thomas blinked as he read the printout. *This is my story,* he thought.

Carter said, "I also have this preliminary report. It charges that you authorized illegal surveillance on two astronauts, received classified information from an officer of the court, and conspired to steal state secrets. I threw that last charge in, 'cause it sounds impressive."

"Who?"

"We've already spoken with Captain Bitters, who, as you know, is an officer of the court and your co-conspirator. These two Marines, here, are ready to arrest you at my command."

"Now, wait a minute. You can't—"

The admiral interrupted, "The police picked up the jokers who tried to bug Sergeant Smith's bungalow. They shouldn't have attacked him. That was in very bad taste. Oh, and a SWAT team caught a couple of guys spying on Gunnery Sergeant McDermott. Along with them, we retrieved some very interesting audio recordings, including a conversation you quoted verbatim in one of your articles."

"You shouldn't have made it so easy for us to connect their activity to you," a grim-faced NASA Captain added.

"Where are my manners," Carter said. "Thomas Jenkins, this is Senior Captain Lewis Wright. He has a special interest in how your guys treated his crew."

"Look now," Thomas said, "don't think you can strong-arm me into retracting my article. I'm onto something and have my rights as a journalist to publish it."

"Do as you wish," Carter said. "But there'll be severe consequences to publishing this particular article."

"You can't dissuade me with empty threats."

"I wasn't talking about you. This article could ruin several astronaut careers, give credence to other crazy conspiracy theories, and undermine the public trust in NASA—"

Thomas interrupted, "So, it's true! You're hiding the truth, and I've gotten too close."

"If you were too close, we'd be having a different conversation," the Admiral said. "No, our astronauts don't need to deal with wild accusations of them conspiring with alien life forms."

"How's that so different from accusing one of your astronauts of killing another in some crazy, made-for-TV, plot? I'm just interested in reporting the truth. I believe this murder trial of your chief is nothing more than a cover-up at his expense."

"Which is true? A nefarious plot to kill a fellow astronaut or a close encounter with a dangerous extraterrestrial life form that exists close to earth?" Carter asked.

"You tell me. You're the one threatening me if I write the latter."

"You're the reporter. The one 'who's only interested in the truth.' I believe those are your words. Do you believe either story?"

"You're the one pushing people to believe this is the work of a rogue astronaut," Thomas said. "Why're you trying to suppress my view of the truth?"

"I'm not trying to push Chief Torres under the bus," Carter said.

"If not, why the sham of a trial?"

"That's the work of a well-connected but grieving and bitter uncle. As to your comment about suppressing your story, we're just saving you from yourself. Why write a story that'll prove that you're guilty of the charges we just listed? Besides, you may have to retract it, anyway."

"What do you mean?" Thomas asked.

"Have you thought about a third story?"

"Like what?"

"It's a less sensational story. It may not sell as many subscriptions, but it can lead to some NASA exclusives for you and a chance to be taken seriously as a journalist again."

Thomas frowned, "I'm listening."

Among the Tombs

Near the Zond 7 Space Craft

S olar Explorer1 was the lofty name of a space vessel that served a not-so-lofty purpose. Owned by ACME Reclamation Services (ARS), Solar Explorer1 was reserved for special retrieval operations. It was one generation earlier than the Osprey. Its engine was slower. Its superstructure was modified for space retrievals. Its cargo hold was divided into a cargo bay, with a retrieval boom (much like that of the 20th century Space Shuttle) and a crew bay, from where the whole process was controlled. It was built so it could retrieve remains of damaged or dead satellites. It could transport them to one of the moon bases or earth for repair or recycle. On occasion, it was used to retrieve, disable, and redeploy live satellites that had been deemed 'unfriendly.'

NASA's Flight Controllers gave the Solar Explorer1 permission to launch with, "Okay, Solar Explorer1, it's time to get your ars in gear and get to work."

This ship was considered unique for several reasons. First, it was operated by former military black-ops personnel. Most of these technicians served honorably during the Asteroid Conflicts. Each technician held a top-secret clearance and, in some cases, distinguished service medals. This was necessary because NASA often requested that the Solar Explorer1 retrieve space objects of interest without permission from the said objects' owners. To that end, the ship had a stealth capability aimed at thwarting any tracking efforts.

She was now on just such a mission. This trip had two unusual wrinkles. It was piloted by Captain Matthew Dirksen and his crew from the Osprey (less Chief Petty Officer Torres, who was residing somewhere in South America). The bridge from which Matt operated was locked down. Two burly Marines stood guard just outside the door. This was designed to stop any attempt by the retrieval crew to join the flight crew. Should someone get past the two somber guards and the locked door, they would have to deal with Gunnery Sergeant McDermott and Master Sergeant Smith.

The retrieval crew cabin, located overlooking the cargo bay, held half a dozen ARS techs. They "handled the acquisition of articles." In English, they ran the boom that grabbed objects and set them in the cargo bay.

On this trip, they were joined by Thomas Jenkins. He, as part of his NASA agreement, had exclusive access to this mission. He was a novice space traveler. This was obvious despite his efforts to appear otherwise. So far, he had observed this team retrieve two ancient communications satellites and one oddly-shaped vehicle that no one could or would identify. He noticed the pattern of activity. First, the flight crew searched for an object, and the retrieval crew relaxed. Once the object was located, the retrieval crew would spring into action. They opened the bay's double doors, ran the retrieval boom, captured the object, brought it into the bay, closed and sealed the bay doors, then inspected and secured the retrieved item. The ship once again went into search mode, with the retrieval crew relaxing. While the retrieval crew rested, Thomas approached the crew chief. "Roger, mind if I ask you a few questions?"

"Sure, but I can't answer unless you have a 'need to know.'"

"This is just for story background. Anything I write is going to be fully vetted so that I don't leak any secret info by mistake."

"Relax, Mr. Reporter. I'm just messing with you. What do you want to know anyway?"

"Is it common for you to work from here and not be on the bridge?"

"No, I'm usually on the bridge."

"Why aren't you?"

"NASA doesn't want anyone but the flight crew to know our exact location."

"Can't others track us?"

"Nope."

"Why?"

"We're running in stealth mode."

"So, you don't have any idea where we are?"

"Sure, I do."

"Then, where are we?"

"Among the tombs."

"What?"

"This place has a dense grouping of non-functioning spaceships, satellites, and space debris. It's off-limits to commercial traffic. It's designated 'tombs' on most star charts."

"Then you do know where we are?"

Roger smiled, "No. many places on the star chart are labeled as 'tombs.' So, I know we are among the tombs. I don't know which ones."

"You're messing with me again."

"Yeah, I am. I don't know where we are."

"Did they tell you what we're picking up?"

"Nope."

"Doesn't this strike you as unusual?"

"No, I'm used to going to places that don't exist and picking up things that aren't there."

Thomas looked out of the portal. "Isn't that strange object with the USSR on its side the same one we passed earlier?"

"Probably."

"Are we just going in circles?"

"Looks as if."

"Is this usual?"

"In this line of work, nothing is usual."

"How do you deal with that?"

"I concentrate on my job and don't ask questions."

"Sorry, force of habit."

Just then, the ship shuddered.

"What's that?" Thomas asked.

"From the feel of it, the Weapons Officer released a search launcher."

"A what?"

"A search launcher. It's a clever way to find a relatively small object. Look, there it's being positioned right now." Roger pointed to a round object that just came into view.

"I'm not following you."

"What do you think we're looking for?"

"A body?"

"Bingo," Roger said. "For example, a body that was ejected from a spaceship. That means the body was pushed in one direction when it was ejected. With no gravity or other resistance, the body has been moving away in the same direction for some time now. To find it, you position a launcher where you think the body started from. Then you launch several hundred mini drones. They spread like a mushroom from your starting point. Then you simply follow the drones as they spread out."

"You've lost me."

"Hm, okay. Imagine you're sitting inside a huge dome filled with smoke. You have a disco ball in your hand, and a friend shines light against the ball. You'll see dozens of streaks of light going from the disco ball to different spots on the dome."

"Okay, I think I follow."

"That's why all the big stuff had to be cleared first. That ensures that the mini-drones have a clear shot at finding their target. Each mini drone senses objects around it with radar. Each one sends a signal back to the ship when it finds an object. Special software cancels out the radar hits on neighboring mini drones. The ship follows, steering toward the mini drones that are getting radar hits. Think of it as a game of hot and cold."

Thomas nodded. "Like when we were kids. We blindfolded someone then yelled 'hot' when they got near what they were supposed to find, and 'cold' when they moved away."

"Exactly. The drones that signal radar hits are the hot ones. Look." Roger pointed out the window. Thomas looked just in time to see the launcher disappear in a ball of red flames. Yellow streaks spread out from it like half a burst of a fireworks shell.

The flight crew on the ship's bridge also witnessed the mini drones launching.

"Drones away," Marci said.

"Very good, Lieutenant," Matt said. "Commander, position us to follow those drones."

Barnabas said, "Maneuvering to follow the drones, sir. So far, we have no radar hits match our search template."

"Are you seeing the drone input clearly on your heads-up display, Commander?"

"I am. So far, no warm inputs."

Matt said, "It's too early. My guess is that the suit was sent straight out from the Osprey. Based on the ship's position when the outer portal door popped open, the pressure that launched the suit, and the number of weeks it has been moving, it'll be some time before we reach it."

Marci asked, "How long do you think, sir?"

"Hard to say, Lieutenant. The drones are accelerating, as are we. Our target isn't accelerating, so we should catch it before time to call it a day."

"Captain, what's with the old satellites we just picked up?" Marc Asked. "A couple of them wouldn't have interfered with our search."

"Good question, Sarge. Back in the day, these satellites left earth from the same coordinates we did. That's all Captain Lewis would say."

"You think they may have made the same trip we did?" Marci asked.

"Or thought we did," Hilda said.

Barnabas said, "Kinda what I was thinking. I mean, about them making the same journey we did."

The crew was silent.

Sensing the crew's mood, Matt tried to ease the tension by changing subjects. "So, was it real or just a drug-induced trip?"

Barnabas said, "It was a trip all right, sir. It was real, for sure."

"Why do you think, Commander?" Hilda asked.

Barnabas said, "It was the smells. I never remember dreaming smells as strong as what I experienced on our trip."

"Such as?" Hilda asked.

"Such as the tar and the rotten egg smell of the sulfur-water. Even the smell of orange blossoms on that carnivorous plant. Every time I get near an orange tree, I think of it."

"Good point. I agree," Marci said. "What about you, Captain? Dream or real?"

"Real," Matt declared.

"Why?" Marci asked.

"The tastes. They were too powerful. I never remember how anything tastes in a dream."

"What about you, Gunny?" Marci asked.

"Dream mostly, Lieutenant," Hilda replied.

"Say what? Really?" Matt challenged.

"Whoa, sir. I'm not saying it didn't feel real. I'm just saying the brain can be very open to suggestions when under the influence of peyote. It's quite able to create its own reality."

"Everyone having the same reality?" Matt asked.

"I admit it's a stretch, sir," Hilda said.

"It's a good thing we didn't have to testify," Matt said. "No one would've believed us if we were divided."

"Don't get me wrong, Captain," Hilda said. "I'd testify to what I thought I experienced. But if asked, I'd have to say it was a dream. I just don't know for sure."

"Hmmm...." Matt nodded his head.

"It's like this," Hilda said. "Bottom line, if there was peyote in the air, we can't be sure if our experiences were real or imaginary."

"Why's it so hard for you to believe what we experienced was real?" Marc asked.

"Why's it so hard for you to believe it isn't?" Hilda shot back.

"My ankle's still recovering from the 'imaginary' sprain I got. I've still got burns on my arms from the 'imaginary' plant that attacked us."

"Look, Sarge, you could've sprained your ankle during the fight we had before we were boarded," Hilda said. "I know it's hard to think of what we went through as fantastical delusions. But no one before us ever went through a wormhole or had any of the experiences we did and lived to tell of it. What we think we experienced just doesn't fit the facts as we know them, of how the Universe works."

Marc said, "Who's to say we aren't the first? I'm not trying to argue, Gunny. But there must be an objective way to figure out if our experiences are real or imagined."

Barnabas eased the ship to a stop. "There is, Sarge. And it's staring us in the face."

Everyone looked out the Bridge's main window. There, in full view, about ten yards away, was Lieutenant Homer Jaeger's spacesuit.

Marci looked down. Matt drew in a deep breath, then let it out. "Commander, commence recovery procedures."

"Aye, Captain." Barnabas announced, "Attention on the salvage deck. Prepare to recover Lieutenant Jaeger."

"Sir, are we about to hang the chief with this retrieval?" Marc asked.

"Could be. But orders are orders."

On the salvage deck, Thomas watched as preparations were made to retrieve the lieutenant's body. He felt his heart beating a little faster as he observed the robotic arm retrieve the body and draw it into the Cargo hold. Then the techs hung it gently on a stand and rolled it to the Salvage crew deck.

Wow, he thought—*the greatest exclusive of my career. I can hardly believe it's happening.* His thoughts turned dark as the reality of what was about to happen set in. *Coming face to face with a dead man is never pleasant.*

Now the moment was about to arrive, and Thomas felt sudden pangs of anxiety. He had thought through all the possibilities of what they would find. And imagined each one in his mind's eye. Still, as they respectfully lowered the astronaut's suit of remains onto the table, he doubted if he could handle what he was about to see. Wait, he heard something. He strained to listen more closely. It was the steady thumping of a heartbeat. Could it be the astronaut was still alive? The technicians didn't seem to notice.

Why aren't they responding? Thomas thought. *Don't they know time is of the essence? They must get the helmet off fast, so the astronaut can get fresh air! Surely, they can hear the pounding heart. Now there is the sound of gasping! Do something!* Thomas's mind screamed.

He started to reach out, himself. Then he realized it was his own heart beating and his own gasping. He inhaled slowly and tried to compose himself. The technicians sensed his unease and took advantage of it for their entertainment.

"This could be grisly," said one. "The decomposition of a body doesn't require oxygen. There's no telling what his face will look like."

"Especially if he was shot in the face," the tech beside him said.

"I don't think he decomposed," interjected another. "But I once heard that dying from a lack of oxygen is fearful, leaving a corpse with a dreadful look — their eyes wide open and all."

"Don't be stupid," replied a fourth. "Dying from a lack of oxygen is like going to sleep. He'll look like he's just taking a nap."

The technicians smiled amongst themselves. Thomas took a deep breath and slowly let it out to calm his nerves. It was time. The lead investigator noted, for the record, that the spacesuit was pressurized as expected. He then reached out and flipped open the Sun visor to reveal the dead astronaut's face. As the visor opened, an eerie hush fell on the cargo hold.

Thomas let out an involuntary gasp. *It's empty!*

Pomp and Ceremony

Arlington Cemetery, Arlington, Virginia

Matt picked up the morning paper. "Lieutenant JG Homer Jaeger was laid to rest, with all the pomp and ceremony due a national hero who gave his life in honorable service to his country." So, began Thomas Jenkin's exclusive article on the search for the recently departed astronaut.

At least he got the pomp and ceremony right, Matt thought as he read the article.

HJ's Ceremony was meticulous in its execution. James Silvertongue made sure of it. Even the weather cooperated. The day was bright, with a cloudless winter sky. It provided the perfect backdrop for the missing man formation fly-over, which happened at just the right moment as the flag-draped casket was set in place above the grave. The rest of the military honors and ceremonies, including the seven-man honor guard firing the obligatory three-volley salute, flawless playing of taps, and closing flag protocol, were well executed. This gave Silvertongue much satisfaction.

It seemed that the whole nation stopped to pay one last tribute to a space hero. Today's News Channel (TNC), who had carried the story non-stop for days, had the largest audience. Their coverage was professional, if not theatrical. The commentary went like this:

"The caisson is rounding the corner and entering the cemetery," the first reporter said.

"It has passed the gathering of dignitaries and arrived at the gravesite," intoned the second reporter. The honor guard presented arms.

"The casket team secures the casket as the officer-in-charge and chaplain both salute," a third reporter said.

"The chaplain is leading the way to the gravesite, followed by the casket team." The second reporter picked up the play-by-play. "The casket team is setting the casket down and securing the flag. The Officer in charge is making sure the flag is stretched out and centered over the casket."

Not to be left out, a fourth reporter spoke up, "As the dignitaries are seated, Dr. Silvertongue is coming to the podium to speak."

The theater was lost on Matt. He felt the weight of losing one of his crew. He had lost men before. Still, *it never gets any easier*, he thought.

Silvertongue stood at the podium and looked around his audience with a solemn air. All waited attentively. He began to speak. "On this sorrowful day, we lay Lieutenant JG Homer Jaeger to rest. Beloved by all those who worked with him, he was a dedicated astronaut well-acquainted with the dangers of space travel. The tragic accident that took his life also exposed, for all to see, his selfless bravery. It was at the very moment the spacecraft door failed, threatening to suck his crewmate, Chief Torres, into the lifeless vacuum, that Lieutenant Jaeger found himself struggling against incredible forces. Grabbing Chief Torres and pushing him to safety, Lieutenant Jaeger traded places and lives with Chief Torres. As the good book says, 'no greater love has a man than he gives his life for a friend.'"

Matt did a double-take upon hearing this twist to their story. Just then, Lewis texted him, *Did I hear that Jaeger is now the hero who saved Torres's life?*

An interesting touch, Matt responded. *Wonder who gave him that idea?*

Matt appreciated Lewis's attempt to raise his spirits by texting during the ceremony. But it failed to relieve the sadness Matt felt over the demise of HJ.

Silvertongue fought to control his emotions. "By his act of heroism, Lieutenant Jaeger set a standard of bravery, devotion, and commitment to which we should all aspire."

"Wow! This bloke absolutely cares about his team of astronauts," an Australian reporter from the news pool wrote on his blog. "You can see it in his eyes and hear it in his voice."

"Our hearts go out to Lieutenant Jaeger's family and crewmates," Silvertongue motioned toward the mourners. A TV camera followed his lead, scanning the two rows of mourners. First, it caught James Christopher Morris II, HJ's uncle, with downcast eyes. Then it picked up Matt on the second row. He also sat erect with downcast eyes. The camera failed to show that his eyes were downcast to read a text from Lewis, who sat further down on his row.

It read *Hope Silvertongue does my eulogy when I die. He'd make even me look good.*

Matt texted back: *Only if I get to set the record straight afterward.*

The camera picked up an image of Marci Gonzalez on the first row. She sat stoically. Her red eyes and hollow stare gave away the depth of her grief.

"I pledge to you our full support as you move forward without your beloved colleague," Silvertongue concluded. He stepped down from the makeshift podium and stopped briefly to comfort each mourner on the first row.

Silvertongue's speech reminded Matt of his inability to save HJ. A sense of failure swept over him. Just then, an incoming text from Lewis caught his eye: *Sorry about HJ. At least you saved the chief.*

Matt appreciated Lewis's text. But found it to be a cold comfort.

Epilogue

South American Jungle

Josh found himself floating just above the Osprey. He had completed the necessary repairs and an inspection of the Osprey. He paused for a few seconds to admire the beauty of Saturn as it rose into view over the craggy wall of Herschel's Crater. The Osprey had set down on Mimas, one of Saturn's moons.

From a distance, Herschel's impact crater caused Mimas to resemble the Death Star from the classic film "Star Wars." Josh thought *Life doesn't get better than this.*

"All wrapped up, Captain," he spoke into his mike while admiring the pale-yellow hue of Saturn, beginning to dominate the Mimas's sky.

"It all looks good here," the captain answered. "Great job, Chief. Now, get back in here, and let's get this bird home."

"On my way, sir."

Josh noticed as he entered the ship's bridge that everyone was already at their stations. "Welcome aboard, Chief," Barnabas smiled. Marci frowned at him and turned to face her station. The captain said, "to your station, Chief. Time's a-wasting."

"Mission Control, Osprey, we've completed our repairs and inspection. Over."

Osprey, Mission Control, how's your ship look? Over."

"Mission Control, Osprey, it looks good enough to get us home. We're completing our pre-flight checklist. Over."

"Flight control computers sync'd and no structural warnings," Josh reported.

"All green on my console," Marci reported.

"Flight control, engines, maneuvering thrusters all good," Barnabas announced.

"Good! Let's get this bird underway," Matt commanded. "We'll begin with a 20% burn on my mark, Commander."

"Mission Control, Osprey, we're beginning our departure protocol."

"Osprey, Mission Control, God's speed. Over."

"Take us home, Commander," Matt ordered.

Barnabas said, "Clearing the surface and increasing to a 40% burn."

Ah, this is the life, Josh thought. Quietly, at first, and then getting louder, was the sound of a warning alarm. *It must be coming from the power plant,* Josh thought. *Oddly, no one else seems to hear the alarm.* For Josh, everything went black, but the alarm buzzing grew in intensity until Josh awoke in his bed. He rolled over and looked at the early morning sky. A sense of loss swept over him as he remembered that he could no longer travel among the stars. He swung his feet out of bed and prepared to face the day. As was the case, whenever he had such a dream, his heart just wasn't in the coming day.

That afternoon, Josh sat on the hotel veranda, overlooking a road running from the riverside wharf past the hotel. An overhead fan provided little relief from the sweltering heat. He was enjoying his iced drink, made possible by the village's new water purification system. His dream from the previous night still troubled him. The dream itself was enjoyable. That was the problem. It renewed his longing to once again travel in outer space. The worst part of his night was waking to a clear sky full of beckoning stars. They seemed to mock him for remaining earthbound. His brooding was interrupted by the whistle of an arriving ferry. Josh observed the typical mass of animals, people, bicycles, and beat-up jalopies as they departed the Wharf. Most of them were making their way slowly up the hill, passing his hotel. A flash caught his attention. He saw two men that were out of place, angling toward the hotel. Josh looked closer. He recognized Barnabas's typical jaunty stride. Even from a distance, Josh could see the familiar broad smile on his face. Walking next to Barnabas was Matt. His back was ramrod straight and his stride resolute.

Josh stepped down from the veranda to meet his two visitors. As he reached them, he realized he didn't know how to greet them. *Should I salute? Or should I offer a hand? Or should I just say, "Hey?"*

The visitors settled his quandary. Matt reached out his hand and gave Josh's hand a firm but warm shake. "It's good to see you, Chief."

"You as well, Captain," Josh replied.

Barnabas grabbed Josh's hand and pulled him close. "How are you, Son?" He enveloped Josh in a bear hug and beat on his back.

"I'm well, sir," Josh coughed and tried to catch his breath.

"Join me for an afternoon drink," Josh invited when he disengaged from the commander's grasp. He almost asked why they came but thought better of it.

The warmth of that afternoon didn't match that of their reunion. The remainder of the day was spent with Josh showing his friends the entire village. He spent extra time showing every aspect of the water purification and delivery system he had designed and built.

Starting from the ingest system, through the four-stage purification process, and concluding with a taste of tap water. Matt and Barnabas tried to avoid tasting the tap water. But to no avail. Barnabas looked skeptically at the glass Josh stuck in his hands. "Are you sure we won't be getting a case of Montezuma's revenge?"

"Naw, I drink it all the time. You've just got to taste how good it is," Josh insisted.

The duo finally complied and found the water tasted good, with no ill effects. Even their compliance with Josh's request failed to release them from his continuous narrative about the water project. Josh left no detail out, despite Matt's thinly disguised impatience. Josh's discourse continued through dinner at the hotel restaurant.

After dinner, the trio sat on Josh's balcony, with coffee and cigars, watching the stars come out. Matt leaned back, took a puff from his cigar, and watched Josh staring at the stars. "How'd you like to revisit the stars, Torres?"

"No, thank you, sir," Josh replied. "I've got my work here and other hydrology projects on our organization's agenda."

"This is all well and good," Matt motioned toward the water purification building. "But it isn't you. You belong up there among the stars," he concluded, pointing at the night sky.

"Sorry, Captain. I'm needed here."

Barnabas asked, "You don't hear the stars calling you?

"Not so much, Commander," Josh lied

"Then why do you have that telescope pointed at the Big Dipper?" Matt asked.

"Southern Cross, sir," Josh corrected. "We're in the southern hemisphere."

"My point exactly. You can take the boy out of the stars, but you can't take the stars out of his heart."

Barnabas said, "Son, you've been dreaming about the stars, again, haven't you? You once told me that you have dreams about traveling in space. If I remember correctly, you've had these dreams for years. Judging by the look on your face, you still do."

"What gave me away, Commander?"

"Your tour. You were trying hard to impress us. Too hard. It felt like you were trying to convince yourself that this is your new reason for living."

"Enough of this verbal sparring," Matt said. "Come back and fly with us again."

"Don't be messing with my head, sir. You know that's a violation of my plea agreement."

"Don't be so sure. A lot can happen in a few months," Barnabas said.

"Yeah, like they buried HJ with full honors. I get the news down here also," Josh said.

"They buried an empty casket with full honors," Matt corrected.

"What do ya mean, sir?"

Matt leaned forward. "I mean what I said. They buried an empty casket. They tossed in a couple of sandbags to make it feel like a human body to the pallbearers."

"You can't be sure," Josh challenged.

Matt said, "I'm as sure it was empty as I am that we're talking to each other right now."

"The news reported that he was recovered floating in space."

"All we recovered was an empty spacesuit."

Josh let out a low whistle. "I was beginning to believe it was all a dream. That HJ, really was in that space suit I stupidly jettisoned."

"Nope, he never made it out of the cave," Barnabas said.

Josh frowned, "That must've upset a few apple carts at NASA."

"More than a few," Matt agreed. "The top brass are rethinking a lot of things. Admiral Carter says he has plans for my crew. That includes you if you want back in."

"Why hasn't this been in the news? What about that Thomas Jenkins reporter guy, who won't stop, 'until I get the truth, the whole truth, and nothing but the truth?'"

Barnabas smiled, "Interesting question. Imagine the panic caused by reporting that there is a place very close to Earth inhabited by intelligent beings who make our technology obsolete. NASA can't let that happen. So, while they let Mr. Jenkins get the truth, they're not letting him report all of it."

"They can do that?" Josh asked.

"Sure, they can. Everyone has a price. His is an exclusive on the recovery effort and a special article celebrating the life of Lieutenant Jaeger, our most recent national hero," Matt said.

Barnabas smiled. "So, kid, are you in or not?"

Josh hesitated, thinking of his previous night's dream. "I'm not sure how Lieutenant Gonzalez will take this. She may not want to work with me again."

Barnabas said, "She's the one who blew up the prosecution's case and saved your hide. I think she'll be okay having you back on the team."

"The commander's right," Matt affirmed. "What do you say?"

"Count me in, sir."

Matt stood to leave. "Good. Now that that's settled, Torres, you need to pack. We leave in the morning,"

Barnabas stood also, but noticing an odd expression on Josh's face, he stopped. "What's wrong, son? You don't seem as excited as I thought you'd be."

"I'm excited about returning to the crew. I'm just puzzling over our return from Portae. I've given it a lot of thought but still don't get it, Commander."

"Get what?"

Josh said, "We never talked about that last message on the plateau. Do you both remember me telling you that Vigilo said we were taking some sort of test?"

Barnabas looked at Matt. "We remember."

"I'm sure that the last test was about going into the cave," Josh said. "Vigilo was very specific about us not going into that cave. We could do whatever we wanted in the garden except going into that cave. It was like … uh … like the Adam and Eve thing."

"What Adam and Eve thing?" Matt asked.

Barnabas said, "According to the Jewish story, God created a garden where Adam and Eve could live. They could eat the fruit of any tree in the garden except for one. God warned them that if they ate fruit from that one tree, they would die. They ate the forbidden fruit. That killed their relationship with God, got them kicked out of the garden, and later they died."

"This is significant because?" Matt asked. "Don't look at me that way, Maalouf. You're the one who has a chaplain in the family."

Josh said, "It's like this. We were told NOT to go in the garden cave, but we ALL did."

"You think that was the great test that we failed?" Matt asked.

"Yeah, I do," Josh said. "Vigilo told me he thought we were from a rebel planet."

Barnabas agreed. "I see your point. The test was a simple obedience test. Obey by staying out of the cave, and we're not rebels. Enter the cave, and we fail the test."

"Exactly, Commander," Josh agreed. "What I don't get is, we all failed the test. We were all supposed to die. But we didn't."

"Came damn close," Matt interjected.

"Yes, we did," Josh agreed. "But in the end, we were rescued. Why?"

Matt said, "Maybe that wasn't the last test."

"If not, the key must be in the last message," Barnabas said.

"Call on me in the day of trouble; I will deliver you, and you will honor me. Signed Alpha and Omega?" Josh asked.

"Yeah, that one. Maybe it meant that when we realized that we were beyond hope of helping ourselves and asked for help, we'd be rescued," Barnabas said. "The final test was, would we ask for help in our situation."

Josh shook his head. "I don't disagree. In fact, that makes sense. But who prayed for help? I know I didn't. Did you Commander?"

"Honestly? No," Barnabas admitted. "I didn't ask for help."

Josh said, "Marc was in so much pain, I don't think he asked for help. Marci was too far gone. Gunny was busy swearing and pounding on the Osprey's door. HJ had already died."

"I didn't ask for help either. So, that's it ... unless...." Josh and Barnabas looked at Matt. "What were you doing while we were dying, Captain?"

Matt shrugged, "Praying to God for help."

The End

An excerpt from THE RETURN OF THE OSPREY,
By DJ Albrecht

The Escape

"Often, you escape by going where those chasing you are unwilling to go."
- Michael Westen [Burn Notice]

Outpost Delta, Mars

J acques's mind was racing. *What woke me up?* he thought. *Was it the food door clicking closed?* His heart jumped. Quietly he swung his feet to the floor, stepped to the door, and opened the food box. He looked at the badge and a small piece of paper lying in the food box. *Finally! My ticket out of here,* he thought while scratching his bushy beard.

The plan, days in execution, was simple. He would exit the prison as a janitor. Each day Jacques had received a note with instructions, which he memorized and flushed down the toilet. The badge was the final item to arrive. It signaled that tonight was the night. Jacques quickly gathered a razor and moved to the sink. Lathering his face, he began to shave off his beard. As he shaved, he went over the plan in his mind. *There'll be a janitor's cart somewhere nearby. As soon as someone bumps into my door, I'll use my badge to unlock the cell door. I'll find the janitor's cart, push it past the guard to the break room. A distraction in another wing of the prison will be in progress to draw attention away from me—a piece of cake.*

After shaving, Jacques removed his prisoner jumpsuit and donned a janitor jumpsuit. *Lucky for me, both prisoners and janitors wear the same kind of shoes,* he thought as he climbed back into bed and pretended to sleep.

He heard the footsteps of a guard making the hourly rounds. As the footsteps passed his cell, he heard a distinct bump of something hard against his door. *This is it. I'd better get to it. The note said, don't be late,* he thought as he rose. He took one last look around the cell. There was a nagging feeling he forgot something, so he looked more closely a second time. *Time's a-wasting,* he thought. He placed his badge against the latch side of the door anticipating the click of the lock opening—nothing. He gave the door a slight budge. It didn't move.

What? Is the RFID on the badge screwed up? Think, man, think. Wait a minute! Of course, the inside of the lock must be shielded in case a prisoner gets a badge. What to do? I'd reach through the food box, but the outside door is locked shut. Or is it?

Jacques opened the inside door of the food box and pushed tentatively against the outer door. It wasn't latched! Jacques grasped the badge and stuck his arm through the passage, waving the badge in front of the cell door latch. Relief washed over him as he heard the latch click to the open position.

He opened the cell door and stepped out into a lava tunnel dotted by a series of cells. The builders of this "facility" carved cells out of several natural lava tunnels. This provided both a secure set of cells and protected the prisoners and personnel from the cosmic rays ever present on Mars. *There it is,* he thought as he saw the Janitor cart just to his right. He took hold and pushed it down the tube. *Almost there! The diversion's in full swing up in cell block A. I can hear it all the way down here. So far, so good.* Jacques crossed the intersection of the three tubes, each one comprising a 'cell block.' He was two steps away from the break room when he was stopped by a shout.

"Hey, you!" a guard yelled at him. Jacques slowly pointed at himself and shrugged. "Yes, you. I'm talking to you. Get your sorry ass over here."

Crap! Jacques thought as he started to comply.

The guard looked at him intently. "Do I know you? Never mind. Get up to cell A-4. The inmate there got food poisoning. They're treating him

314

right now and are about to take him to the infirmary. He's tossed his cookies and has diarrhea. You need to clean it up pronto."

"But my shift's over," Jacques replied.

The guard glared at him. "I don't care."

"I need to meet someone – it's urgent," Jacques explained.

"Quit wasting my time. That cell stinks, and we'll not put up with the stench until the morning shift. The faster you get to work, the sooner you can leave for your urgent meeting."

"Yes, sir." Jacques began pushing his cart toward cell A-4. He was careful to look down as he passed the guard and the EMTs who were removing the sick prisoner.

The stench is worse than what that guard said, Jacques thought. He worked as quickly as he could to clean the floor, bed, toilet, and sink. *Bet whoever planned this little distraction didn't count on me being part of it. I'm going to be sooo late!*

Finally, with the mess cleaned, Jacques stored the janitor cart and approach the final prison door. Even though that guard waved him through, his heart was racing. *Twenty minutes late. This'll never do. I hope I'm not too late to catch my ride.*

Outside the prison, Jacques found himself overlooking a park of sorts. It was about the size of a football field and descended gently into a bowl. Jacques guessed that straight ahead, on the other side of the park, was a gated lava tube that led to where the actual Delta 1 colony was located. To his left was another gated lava tube that probably led to the living quarters of the prison staff. Snuggled against the lava outcroppings, the park's exposed side was enclosed by a partial geodesic dome structure that extended over the garden to form its roof. The structure of stainless steel and heavy plexiglass was covered with a thick layer of ice. This translucent combination allowed an airy feeling during the day. It was a clever way of reducing exposure to cosmic rays. He smelled pine needles.

Looking around the park, Jacques saw several small stands of neatly trimmed evergreens. The park also featured a lawn of moss and many raised beds of growing vegetables.

Quit gawking and get moving. You're late! he thought. Jacques turned toward his right and followed a path that led through a stand of trees to an obscure door. Next to the door was an RFID reader and keypad. One needed to have the correct badge and key in the valid code to gain access, which changed daily. Jacques swiped his badge over the RFID reader and keyed in the code that he remembered from the note that came with his badge. Nothing! He tried again—still nothing. *Think, man, think. What was the code anyway?*

Was it 2463 or 6324 or … if I don't get this right, I'm toast! Jacques had already tried both combinations, with no success. *Wait, I forgot to swipe my badge when I keyed in the second combination.* This time he did both. To his relief, the door unlocked. Jacques opened the door, squinted at the lights' brightness, and entered the prison's service hanger. It was big enough to hold three large starships. Currently, no such vehicles were present. Jacques saw an assortment of half-track service vehicles, hovercraft, and small pursuit aircraft. *Jeez, I'm a full half-hour late,* Jacques fretted. He dashed behind Halftrack #8 as the note had instructed. No one was there. *What now?* Jacques thought. He picked up a nearby broom and started to sweep, trying to fit into his janitorial role.

"Hey, you!" Someone yelled across the hanger to get his attention. *Here we go again,* Jacques thought as he answered, "Yes, sir."

"You're late," the sergeant said as he walked over to Jacques. "This is no way to start your first night. Follow me, and we'll find the captain." Jacques followed him to a large office on the far side of the hanger. When they arrived, several other maintenance people were leaving. The sergeant introduced Jacques. "Hi, Captain. Here's the new janitor."

The captain said, "Hmph! Being late is no way to start your new job. Sergeant, take him over to Hovercraft Station #3. I noticed that the floor over there is in desperate need of mopping."

"Yes, sir," the sergeant replied. "Come with me," he said, looking over his shoulder at Jacques. Just as they arrived at the hovercraft station, a tall, husky fellow suddenly grabbed the sergeant from behind and applied a sleeper hold. The sergeant flailed, trying to get leverage and break free. But the attacker was too large and strong. Soon, a lack of oxygen to the brain left the sergeant limp. The attacker lowered him to the ground, tied his arms and legs with zip ties, and gagged his mouth. After rolling the sergeant under a workbench, the assailant opened the hovercraft door and motioned for Jacques to get in. Once inside, he motioned for Jacques to sit in the right seat as he slid into the pilot's seat.

"You're late!" The attacker challenged.

"I'm getting that a lot lately," Jacques said.

"What? Whatever, the boss won't be happy."

"Had to clean up a—"

"Save it for the boss. We need to boogie," the assailant said. He spoke into his mike, "Traffic Control, this is employee 673682 requesting permission to take hovercraft 492 out for a test spin."

"Hey, Chuck, did the Sarge OK this?" Traffic Control asked.

"Yep, and he said I should've started a half-hour ago," Chuck answered.

"Good enough. I'm opening the door. When it's full up, feel free to leave. Just stay well away from the frontier. Understood?"

"Understood," Chuck answered.

Jacques jumped at the sound of alarms and red lights flashing.

"A little jumpy are we, tonight? That's just the notice that a flight door is open. It's a safety precaution. They aren't coming for us yet," Chuck said. "By the way, I'm Dimitri. But my friends call me Chuck." He eased the craft out into the night.

"How do you get Chuck out of Dimitri?"

"Don't ask. I'm getting you out of here pronto."

"Don't we need a spaceship?" Jacques asked

Dimitri continued flipping switches and communicating with Traffic Control but didn't answer Jacques's question.

"You know – something that can actually fly."

Dimitri took a deep breath and hit the accelerator. The hovercraft swept forward with a vengeance.

"I have a question Di … uh … Chuck," Jacques said.

"You've got a lot of questions. What is it?"

"Why did you take the time to tie up the Sergeant? You could've just killed him."

"Yeah, but strangling someone takes more time than you'd think. Besides, if this little adventure goes south, I'll only face an assault charge, not murder."

"*This better not go south,* Jacques thought.

"Switch on the toggle marked 'com,'" Dimitri said.

Jacques complied. The voice of Traffic Control could be heard speaking with other vehicles.

"Who is Traffic Control talking to?" Jacques asked.

"Researchers, travelers between Moon Base Alpha and Moon Bases Beta and Charlie. Mostly civilian traffic. OK – now's when the fun begins." Dimitri made a sharp turn and accelerated. Shortly after completing his turn, a warning alerted Traffic Control. "WARNING! WARNING! THE FRONTIER BORDER IS BEING BREACHED."

"Sentries, intercept the intruder."

Jacques laughed. "That's funny. We're going in the wrong direction to be intruders."

"You're laughing now, but the party's over as soon as the pursuit ships arrive."

"STOP! YOU ARE ENTERING A RESTRICTED ZONE," a sentry drone warned.

"Here, take over the ship while I occupy those little buggers," Dimitri said. "Steer toward that slot canyon over there." He hopped out of his seat and made his way to the back of the ship. Climbing into the port side gunner's seat, he started shooting at the drones.

"You got it," Jacques said as he grabbed the controls and began steering.

"Damn those buggers, they're too quick dodging my energy bursts. Drop into the slot canyon, an' they'll have less room to maneuver."

Jacques accelerated the ship into the slot canyon.

"Hey, a little smoother, man! I can't line up my shots."

"Excuse me," Jacques rolled his eyes. "I'm trying to keep us from decorating a wall."

"Yeah! I just got one of those buggers! Yes! Another just lost a wing to the canyon wall."

Two other security drones hit the canyon wall and exploded, trying to evade his fire.

"Take that, you little bugger," Dimitri gloated as he shot the last drone out of the sky. "Go ahead and set this baby on the ground, Jacques. That was easy."

"Yeah – too easy, if you ask me."

"I'm not asking, chump. Just set 'er down."

"Really?" Jacques asked.

"This is where the boss wants to meet us."

Before Jacques could reply, a middle-aged man in a NASA flight suit appeared in the pilot's seat that Dimitri had once occupied. The man was looking straight ahead and seemed not to notice Jacques.

Jacques jumped and said, "What the Hel—"

"Oh, don't mind him," Dimitri interrupted. "That's just a hologram of the Boss."

"Could've fooled me."

The hologram looked at Jacques. "You're late."

"I had to clean up a mess left by your planned distraction back at the prison," Jacques complained.

"You two, being so late, could've ruined this whole endeavor," the Boss chided.

"We lost our escort anyway, Boss," Dimitri said.

"The sentry drones are nothing compared to the pursuit ships. They'll be waiting for us as we exit the canyon," the Boss said. "Jacques, go take over the starboard side guns. You'll both have to keep after the pursuit ships if we are to survive."

Jacques took up his gunnery position. "Who flies?"

The Boss said, "I'll fly remotely."

Jacques felt the ship lift and shoot forward. He was pushed hard against his restraining harness as the ship got up to full speed and blasted out of the canyon. *Just like a bat out of Hell*, he thought.

Just as the Boss said, they were waiting, and their initial blasts took out the ship's shields. But the Boss was flying too fast to be brought down. Soon the escaping vessel was lengths ahead of the pursuit ships as they turned and followed. The transmissions from their pursuers could be heard clearly over the ship's speakers. Occasionally, a message would be aimed at the hovercraft. "Halt! Set your ship down. You cannot escape!"

"Take careful aim, boys," the Boss said. "These pilots should be easier to hit than those pesky drones."

The ship rocked and pitched wildly as the Boss maneuvered to avoid the pursuing ships' fire. Jacques and Dimitri aimed carefully, but the motion of their ship kept them from scoring any hits. Fortunately, their firing and the Boss's maneuvers kept them safe for the moment. *We can't keep this up much longer. We need to find shelter soon,* Jacques thought as he felt a ball of fear knotting up in his stomach.

Jacques glanced forward and saw nothing but an open barren landscape ahead. "Feeling a little exposed back here," he said.

"Not to worry," the Boss said. "I have a plan." With that, he made a hard-right turn, angling toward a small bluff in the distance. The pursuit ships followed and drew closer.

The speakers came to life again. "WARNING! WARNING! YOU ARE ENTERING A HIGHLY RESTRICTED ZONE. TURN BACK NOW!"

An annoying alarm sounded. Jacques looked at his console and saw a red radiation alarm was blinking. He glanced at the radiation meter. *The radiation meter is off the charts,* he thought.

"Uh, Boss, we seem to have wandered full speed into a radiation zone," Dimitri said.

The Boss just laughed. "What's a little radiation among friends?"

"You heard it, boys," the pursuit leader said over the speakers. "These clowns are flying us into a radiation field. It's time to pull out."

"Roger that," was the reply as the pursuit ships pulled up and set course for home. Their leader hovered at the radiation boundary to guard against Dimitri and Jacques circling back.

"Go ahead and fry your hearts out, you fools," he said.

The alarms grew louder as their boss flew further into the restricted radiation field.

The Boss chuckled. "The secret to any successful escape is to be willing to go where the pursuit won't follow."

"What about us?" Jacques asked. "We're the ones getting fried!"

Together Jacques and Dimitri jumped out of their seats and dove for the ship's controls. But they couldn't change the hovercraft's relentless dive into the radiation.

The Boss laughed and said, "Nice try, but the ship is totally in my control. You shouldn't have been so late."

The pursuit leader, hovering at the radiation boundary, listened to the escaping ship's internal communications. He thought, *by my calculation, you'll be fried in three more minutes. I guess your boss was more interested in seeing you die rather than escape.*